R A Y

MW00999942

SECRETS, LIES, AND SNEAKY SPIES

Secrets, Lies, and Sneaky Spies
Red Adept Publishing, LLC
104 Bugenfield Court
Garner, NC 27529
https://RedAdeptPublishing.com/

Copyright © 2023 by Rayna Flye. All rights reserved.

Cover Art by Streetlight Graphics[1]

No part of this book may be reproduced, scanned, or distributed in any printed or electronic form without permission. Please do not participate in or encourage piracy of copyrighted materials in violation of the author's rights. Thank you for respecting the hard work of this author.

This is a work of fiction. Names, characters, places, and incidents either are the product of the author's imagination or are used fictitiously, and any resemblance to locales, events, business establishments, or actual persons—living or dead—is entirely coincidental.

---

1.   http://StreetlightGraphics.com

For my mom and my husband

Chapter 1

S*omewhere in the Pacific Northwest*

WORST CASE OF THE MONDAYS ever.

At barely nine in the morning, Katrina Foster had already found herself stalked.

Hooded.

And in her current position, dumped unceremoniously into the back of a vehicle.

Her situation was made all the worse by the fact that her day had started out so well. The early summer morning was beautiful. She snagged the last seat on the light rail, the line at her favorite café for her daily vanilla rooibos was short, and she later managed to avoid spilling said drink while weaving her way past her fellow distracted pedestrians on the sidewalk. All in all, she'd been having a win of a Monday.

But then she sensed something. It began with a prickly sensation on the back of her neck. Katrina had learned long before not to avoid that feeling. She paused to sip her tea and take a surreptitious glance around. She couldn't explain why, but a tall, slender man in a navy Savile Row-looking suit caught her attention—and not because he was attractive. On the contrary, the man had a disturbingly large mole on the right side of his forehead and suede lug-soled shoes.

1

Not your everyday look for someone in such an expensive suit, she thought in reference to the shoes, not the mole, although the observation might have applied to both. *Although…*

She went another block before crossing the street and turning the corner, only to notice he mirrored her pattern. She walked another two blocks before making a left. Mole Man did the same. She briefly ducked behind a courthouse statue.

Clearly, none of it was a coincidence, and Mole Man's intentions were obviously not good. If they were, he would call out and try to catch her attention. What Katrina really wanted to know was whether the chase was about her—or her employer. She kept moving.

Like most wage earners on a Monday morning, Katrina did need to be at work, and she found the little game was getting tedious. Moreover, her employer would be significantly displeased if the man successfully followed her to her workplace. *Time to end this nonsense.* So she paused at the nearest window, pretending to fix her hair. As she did a few quick finger curls with her dark-brown hair and checked to make sure her makeup was perfect on her golden-brown skin, making it a dual-purpose stop—Katrina did value efficiency—her eyes locked with her pursuer's in the reflection. *There.* At least the games would end, seeing as the cat knew the mouse knew about the cat. Or something like that.

His eyes narrowed, and he abruptly turned and stalked off in the opposite direction. Katrina congratulated herself.

"Much easier than I expected. You've just got to stand up to creeps and scare 'em off. Wait till I tell Izzie. She's gonna love this." She took a long swig of tea. It, too, tasted of victory. Her fabulous Monday was back.

She was just a few more blocks away from her job at Safety's Sake Insurance Corporation. With a renewed bounce in her step and distracted by self-congratulatory thoughts, Katrina didn't see the beefy arm that shot out and yanked her into an alley.

IT'S A RARE SORT OF person that views abduction as an opportunity for adventure. Given the adrenaline flooding her nervous system, Katrina supposed she qualified as a member of that class.

She didn't hyperventilate when her assailant stuffed a greasy rag in her mouth and yanked her arms back in order to better bind them with zip ties. Nor did she freak out when she felt her legs being treated similarly. Indeed, as a hood was roughly pulled over her head, her first thought was *Oh, that's gonna make me frizz something terrible...*

So while most would've crumbled, Katrina Foster lived for those moments. And she probably wouldn't die for it either. *Because really, who dies zip-tied on a Monday?* In a circumstance such as the one she was in, Katrina was fairly certain the fates would more likely reserve such a ridiculous way to perish for a weekend—insult to injury, and all that.

Fates' whims aside, she also lived for that sort of moment because her livelihood, via her cover as a Safety's Sake Insurance employee, was as an agent for the Division. A sort of covert Interpol, the Division was a multinational, multibranch agency that collected and trained the world's top agents from select countries around the world. And from that training, Katrina knew how to fight back and how to get out of nearly impossible situations. Well, she understood the theory, anyway. She'd trained but had never actually been face-to-face with a real assailant. That was generally left to the Level Fours.

Katrina felt herself being hoisted over the man's shoulder. Seconds later, she was face down on a surface. It was cool and hard against her stomach, leading her to conclude she was on metal. She heard doors shut and sensed her kidnapper sit next to her.

"She's in. Yeah, I got her hooded and trussed up like a turkey. Let's go."

What sort of goon uses words like "trussed"? Katrina wondered. That should've been her first clue that she was in the midst of an atypical abduction. She gave a tentative wiggle to see how tightly her ties were on. She felt no slack. Unless she was willing to leave a hand behind, Katrina wasn't going to be escaping her bindings anytime soon.

"Don't bother. I know who you are and who you work for, so I made 'em extra tight. And, cute as it is to see, there's no point to wiggling that around to tempt me, either."

Katrina had the distinct displeasure of getting her bum pinched. The thug laughed.

She gasped at the indignity of it all. That was a bad choice, since it allowed the pure unadulterated funk of her kidnapper to finally assault her nostrils. Although she couldn't see her kidnapper, she could certainly smell him, a wretched sensory compensation.

Good lord. Exactly how hard is it to use deodorant and bathe? Is there some Villains 101 *manual that determined the best way to knock out an opponent is through overpowering their olfactory senses?* If so, Katrina figured her attacker was well on his way to a TKO.

Concentrating on her other senses, Katrina determined she was in a van. A series of bumps jostled her around, briefly knocking the breath out of her. The van desperately needed its shocks replaced.

The engine revved hard. Either the streets had miraculously all cleared of morning traffic, or they were entering the on-ramp of a freeway. Katrina noticed her kidnapper move away from her and toward the front of the van. He whispered to the driver, but she couldn't make out anything he said.

As she bounced along, Katrina wondered who would be the first to notice her absence and what, if anything, they might do about it. She was certain someone would notice. Katrina was always on time.

Will anyone come for me? Or will I just be written off as disposable?

From her previous observations, only high-value agents tended to warrant immediate action, and as a Level Three, she didn't think anyone would authorize a search party for her, based on what she guessed was a forty-five-minute absence.

Katrina felt the van slowing down and taking a curve. Her kidnapper and the driver were arguing over directions.

"I'm tellin' ya. Take the side streets! I know it's only twenty-five miles per hour, but there're fewer cops around."

"Yeah, but no one pays attention to who's driving what on the main roads. Last thing we need is some snoopy old biddy calling the police to report a suspicious-looking man in a windowless van."

Katrina could use that information to try to determine where they were taking her. She would find out soon enough—the van came to a stop.

That revolting and all-too-familiar smell returned as her kidnapper clipped the ties around her wrists and ankles. "Don't get excited. You're going to walk on your own volition, but know that I'll be gripping you the whole time, and there'll be armed men the entire way, ready to shoot if you try to run for it."

The doors opened, and Katrina was pushed out of the van. The air smelled of a paper-pulp mill: chemicals and warmed-over dog food. It was somewhat better than the *eau de stink* coming off of Mold Spice, but not by much. She would take it, though. At least it told her she was in the industrial district, about twenty miles south of Division headquarters.

Katrina counted the paces as she walked. Someone whistled and said, "Dead chick walking." Several other men laughed.

After one hundred twenty-five paces, Katrina and her smelly escort stopped. She heard a door slide open, and Mold Spice yanked her inside. She was pushed down into a chair, and her arms and legs were bound to the back of the chair with a nylon rope. Obviously, she couldn't expect that her comfort would be taken into consideration in a situation like hers, but Katrina would've preferred a softer cotton option.

He yanked the hood off her head, knocking her curls forward over her face. She flipped her head back and saw the room was dark and empty, save for swirling blue and red lights. He pulled the rag out of her mouth and pocketed it.

"Nice knowin' ya." He chuckled before walking away.

She heard the door slide open and slam shut, then she exhaled. At least the smell was gone.

The swirling red and blue strobes were starting to nauseate her. Katrina pushed aside the sensation and took stock of her situation. Even with the rag gone, she saw no point in screaming for help. Anyone who was near enough to hear definitely would not be running to her rescue. She'd long since been divested of anything and everything that could be of use. All she had in her possession were her wits and instincts, and every instinct told her something about the entire scenario wasn't right. Or at least, it was more *unright* than she would expect after being abducted, chucked into a van, and dropped off in a seemingly abandoned warehouse with disco lights.

Katrina didn't have long to contemplate this, however, because at that moment, the figure of a tall man entered the room. As the lights swirled over him, she could make out his face. She heaved a sigh. It was Mole Man again, but he wore a black Nehru jacket and pants, looking for all the world like he'd grabbed the last-chance items at a supervillain's yard sale. His hair was slicked back and greasy.

Really, now. This is a bit much. All he needed to complete the look was a monocle and a hard-to-place European accent.

"Vell, vell, vell, Agent Foster."

She rolled her eyes in disgust. *Will there be* no *originality at* all *in this abduction?* She almost took pity on him—almost.

"Vut are ve going to do vit you?"

She shrugged as much as her ropes would allow. "You're the criminal mastermind. I figured you'd have a plan."

"It vuz a figure of speech!" His mole pulsated in commiseration with its owner's irritation. He snapped his fingers, and a bright light shone in her face.

Ah, the old spotlight trick. She'd been trained to experience the intense lighting during her Getting Out of Your Comfort Zone: Interrogation Tips and Techniques of the Division training. She closed her eyes and gave a tentative tug on her ropes. The abrasive nylon meant she wasn't going to be able to rub and wriggle her way out.

Despite her current circumstance, Katrina couldn't deny that being abducted was somewhat flattering. They must have thought she knew something valuable.

She couldn't help but wonder why they chose her. *What sort of information do they think I have?*

"Katrina Foster, who are you vehrking for?"

"If you know my name, then you know the answer: Safety's Sake Insurance Corporation." Feeling defiant and more than a little indignant at her treatment, she asked Mole Man, "Who are *you* working for?"

He made an irritated face. "Clever," he said sarcastically. "But to answer your question—see how easy it is to do—I'm a bit of a freelancer, hired for occasions such as this." He leaned over her. "Let me remind you that *I* vill be asking the questions, thank you. Now again, I vill ask, who are you *really* verhking for?"

Katrina continued to parry verbally and avoided answering her interrogator's questions. The spotlight still glared down on her, and Katrina periodically closed her eyes against it in an attempt to fight the effect it was having on her. While Mole Man grew increasingly angry, she flexed her fingers and reached up to feel the knot. Her eyes sprang open in surprise. *A square knot?*

"Ah! I see I have finally hit your veak spot!"

If Katrina could just stretch her fingers a little higher up, she was going to show him what it meant to get hit in a weak spot. She pulled at the loops to loosen the knot while trying to squeeze some feeling into her hands.

Well, that was easy. Maybe too easy. Tying the ropes into a square knot? Amateur hour. Any thug who expected to get hired for another job would never be so sloppy.

Then again, Katrina considered, she was quite clever. Maybe the assailant had underestimated her, which wouldn't have been the first time. She smiled and shimmied her shoulders to escape the ropes around her. Mole Man's mouth dropped open in surprise.

"That rope tying would've embarrassed a Cub Scout," she said. "You really need to hire a better quality of henchmen."

He shrugged. "Vell, you know, it's hard to get good help these days. The best ones alvays vant the benefit packages, dental..." He whipped out a jagged-edged knife. "I vouldn't bother to make any sudden moves." He stroked the tip of the knife lovingly. "Vehr the hired help failed, I vill not!"

Her legs were still bound, and Katrina wasn't foolish enough to think she could bend over and untie her bindings, not without getting a knife in the back. She figured she had only one option, which was probably going to hurt her as much as him.

As Mole Man lunged, Katrina hurled her body to the side with as much force as she could. The chair cracked as she fell to the floor, and Katrina grunted in pain. She flung her legs against the floor again to break the legs of the chair, ignoring a sharp stab as a chunk of wood was embedded in her hip. The chair fell apart. She grabbed the seat and knocked the knife out of his hands, making it skitter across the floor. Swinging the other way, she cracked the seat across the man's head. With a rewarding smacking sound, Mole Man fell to the ground.

At that moment, all of the lights in the room suddenly turned on.

"Congratulations, Agent Foster," a tinny, familiar-sounding voice came through a ceiling speaker. "You have now achieved Level Four status."

Chapter 2

There's nothing quite like reaching Level Four status to get a girl out of bed in the morning.

Her whole body was stiff, but Katrina wasn't going to let a few aches and pains keep her from her first official day as an advanced agent. The pain was good. It reminded her that the events of the day before weren't a dream. Having been stuck at Level Three for three years and fifty-seven whole days, she'd often worried she would languish there forever. Forever, of course, being a relative concept.

After a gratifyingly hot shower, Katrina set about assessing the damage. Everything looked worse the next day. Bluish-black bands crisscrossed her chest and stomach where she'd bounced against the hard metal floor of the van. Red welts were still visible against her light-brown skin. She daubed some antibiotic cream on the abrasions left by the zip ties and rope then gently wrapped her wrists and ankles with soft bandages.

As Katrina methodically tended her various injuries, she thought back to the day before. Everything had happened so quickly. One minute, Mole Man—who turned out to be a delightful actor whose real accent was pure New Jersey—was congratulating her, and the next, she found herself being whisked away in an ambulance for a medical assessment. Then came the lawyers who had, indeed, lived up to their reputation by being right behind the ambulance, confidentiality agreements in hand. Before she could be released from the doctor's exam table, she signed documents swearing she would never reveal her experience to any Division employee lower than a Level Four, which made sense. Otherwise, all the Level Threes would be alert at all times for their big chance to reach Level Four status, and the whole point was to catch them off guard.

The ink was barely dry when she was smuggled back into Division headquarters for a meeting with someone in human resources. The man droned on and on in a seemingly never-ending recitation of the rights and responsibilities of a Level Four agent. The main message Katrina took home was "Succeed in your mission, and get rewarded with another. Fail, and well, don't expect anyone to write you a letter of reference." One hastily taken identification-card picture later, she was free to go. The driver of the same windowless white van that had started Katrina on her day's adventure dropped her off a block from her apartment, and she'd limped inside before passing out gratefully in bed.

Bringing her musings to the present, she smiled as she carefully slipped into her clothes. *Level Four. Incredible what can happen in twenty-four hours.* She'd gone from being a mere spy lackey, stuck doing case maintenance and cleanup, to a *real* spy—with a real mission. Feeling sentimental, she put on the gold necklace her mother had given her as a child. With a series of swirls on top of a forty-five-degree angle, the pendant resembled an ice cream cone. Maybe it looked juvenile, but she still liked to wear it on occasion, and that day was a big occasion. It slid down to her cleavage and hid out of sight.

As she hurried to finish, Katrina brushed a final light layer of powder over her skin and checked the status of her hair. Her curls were perfectly glossy without the slightest hint of frizz. *There. That proves it—a sign.* Even her hair recognized the momentous occasion by calling a truce. She fixed her starched collar and checked one last time in the mirror. *Crisp. Professional. Orderly.* She glanced down at her velvet-embossed heels. *And with just a little bit of flair.* In short, she wore the uniform of the perfect secret agent.

Before heading out the door, Katrina pressed her fingers to her matte-finished lips and touched a photo of her parents. They'd worked for the Division as well, and she liked to think they would've been excited for her too. Then she grimaced. Perhaps, given what had happened to them, maybe not. She set the alarm, turned both locks, and prepared for the morning's commute.

Looking around with greater vigilance, Katrina approached the tall glass doors of her official workplace, Safety's Sake Insurance Corporation. An entirely nondescript building, it served as the perfect location to house an ultra-top-secret spy organization, its innocuous exterior cleverly masking the bustling agency within. The Division might have been small by bureaucratic standards, but it delivered outsized results.

Katrina sailed through the first set of doors, past the Level Ones busy developing their deception skills while selling insurance policies, and right toward the second entryway.

"Hey, Katrina, have you heard about the new Level Fours? Boy, the Division is really dropping their standards. Nowadays, they promote just about anybody who can solve a sudoku puzzle and keep a secret." James Brickman, the secure-entry technician—also known as the doorman—grinned as he gave Katrina her updated identification badge.

Katrina returned his smile and followed it by sticking out her tongue for good measure. "Thanks for the vote of confidence, James." She sneaked a glance at her badge before clipping it on. Judging by her half-closed eyes and a mouth opened as though to object to the impending indignity, the agency's photographer—if she could be so generous—had clearly gone through the same photography program as the Department of Motor Vehicles.

"Eh, you know I'm just joshin' you. You'll be great. You can't help it. It's in your genes."

"In your genes." With that statement, Katrina's already ramped-up emotions went into overdrive. Her parents had also held Level Four status and had a well-deserved reputation for getting results no one else could.

Can I match their accomplishments? Should I even try?

Gripping a steel railing as she ascended gleaming marble steps, Katrina told herself that, no, she would just be the best agent she could be. Naturally, that was a lie. She'd never been the type to be content with "just good enough," and she certainly wasn't going to start. She'd been at the top of her class, and confidence, along with maybe a little arrogance, came naturally to her.

But this is something else.

Even with her frustration at staying a Level Three for so long, she'd felt some comfort in knowing she was the best at her level. As a Level Four, though, she wouldn't be an expert anymore. With her advancement, she became a veritable little fish in a big spy pond. She wasn't entirely certain what that would mean for her, but she knew she would give it her all. She took a deep breath and opened the conference room door.

Inside was one other newly upgraded agent, appearing both nervous and excited. Katrina joined her at the table with a quick smile. She'd known Isobel Figueroa since her first day with the Division. She was as goofy as Katrina was serious. Surprisingly, the contrast worked well. Together, they rose through the ranks and had been through much, from the Filing Cabinet Caper of 2008 to learning how to induce projectile vomit on command in their Bodies as Diversions course. That was *not* Katrina's finest moment. If she was going to be on her first assignment with anyone, she was glad it was with Izzie.

Director Samantha Jones entered, stalking around the room at a brisk pace. She had frosted blond hair that seemed to match the iciness of her personality. Outside of seeing her "inspirational" closing messages in training videos—"And should you die, take pride that you were fortunate enough to die for the Division"—they'd never interacted with the director in person while in the lower levels. But they had indeed heard rumors. Most definitely. One glance said Director Jones had earned every bit of her fearsome reputation. Katrina had the clear impression that she never trifled or suffered trifling. The director did not formally introduce herself as it was a given that everyone knew of her. She didn't ask their names and did not need to. They would never have advanced if she were not fully apprised of their backgrounds.

A nameless assistant gave them tablets while Director Jones began speaking. "Congratulations on the end of your Level Three tenure and your subsequent promotion. To celebrate, I got you a present: your first Level Four case."

Her assistant began projecting information on a large screen.

"Get your Division passports ready, ladies. Your first mission—which I will oversee—is taking you to Sweden."

Oooh, travel. This sounds intriguing...

"One of Sweden's top agents, Oskar Reinfeldt Blomqvist, code name Noll-Noll-Sju, has gone missing."

Katrina spoke first. "And by 'missing'..."

"I mean dead, Agent Foster," Director Jones said.

Katrina's eyes met Izzie's. *Figures.* The Division loved to employ euphemisms—like how rogue agent Sparrow didn't get electrocuted, she was just simply found to be a rather excellent conductor of electricity.

"Alright," Katrina said, feeling cowed but not willing to show it. "So the 'missing' agent—what's the story?"

"Two days ago, we were informed that Blomqvist was killed. As you well know, that's not exactly a newsworthy occurrence in our line of work. However, that the death of a high-profile agent was under mysterious circumstances did capture Division attention. His body was found on the twenty-eighth floor of Kaknäs Tower, but preliminary evidence indicates that he was transported there postmortem. Given the high visibility of the site and the fact no one should have been allowed access, the Swedes believe his death was intended to send a message."

"What was he working on at the time?" Katrina asked.

"Good question. He was working several missions simultaneously, but the Division suspects he was on an unsanctioned assignment, based on forensic evidence. Agent Blomqvist must've known his time was up, because the pathologist discovered Blomqvist had managed to insert a small recording device inside himself before he was killed."

Isobel made an "eeew!" face. Katrina involuntarily clenched.

"Other end, Agent Figueroa. The sound file was mostly corrupted by the stomach acids, but they were able to obtain the following, and I quote, 'The V is the key. Surikov knows. What's past isn't past.'"

"At least there's a name," Katrina noted.

"Indeed," Director Jones said. "Using the name Surikov, they were able to trace it back to an assassin who was responsible for the murder of a Swedish politician, Johanna Lindström."

"Then what's the problem? What do they need us for?"

"The problem, Agent Foster, is that the case was closed a decade ago, and the assassin has been confined the same length of time. Adding to the Swedish Division's difficulties is that all of Blomqvist's records are written in a way that no one there can decode. They need a code breaker."

The director turned toward Katrina. "This is where you come in. With your specialization in enigmatology and your ability to speak

Swedish, you will be the lead on this. Your mission: find out what Blomqvist uncovered and why it was worth dying for." She turned toward Izzie. "Whoever managed to kill a top agent was obviously skilled. Agent Figueroa, with your background in armaments, you are being sent for additional protection."

"Contacts?" Katrina asked.

She looked at her notes and flipped a few pages. "You've been assigned to Agent Magnus Svensson and his partner, Lena Holmberg. Both are experienced agents, and you would do well to listen to them and follow their lead."

At that moment, the director's assistant slipped behind her and whispered in her ear. She grimaced. "Alright, I can't waste any more time on this. You leave tomorrow. Don't screw this up."

With those encouraging words, she straightened, turned sharply on her stilettos, and left the room. Her assistant quickly scuttled after her.

The two women looked at each other in surprise. Whatever concerns they might've had about having less than twenty-four hours to prepare were clearly not shared by the director.

"Uhh... okay..." Katrina turned toward Izzie. "Not a lot of guidance, was there?"

Izzie shook her head. "Nope. Guessing this is trial by fire."

"Alright, I'm going to hit the code books and keys and start brushing up on techniques. While I do that, why don't you work out the logistics of getting us there? Also, I'm leaving it up to you to figure out what hardware we'll need."

Izzie's eyes lit up. The woman had an unexplained and unabashed love for weapons of destruction, so letting the agent work within her strengths only seemed advisable.

"I'm on it. Catch ya later."

Katrina left the conference room and headed one floor up to her new office. She'd been moved in with the Level Fours. While not luxurious, her own office had her name on the door and a plant in the corner, which she was determined not to kill. She sat down at her new desk and smiled. Even the office chairs were better as a Level Four. She was absolutely convinced that the increased lumbar support would undoubtedly aid in her progress.

Alright, time to hit it.

While Katrina had no idea what techniques Blomqvist had used, she was determined to figure out what he knew and to make her mark as a Level Four who could get results. That wouldn't be easy, though—if it had been, the Swedes wouldn't have needed her and her skill set, so she was just going to try to cover as many bases as possible.

Broadly speaking, Katrina was an enigmatologist, someone who studied puzzles. Puzzle creation, cryptology, ciphers, and code breaking all fell under that umbrella. At the most fundamental level, Katrina liked things to make sense, and when they didn't, she viewed it as a personal offense. She derived a lot of satisfaction from making sense of the incomprehensible. So much of her childhood didn't make any sense that she was glad to have a skill set that solved mysteries. Family legacy aside, no one was surprised that she decided to become a spy.

She was in the middle of reviewing the Feistel cipher when Izzie flung open her door and came toward her, juggling a black leather briefcase in one arm and a stack of papers under the armpit of the other. Izzie pulled out the papers that had taken up residence under her arm and tossed them carelessly onto Katrina's desk. She then picked up the black leather briefcase and rested it gently next to the strewn papers.

"Okay, pick your poison—not literally, mind you. Do you want to review logistics first or your weaponry?"

"Oooh. Weapons first, please."

"That's what I hoped you'd say." Izzie snapped open the leather case. "I'll do most of the heavy lifting—we can't all be selected as the lead. Some of us have to have an actual talent in getting our hands dirty," she said without heat.

As Izzie was probably the best, most diversely skilled fighter in their class, Katrina had no disagreement there.

"I will, however, allow you to have this small pistol with a silencer." She carefully handed her the gun.

Katrina examined it and had to admit that Izzie had good taste, as it was both sleekly beautiful and functional.

"And because I'm a traditionalist, I am also bestowing upon you this V-42 stiletto." Her eyes took on a rapturous fervor that warned Katrina that she was in for an overly poetic treatise.

"First issued in World War Two, this beautifully crafted high-carbon-steel dagger is narrow enough to be discreet but designed to operate well for both slashing and thrusting. The pommel, known for its skull-cru—"

Katrina had to shut this dissertation down. "I will let you tell whatever ridiculously embarrassing story about me from our training days to our Swedish counterparts if you will wrap this up."

Izzie's face took on a frighteningly excited expression that made Katrina instantly regret not sitting though Knives 101. "Deal. Shiny knife. Kills good. Moving on."

Izzie pointed at the papers she'd given Katrina. "In that pile are your plane tickets, hotel reservations, meeting times with the Swedes... Oh, and some bad news: we're sharing a room."

"What? We have to share? Are you kidding me?" Sometimes, Katrina couldn't tell when Izzie was serious or just working her way to a punchline.

"I know, I know. But the director's assistant said that the dollar doesn't carry the weight that it used to and that, as two of the newest Level Fours, we should be glad we're only sharing a room and not a bed." She then turned on a pitch-perfect imitation of the director. "Even the Division has to be fiscally prudent in this economy."

Katrina did a quick dollar-to-crown conversion in her head and considered what hotel rates were likely to be during the summer in an expensive city like Stockholm. *Rats.* The director was right—they were stuck together. Izzie was a good friend and colleague, but she was notorious among the other spies as someone who alternated between night terrors and snoring like a beast. Katrina made a mental note to add earplugs to her packing list.

"But no matter. We'll be great roomies, right?" It was less of a question and more of a statement from the confident Izzie.

Katrina nodded. Getting her weapons and paperwork made it real—like, real-real. She glanced at Izzie, who didn't seem the least bit stressed about what they were getting ready to head into in less than twenty-four hours.

"Aren't you worried about our first mission? I mean, I know it'll go great and all." Katrina had to at least project confidence. "But what if it doesn't? It could set our careers back and damage our reputations in the Division."

Izzie shrugged as she carefully packed the weapons back into the briefcase. "Yeah... totally not worried about that. We'll be joining two seasoned Level Fours, so I'm going to go in there, do my best, and try to come home alive. If I can do that, hey, mission accomplished."

Katrina seemed unconvinced.

"I get where you're coming from, though. It's just that we're going into this from different angles. You're all 'Be the best, and make your mark!' and I'm more 'Did I live? Sweet.' Although, to be fair, I don't have two famous parents who were top agents, so there's that. I don't have the same baggage you do, so it just means I can focus my attention elsewhere." With that, Izzie stood up to leave. "Besides," she said with a mischievous grin, "You're the lead on this, so if we screw this up, it's all on you."

"Thanks, Izzie," Katrina deadpanned. "That was helpful."

"Anytime, friend. Anytime."

BACK HOME FROM WORK, Katrina was heading up the front steps to her apartment when she spotted Hector Ochoa by the mailboxes. She didn't have many close ties, given her history and profession, but they'd been friends ever since the day she moved into the building, and he was her go-to person for anything to do with technology—or food. He was an excellent cook, and as Katrina's culinary skills were largely relegated to expertly peeling back the film on a frozen dinner, that was a very nice benefit of their friendship. She gave a big wave, which Hector returned by shaking his left foot as he was in the act of carrying a box. They walked down the hallway together.

"What's going on, Kat?" Hector set down the box in front of his apartment door and started absentmindedly patting his cargo pants' many pockets for his keys.

Katrina lifted Hector's keys from his shirt pocket and unlocked his apartment door. "Just coming back from work. I got a promotion today, and you know the saying: with great power comes great responsibility." A quote from Voltaire for her, most likely a comic book quote for him.

"Well, congratulations on making your way up the insurance-investigation ladder. You were in your other job for what, a little over three years?"

"That's right!" Katrina tried to not look wary. "Crazy you remembered that."

He dropped the box on the floor inside his apartment and ran a hand through his dark hair. "Well, you know, I guess I have a knack

for that sort of thing. I'm always retaining one factoid or another."
He paused. "Want to come over for dinner to celebrate? It's only left-
overs, but you know they're even better the next day."

"Aww, I'd love to, but I've got an early start in the morning. I'm
heading to Stockton first thing. Maybe not my first choice in location, but at least it's an intriguing case. This guy's farmhouse was destroyed under suspicious circumstances. Quite the exciting hubbub,
really. See, his policy had two subsections pertaining to the proper
storage of asparagus in relation to—"

Hector groaned and put up a hand. "Let me stop you. No details,
please. You may find this hard to believe, but I'm simply not interested in the scintillating world of insurance."

Katrina actually found that quite easy to believe, as did the Division. No one ever got overly curious about insurance companies,
which is why Safety's Sake Insurance Corporation made the perfect
cover. Just mentioning actuarial tables and policy riders would make
an otherwise attentive human being's eyes glaze over. No one but the
most polite or masochistic would be foolish enough to risk a follow-
up question, which was exactly what Katrina counted on.

"Anyway, I may be gone for a few weeks. Keep an eye on my
plants, will you? The ficus nearly went to the big plant nursery in the
sky last time."

Hector nodded. "Sure thing. They might go into shock from receiving such good care, though."

She grinned. "Thanks. I owe you. I'll slip my spare key under
your door before I leave, and you know the code for the alarm."

"Got it. I'll be on the lookout. Let me know if you need anything
else. Have a good time in Stockton."

Katrina snorted. "I'll try. It's not exactly the big city I was hoping
for."

He frowned in sympathy. "Well, have a good time there anyway.
See you when you get back."

Stockton. Stockholm. Good to have similar-sounding locations.
That made accidentally saying the wrong name a lot easier to avoid.
She wondered if the same thing ought to apply to men, but proper
dating was such a rarity for her anyway that she supposed it hardly
mattered.

Katrina waved goodbye and made her way down the hall. She
probably should have felt regret for lying to her friend, but she didn't,
and she didn't think that made her a bad person, especially since he
was her only friend on the "outside." Not knowing the truth could
save his life. More than plausible deniability was at stake.

She unlocked the door, turned off her alarm, and kicked off her
heels into the corner piled high with the others. She grabbed her spy
bag—a large bulletproof four-wheeler with Safety's Sake Insurance
Company emblazoned in blue across the sides and an extra compartment undetectable by airport scanners—and started to pack. In went
her passport, the one that said Katie Foster and blocked transmission signals. In went the map of Stockholm coated in a bulletproof
polymer. In went the platform sandals that concealed one small in-a-
pinch knife in the left heel and one loop of piano wire in the right.
In went the blue-and-yellow sundress that doubled as, well, nothing,
really. A girl plain needed to look good, no matter the mission. Katrina threw in a few more clothes, toiletries, and Division-sanctioned
items, and she was set.

After fixing a steaming cup of tea and one of Lean Cuisine's finest
culinary exemplars, Katrina grabbed a book off her top shelf and
flopped on the couch. She cracked open one of the dog-eared pages.
Time to brush up on my Swedish.

Chapter 3

Well before the sun rose, Katrina hopped in the shower, threw her wet hair into a high bun, and tossed on what she liked to refer to as her early-summer travel ensemble: a long-sleeved, salmon-colored shirt, brown jersey-knit pants, and a cream pashmina that could double as a blanket in a pinch. She wasn't much of a believer in good luck charms, but on the off chance they were actually a thing, she put on her gold necklace again. She grabbed her bag and a preschmeared bagel, slipped her key under Hector's door, and hopped on the train to the airport.

On the way, she checked her phone.

Izzie had texted, *In front of the security checkpoint to Gate D. Where R U?!*

Next was an encrypted video transmission from the director: "Please memorize this message, as it will be deleted upon the video's completion. Your first point of contact at Skavsta airport will be Jens."

Katrina noted that no last name was given. A man's picture appeared on the screen. He resembled a really Jeevesy sort of character, impeccably dressed, with slightly jowly cheeks that made Katrina think of a bulldog.

The director continued, "Upon encountering Jens, use the code phrase 'Beautiful day. I bet the water is nice in Nynäshamn.' He'll deliver you to the Swedish Division headquarters."

Katrina committed the phrase to memory. Something about his profile told her Jens wasn't exactly the type to offer second chances.

"Oh, and one more thing. Do be sure to keep Isobel reined in, will you? While she's eminently qualified, I'm not fully of the opinion that her loose-cannon nature will do well in foreign places. We do not need an international incident. Do also remember that public knowledge of this agency is disavowed by all heads of state, so no one outside of the US and Swedish Division will assist you. Do not even bother setting foot in an embassy or any governmental branch."

Her assistant handed her a note.

"Yes, yes. Just let me wrap this up," she said impatiently. Then she turned back to the camera. "Good luck on your inaugural mission, Agent Foster. I do hope you don't die, but remember that if you do, take pride that you were fortunate enough to die for the Division. Director out." With a strained grin—smiling did not appear to come naturally to the director—she disappeared from the screen.

Katrina wondered if Director Jones's encouraging catchphrase was her own or if that was a verbal baton passed from director to director over time. She would've liked to ask her parents, if that was an option.

No time to dwell on that. She had a loose cannon to find at the airport.

AT THE AIRPORT, KATRINA spotted Izzie's mass of short black curls near the security entrance. She was shorter than Katrina but curvy and strong. Izzie was rocking back and forth against a wall, reading her copy of *Welcome to Sweden: When You Want to Know More than Abba, Volvo, and IKEA.*

She looked up as Katrina approached. "About time you made it."

"I'm not late."

"Well, you're certainly not early." She lowered her voice. "We can't mess around when it comes to getting through security. I don't want to have to explain to the director why we missed the plane... especially since I was the one who set the itinerary." She transitioned to tapping her toes, appearing distinctly anxious—not a good look on the ordinarily devil-may-care Isobel.

Katrina sighed. "Well, I'm here. You're here. We've got plenty of time, so quit being antsy. If anyone should be worried, it's me. As you so aptly noted yesterday, if there's a screwup, I'll get the blame."

"I'm not worried, and I am certainly *not* antsy," she said. "Let's just get going and hope our bags get through without any problems."

When Katrina finally made it through the security line, she had a moment's hesitation before putting her suitcase on the conveyor belt to be scanned. She didn't want to think about what might happen if the alarm went off. While she suspected the Division probably had some of their own working in airport security, that wasn't a theory she wanted to test out. As she passed through the detector and collected her shoes, she exhaled in gratitude. The specially lined compartment in her suitcase had done its job. No questions were asked.

The two women boarded the plane, and as they headed down the aisle, Izzie gestured for Katrina to take the window seat. "I'd rather not know what's going on out there. Just staring out at the clouds reminds me of how far I have to plunge."

When Katrina noticed a sheen of sweat building on Izzie's brow, everything made sense. The otherwise brave Izzie didn't like to fly, and a US-to-Sweden flight was not exactly a quick jaunt.

"Huh. I guess I've never traveled with you by plane before." She gave her friend a pat. "Don't worry, Izzie. It'll be fine."

Izzie gave Katrina a Look. She was well beyond the reassuring-pat stage. "And you know this how? Are you a pilot? No. Are you a mechanic? No. Did you make sure the wing bolts were screwed on right? No. Did you scan every seat for potentially explosive residues?

No. Did you make sure the food trays contain no harmful bacteria so it won't make the pilots sick..." The more doomsday scenarios Izzie came up with, the more agitated she became, her breath coming in big huffs. She glanced over at the exit as the flight attendants closed the door. "And the next thing you know, it's 'Farewell, America' and 'Hello, bottom of the Atlantic.'"

"You do realize that, statistically speaking, you're more likely to get killed by a car or heart disease or even a homicidal maniac than by plane, right? It's just basic mathematical probability. You are perfectly fine."

"Well, you rely on your 'basic mathematical probability,' and I'll rely on *this*." Izzie whipped out her rosary and began working the beads and murmuring at a frenetic pace.

Katrina shrugged and nestled into her seat. As the plane—safely—took off, she stared out the window, lost in the contemplation of old memories.

Yes, Katrina knew about the statistics of life and death. She'd been with her parents the day they died. At ten years old, Katrina was in the car with them when it burst into flames. She couldn't remember much: bright sunshine, brighter flames. The stench of burning plastic and skin. Katrina supposed she should be grateful for the explosion—the sheer force of it ejected her from the vehicle and ultimately saved her life. The only physical evidence of that day was a large scar on the back of one leg, between the bend of her knee and upper calf. It bore a strong resemblance to the profile of one Richard Milhous Nixon. Some days when the scar itched, she liked to say that "Ol' Tricky Dick is acting up again." No one got the joke except her, but it was better than saying, "Excuse me while I scratch at a horrific reminder of my parents' death."

Since Katrina somehow survived a massive car explosion with only one Nixonian scar to show for it, she wasn't the least bit concerned about plane safety—or any safety statistics at all, really. She'd already beaten the odds.

And with that comforting thought, thirty-six thousand feet in the air and nowhere near a car, Katrina fell asleep.

THEY ARRIVED IN THE late afternoon at Skavsta airport. Poor Izzie was the worse for wear, having foregone sleep in lieu of keeping a one-woman lookout for terrorists and any potential loose screws on the plane. Katrina suggested that the only thing she noticed with a screw loose happened to be located in the seat next to her. She received several choice words from her irritable, flight-traumatized seatmate in response.

In contrast, Katrina was refreshed and eager to get to the Swedish Division headquarters. They retrieved their bags and headed toward the exit.

"Okay, keep an eye out for a Jeevesy sort of character. Probably in a dark, well-tailored suit. From the picture the director sent, he seemed to be in his early forties."

Izzie gave a drawn-out yawn in response. "Keep an eye out? I can't even keep an eye open."

"No one told you to stay awake the entire flight, contemplating your doom." Before she could continue her lecture, she saw a mid-sized, nattily dressed man with slicked-back brown hair and a face that indeed gave a rather good impression of a bulldog. He was crouched on the ground, intently polishing the tip of his right shoe with a handkerchief.

Katrina nudged Izzie and gave a slight nod to the right. "Over there, by the newsstand. That's our Jens."

They approached, and Katrina remembered the designated code phrase. "Beautiful day. I bet the water is nice in Nynäshamn."

At those words, Jens rose and gestured toward a black sedan parked in the loading area by the curb. Izzie ran for coffee while Jens loaded their bags.

On the drive into Stockholm, a freshly caffeinated and re-energized Izzie attempted to engage Jens in conversation. That went as well as Katrina could have expected, which was not well at all.

"So, Jens, how long have you worked for the agency?"

Silence.

"You originally from Sweden?"

Silence.

"What's the most interesting mission you've ever been on?"

Silence.

"Ever killed a man?"

Silence.

Impressed by Izzie's dedication but tiring of the one-sided conversation, Katrina turned her gaze toward the window. As she watched a herd of reindeer prance through the tall yellow-green grass, Katrina was reminded of how beautiful Sweden was, especially in the summer. She'd been there several summers as a child with her parents and had hazy memories of crayfish and laughter and strawberry cakes. Only later did she find out that they were actually on missions and not family vacations. That made the whole thing feel a bit more calculated but not any less enjoyable.

"Alright, Jens. It's been lovely talking with you, but I'm all tuckered out." Izzie turned toward Katrina and stage-whispered, "Such a chatterbox! You can't shut the guy up."

In the driver's mirror, Katrina saw Jens roll his eyes, but true to character, whatever response he might have wanted to make stayed within.

Once they reached central Stockholm, the car pulled into a parking garage. Jens opened their door and brushed an invisible piece of lint off his shoulder while he waited for them to exit. Unable to further avoid the necessity of talking, he grunted, "This way."

Katrina and Izzie followed him down Hamngatan. They stopped in front of a large stone building with flags out front and a glowing red NK symbol.

Izzie silently read the placard and turned toward Katrina, whispering "*Nordiska Kompaniet*?"

"Yeah. It's called NK for short. It's an upscale store. Any idea why he'd take us here?" Izzie shrugged.

Katrina peered down at her own serviceable attire. "I have the impression that Jens is sartorially intense, but I don't think he brought us here for a wardrobe change."

Knowing they couldn't count on an explanation from Jens, they followed him through the doors. Once inside, Katrina watched with a smile as Izzie took in the interior. It was an impressive display of gleaming marble and brass. Her eyes lit up, and both women slowly looked upward. Above them were four glorious floors of *shopportunities*—a nearly endless display of handbags, expertly lit makeup counters, and dresses that had to be for display only as they appeared to be well outside an ordinary Swede's budget.

"I am liking Sweden more and more, I think," Izzie said with a grin. As they followed Jens up the escalator, she pointed at a pair of fluorescent-pink heels. "Do you think I could get these written off as a mission expense?"

Katrina shook her head. "With our director? Think again. This is the woman who's forcing us to share a room, remember?"

Izzie pulled a face. "Fair point." She gazed back wistfully at the shoes as they passed by, continuing to trail after Jens.

On the fourth floor, they walked down a narrow path between a cloakroom and a delicious-smelling restaurant. They went farther and farther back until they reached the rear of the building. There, they found a freight elevator with an out of order sign.

Disregarding the signage, Jens pressed the down button, and the doors slid open. Inside the elevator, Jens lifted up the button panel. Underneath was a keypad with a touchscreen above. Apparently, this elevator served a purpose other than transporting freight. He cut his eyes over to the women, who quickly became interested in the lighting fixtures above.

Katrina surreptitiously slid her eyes downward to watch Jens punch in a ten-digit code, which he followed by pressing his hand against the touchpad. After three beeps and a jolt, the elevator descended.

"I guess there is more to NK than meets the eye," Katrina murmured. "I had no idea that all this time, it doubled as the Division headquarters."

Several moments later, the elevator finally reached its destination. Jens readjusted his tie before exiting. Katrina saw two figures standing halfway down a dimly lit hall. She turned back to see what Jens would do next, but he'd already disappeared. Katrina and Izzie were on their own.

Chapter 4

Katrina had a brief moment of nervousness, feeling intimidated at the prospect of working side-by-side with two real-deal Level Fours. Then she realized that, having reached Level Four status, she too was a "real-deal" spy and not just another member of the agency.

As she walked down the hallway, she could see the Swedish agents a bit better. Both appeared to be in their early forties. Maybe the woman was a little older. The man was tall, about six-foot-three, with a sharply angled face that made his warm blue-gray eyes look curiously out of place. His partner was short, with an even shorter pixie cut dyed a bright shade of red not normally found in nature. The cropped style served to emphasize arctic eyes and scowling eyebrows.

Katrina heard what sounded a lot like a heated argument between the two of them. From her college coursework and supplemental language work with the Division—unsurprisingly, most college language classes didn't teach the translations of terms like "grappling hook" and "cyanide capsule"—she was fairly fluent in Swedish, but she still had to listen intently while trying to seem as though she wasn't doing exactly that. Katrina smiled. Izzie peeked over and quickly followed suit with a pearly grin of her own and a wave.

The female spy sneered and said in Swedish, "Just look at them, with their giant American smiles. All perfectly straight, shiny white teeth. So superficial."

Katrina's smile briefly faltered before brightening again.

"I didn't realize having a decent mouth was a character flaw," the male deadpanned.

"Did you see their weapons that arrived yesterday? What, like we don't have a perfectly fine arsenal at our disposal? I guess our armaments are not good enough for the cowboys. Not like they are likely to need them anyway."

"Unless my vision is faulty, I believe you meant to say cow*girls*."

Katrina decided that she preferred the man over his grumpy Ameriphobic partner.

The woman scowled even more deeply somehow. "Yes, I'm sure you're excited by your new prospects. I know your type—all boobs and brashness."

He chose not to respond to that and instead said, "They're part of our team now, Lena. That's just the way it is."

"And why is that, exactly, Magnus? I mean, I know why *we* were given this mission, but why are they here? They're a couple of newbies." She verbally barreled on before Magnus could reply. "Whatever. Just keep them out of my way. The less I have to deal with them, the better."

The man had clearly lost his remaining shred of patience. "Enough, Lena. In case you forgot, our director demanded we bring over the Americans. I couldn't have prevented it even if I wanted to. Which I don't." Though Katrina and Izzie had nearly reached them, he continued to ignore them. "We all have a job to do. So try to do the bare minimum to be civil—difficult for you, I know—and let's get through this."

Lena huffed in irritation. "If I had known *this* is who we would be stuck with, I wouldn't have told the new director where he could shove his *knäckebröd*."

Katrina and Izzie reached them before Magnus could reply. They immediately stopped arguing and turned toward the two Americans.

Katrina spoke directly to the male agent. *"Hej. Är du Agent Magnus Svensson?"*

He seemed momentarily nonplussed before responding. *"Ja. Agent Foster?"*

"Precis. Trevligt att träffas. Kan vi prata engelska? Min partner förstår inte svenska."

Izzie nudged Katrina in the ribs and murmured, "Are you talking about me? What are you saying about me? What's this about not understanding Swedish? I understand it *perfectly*." Izzie pasted on a big cheery American smile and with her finest accent said, *"Hej! Om dig, jag hora mycket bra!"*

In response, Katrina bit her lip and rolled her eyes upward, Lena looked like her greatest fears had been realized, and Magnus tried to hide his grin but failed.

Magnus cleared his throat. "Yes, I think English would be best. It's a pleasure to meet you as well. Agent Foster, let me also introduce you to my partner, Lena Holmberg."

Lena gave a curt nod.

"No need for formality on my part. Just 'Katrina' is fine." She focused on Lena. "It is a pleasure to meet you, Agent Holmberg." She noticed the woman did not return the offer of informality. She gestured toward Izzie. "This is my partner, Isobel Figueroa. We're excited to assist in any way we can." She then smiled at Lena in a way that put all her teeth on display. "I know we look forward to sinking our shiny white teeth into your case."

Magnus's eyes grew wide, and he quirked his lips.

But if Lena was the least bit ashamed that she'd been overheard and understood by her new colleague, she didn't betray it.

Lena sucked her teeth for a moment and said, "Well, if your partner there can stay out of the red-light district long enough, maybe you two might actually be of some use to us."

Angered, Izzie stepped forward. "Red-light district! What the hell?" She turned back in bewilderment to Katrina before returning to Lena again. "All I tried to do was be nice. I told you that I heard nice things about you. And you turn around and act like a jerk."

Katrina sighed. "No, actually you said to them, 'Of you, I whore very good.'"

Izzie looked abashed and groaned. "Oh. Sorry. Obviously, that's not what I meant."

"No worries. Ours is not an easy language," Magnus replied, clearly ready to change the subject. "Shall we head into the processing room? I know you just arrived and are probably quite tired, but I am afraid you will need to do some paperwork and undergo an initial briefing this afternoon before we can have Jens deliver you to your hotel room. We will fully begin tomorrow morning at eight o'clock."

"That sounds fine to me," Katrina said. To cover for Izzie, who'd suffered enough embarrassment for the day, even if it was of her own doing, she added, "I didn't sleep well on the plane, so I'd like to get this over with and rest up for tomorrow."

"Of course. Come this way. Room A7." Magnus led the way.

Lena side-eyed the women briefly before joining her partner.

As they walked down the hall, Izzie and Katrina lagged a little behind.

Izzie whispered, "Jeez. How was that for a first impression? 'I whore very well.' And here I thought my Swedish was quite good."

Katrina shook her head. "You know, all those little circles and dots above the letters they taught us about in our Languages of the Division classes actually *do* serve a purpose. It's how you know how to pronounce things. You said 'höra' without any 'ö,' which totally changes the meaning, as you just found out." Katrina gave her friend a small smile. "As far as first impressions go, it wasn't your finest moment. But hey, now the Swedes have a great story to share about the US agency's newest Level Fours."

Izzie had the good grace to be embarrassed. "Great. Well, let the redemption arc begin, then."

Ahead of them, Lena leaned against an office door, tapping a foot noisily. "If you both are done taking your sweet time, everyone is in the room, waiting patiently for you to grace them with your stars-and-stripes presence."

Katrina made eye contact with Izzie before quickening their pace down the dim hallway.

"Well," Izzie whispered, "this isn't going to be awkward at all."

Chapter 5

Katrina and Izzie entered the processing room to find a bustling environment of perhaps fifty agents, some in normal attire and some in long-sleeved white dress shirts. Katrina supposed those might be the desk job agents.

After a fingerprint analysis and a retinal scan, their identities were confirmed, then they entered the main facility. With lighting specially designed to simulate sunlight, Katrina noted that working in the windowless facility would not be a problem. Despite the building's age, the Swedish Division's interior was strikingly modern. The Swedes had made workplace aesthetics a priority, apparently.

Magnus beckoned them forward as he addressed the room. "*Ursäkta*. Excuse me. I want to introduce to you our visiting US agents, Katrina Foster and Isobel Figueroa." The response ranged from complete disregard to tentative smiles.

He took them over to their workspace. "Here's where you'll be working, Agent Foster."

It was the dreaded open desk. All that workplace theory that an open layout was best for collaboration was all well and good unless a person needed quiet to focus on decoding. Katrina groaned inwardly.

"You have a space, too, Agent Figueroa, but most of your work will probably be in the armory, at least to begin with," Magnus said. "And Lena is... over there." He indicated a small desk shoved as far away as possible from the rest of the workspace. Then he pointed at a large enclosed room with blinds pulled in front of the windows. The door was open, though, and a large desk had several chairs positioned in front of it. "There's my office. We will hold group meetings in there."

Katrina nodded and wondered what sort of successes she would need to rack up at the Swedish Division in order to move from her crappy open-space desk to an office with a door.

"Okay, I'll leave you to it. I know you are tired and probably hungry. Head out and rest up." Magnus glanced down at his watch. "I need to meet with my director. Jens will take you to the hotel. See you tomorrow at eight."

As if on cue, Jens appeared next to them, tugging on the cuffs of his shirtsleeves and looking vaguely uncomfortable at the idea of transporting Izzie anywhere. Katrina gave a nod, and they followed Jens back to the secret elevator and through the department store. None of the shoppers paid them any mind.

After a short and silent drive past the national library, they reached their hotel. Jens carried their bags and waited while they checked in. As he followed them up to their room on the third floor, he shocked the women—and perhaps himself—by speaking. He coughed once to get their attention.

"I don't know if you've been told by Magnus, but in addition to ensuring your safe transportation during your time here, I am also available to fulfill any requests—to get you what you need. The director—ahem, the Swedish one—says that I am to be at your disposal."

Katrina and Izzie eyed each other in mutual understanding. In other words, Jens was a spy for the spies.

"I am in Room 106." His voice was creaky.

"Thank you, Jens," Katrina said. "But I think we'll be fine."

Jens looked relieved, as though getting all that out had cost him greatly.

"Good evening, Jens."

He tipped his hat, quickly readjusted it, and headed downstairs.

They stepped inside their room and quickly shut the door.

"I don't know if I want that guy around," Katrina said. "The two floors separating us might not be enough."

"I'm sure he's harmless enough," Izzie replied. "Worse comes to worst, we'll just throw a wrinkled shirt over his head. The horror of that alone will keep him occupied and out of our hair."

They scanned their room. The beds were Scandinavian style: light-colored wood with clean lines and a thin mattress with a brightly colored duvet in lieu of sheets.

Katrina reached down into her bag and pulled out a small sweeping device.

"Before we get settled in, I'll check the mattresses for bedbugs."

Izzie nodded silently. That was US Division code for "sweep for bugs."

They worked around the room in quick and efficient silence, spending extra time on the light fixtures, where they only found bugs of the literal kind—and dead at that—the outlets, and the balcony. And they also checked the beds for actual bedbugs as well—all clear.

Satisfied that no eavesdropping devices were in their room, they popped downstairs for a late dinner. Too tired to bother with a restaurant, Katrina introduced Izzie to *tunnbrödsrulle* from a food cart. After finding a park bench overlooking the Nybrovikan Bay, the two plopped down and ate.

"Man, this is, like, the best food ever invented," Izzie managed to get out between bites.

Katrina agreed. "I know, right? Whoever came up with the idea of stuffing a hot dog, mashed potatoes, lettuce, and beet salad into a conveniently rolled-up flatbread cone was a genius."

"Pure genius," Izzie agreed.

"Alright, before we lapse into food comas, let's get back to the hotel. I'm hoping the carbs will overwhelm the jet lag, and we'll have a nice, deep sleep..."

Chapter 6

Katrina did not have a nice, deep sleep. The stress and jet lag must have done a number on Izzie because she managed to treat Katrina to a display of both night terrors and some nearly room-shaking snores. Despite all the racket, Isobel woke up fresh as a daisy, while Katrina needed two hits of Earl Grey before she could even form words.

Bleary-eyed from the lack of rest, Katrina dragged herself into Division headquarters—not how she wanted to start her first day on the job.

"*God morgon*, Agent Foster. Ready to get started?" Magnus was annoyingly cheery. He probably hadn't had anyone alternating between screaming and snoring in his ear all night.

"Ready as I'll ever be," she replied as she sat down at her desk. At least the statement was honest.

"Here's everything that we could find from Blomqvist in his Lindström file. Odd guy. His files all had names, but most of what was in them was coded."

With that, Magnus rolled a little wagon toward her. It was stacked high.

Katrina looked at the massive files. Collectively, nearly three feet of paper had to be piled in the cart. She was going to need more tea if she was going to tackle all that.

"Paper? Really?"

"Yeah. I didn't know him particularly well, but I know he was old-school. Said it was easier to destroy paper records."

Katrina thought back to that partially digested recording device found in Blomqvist's body. She couldn't fault him there.

"If it helps, I also have the official file on the Lindström mission. Should help you with decoding." Magnus looked more hopeful than confident.

"Can't hurt," she replied. "Thanks."

"Alright. Well, I'll leave you to it. We'll meet at the end of the day for a meeting, but reach out sooner to Lena or me if you have any questions."

By the end of the first day, Katrina had no luck, but that was to be expected. After all, if the mystery surrounding Blomqvist's death wasn't complicated, she wouldn't have been sent there.

By day two, she was starting to get irritated at the dirty looks Lena would constantly shoot her way. Matters were not helped when she walked past Magnus's office to get some tea and overheard Lena saying to him, "They knew Blomqvist's ability with codes—they're betting we can't succeed, and sending Foster only guarantees that this is how they dump us..."

That enraged Katrina, but instead of throwing her off her game, it made her even more determined to crack the code.

By day three, she began to catch the rhythm of Blomqvist's writing and started to figure out how he formed his letters. Often, an *a* was indistinguishable from an *o* with him, which made it even harder to determine an *ä* from an *ö*. From what she could determine, it looked like he was employing a mashup of a rail fence transposition cipher with a polyalphabetic Vigenère one—with a little something extra.

She sat stumped. Some of the words would start to make sense, but not others. She could find no consistency. She was close, though. She could feel it.

Then a familiar sensation hit her. She experienced a rush that said her subconscious was heading in the right direction even if she wasn't fully aware of it herself. The answer to the puzzle started to tumble into place. *Can it be? Good grief.* The man was writing in Swenglish, a mashup of Swedish and English. That explained why some of the words made sense and others didn't and why her decoding tricks never quite added up.

She gave him credit—his technique was something a native speaker wouldn't look for, but it came naturally to someone who had acquired the language secondhand. If he was paranoid about others in the Swedish Division catching onto what he was working on, he'd found a good way to hide it. She did a few sentences to confirm that it worked. She sat back in her chair, exhausted but elated from the rush of figuring it out. *Time to share the good news.*

Katrina looked for Magnus and finally found him in the break room. He was sitting slumped on a couch, staring at the simulated sunlight. He looked exhausted. She took advantage of the moment to observe his profile. Though his face might be considered a little overly angular, it certainly had the potential to lean in the direction of handsomeness. Katrina rather thought his eyes were what tipped the odds in his favor. She wasn't convinced that eyes that blue were even possible, yet the evidence was there before her. Shallow crinkles spread from the corners of those eyes. She wondered how old he was, exactly. Earlier, she'd guessed he was somewhere in his forties, but she was no longer sure. The rest of his skin seemed pretty smooth. Maybe the stubble was what aged him, making him look more tired.

He turned and caught her staring—so much for stealthy spy tactics. He patted the couch.

"*Hej*, Katrina."

They were on a first-name basis. The formality of "Agent Foster" from their initial meeting seemed to have dropped away. That was fine by her.

"Not trying to pressure you... but any luck?"

She joined him, taking care to keep the space of a cushion between them. As the US Division divided their agents by gender, she wasn't quite sure how to interact with a male colleague and didn't want to send the wrong message.

"Actually, yes, Magnus. I've been trying to find you." She relayed what she'd discovered. She didn't want to toot her own horn—yes, she did—but she was feeling pretty self-satisfied.

"*Fantastisk!*" Magnus said. "I must hand it to you, Katrina. You always did have a good eye for seeing details and linking them together."

"Excuse me?"

He smiled. "Clearly, you don't recall me from your past."

"I've never seen you before in my life!"

Magnus smiled and shook his head. "Yes, you have—we have met. You just don't remember. I almost didn't remember, myself. It took me a moment to place you, what with your different name and ability to speak Swedish."

Katrina was skeptical.

"Sorry, but it's true. You were ten, and I was fifteen—"

"Wait, you're only thirty-five?" she blurted out. Katrina clasped a hand over her mouth, but it was too late. Cows gone and barnyard doors open and whatnot.

He self-consciously dragged a hand over his face. "It's been a bit rough lately, you know," he said, slightly defensive.

"You look perfectly all right. I'm just bad at guessing ages." Katrina could tell he didn't buy that lie either. The increased octave she hit when she'd said it didn't help. "Well, if I can dig myself out of this embarrassingly awkward hole, it's not like I thought you were *applesauce and diapers* old, just a little older than thirty-five." She stared down at her hands. "Anyway, I still don't think we've met. You must have me confused with someone else."

He shook his head. "My apparently decrepit appearance aside..." He gave a slightly wry grin. "My memory is still quite sharp, and I can assure you that we have indeed met. I definitely remember because you were the first American I'd ever met. First black person, actually."

Katrina raised an eyebrow.

"Multiculturalism was a relatively new concept to Sweden back then, and I grew up in Lidingö," he said, as though that explained everything. "I also recognized you by your necklace." He pointed at her chest, and Katrina instinctively peered down. Her necklace was well hidden under her shirt and always had been. Indeed, he never would've had an opportunity to know she was wearing one unless he'd peeked down her shirt at some point.

They both seemed to come to that realization as Magnus slowly lowered his finger. "Er, point being, I remembered it because it looked just like *mjukglass*—soft ice cream swirled on a cone." He shrugged. "What can I say?"

"You can start by going back to the meeting-my-parents part. If the last time you saw us was when you were fifteen, then they died later that same year."

He leaned back on the couch and stared at the ceiling as though the answers might be found there. "It was on National Day. The Division was having a conference under the guise of a party. You introduced yourselves as the Huxtables. My parents pushed me toward you and told me to play a game of I Spy with you." He made a face. "I told them fifteen-year-old boys don't play little children's games. That's what I said, anyway. The truth was I hated playing that game with you because you always won."

His admission and pronunciation of *children* as "sheeldren" made Katrina smile. The memory was a bit fuzzy, but she thought she could remember playing I Spy. But her parents' deaths had blocked out most of her memories from that time. She needed more.

"If it was National Day, then my parents died about two weeks later. Did you hear anything of the adults' conversation? Did anyone seem worried?" She often wondered if her parents knew they were going to die or if it came as a surprise. She'd never believed what happened that day was an accident. No engine just combusted like that.

He squinted as he pondered her questions. Katrina noted that it made his crow's feet all the deeper, yet somehow, it didn't look bad. She wondered how men got away with looking more "distinguished" with them.

"You have to remember this was a long time ago. I remember the adults were doing that thing where you act nice but you're really angry. I kept hearing my parents say, 'Berlin, why Berlin?' And then your father said, 'Because it must be done. It can't be long. Will you help us or not?' And that's when—" Magnus stopped whatever he was about say.

At the mention of Berlin, Katrina's brows furrowed in concentration. "Germany? That's where the car exploded. But who—"

With an unfortunate sense of timing, Lena and Izzie entered the room with a trail of other Division employees behind them. Magnus immediately turned his attention toward the group. Katrina noticed he seemed more than a little grateful for the distraction.

Two carts filled high with pastries and coffee were rolled into the room.

"What's this?" Katrina asked Magnus.

He checked his watch. "*Fika*. It's like an American coffee break."

Izzie flopped onto the couch between them and crammed a bun into her mouth. "What is this cinnamony goodness?"

"It's called *kanelbullar*," Magnus answered.

Izzie tried it out on her tongue. "Kah-neel-boo-lar. Delicious. I'll have to find a recipe."

Lena shook her head. "Yes, you do that."

Katrina sighed and reached for a bun. "Well, I might as well get a snack since I don't think I'll be getting anymore of the information that I really want."

Magnus smiled but remained silent on the topic. It did not escape her notice that his eyes hadn't met hers since he mentioned Berlin.

"Good news, team," he said. "Katrina has cracked Blomqvist's code."

"That's great, Kat," said Izzie. "Now, we can figure out what he knew... and why it killed him."

"You figured it out? Great. Take an extra bun with you for the journey back home," Lena said.

"No one's going home yet," Magnus said. "Katrina, get as much decoded as you can while Lena and I pull everything we can from the Lindström case. We'll then compare to see what we're missing. As our head researcher, that should not be too difficult for you, will it, Lena?"

Lena responded by rolling her eyes and clomping out of the room.

"Well, let's get to it and reconvene tomorrow afternoon." Magnus got up to leave.

Katrina followed suit and went back to her desk. With the knowledge of Blomqvist's method, she programmed an algorithm into her computer, and she and Izzie fed papers into the scanner.

Izzie seemed to have liked the gig so far, as she'd spent most of the past three days cleaning and archiving Blomqvist's weapons. It wasn't glamorous, but she was content.

"Dude had a fine arsenal. Had a real appreciation for the classics."

While Katrina had been largely left alone, Izzie had worked alongside Lena, researching the provenance of some of the older or rarer weapons. "Despite her first impression, she's actually not that bad, believe it or not," Izzie said.

Based on Katrina's interactions with her, she didn't. "Well, just keep your eye on her. Something about her just doesn't seem right."

Izzie shrugged and continued feeding papers into the scanner.

Later that night, Katrina lay in bed, thinking. Izzie was snoring away in the neighboring bed. Even though she was exhausted, Katrina couldn't sleep. Between the case and Magnus's revelation about her parents, she had too much to process. *What did the reference to Berlin mean?* Katrina had found a new mission, one that certainly would not be Division sanctioned: she was going to find out the truth about the day her parents died.

Chapter 7

Oskar Blomqvist had secrets.

In reviewing his documents, Katrina discovered that Oskar had official reports, yes, but that he also had the unofficial, *real* reports. The official report on Johanna Lindström was pretty straightforward, not giving much more than the who, what, when, where, and why.

Ten years before, the Swedish Minister of Defense, Johanna Lindström, was assassinated on her way home from shopping. It happened at night, and no one searched for her until the next day when her husband called the police. The killer, Viktor Surikov, was captured, confessed, and was convicted. He was later found by Sweden's National Board of Health and Wellness to be mentally disturbed and was sentenced to psychiatric care.

Case closed.

The *real* report, on the other hand, was considerably less dry. It consisted of Oskar's notes that didn't make it into the final report and showed his fascinating personal insights into the mission. Apparently, the well-publicized death of a high-profile politician threw the Division into chaos—no one was happy that an assassination had occurred on their watch.

The first things that stood out to Katrina were the dates of each entry. The bulk of them, reasonably so, were from a decade before. The odd thing was that his notes started up again about a year ago, with the last entry made just two days before he died. Apparently, the closed case was still very much open in Blomqvist's mind.

The second thing Katrina noted, with some disappointment, was that despite the large pile of papers, the documentation was not complete. Certain pages—ones she suspected were even more sensitive—were missing. She wanted to know where they were and what they said that was so troubling that he'd determined they needed to be kept off-site.

From what she could make of his notes, Blomqvist was obsessed with politics. He made multiple references to rallies, election years, party members, and party platforms. Katrina supposed that made sense to some degree, considering Johanna had been a politician. Yet his interest continued long after her murder was resolved. He wrote about going "back to the original," but Katrina wasn't yet clear on what that meant. It could have meant the original scene of the crime. It could have referred to an original theory of some kind. Katrina simply didn't know.

The third discovery that stood out was that Blomqvist had made a point of tracking anyone at the Division who might've had ties to the case. He'd gone so far as to constantly track the whereabouts of his own partners on the mission. She saw notations that indicated they'd all died. Blomqvist had been the last of the *Lindströmsgruppen*. She would need to ask what happened to the others.

In one interesting note, she saw a familiar name listed: Lena Holmberg. She'd been pegged to work on the mission until he uncovered that she had ties to the victim. Lena had once done security work for Johanna, which disqualified her from participating. Katrina mentally filed that fact away. Something more than Lena's grouchy, condescending nature was making her feel ill at ease. She didn't know what, but she knew she would find out.

"LET'S START BY EXAMINING the body," Katrina said.

The team had gathered in a conference room, and Magnus projected images of Lindström's corpse. They all watched the screen, with Izzie paying rapt attention.

One showed Johanna on the coroner's table, and the other had been taken at the scene of her death. Taken by forensics, the latter showed an above-body view of the dead woman lying in the snow. Her shirt was torn open, and at least three stab wounds had stained the white ground around her.

"Stomach. Throat. Upper chest. She was stabbed only three times, but it was more than enough to kill her," Katrina said. "According to the coroner's report, while she was quickly taken to the hospital, she had in all likelihood died before she even made it into the ambulance." No one said anything, so she forged ahead. "Which makes sense to me because those are the areas you'd target for a quick death. If done correctly, it would've only been a matter of minutes."

"Can you get in closer on the wounds?" Izzie asked.

"What's the point?" Lena asked. "They are just basic knife wounds, and we know those wounds killed her." Things might've improved between her and Izzie, but Lena's prickliness wasn't going away anytime soon.

"Learning about the body tells me more about Johanna's killer than anything I've heard so far this morning," Izzie said. She pointed up at the stomach. "See that? That is not the slash of someone driven by emotion—it would've been more ragged. Instead, it's smooth and precise, like what you'd expect from a professional, be it a surgeon or a hired hitman."

Lena looked on with reluctant approval. "I didn't notice that."

"Nice work, Isobel." Magnus shuffled some papers. "And you were right about the professional part. The assassin Surikov is a former Russian soldier."

"So the Russians were involved?" *That wasn't in any of Oskar's notes.* Katrina might not have been able to identify the intent behind a knife wound, but her ego was determined not to be left out of the conversation.

Magnus shook his head. "I think that was everyone's first thought, but we don't have any evidence to support that."

"Which explains why that didn't appear in Agent Blomqvist's documentation. And now that I think about it, poison is more their style." She made a motion for Magnus to move to the next slide.

"Let's continue to look closer, this time at the center of her chest," Katrina said.

Magnus zoomed in the image. In the center of Johanna's chest was what could only be described as a carving. Carved with shallow precision was an ornate upper-case *V*, with what appeared to be snakes intertwined around the letter and trailing off from it. Not enough to kill, its purpose seemed more decorative.

Izzie squinted in concentration. "That looks like a fancy roman numeral five or maybe the letter *V*... Hang on a sec!"

"Yep," Katrina said. "Remember what our director told us about Blomqvist's final words? 'The *V* is the key'? I think that could be a *V* for Viktor. As in Viktor Surikov."

Magnus spoke up. "Yes, that's what made it so easy to believe Surikov when he confessed. I read the official report, and the police withheld that part from the media. The news media reported that she had been stabbed, which of course was the truth. When Surikov described the stabbing and the carving precisely, they knew they had their man. Which was convenient because while they had had some suspects, Surikov had certainly not been one of them. With his admission, they were able to wrap up a politically explosive case."

"How do we know it wasn't someone else?" Lena asked. "An accomplice."

"Nope," Izzie said, still studying the screen. "The knife technique is consistent throughout."

"Okay, so other than being a killer with excellent knife skills and a penchant for autographing his kills, what else do we know about the man?" Katrina asked.

A mug shot of Surikov appeared on the screen. His brown hair was cropped in a buzz cut, and his dark eyes had a deadened quality to them that creeped Katrina out. His face and scalp were criss-crossed with scars. She wondered if they were all from his time in the military or if he'd picked them up throughout life as one picked up souvenirs.

"Lena, I know research is your specialty," Katrina said. "Were you able to find out more on his background?"

She didn't look particularly thrilled to do so, but Lena responded, "Here's what I know so far. He spent time in Finland before finding work here. Once in Sweden, he worked in scrap metals. His coworkers said he mostly kept to himself but was friendly enough."

Friendly didn't seem to describe the image Katrina saw. "What do we know about his personal life? Wife? Hobbies?"

"Not much. We know his girlfriend broke up with him a few months before the assassination took place. It came out in the trial that he'd spent a lot of time in political forums on the internet."

Katrina spoke. "What kinds of politics were discussed in the forums? Anything extremist? I'm afraid I don't have more than a perfunctory understanding of Swedish politics."

"The forum is no longer active, but the old comment threads were still available. I checked, and mostly, he just railed against Lindström. Didn't like her politics, especially her campaign for trade sanctions in the Middle East over their treatment of women. One particularly hateful post suggested she go there and get her tongue cut out—maybe then she'd learn to keep her opinions to herself like women are supposed to."

"Guess that explains the ex-girlfriend part," Izzie murmured with a scowl.

Lena nodded in agreement.

"So he was a woman-hater, a misogynist," Katrina said.

"With exceptions," Magnus said. "He seemed to revere his mother and his ex-girlfriend. As you might imagine, neither wanted anything to do with him after he confessed to the killing. I went through the court transcripts. Both testified that Surikov seemed to have 'snapped' in the months leading up to the assassination. Not that he needed evidence against him. He contacted the local police to tell them he did it and mounted no defense of any kind. The trial was pretty perfunctory. His lawyer did claim insanity on his behalf, but that was readily obvious, so it was just a matter of going through the legal motions, so to speak, before they sentenced him to psychiatric care."

"Ugh. Enough about this creep," Lena said. "Get him off the screen."

"Yes, what about Lindström?" Katrina asked. "We know about the corpse. What can you tell us about the person?"

Lena answered. "She was a powerhouse, a force to be reckoned with. She started off as a youth member of the Kvinnor på Toppen, a feminist party. Lindström quickly worked her way up the ranks there. I liked her," she added as though that was the most important endorsement of all. "Well, I did before she decided to go big and make a name for herself at Kvinnor's expense."

"What do you mean?" Izzie asked.

"I mean she ditched Kvinnor and switched to a more mainstream moderate party. At the time, everyone knew once she joined up with the Liberalkonservativa party—the Libcons for short—it was obvious that she was going to be the party's choice for prime minister," Lena replied.

"Okay, so she's this big-time politician. I get that," Izzie said. "But here's what I don't get. Why didn't she have some people with her? Bodyguards or something? How is it that she was just out there all alone, walking at night?"

"We're a relatively safe country," Magnus said. "You might hire security to prep a venue or to hold back crowds from getting too close to a politician, but when a politician wasn't doing an event? It wouldn't have crossed anyone's mind to do so."

"Not like the US," Lena muttered.

"No one imagined something like this would happen," Magnus continued as though Lena hadn't spoken. "You can bet that afterward, most major candidates have some sort of security with them when they are out in public now, though."

Katrina thought back to Blomqvist's notes about Lena but chose to keep quiet. If Lena wasn't going to mention she'd been on Lindström's security, then Katrina wasn't going to volunteer it. Not quite yet, anyway.

As if sensing Katrina was thinking about her, Lena turned her way. "Okay, so what are we supposed to do with this? As far as I can tell, there's not much new to go on."

"Well, here's what I think we should do," Katrina replied with more confidence than she necessarily felt. "We piece together what we know from the case with what we know from Blomqvist. What is undoubtedly known is that Surikov stabbed Johanna Lindström. Blomqvist's final words were significant enough to him that he tried to save them to be shared later, right? So let's follow the clue from a top agent. If Oskar believed Surikov knew something, let's shake him up and find out."

"Okay, I agree," Magnus said. "Let's start with Surikov."

Lena volunteered herself, but Magnus shook her off.

"No, I think this is a good first opportunity for Katrina and Izzie to do some fieldwork. Go see Surikov, but first, a visit to Professor Rasmusson is in order."

Chapter 8

Katrina liked Professor Rasmusson from the moment she met him. Professor Andreas Rasmusson was an impossibly old man with intense eyes that indicated he would not be retiring anytime soon. An air of warmth and professionalism radiated from him.

"It's a pleasure to meet you both. I've been directed to equip you with all the necessary technology for the duration of your time in Sweden." He swept his arms wide. "Please look around and know that anything you see is at your disposal." He gestured toward some of his technicians. "And don't mind them—they're used to disruptions when people try out my gadgets."

Katrina and Izzie took in the large room, which was wall-to-wall with seemingly innocuous gadgets that undoubtedly served less-than-innocuous purposes. Everything from conventional earpieces to mustard squeeze bottles was there. Katrina didn't know where to begin or even what she should be asking for. Somehow, she hadn't been trained for this. The use of spy gear she absolutely knew, but knowing how to choose the right items for the mission was something else entirely. She felt that the moment she regained her footing as an agent, she just lost it again. She somewhat suspected that attaining this skill was a "test," courtesy of the Division.

Take a breath, Kat. You can do this. She looked back at Professor Rasmusson. His eyes crinkled into a smile, and he gave a knowing wink.

"If I may be so bold, for your particular mission, you may want to consider, shall we say, more nuanced forms of technology." He hobbled over to a counter with a bag of what appeared to be Swedish coins of some kind. Professor Rasmusson held one up and wove it through his gnarled fingers.

"What you have here is seemingly your everyday five-*kronor* coin. Yet press against dear King Carl's head—"

At that moment, the electrical buzz of all the gadgets nearest to them stopped. Two lab techs' heads popped up, then they recognized what was happening and returned to work.

Pushing the coin again, he continued, "Sometimes, a crown is just a crown. Other times, it's a device that emits an electromagnetic pulse, blocking electronic transmissions. Don't get the two mixed up, or it will be a costly mistake."

"Heh, costly. That's funny. Get it?" Izzie nudged Katrina.

Katrina elbowed her back. "Hush."

"With this coin, you can temporarily block all forms of electronic communication devices within a five-foot radius," Professor Rasmusson noted. "Very useful when wanting private conversations and signal blocking."

Katrina took a coin and carefully examined it. "Very impressive, Professor."

He gave a self-satisfied smile. "I think so, yes. But do be cautious with its use. What might block the mobile phone reception of the enemy will also block *your* ability to communicate."

Professor Rasmusson moved farther down the counter and opened a jewelry box. He held up a pair of very pretty teardrop-shaped garnet earrings and passed them to Katrina with a little bow. "For the lady."

She held them up to her ears. "What do these do?"

"Well, in addition to being an exquisite accompaniment to any evening wear, those earrings also serve as both an optical and tracking device. With each earring, you get a GPS tracker and a camera with a one-hundred-eighty-degree visual that is sent to headquarters in real time."

In no time at all, Katrina had them in her ears and was admiring them in a mirror. She was a sucker for sparkly jewelry. Professor Rasmusson smiled in appreciation.

"They are a bit old-fashioned in style, yes, but they are so lovely—and so functional—that I cannot bear to remove them from the collection."

He turned to Izzie. "I was informed of your reputation as a lover of weaponry. I will leave you to your more blunt instruments, which I hear you have had transported here. But I would advise you to consider some more subtle weapons of choice." He tossed Izzie a watch. "Turn the dial."

Izzie turned the dial to six o'clock, and a small needle popped up from the six.

"Use with caution. Each needle contains only enough drug or poison for one person. And it goes without saying—although I will say it—do be careful not to accidentally use it on yourself. Former Agent Berg—very smart but very clumsy—once jabbed herself with the three o'clock, that is, sodium pentothal. Blabbed so much she caused three divorces, two internal investigations, and a military coup. Needless to say, you don't want to end up like her." He gave a twitch that indicated the Swedish Division had not been particularly forgiving of her mistake. "Make sure to have a tech tell you what's in each number, Isobel."

He flipped a coin at her. "Take a crown too. Maybe it's not as good as a knife, but you never know when it might come in handy."

After gathering a few more gadgets from the Professor, Katrina and Izzie took their leave.

Professor Rasmusson shook their hands. "Come back anytime. I imagine we'll be seeing a great deal of each other before this mission is through."

Chapter 9

Katrina was given three days to put together a mission. The tight timeline meant they had to work quickly and efficiently. With all the interaction, the somewhat awkward international team began to gel. While Jens was helpful for procuring whatever they needed, he very much took his job as "a spy for the spies" seriously, silently escorting Katrina and Izzie around. Katrina was relieved to find that when they weren't arguing, Izzie and Lena actually worked well together. That unfortunately did not carry over to Lena's interactions with Katrina. She would see Lena regularly slump in and out of Division headquarters, but Lena never described her whereabouts other than with a terse "Out." Katrina hadn't forgotten Lena's previous ties to Johanna or her attempt to be the one to visit Surikov.

She was also a familiar face in Professor Rasmusson's lab, where she and Izzie had amassed quite the collection of spy gadgets.

Magnus remained as capable and mysterious as ever and, to Katrina's frustration, seemed determined that the two not be left alone. Whatever questions she had about her parents, they were not getting answered anytime soon. Not that she was able to spend much time thinking about her mom and dad. She'd been so busy on her assignment that she hadn't had any time to see Stockholm, let alone do any side investigations. Espionage was very much an all-consuming job. If she wasn't in the basement of NK, she was back at the hotel, trying to grab a few hours of sleep between Izzie's snores and planning out their next steps.

In preparation for meeting the assassin Surikov, Katrina decided that she would pose as a psychologist with a research grant to study the mind of fanatical killers. That way, she could ask questions surrounding Lindström's murder without raising suspicion as to why she might be speaking to someone about a decade-old assassination. She could also ask probing questions to try to tap into whatever had made Oskar so curious. Izzie was to accompany her as her graduate student assistant and as her lookout in case any complications arose. Lena retrieved the building's schematics so that Katrina and Izzie could memorize their exits and any rooms of importance. A great deal of preparation leading up to the first expedition needed to be done, but Katrina was most definitely ready. And she repeated that to herself hourly until she was at least halfway convinced.

THE NEXT MORNING, KATRINA and Izzie went to Jens's hotel room.

Never one for subtlety, Izzie reached Jens's room first and promptly pounded on the door. Despite her strong sense that Jens might be afraid of Izzie, Katrina let her take the lead.

"Jens!" Izzie shouted at his peephole as though it was an intercom. "We need you."

The door swung open. Jens represented the only unironic example of "I woke up like this." He was clean-shaven and without a hair out of place, despite having been roused from his bed at five in the morning. He peered down at his watch. He looked back up at Izzie.

"Jens," Izzie said, "I know it's early, but we're desperate, and I know you have what we want."

At this, his eyes grew wide, and he readjusted his fluffy Turkish cotton robe. "*Urs*—er, excuse me?" He rubbed his throat to reawaken his still-dormant vocal cords.

Izzie showed impatience. "Isn't it obvious, man? We're visiting Surikov today, and we can't exactly show up as ourselves. We need clothes. Disguises. At least a week's worth, just in case." She then smiled. "And if there's anyone I trust to provide the appropriate costuming, it's you, Jens."

Seemingly relieved, he grunted, "Yes," sounding more enthusiastic than he'd ever been. With a renewed sense of aplomb—although the bar was quite low for successful displays of enthusiasm from Jens—he shut the door.

At any rate, Katrina was glad that the first part of her plan was on target. Then, back in their shared room, they continued to review while they waited.

Jens arrived promptly at eight in the morning with six large suitcases in tow. After overseeing their safe entry into the room, he gave his signature curt nod and left. As Katrina had hoped, Jens did not disappoint in his selection of disguises.

Katrina assembled what she imagined a stereotypical psychologist might wear: comfortable flats, a pair of khaki pants, and a button-down blouse—slightly frumpy but professional. The frumpiness was also the apparent result of Jens thinking she was a size larger than she really was. She was not amused.

She then searched for a head covering of some kind. That task was quite easy since one suitcase had been solely dedicated to hats, wigs, and assorted hair accessories. Clearly, Jens had understood the importance of being prepared for any hair scenario. She pulled out a wig of box braids and decided it would do nicely. As she played with the braids, she briefly wondered if it came equipped with any additional gadgetry. She gave one of the braids a tug. It hung limply. No sign of Professor Rasmusson's handiwork—it was just an everyday synthetic wig. Watching her reflection, she put on the wig and collected the braids into a loose, low ponytail, checking that none of her real hair peeked through. Finally, she put on a pair of Professor Rasmusson's black-rimmed glasses that served as a camera and communication device. *There.* Her transition to Dr. Foster, PhD, was complete.

Izzie came out of the bathroom. "So... do I pass as a proper grad student?" She was clad in slightly faded bootcut jeans and a navy T-shirt. Jockeying for position before Katrina's mirror, she loosely wrapped a light-blue-and-white-checked scarf around her neck. She grinned as she checked out her reflection. "Yes, I do believe the scarf classes things up a bit. It says, 'I'm poor, but I can still look nice.'"

"You *do* make a convincing doctoral student," Katrina agreed.

Izzie gave a small twirl back and forth. "How did Jens know my exact size? It's actually quite impressive."

"Something tells me that among his many talents, he's good at sizing people up." Katrina smirked.

Izzie blushed a bit in response, a novel look that puzzled Katrina, but she didn't have time to pursue what appeared to be yet another mystery.

"C'mon. Grab your notebook, and let's go," Katrina said. "We've got only fifteen minutes to catch the train."

THE TRAIN WAS LATE. Katrina was soon finding that their train system, *Statens Järnvägar*, otherwise known as SJ, did not have the best record for getting people where they needed to go on time. Izzie took it as a sign that she was meant to go to the *Pressbyrån* for some *kanelbullar*. Katrina suspected Izzie was developing an unhealthy obsession with those cinnamon buns.

While she waited for both Izzie and the train, she read over the headlines on the newsstand. Apparently, a big political debate was coming up. Two images were prominent: a fierce-looking female and a man with a thousand-watt smile were head-to-head in a spliced shot. "Siggi vs. Tore: Battle Royale!" the headline screamed. "The woman who hates men and the man who loves (too many) women battle it out." Katrina didn't have a chance to read more as the train had finally shown up, with Izzie not far behind.

Soon, they arrived at St. Gustav, the hospital housing Surikov. Katrina took in the building. It was seriously imposing. The giant concrete slab walls and the tiny windows practically screamed "institution," which was quite fitting as it was, in fact, a mental institution. She tapped the left corner of her frames to turn on the camera.

"Hopefully, they can see this," Katrina murmured to Izzie.

With the glasses, Magnus and Lena could see and hear her but couldn't communicate to her in return.

She took a deep breath and turned toward Izzie. "Are you ready?"

Izzie gulped as she took in the building. "*Dios mio*. If a person wasn't already nuts, they would be after a few weeks at this place."

"I have no idea what we're going to encounter with Surikov. His Division file says that no one was able to do a conclusive psych profile. The Division has only conjectures based on what they recorded from his trial and from interviewing the people who knew him."

"That's not much to go on."

"I know. The best they have is a vague report where people say it's like he's two totally different people. So be ready for anything."

Izzie nodded. "I'll stay in the lobby, and if there's any sign of trouble, I'm giving myself full authorization to start shooting."

"Slow down, Calamity Jane—" Katrina cut herself off as a worker strolled past them with a patient in a wheelchair. "If you'll recall, in training, we were told that the moment an agent has to brandish a weapon, they're already at a strategic disadvantage."

"Yeah, yeah, that's what they said, but I never put much stock in that." Izzie made a dismissive gesture. "Just know that if you need some firepower, I'll be ready."

"Let's hope it doesn't come to that."

Katrina took a deep breath as the automatic doors slid open. As they walked down the corridor and into the lobby, she whispered to Izzie, "Now, don't break character. If I'm not out of his room in thirty minutes, you know what to do."

Izzie gave a curt nod before taking a seat in one of the orange chairs near the receptionist's station.

Katrina walked up to the counter to meet a nurse who might've labored as an ox or some other equally unfortunate beast of burden in a previous life. "Hello, my name is Dr. Katie Foster." She gestured over to where Izzie sat. "And that is my assistant, Isobel Maria Francisco. I'm here to see Viktor Surikov."

The nurse stared at her before pointing at a sign. "Sorry. No visitors today for those in forensic psychiatric care. Only on the first and third Saturday of each month."

Katrina's eyes grew wide in confusion. "Oh. But I'm not a visitor. I'm a scholar, a behavioral psychologist." She quickly flashed a fake university identification card.

The nurse pointed at the sign again. And again, Katrina reacted with oblivious befuddlement.

"Oh, but you don't understand. I scheduled this interview a long time ago and came to Sweden specifically to use Surikov in my research."

The nurse remained unconvinced.

"It's part of the fellowship I was awarded from the International Membership of Psychiatric Observatory Scientific Treatment for Epistemological Research." She chuckled inwardly at her own cleverness. "I'm working on a cross-national project on the transition from internet-based fantasy violence to real violence in the mentally ill.

Fascinating stuff." She pushed up her glasses and leaned in. "I mean, what makes someone go from *saying* they want to kill someone to actually *doing* it?"

The nurse crossed her arms. "Simple. Crazy people do crazy things. End of story." Clearly, the nurse was not the philosophical sort.

Katrina changed tactics. "Can you check the calendar records? I'm sure you'll see my name in your computer." Before their arrival, she'd asked Magnus to hack into the facility where Surikov was housed. She hoped she'd given him enough time to insert an eleven-thirty appointment.

"Hmm... You *are* listed here. Along with a Ms. Francisco." She stared at the computer screen and murmured, "I don't know why I didn't see it when I first came in this morning..."

Katrina had the distinct impression that being incorrect had ruined the nurse's day, maybe even her week.

Not wanting the nurse to dwell too long on the recently entered appointment and why it would be scheduled on a nonvisitor day, she sought to distract her with flattery. "I'm sure the stresses of your job are what caused you to overlook my appointment. It must be very intense working in a place like this."

The nurse stared at her with a narrowed squint—so much for flattery.

"I'll escort you to his room. A guard will stay in the room to observe and ensure safety. You should know that Surikov really only speaks Serbian or Swedish. Maybe a little English that he hears on the TV. Interpreters need to be arranged in *advance*." She looked smug.

"Not a problem," Katrina answered in Swedish.

The nurse scowled.

Katrina and the nurse had to pass through the facility to get to Surikov. They'd passed the compulsory care section and moved down to the forensic psychiatric area, where offenders were kept. It didn't seem as nice as the previous section. Despite its general dinginess, the building smelled strongly of bleach and antiseptics. However, a general undercurrent of psychological unmooring lingered, resistant to being scrubbed away.

"This facility certainly appears to be clean and well operated," Katrina ventured.

"Yeah, well, we had a bedbug outbreak a few weeks back. An entire week was dedicated to heating, cleaning, and purging. That meant we had to transfer all the patients for a week too. Threw everything into chaos."

Katrina noticed the nurse's normally dull eyes glittered slightly when she used the word "chaos." *What sort of people are they hiring here?* They continued along the hallway. She heard wailing and wondered if it was coming from the inmates or the staff. Listening to Nurse Ox muttering to herself about how "they" kept changing her appointment schedule to keep an eye on her and how "they" were the source of all her problems, Katrina determined it would be better if she didn't pursue that line of thought further. She heard more murmurs and moans but kept her eyes straight ahead to avoid getting distracted.

The nurse huffed and puffed sweatily alongside her, flinging sweat left and right as she trudged along. "Why'd they have to put him all the way at the end of the wing?" she grumbled.

As they continued their trek, Katrina tried to casually make inquiries without attracting even more suspicion from the nurse. "So, I know you said he's only allowed visitors on the first and third Saturday, but has anyone come to visit with Mr. Surikov recently?"

The nurse snorted in surprise. "Other than doctors? No. No visitors. No outside contact from anyone that I'm aware of. He *is* a convicted assassin, you'll remember." She still came across as skeptical at Katrina's presence there. "Research or no, I still don't understand why you were authorized to come in—"

"Well, it is a very prestigious fellowship. So no phones, no internet, and no letters?"

"That would be the meaning of 'no outside contact,' would it not?" the stern nurse snapped. She let Katrina into the room and beckoned a guard over before huffing away, muttering something about "more education than sense" and "*javla amerikanska*."

Surikov's room was narrow and cramped, not unlike a dorm room from Katrina's college days. He was sitting on the bed by a window. He stared silently at the unexpected visitor but made no other movements. He was thinner than the pictures she'd seen, with eyes made large from the weight loss and glassy from whatever medications they had him on. The idea crossed her mind that he looked like a man tired of being haunted. Before Katrina saw him, she'd briefly wondered if all this was just an elaborate act. However, if his appearance was any indicator, either his mental frailty was very real, or he was giving the performance of his life.

The guard pushed a chair next to Surikov's bed and gestured for Katrina to sit there. He went back to his chair by the door and sat down, seeming to settle in for a nap. Katrina interpreted that as a sign that Surikov was sufficiently drugged as to be harmless. Or maybe the guard just didn't care either way. If her interactions with the nurse were representative of staff there, the latter possibility was more likely.

Katrina sat down and pulled a yellow notepad out of her bag. She flipped it open and smiled. "Hi, Mr. Surikov. May I call you Viktor?"

He nodded, still staring.

"Good. Thank you." Katrina tried to make her voice sound warm but not patronizing. For a brief moment, she considered it a little bit pitiful that soft empathy didn't come naturally to her. But then she reminded herself that that characteristic wasn't exactly conducive to spying.

"It's very nice of you to allow me to visit with you." Not quite knowing what possessed her to do it, she repeated her statement in English.

Surikov's eyes grew momentarily lucid. "English is good."

He must have picked up a great deal more from TV shows than he was letting on, Katrina determined.

"Well, Viktor, my name is Dr. Katie Foster, and I'm doing a project on people like you, people who have killed while struggling with mental illness." She decided to leave out the part about online postings about violence in order to not rile him early on. "I'm trying to understand why you killed that politician, the minister of defense, all those years ago. Do you mind if I ask you a few questions?"

He shrugged.

"You're Russian, correct?"

"I was born... along the Chechen-Georgian border."

That seemed like a careful distinction that she would need to investigate further. Katrina asked his age, how he ended up in Sweden, and what type of work he did. All his responses matched what they already knew. Also, she noticed his unusual speaking style. He had an odd, halting way of speaking, which she attributed to trying to speak in a non-native language while medicated. The only way she could describe his body language and affect was flat—not listless, just not remotely engaged. She needed to ramp things up.

"You used to spend a lot of time online in political forums, didn't you?"

"In the past, yes. No more, though. Not allowed."

"You wrote a lot about Ms. Lindström online?"

He nodded. "Yes."

"Why did you start doing that?"

He started to speak then stopped. He screwed up his face in contemplation then finally said, "Pol... Politicians are no good. Talked about it."

"Politicians are no good," Katrina slowly repeated.

He nodded again with a little more energy.

"Viktor, why did you do it? Why did you kill Johanna Lindström? Was it because you didn't like her politics? Was it because 'politicians are no good'?"

He shrugged. "She needed to die. Stupid politics. Stupid woman. She needed to die. So I did it."

"I see." Katrina scrawled some notes, which was pointless as their conversation was being seen by her Division colleagues, but Viktor didn't know that.

"Had you tried this before? Contacting her?"

He shook his head and started tapping his left foot.

"Did you plan to do it that day, or was it an impulse?"

He looked down and fiddled with a hole in his blanket. She could tell he was starting to get agitated.

"Planned. It was planned. I did what I was told to do that day." He stared at Katrina. "I'm very obedient that way."

She peeked over at the guard. Either he was sound asleep, or he was giving an Oscar-worthy appearance of a champion napper. She leaned in a little closer and lowered her voice. "Are you saying someone told you to kill? Did you have an order?" Perhaps this was what Blomqvist was talking about.

His eyes grew wide. "Yes."

Her breath caught in anticipation. "Viktor, please tell me. Who told you to kill her?"

"The voices told me to."

"Now, when you say 'the voices,' who exactly do you mean?"

He was starting to sweat. His left foot was now tapping out a steady rhythm. "The voices. In my head! The voices. I keep telling everybody that, but no one will listen! No one will *do* anything!" The more agitated he got, the more clearly he spoke. He started to cradle his head and began rocking back and forth. "I told you. I told you. It was them. The voices. You have to do something about the voices!"

For the first time, Katrina was truly frightened of the man. He truly did believe that voices in his head had commanded him to kill. He might've been a skilled killer, but he didn't seem to be one of the cold-and-calculating variety, just a sad schizophrenic. The courts were right—the institution seemed to be a better place for him than prison.

Given how things had gone, Katrina didn't have much hope of getting anything useful from him, but she gave it one last try. On her notepad, she quickly sketched out the ornate *V* that had been etched into her brain. She knew she was taking a risk with the guard there, but she wanted to push him. Maybe learning more about Viktor's mind when he carved the letter would give her the insights she'd been searching for.

"Viktor, let's do an image test. Sometimes, that can help us focus and better express ourselves." Katrina held her notepad up to his eye level. "When I show you this, what does it mean to you? What do you think it should mean to me?"

With a speed that surprised her, he tried to reach for the notepad. Katrina pulled back.

His eyes grew intense, and he shook his head rapidly. "No, no, no, no, no. You need to help. Help me. Tell the voices. Tell the voices I did it. The voices said if I did it, they'd get me out of here!"

Katrina eased the notepad back into her lap and crossed her legs. Crossing her fingers would've been too obvious. "Sure," she said placatingly. "I'll tell the voices. I promise."

Surikov growled in frustration. "Liar!"

The guard woke up just as Surikov lunged for Katrina's throat. She gasped as his fingers tightened around her neck. The guard leapt between them, accidentally knocking Katrina in the face. Her glasses flew across the room and snapped in half as they hit the wall. The guard held Surikov down on the bed, and Katrina hurried across the room to grab the broken frames. She stuffed all her belongings into her bag and ran for the door. It was locked. She looked back. The guard was wrestling to restrain Surikov. For a man that had seemed so frail earlier, he fought like a wild animal—arms and legs kicking and punching, teeth gnashing. The door beeped.

"It's unlocked now!" The guard grunted as one of Surikov's knees connected with his stomach. "Go!"

Katrina flung the door open and ran out. The first person she had the misfortune to see was Nurse Ox.

"See, Doctor?" The nurse smiled smugly over the sounds of the guard still trying to settle Surikov down. "I told you he was crazy."

Still shaken, Katrina agreed. "I don't know that I'll be coming back. He may not be such a good subject for my study after all."

ESCORTED BY THE NURSE, Katrina returned to the lobby to find that Izzie wasn't there. After her ordeal with Surikov, her nerves were on edge. In a moment of panic, she shouted, "Isobel! Where are you?"

The nurse scowled and shushed her. Izzie came strolling around the corner, holding a plastic cup filled with green gelatin.

"Ah, Dr. Foster. You finished up early. Sorry I wasn't in the lobby. I was just having a tasty snack with some of my new friends."

Katrina scowled at her and gave her best Nurse Ox impression before dragging Izzie out of the facility. Once they were off the premises, she turned on Izzie. "You were supposed to stay in the lobby, not go on a snack run! I damn near got strangled to death by Surikov, and you're out here getting a sugar fix! What is wrong with you?"

Izzie took her time, calmly chewing a mouthful of gelatin, before she replied, "Well, one, I'm happy you're still alive, and two, while you were off conducting *one* interview, I went off to conduct several." She paused. "Would you like to know what I found out about our dear friend Surikov?"

Katrina didn't like that the lecture she had just warmed up was being tempered by the prospects of new evidence. "Okay, since I didn't find out much other than he's a garden variety psychotic, what'd you find out?"

Izzie smiled. "Well, I was chatting with King Carl, Queen Silvia, and Princess Victoria. At least, that's who they claimed to be. Something makes me suspect they're not—"

Katrina was exasperated. "Get to the point."

"The point, my impatient friend, is that they had a clear consensus about Surikov, and that was that if anyone really needed to be in that facility for his own safety and the public's, it was him."

Katrina was doubtful of the idea of accepting testimonials from patients masquerading as royalty, but she let Izzie continue.

"And yes, apparently, there is a hierarchy of sanity in that place. Those who are saner can detect the truly, fully insane and make a point to stay away from them. No one in there is friends with Surikov. No one."

Katrina chewed her lip in contemplation as they made their way back to the train. "Well, that about confirms my brief experience with him. He had what I thought might have been a moment of sanity, but then he started talking about the voices in his head."

"Exactly," Izzie said. "Most patients there seem to have moments of lucidity, however fleeting they might be. According to them, however, Surikov is *always* unbalanced. He's always communicating with the voices in his head, and when he does things, it's like he's responding to a set of instructions, not following his own instincts, however delusional they might be. They described him as a shell, that there's no *him* in there anymore, only the voices in his head, guiding him along."

Katrina believed she could see where Izzie's circuitous train of thought was heading, but it seemed entirely implausible.

"Indeed, based on their description, he behaves almost, you might say, like he had been…" Izzie gave a dramatic pause. "Brainwashed."

"Mind control, Izzie? Really?" Katrina didn't bother to hide her skepticism since Izzie's theory was too much.

Izzie threw up her hands in the universal gesture for *go figure.* "I know, I know. At first, it sounded insane to me too. Which would be fitting, given where we were. But think about it. How does a guy without friends or resources suddenly go out and orchestrate the assassination of the minister of defense?"

Katrina drifted back to her interview with the assassin. She had to admit that she didn't detect anything particularly cunning or clever about the man. If anything, his strangulation attempt was more consistent with someone who was a blunt instrument. His comment about having an order and being obedient took on a new light. It was improbable, yes, but then, so was having the murder of a top agent take place due to a case that was supposed to be closed. Maybe suspending disbelief would be the key to figuring things out. *If I'm not willing to think beyond the surface level, beyond the obvious, how am I going to solve this?* she wondered.

Katrina turned her attention back to Izzie. "Okay, I'm going to open myself to your theory." She told Izzie all about her conversation with Surikov.

She spoke her thoughts aloud, partially to herself and partially to Izzie. "From what we know, he went on websites and wrote nasty things. People say disgusting things on the internet all the time—they don't go out and act upon them. The ones that do practically advertise their actions in advance. They build up to it. A threatening letter here, a phone call there... trying to go to her office or see her at a rally—that's what you'd expect.

"So yeah, the idea that an otherwise inactive individual could've been subjected to coercive persuasion to make them behave in a way that they ordinarily would not... makes a certain level of sense," Katrina concluded.

Izzie nodded. She seemed happy that Katrina was going along with her theory.

"But we're also not doing our job if we don't consider the messengers. I mean, it's not like they're the most reliable of sources... After all, they're under the impression that they're members of the royal family."

"Well, there was some disagreement about that," Izzie said. "Queen Silvia was quite adamant that King Carl was, as she so perceptively put it, 'a complete and total imposter' because he looked nothing like he does on the coins. But you have to admit their description of him doesn't seem too far-fetched."

Having reached the station, the two women headed down the platform. Katrina paused before passing through the gates. "Okay, let's say it's true. Maybe he was brainwashed. That still doesn't tell us who was really behind the assassination. It still doesn't tell us who killed Blomqvist. It only rules out that it started and stopped with Surikov."

Izzie agreed. "Which is also not much further than where we were when we first heard about the Lindström case." She brightened. "But now, we have a new angle to pursue when previously we had none, and we did learn something else." She tossed her cup and spoon into a nearby trash can before boarding the train.

"What's that?"

"Institutions serve excellent snacks. I may have to visit again on pudding night."

Chapter 10

As they were alighting from the train station at their destination, Katrina saw Magnus and Lena before they saw her. Magnus's features were hard-set and determined. Then Lena glanced up and touched his arm. His eyes met Katrina's. Looking relieved, he jerked his head toward an elevator. They all boarded and headed down to the lower platform to make their connection.

Magnus was the first to speak. "We lost contact with you, and the last thing we saw was Surikov's hands going toward your neck."

That wasn't a moment Katrina wanted to recall. "I extricated myself without problem and retrieved the glasses. I'm hoping Professor Rasmusson can fix them."

"Yeah, and I would've had my girl's back if she didn't show up on time," Izzie added.

"Everything was fine, and I believe we've developed a potentially valuable theory." Katrina wasn't about to admit how scared she was the moment Surikov lunged at her, especially not in front of Lena.

"Not exactly a damsel in distress, then," Lena said wryly. She looked over at Magnus. "I guess there was no need to play knight in shining armor."

Magnus coughed and turned away. "Not that anyone was, of course."

"Of course not," Katrina said.

"We're a team, and..." He trailed off.

"And...?"

Just then, the train arrived.

"Oh look. The train is here," Magnus said, pointing out the obvious. And as discussing spycraft was impossible on a packed train, his deflection succeeded.

BACK AT HEADQUARTERS, Katrina relayed what had happened during her meeting with Surikov.

"What did you show him on the notepad?" Magnus asked.

"I sketched out the *V*. And, well, you can see how he reacted. It triggered him straight into strangling me."

Izzie told her tale of meeting with the other patients, complete with dramatic flair. "Even they were worried about being tossed in the loony bin with him."

Magnus closed his eyes and rubbed his temples. "We don't say he was 'tossed in the loony bin.' In Sweden, we prefer to say that he is receiving forensic mental care."

"Sounds like semantics to me."

To put an end to the exchange, Katrina took a deep breath and told Magnus and Lena their theory on Surikov. Lena laughed hysterically until she realized that Katrina and Izzie weren't laughing with her.

"Wait. You were serious? Brainwashing? You have *got* to be *kidding* me." Lena turned toward Izzie. "And I was just beginning to think you were alright."

"It was both our idea," Izzie said, although it was unclear whether she said it to share the credit or the blame with Katrina. "And it's a good one."

Katrina stood up for Izzie. "I know it sounds crazy, but if Blomqvist was right and there is more to Johanna's death, Surikov may know something, but he's in no condition to share it, and it may be due to more than mental illness. I mean, he doesn't have access to the outside, and he clearly didn't have the ability to get Blomqvist killed. Someone else is taking matters into their own hands for what they think Blomqvist found out. It's thin, yes, but we need to investigate."

Lena continued to look skeptical.

To his credit, Magnus didn't laugh at Katrina outright. "Well, this is certainly an unorthodox theory."

"It's unorthodox, I'll grant you, but a good agent pursues all avenues, no matter how unlikely." She shrugged. "If it was easy and straightforward, then we wouldn't be here in the first place, would we?"

"Okay, I'll bite, Agent Foster. Play this out for us convincingly. What's your train of thought on this?" Magnus asked.

Because she'd already spent time being equally skeptical with Izzie's theory, Katrina was ready. "Maybe they—and by 'they' I mean whoever's really behind this—went on political forums to see who might make for a likely candidate for mental reconditioning. They'd need someone susceptible. Finding a foreigner to do the job was good too. If you think about it, Surikov was the perfect candidate, an immigrant with a bad attitude and a clear trail of statements against Lindström."

"I can't disagree with you on that front," Magnus said.

Katrina was starting to get excited the more she thought about it. "Think about this: he's military, so he knows how to take orders, and he knows how to kill efficiently. And because he's just the sort of person that everyone would think would act alone—isolated and crazy—the real leader or leaders in all of this don't have to worry about anyone looking any deeper. Until Blomqvist." She turned to Magnus. "Just think about it. Even if you don't buy the brainwashing, him being a patsy makes sense. There's somebody else out there, and that's who Blomqvist was after."

"It's more than we have at this point," Magnus said. "We can either confirm it and move forward or debunk it. I'm not going to get bogged down on a single theory, though. We need to be pursuing as many parallel avenues as possible. Katrina? It was said that everyone was relieved when Surikov confessed, because it meant they didn't have to investigate anyone else. Go back to the file and see who their initial suspects were."

Katrina nodded.

"Lena, start by searching deeper into that political forum, and get me information on who ran it, who the members were, and any conversation threads from that time that looked like someone tried to do some recruiting."

"Sure. I'll put aside my equally useful work on searching for yetis and space-time portals to get right on this." Lena gave an ironic salute before heading to the door.

Katrina turned to Izzie. "Can you see what you can dig up on different types of persuasion techniques?"

"You got it."

Katrina left to get the file and quickly returned. Only Magnus was there, at his desk.

As she sat down across from him, he leaned forward. "Brainwashing, Katrina. Really?"

Katrina could feel her irritation rising. "Look, when Izzie proposed it to me, I reacted the same way, but—"

"Of *course* Isobel is behind this," Magnus muttered.

"It may have been her idea, but it has my support. You saw what I saw. No way is Surikov directing this. He's described by others as being pretty much a shell of a man."

She stared beyond Magnus, reliving her interview with Surikov. "Do 'the voices' mean anything to you?"

"Other than he's mentally ill? No."

"Something about it is sticking with me. It's the weird the way he said it. Not like there were assorted voices going through his head, but more like it was a particular grouping or group: The Voices."

"I've never received any intel on any group called The Voices, but then, I'm almost starting to think that anything is possible with this case." He put his hands behind his head and leaned back. "Alright. Let's pursue it. I don't want to give Lena any fuel, though, so we're not tying up all our resources on the 'brainwashing' angle."

"Fine. Works for me." Katrina folded her arms. "At least I know Izzie's got my back."

"Don't be that way. Brainwashing theories aside, your overall mission went quite well. You came up with a clever disguise and backstory for being there. And not only were you able to get in and out without getting caught—which counts as success in our line of work—you were also able to get some intel. Surikov is an innocent... other than the assassination part."

Appeased and pleased, Katrina said, "Surikov killed her, yes, but someone close to her had to have known her movements, would have anticipated when and where she'd go shopping that evening. I think we should go back and reevaluate the people in Lindström's world. See who may have wanted to do her harm." She opened the file and flipped through. "The notes say that while she had a lot of enemies, before Surikov came on their radar, the *Lindströmsgruppen* was focused on three potential suspects, all listed as highly sensitive: her husband, Petter Lindström, a woman named Sigrid Ekstrand, and a man called Tore Pantzerhielm."

"Yikes. I know who they are. Those last two are top politicians. Makes sense that they checked into them, though. Most of the time when there's a murder, it's usually someone close to the victim—like you said, someone who would have known where she would be. If I was on that team, I would want things wrapped up as quickly as possible. That would be the politically expedient thing to do, especially when their top three suspects consisted of two high-level politicians and the husband."

"Politically expedient, yes, but not accurate. At least not according to Blomqvist," Katrina replied. "From his notes, he was following politics pretty closely as well. Do you know anything about Johanna's personal life? Any drama in the media?"

Magnus said, "Well, we know pretty much what any politician wants us to know, the image and story they project. We know she was married to Petter Lindström—happily, by all accounts—and had two kids."

Katrina had seen enough political scandals in the US to know the politicians that thumped the hardest for family values were usually the most dysfunctional ones. "I think I'll start with Petter, then. After all, who would know her better than her husband?"

Chapter 11

A few days later, Katrina found herself in front of the summer home of Petter and the late Johanna Lindström. She noted that the *falun*-red house and the lawn were well maintained, with the exception of sports equipment littered about. The front door opened, and a medium-sized man with sandy-brown hair stepped out onto the porch. Petter wore a yellow polo shirt and blue cargo shorts. He could've been considered good-looking in that typical characterless political spouse way. With no beer gut and clean-shaven, he would've been equally at home at the Kennedy compound. He smiled and gave a wave.

"Good morning!" Katrina pasted on a cheery smile as she approached the steps, where he met her. "My name is Katie Franklin. Thanks for meeting with me on such short notice." She reached out a hand to shake Petter's—new day, new persona.

"Nice to meet you. So you said you were doing some kind of research?"

Katrina had her cover story down pat.

"Yes, I'm a political scientist doing qualitative research on the families of politicians, how a political career can change family dynamics, and what life was like for you before your spouse attained office, during, and after. So while most researchers are interested in the politicians, I want to examine the lives of their spouses and children." She pushed her recently repaired glasses farther up on her nose. "There is surprisingly little work done on this, on political families. As you probably know, they tend to get lost in the mix. Very understudied."

Petter agreed. "I can certainly understand that. We tend to be overshadowed." He gestured toward a pair of plastic lawn chairs near the steps. "Please sit."

"Thank you." Katrina gathered the back of her sundress before sitting down. She further explained the research and informed him that he didn't have to answer any questions he wasn't comfortable with. He signed a consent form with surprisingly loopy handwriting. Then she began with a softball question.

"I want to start off by asking what it was like, being married to a politician. What was it like with all the media attention when Johanna was alive?"

"Our dinners out would be interrupted all the time by either the media or the public. They'd come up for autographs or to talk about the issues of the day. Johanna was very accessible and welcoming with the people. She considered it an honor."

"And what about you, Petter? How did you feel about living in the public eye?"

He shrugged. "It was expected."

Katrina asked about canceled vacations, late nights working, and international assemblies where Lindström might be gone for weeks at a time. She asked what it was like to be the primary parent. Petter's responses were all variations on a theme, that it was just part of being a political spouse. Katrina noted he was fairly matter-of-fact about everything, emotionally neutral. None of her questions elicited anything more than an anodyne response. She needed to find out more, needed to see if she could rouse any kind of response from him that would offer a clue.

She leaned forward slightly in her chair, the plastic woven seat squeaking a bit. "Thinking about you, thinking about your family, I'd like to now ask you how your lives changed with Johanna's death."

For once, he did no "that's just the business" shrugging. Petter's face became grim. "I lost my soulmate, and my kids lost their mother. The youngest was just a few months old when that *invandrare*, that immigrant, killed her."

"And how did it affect *you*?"

"Other than my heart breaking?" He looked wry. "Well, it changed my politics, for one. I joined up with Svensk Sanning, or as you might know it, Swedish Truth."

Katrina definitely knew it. Svensk Sanning was a far-right party dedicated to fighting for the "cultural purity" of native Swedes—to make Sweden great again. It did not escape her notice that the party's initials were SS. *How apropos,* she thought cynically. It wasn't very politically savvy unless it was purposely meant to be provocative, and she suspected it was.

"You support Svensk Sanning? That's quite the switch from Kvinnor på Toppen and Liberalkonservativa."

"Well, times change, and so did I. I'm not a dreamer anymore," he said. "Johanna's killer took that away. Now, I'm just a realist trying to create a better Sweden. Through joining the party, I got my closure. And every day we get closer to closing the borders against that kind of filth, I feel closer to peace."

"I see." Katrina was repulsed but knew she had to keep her opinions to herself.

"Look, I used to share Johanna's views. But we were naïve. I don't have a problem with people who come to this country to work. But then the EU took over, and all the politicians just let everyone and everything in. These people, they don't work, they don't speak Swedish. They don't even look—" Petter caught himself. "Now, don't get me wrong. I'm not a racist. We had some good friends who were immigrants."

Said every racist ever.

"But we have a culture and a way of life to preserve. That's what Johanna worked for, and that's what I want for our kids. It has gotten to the point that I don't even recognize Sweden anymore. I read my kids' school list: 'Hassan, Onyewu, Surikov...'"

Katrina's ears perked up at that last mention.

"I mean, whatever happened to 'Svensson'?" He got up and grabbed some wayward soccer balls from the grass and tossed them into a nearby bin. "If anything, I don't hate the immigrants." His eyes went steely. "After all, we're the ones who opened the doors and let them in. No, I hate everyone left in the system who let this happen to her, her so-called friends. They let her down. They all let her down, and yet here they are, like that Sigrid and that greasy Tore. Every year on the anniversary of her death, they make a point of pretending to care. Not a tear shed, though. They just stand there, smiling for the cameras, still in office like everything is fine. But it's not fine—not for me and not for Sweden."

Katrina took note of those two names, remembering them as potential suspects. "I take it you haven't remained in contact with either since Johanna's death."

He gave her a bewildered look. "It is not like we were ever friends to begin with. Both of them were users. They used Johanna in their own way. As you know, my wife was charismatic. She could draw anyone to her cause, and it didn't matter how far from the mainstream. Sigrid was happy to capitalize on it, as long as it benefitted Kvinnor. Tore, too, until she began to overshadow him."

He paused from picking up sports gear long enough to stare directly at Katrina. "I'm the only one who keeps the true memory alive of what happened that night, and that's why I fight alongside Svensk Sanning—for Johanna and for Sweden."

"You sound like you might have the makings of a politician," Katrina said in response.

He smiled. "Perceptive. I am running to represent Stockholm's *län* in the upcoming election."

He resumed his task of picking up wayward sports gear. "Like I said, Johanna and I believed we knew what was best for the country. And maybe we were right... for the time. But now? Now, I just want a safe place for my kids to grow up. And we don't have that anymore in this new vision of Sweden."

A handler walked up the driveway toward them with his children in tow. They were carrying fishing poles and a cooler. The older one came up cautiously, warily watching Katrina while the younger came running up to Petter, waving a net with a small fish flopping around in it.

"Pappa! *Titta*!"

"Yes, yes! I see you caught a big one! It's going to make for a good dinner tonight." Petter took the net from his son, kissed the top of his head, and ruffled the hair of the older one.

Whatever his current affiliation, the man clearly loved his children, and in all likelihood, he believed he was doing the best for them. Petter smiled an apology as his children continued to take his attention, and Katrina knew the interview had concluded.

"Thanks for sparing a few minutes of your time, Mr. Lindström. It will really help in my research."

"Good luck with your book. I hope you'll be able to find some people left who speak the truth and don't just say what is politically correct."

ON THE WAY BACK TO Division headquarters, Katrina wondered about one comment Petter made in particular. It had been a rather odd way of phrasing it: "I hate everyone left in the system."

It sounded a lot like someone who might be motivated to systematically remove anyone associated with his wife's assassination—anyone who could've done something but did not or who knew something but did not say it in time. Petter had been, by virtue of his wife, affiliated with the government. She wondered if that meant he could've known about the Division and, more specifically, about Oskar. As next of kin, he had access to Johanna's body, so he would've been one of a small circle of those who knew about the carving on her chest.

Yet other aspects didn't add up. It didn't make sense for Petter to be a killer when he had two young children to care for. Nor did taking such risks seem wise when he seemed so politically active and in the public view. That all seemed like too much of a gamble.

Kat wasn't surprised that he was running for office. Despite his words, he sounded ready to get out of Johanna's shadow. Maybe by eliminating everyone who ever knew or suspected the truth behind Johanna's death, he saw himself creating a fresh start for a new career.

She found Magnus in his office. He looked up as she entered. He wiped away a vaguely guilty expression and quickly shuffled some documents into a manila folder as he greeted her. The papers, whatever they were, appeared old. She gestured at them and asked what he was reading.

"Nothing that ought to be relevant to you."

He tried the "don't question me further" single-eyebrow lift, but she wasn't cowed. No one moved that quickly unless they were trying to hide something from prying eyes. And Katrina's eyes were definitely set to pry.

"I see. Well, they looked pretty old to me."

"We've already established that you're not particularly skilled at ascertaining the age of things... or people."

Katrina scowled in response.

"But yes, it shouldn't be surprising that I'm going through old records. It has been years since Lindström's death, remember?" He seemed satisfied with his explanation.

Katrina was not. "I am unfortunately well-versed in what old records look like, and I can tell you that those appeared older than anything associated with Johanna Lindström. They have that bluish-purple tinge of an old Xerox machine. Like from the nineties."

He seemed mildly exasperated. "Clever as usual," he acknowledged. "Just researching. You never know what documents might come in handy. As I said, nothing for you to concern yourself with."

Magnus did not elaborate further, and Katrina knew enough about him at that point to know he would not. She tamped down her irritation by remembering that he was a spy, and from a different branch, so sharing information did not come readily. *But how is collaboration possible if he always holds his cards so close?*

"We're on the same side, you know. No secrets."

"We're spies, Katrina. There are *always* secrets."

She didn't pursue it further, but that didn't mean she would let it go. Something in those files was worth knowing and, she suspected, worth keeping from her. Katrina would find out what was in that folder, one way or another.

"Anyway, I assume you came here with another objective in mind, other than irritating me with the pointless conversation we're currently engaged in."

She eyed him as he slid the manila folder into his bottom right-side desk drawer.

Katrina harrumphed. "Yes. I just got back from meeting Johanna's husband."

"So what'd you think of him?"

"I'm not entirely certain what to think of Petter Lindström. On the one hand, he seems like a husband who loved and respected his wife and her career. When his kids arrived at the end of the interview, it was clear that he adored them."

"But…?"

"His views. Petter's done a complete one-eighty. I think Johanna's murder broke him. He's turned into the spokesperson for Svensk Sanning, and it's definitely *not* for show. He truly believes what he's advocating."

Magnus leaned and rested his head against a palm as he listened. "He has repulsive views, yes. But does that make him a killer?"

Magnus looked handsome, but she quickly brushed aside the flittering thought in order to answer his question.

"Of course not, but anytime someone changes so dramatically, it makes me want to find out what other dramatic actions they're willing to take. What I took from meeting with him is that he definitely needs to remain a person of interest. He said a few things that gave me pause."

She told Magnus more about his views and, in particular, his peculiar reference to hating everyone remaining from the time of her assassination, as well as his own burgeoning political career.

Magnus leaned back in his chair and gave a low whistle. "That does stand out, but you're right, it's far from conclusive. We'll have to watch his movements more closely. I'll see if I can get some Level Threes to set up heightened surveillance—get some feet and eyes on the ground.

"He also mentioned two names specifically," Katrina said. "Sigrid and Tore. I remembered them from the file. You said they were politicians?"

"Oh, yes. That'd be Sigrid Ekstrand and Tore Pantzerhielm. Both are very well-known politicians. They're fighting it out pretty hard this election year."

Katrina flashed back on the newspaper stand she'd seen on the way to the institution: "Siggi vs. Tore: Battle Royale." She considered

Petter's new party affiliation and, now, the two politicians running for reelection, becoming convinced more and more that Blomqvist was right to keep politics in mind.

"Ekstrand is the current head of Kvinnor på Toppen, and Pantzerhielm heads the Liberalkonservativa. As you'll recall, Kvinnor was the party where Lindström got her start. What's surprising is that Ekstrand and Lindström never seemed to be rivals. By all accounts, they were good friends and political allies even when Lindström switched parties, so I honestly don't know why Petter reacted that way."

"Maybe Ekstrand never really forgave her for leaving the party."

Magnus frowned. "Maybe."

"What about Pantzerhielm?" Katrina asked.

"Now, that one seems more plausible. I think that Pantzerhielm, for all his smiles and glad-handing, considers *everyone* a rival, if only for camera time. Even though he and Lindström were on the same team, so to speak, I don't think it would be unreasonable to say that he viewed her as a threat to his ascension in the party."

Katrina nodded slowly. "I can see that. Young, pretty, smart, and with a telegenic family... That's a lot to go up against."

"And with enough charisma to match his bigger-than-life personality," Magus added.

"Then I think we'll need to take a closer look at her political rivals... and her allies."

"We'll see if we can coordinate a meeting for tomorrow."

"No can do. You're forgetting something." Lena had entered the room and was leaning against the doorframe. "Tomorrow is Sunday. All party offices are closed."

"Well, what do you suggest we do in the meantime?" Katrina asked.

Magnus smiled. "I think it's high time you and Agent Figueroa had a proper tour of Stockholm."

Chapter 12

The team had a new temporary mission: visit as many tourist traps as possible. It was not as easy as one might expect as Stockholm had no shortage of things to see and do. They started off with the serious, respectable museums, followed by a ferry ride around the archipelago. Katrina loved it all. Along the way, Izzie spotted what appeared to be a massive amusement park.

That effectively ended any more museum visits.

Katrina put up a brief protest in favor of visiting *Kulturhuset*, the cultural exhibition hall, but was outvoted by Lena and Izzie. Jens and Magnus wisely abstained from offering their opinions.

In response to Katrina's grumbling about the importance of educating oneself in the cultural traditions of other countries to become better spies, an exasperated Izzie responded, "I think we've had enough 'culture' for today, Katrina. Let's go have some fun!" In Izzie's world, those two things were mutually exclusive.

So the amusement park, it was.

Twelve rides, two ice creams, and one ghost house later, Katrina could admit that the right decision had been made. Within the Division, nobody had a concept of "the weekend," so this was really her first chance for a break. Even Lena—whom Katrina would never take both eyes off of—seemed to be enjoying herself. Winning a giant Kex candy bar at the water gun booth might have had something to do with that. On the way back, they stopped at a few stores but bypassed the souvenir shops.

"Who would I buy for?" Katrina pointed out. "I'm supposed to be in Stockton, California, not Stockholm."

Magnus looked down at his watch. "Alright, everybody, I think we've almost had enough 'team building exercises' for today. Let's reconvene around twenty hundred hours at *Keruben* in Old Town. Stagger your entry times, and we'll find each other on the inside."

That was just fine by Katrina. After the heat of the day and the stickiness of the amusement park, she was more than ready for a shower and a change of clothes.

Back at the hotel, Katrina and Izzie got ready for the evening. The humidity was doing neither agents' curls any favors, and how they dealt with it was a perfect representation of their personalities: Kat carefully twisted her hair up in an elegant knot, while Izzie let her short curls fly free and frizzy. After a moment's deliberation, Izzie wore a white minidress—with a hidden thigh holster for her beloved knife—and platform sneakers, and Katrina wore a slinky black sleeveless jumpsuit and a pair of walkable heels.

They arrived with Katrina going in first and Izzie lagging ten minutes behind. Katrina spotted Jens at the bar. Izzie waved to Lena, who was already on the dance floor. Lena cleaned up surprisingly well. She had on leggings and a slouchy hooded sleeveless dress that managed to make her look both edgy and carefree. Izzie grabbed the nearest man she could find and joined Lena on the floor.

After ordering a drink, Katrina sat with Jens in their customary silence. After several minutes passed, she examined him more closely. He was well dressed, as usual, but looked awful and seemed to have a couple of drinks in him already. He must've been the first to arrive, to get that much of a head start.

"Um, Jens. Are you okay?"

"Sure." Jens watched the dancers gloomily from his barstool and tipped back his pint.

She gently nudged him in the ribs. "Hey. I thought we were supposed to be team building and getting closer?"

He heaved a sigh and clinked glasses with her. "*Skål*."

"Cheers, Jens," she said. "But I must say, you don't look cheery."

"You'd look like this, too, if you had just spent the day with a beautiful woman who barely notices you exist."

That's when Katrina noticed he was staring at her friend. "Izzie?"

"Izzie."

That was all it took to open the verbal floodgates. Apparently, Jens had been attracted to Isobel since their first encounter at the airport. He asked Katrina what kind of guys Izzie usually dated.

"Honestly? I've never actually seen her date anyone. But if I had to guess, she strikes me as the type who likes a man who's strong. And probably silent, since she can talk enough for two people." She considered her friendship with Izzie and was surprised to find that she really didn't have any insight into Izzie's love life. Of course, that could simply be because she was just like Katrina and didn't have one. *Hmm... I'm going to have to investigate this.*

Jens's eyes turned dreamy. "She's just so free and easy. And the way that woman handles a knife..." He seemed to catch himself and looked over at Katrina. "You won't tell her, will you?"

"I won't tell her you like her, but I think you should. What's the worst that could happen?"

"Other than total public humiliation?"

"Give it a chance. I can guarantee that Izzie wouldn't throw it in your face. She may be a jokester, but she's also incredibly kind. She wouldn't parade it around the Division hallways." *I don't think.* She kept that to herself, though, as Izzie could sometimes be a bit unpredictable.

Maybe what people said about Swedes opening up once alcohol was involved was true, because that was quite possibly the longest conversation she'd had with the man. She knew things had taken a turn when his hair flopped in front of his face and he didn't even bother to fix it.

Jens leaned in confidentially, his breath smelling of the entire top-shelf selection of the bar. "Since you were so generous with me, here's a little something you might be interested in knowing. Magnus thinks you're pretty hot. He spends more time than he ought to looking and talking about your—"

A heavy hand clapped Jens on the shoulder. "I think you've had enough, my friend." Magnus sidled up between Jens and Katrina.

Absentmindedly, she rubbed her gold pendant, which was, along with other assets, well on display in her low-cut jumpsuit.

"*Titta*, Jens. Look. Now's your chance. Izzie's over there, all by herself. Go make your move, man." Ignoring Jens's unmistakably frightened expression, he called over to Izzie, "Isobel! Jens needs a dance partner!"

Without giving Jens a chance to refute the statement, Magnus pushed him toward her. Isobel grabbed his hand and smiled, and a bewildered Jens let himself be dragged along.

"Poor bastard," Magnus muttered as he took Jens's unceremoniously vacated seat. He signaled to the bartender for another beer. "Mopes over her, then when he gets his chance, he doesn't know what to do with her."

"Talks to you about her, does he?"

"Won't shut up."

"When he's drunk?"

"*Nej*. Stone-cold sober. Hasn't had a drink on this case until now."

"A sober Jens chattering nonstop? I refuse to upend my impression of the man by believing that."

"Believe it. Just because you don't see him talk, doesn't mean he can't."

Katrina gave him a look of clear disbelief.

"Honest! Think about it. A man that silent all day long? By the end of the day, he's like a dam ready to burst."

She took a sip of her drink. "Well, damn."

He smirked at the joke. "Exactly."

Katrina turned back toward the floor. Apparently a liquored-up Jens became all limbs on the dance floor. He was smiling, though, so Katrina ruled out the possibility that she was bearing witness to a seizure. She turned back to Magnus.

"Before you interrupted us, he was telling me some rather interesting things. You talking about me and my most wonderful—"

Magnus looked mildly disgusted. "Jens. Can't hold his liquor, and the liquor can't hold his tongue."

"Well?"

"Quit fishing for compliments, Katrina."

She shrugged and took a drink to further her own courage. "Well, if you won't talk about that, why don't you tell me some more about my parents."

"How 'bout we talk about Jens some more? Or Lena?"

They both watched Lena. She had stopped dancing and was at a table with her right bicep flexed, comparing tattoos with a heavily bearded biker.

Katrina raised an eyebrow, more than aware of his blatant deflection technique. "What made you decide to join the Division, Magnus?"

"Probably the same reason as you—because my parents did." He took a drink and shrugged. "Well, that and the fact I was heavily recruited by the director at that time. Director Hagglund. Odd guy. Always said my genetics were the key to spying success. That it was the self-selected inherited qualities of the children of spies that made them so exceptional."

Katrina was baffled.

"Exactly." He laughed. "And you wonder why people only think I'm here due to nepotism. Needless to say, a year or two after I joined, he was forcibly retired."

"Ah. Your Division likes to employ euphemisms as well, I see."

"Indeed. I'm pretty sure his retirement package involved cyanide. We have a new director, brand new. He's convinced my advancement in the Division is because my parents are spies. Never mind all my successful missions."

"Paranoid, much?"

"Uh, no. The man literally said he was just waiting for an opportunity to demote me and get someone into my position who didn't get there based on nepotism."

"Ouch."

"I think that's why he assigned me this mission—he expects me to fail, giving him the excuse he needs."

"And Lena? Does she have relatives in the Division as well? Is that why she's on this mission?"

Magnus gave a short laugh. "If she did, that might actually have been to her benefit. No. You've met her. She's an excellent agent, but she's constantly rubbing people the wrong way, and I suppose she has finally rubbed the wrong person the wrong way for the last time."

"I can see how that could happen," Katrina replied dryly.

They continued to drink and people watch. The bartender had turned on a local football match. The dancing crowd moved to the room downstairs, and the footballers got in position to cheer on their teams. Katrina had little interest in watching the game, but she wasn't going to leave her seat and give up the opportunity to try to quiz Magnus about her parents. She needed to find out more about Berlin.

"So, family ties aside, how long have you worked for the Division?"

He took a moment to consider. "Almost fifteen years, I guess, but it doesn't seem that long."

"I bet during that time, you've been on some pretty memorable missions."

He looked a little lost in the past. "*Ja*. I've had some definite close ones."

Go for it, Kat.

"Any of those close ones ever take you to Berlin?" Katrina kept her expression blank.

He narrowed his eyes. "Don't play spy with a spy, Agent Foster."

She gave an unrepentant grin. "I wouldn't be doing my job if I didn't try."

Her cheekiness was sufficiently disarming, and he relaxed. From there, they slipped into easy conversation. Granted, it was about everything *but* her parents, but Katrina liked to think she was getting through his defenses. Although truth be told, he was getting under hers as well.

After a while, Magnus lightly stroked her arm. "It's getting too hot and rowdy in here, and I don't think I can watch Jens make a fool of himself anymore. How about we step outside for some fresh air?"

Given the tingling that had begun in her arm, Katrina found she could use some air herself.

They passed Jens, who'd gone back to the bar for yet another drink for himself and Izzie. He had, thankfully, given up dancing in favor of the game. He gave them a huge smile and two eager thumbs up. Katrina gave him a wink as she followed Magnus.

As they moved toward the exit, the lighting improved, and Katrina was able to see him better. Magnus had on a dark-gray short-sleeved shirt and a pair of snug black pants cut in the way that Europeans excelled at but American manufacturers could never quite figure out. It was doing him all kinds of favors from behind, Katrina noted.

After making their way outside, they stood under a green awning and talked as they watched locals and tourists cross over the bridge. Slowly, though, they reached that awkward moment when they ran out of things to say.

"Well..." he said.

"Well?" Katrina studied Magnus's face. His eyes had taken on a slightly sleepy look.

He leaned down over her, and Katrina tilted her face upward. If she was reading the signs correctly, she wasn't going to turn down a perfectly good—*please, please*—kiss. He smiled and came in closer, his lips inches away.

"Yearghhh!"

They looked up in time to see the bartender push Jens outside. The two men were angrily jawing at each other. Katrina and Magnus both winced as the bartender's right knuckles made contact with the left side of Jens's face. Jens's head snapped back, and he promptly stumbled over a trash can. Loud whoops were coming from the crowd, which had lost interest in the game the moment Jens was pushed out of the bar. Izzie tried to get between him and the bartender, and Lena came running out not far behind.

The bartender stormed over to Katrina and Magnus, brushing his hands on his apron.

"Tell your friend that if he's gonna say Hammarby is a better football team than Djurgården, he better be able to back up that statement with his fists."

At those fighting words, Jens ineffectively flailed out an arm, his hand in some semblance of a fist. "Then let's dansh, buddy." Coordination, however, was outmatched by momentum, and Jens promptly spun around and fell over. Magnus went to pick him up off the ground.

Eager to see what the ruckus was about, the small crowd started to grow. Izzie and Katrina tried to distract them, while Magnus handed Jens over to Lena and went to calm down the angry bartender. The last thing they needed was four spies and their not-quite-a-spy, not-quite-a-chauffeur ending up on the news.

"Sorry about my friend. I'm a Djurgården man myself, and I make a point not to talk about football with him. It's like talking politics or religion in a bar—it rarely ends well."

The five-hundred-crown note he placed in the bartender's hand seemed to appease him.

"It's alright," the man grumbled. "Just get him out of here."

When the crowd realized the fight was over, they dispersed, going on to find better entertainment for the evening. Izzie dabbed at the blood on Jens's face as Lena deposited him back on Magnus, shaking her head in disgust.

"Men," Lena muttered as though that explained everything. "Have fun dealing with..." She waved her hands at the human mess that was Jens. "Well, with all of that. I'm going home. See you at the office." She walked away from the sidewalk farce.

Katrina stared after her. Lena had totally blown them off. It might've surprised her, but given what she knew of Lena, it didn't. The woman had a colleague that was clearly in poor shape, and she'd completely abandoned him. *Jerk.* Not that Katrina was super eager to drag a drunken Jens home, but not only was he on their team, if they didn't deal with him, his antics were going to be a security risk.

She turned back toward Magnus, who glanced at Katrina somewhat wistfully. "C'mon, Jens. Let's get you back to your room."

Following the five stages of drunkenness, Jens seemed to have transitioned from feisty to remorseful. "S'pose I shouldn't have done that. Was stupid," he told Magnus.

"I can't argue with you on that."

"But if I didn't stick up for Hammarby, who would? They need me."

"I'm sure they appreciate your support."

As she watched Magnus handle Jens, Katrina wondered how often the two of them had been in that situation.

They were slow-moving with their stumbling companion, but they eventually made it back to the hotel and headed into the elevator.

Jens lifted his head to look at Magnus. "Hey, did you see me dancing with Agent Figueroa? Me?"

"Yeah, mate, you were something," Magnus deadpanned.

Something indeed.

"Mag... Magnus," Jens whispered loudly. "I tried to shtay cool, like you said." He let out a large burp. "Do you think she could tell? Agent Figueroa? She says I can call her Izzie, though. Izzie!" He seemed to be cheered by the fact he was now on a first-name basis with Izzie. The two women turned to hide their smiles as they all left the elevator.

Magnus tried to grab the thread of the conversation.

"No, Jens. You were as cool as a cucumber."

They finally reached Jens's room. After several failed swipes by Jens, Magnus gently took the room key card out of Jens's hand and opened the door.

"If you'll excuse me, Agents Foster, Figueroa." He nodded curtly, dragged Jens inside, and shut the door.

Dismissed, Izzie and Katrina continued up the steps to their own room—a little tipsy, yes, but no worse for wear.

"Good lord. I did not foresee this evening at all," Katrina said as they reached their floor.

"You mean you didn't anticipate our normally reserved Jens transforming into an antagonistic drunk given to pugnacity?" Izzie was in good humor.

"So there won't be any plans for a date, then?"

"You just heard my description of him, didn't you?" Izzie waggled her eyebrows. "Not necessarily a turnoff."

Katrina rolled her eyes. *Figures.*

"He's kinda cute. He's normally so unflappable. I gotta say I kind of like him flapped." Isobel smiled thoughtfully. "That said, I don't think I'll be dancing with him again anytime soon. That man dances like one of those inflated air dancers you see in front of the car dealerships." She started wiggling and flailing her arms, which cracked Katrina up. "It's not funny," Izzie protested, laughing all the while. "I nearly lost an eye a couple of times!"

They reached their room, and Katrina pulled out her keycard.

"What about you? Don't think I didn't notice you slipping outside with Magnus."

Katrina smiled as she opened the door. "I don't know. There might be something there. Maybe not the fiery heat that burns between you and Jens, but..." Her voice trailed off as she surveyed their room.

It was completely destroyed.

Chapter 13

"Someone was in our room last night."

At his desk, Magnus snapped to attention. "Details."

Katrina shook her head. "Not much, I'm afraid. It happened while we were out, so I couldn't say when. It was completely trashed, but nothing was taken. We dusted for fingerprints and found none."

Cleaning up the mess had taken them nearly four hours. Clothes were strewn everywhere, and toiletries had been emptied all over the floor. Given the dearth of evidence and the fact nothing was taken, Katrina was sure professionals were involved. Most thieves might be pretty careless—a fingerprint here, a strand of hair there—but most generally remembered to actually steal something. Katrina wasn't afraid to admit she was worried. Neither Katrina nor Izzie had slept, and Katrina felt better for being back at Division headquarters and ensconced in Magnus's office with the team. At least she was safe there—probably.

"Why didn't you call Jens?" Magnus asked.

All eyes turned toward Jens. He looked pitiful, and if appearance was any indicator, he must've been feeling quite poor indeed. Katrina didn't want to indict him, but she wasn't about to be accused of incompetence, either.

Luckily, Jens solved the conundrum.

"I'm afraid that I may have, well, passed out after last night. Unprofessional and will never happen again." He cringed and stared down. "I can, however, verify that I had several missed calls from them."

Magnus looked disgusted and turned to Lena. "What about you? Any signs of entry at your place?"

She shook her head.

Magnus turned back to Jens. "Jens, I'll deal with you later. In the meantime, go get someone to access and analyze the hotel's security camera feed. Maybe we'll see a familiar face or two making a visit to the hotel. Also, set up some one-hundred-eighty-degree sensor cameras outside their front door and monitor them. If anyone is going to mess with my agents again, I want to know."

Jens glanced sadly in Izzie's direction before leaving.

"Lena, go get some Level Threes over there to comb their room for clues."

Lena gave a short nod and left.

"Isobel, go with Lena, and give her a detailed report so the Level Threes will know where to begin." Izzie followed Lena.

Magnus softly tapped on his desk in Katrina's direction. "Do you have a minute?"

"Sure, do you need more details from the room? I'm afraid the Level Threes really won't find much, although I suppose it will be a good training exercise for them."

He listed to one side in his chair and leaned his head on a hand. He looked a troubling combination of worried and weary. "No, I don't think they'll find anything either, but I have to check anyway. It's pretty obvious that this wasn't a robbery—someone was either trying to do some fact-finding, or they were trying to scare you."

"To be honest, they may have accomplished a little bit of both. I'm more concerned that someone seems to know where we would be. But Izzie and I are fine, though. We're ready for the next time, should there be one." Katrina stood a little straighter.

"I know. But that's not what I wanted to speak to you about. I mean, we'll discuss that

when we know more, but I mean to say that I wanted to talk about something else..." He looked uncomfortable. "It's about last night. Outside of Keruben."

Katrina had the sense she was walking into what was going to be an awkward conversation and waited for Magnus to continue.

"Agent Foster, much like Jens, I'm afraid I may have overindulged as well..." He shifted awkwardly.

The hell he had. Katrina could see where this was going.

"I apologize for being anything less than one-hundred-percent professional."

Katrina held up her hand. "No need to continue, Agent Svensson." She could pretend to be perfectly professional as well. "We have a mission, and we can't afford any distractions."

He breathed a sigh of relief. "As you know from last night, I am already on thin ice, with the director determined to find a reason to dispose of me. I am pretty sure that looking cozy with a subordinate would count as a good reason."

She nodded.

"Good. I'm glad we are in agreement."

Something like that, she thought sarcastically.

He cleared his throat. "Who are you meeting with today?"

"Sigrid Ekstrand. Her assistant was able to squeeze me in for fifteen minutes this afternoon. I want to see if she matches Petter's impression of her. Hopefully, I'll get something to push this mission forward."

"Good luck out there with Ekstrand," he said.

"Thanks."

While Katrina knew this was the correct and properly professional decision for both of them, if she was fully honest with herself, she wanted to see where that almost-kiss would've led—nowhere good, probably, considering her dating track record. She'd never had much luck with men, and her interaction with Magnus was just a continuation of the trend.

Katrina left his office to find Izzie leaning against the wall right outside.

"You were in there for a bit. Picking up where you left off last night?"

"Nope. We have decided to remain professional." Katrina tried to appear nonchalant, but Izzie had known her since they were Level Ones.

"Sorry, buddy," she whispered.

Katrina shrugged. "I'm fine. It's fine. Besides, it just helps me to get into screw-the-oppressive-man mode."

That was perfect for meeting with the feminist leader of Kvinnor på Toppen.

Chapter 14

Katrina stood in front of the office of the feminist political party Kvinnor på Toppen—Women on the Top. Katrina smirked at the double meaning and wondered if it had been intentional.

She'd arranged a meeting with Sigrid Ekstrand, the head of Kvinnor, under the guise of a journalist. To fit the role, her ensemble included a deep-purple pantsuit and a bouffant wig.

Once inside, she showed her forged media credentials to an intern and was led to Ekstrand's office, where the woman was sitting. The intern quickly positioned herself by Ekstrand's side.

She approached with a smile. "Hello. My name is Katie Freedman. I'm a reporter with *The Evening Post* in America. Thank you for meeting with me."

Ekstrand gave Katrina a warm but intense smile. She was on the short and plump side, with mousy brown hair cut into a severe bob. She had on a black pantsuit that only emphasized the severity of her appearance. "Yes. *Absolut.* Welcome, sister. I'll confess I hadn't heard of you, but the internet tells me you're a pretty prolific writer in the US."

Thank you, Izzie, Kat silently said as she nodded. Before she set up the appointment, she'd had Izzie hurriedly post articles on the internet with her alias in the byline. The Division always kept an assortment of prewritten articles on hand for that very type of situation. After a change to the name and date and the addition of a couple of current references, no one could be the wiser. Each article was then set to autoerase within a preset time limit without caching, leaving no trail.

Ekstrand gestured for Katrina to help herself to some tea and Kex cookies. Katrina passed on the cookies but helped herself to a chai before taking her seat. She set out her digital recorder on a small side table. "I'm working on a series on influential female politicians from the 1960s to today. When I started researching internationally, Johanna Lindström's name came up repeatedly."

"I'm not at all surprised. Johanna was a real trailblazer."

"As someone who knew her well, can you tell me a bit about her?"

Ekstrand settled into her seat. "She was very pro-environment. Most Swedes are, of course, but she was particularly adamant that not only should Sweden practice environmental stewardship, but we should impose our standards on other countries. By aggressive means, if necessary."

"When you say 'aggressive,' what's an example of this?"

Ekstrand smiled. "I'm talking about advocating for entering other countries and forcing them to stop negative environmental practices such as strip mining or deforestation."

Katrina's eyebrows rose. "Well, that certainly *is* aggressive."

Ekstrand nodded, looking amused. "It wasn't agreed upon for Kvinnor's platform, but she lobbied hard for it. 'Can't you see it, sisters,' she said, 'us blazing into rainforests like the Amazonian women of old, capturing the evil clear-cutters and destroying their equipment?'" Ekstrand laughed and shook her head. "Everyone was convinced she was *nuts*. Absolutely nuts. But that was our sister—always a warrior, always finding a new cause for us to advocate."

"What can you tell me about Kvinnor's platform? As the party head, what are your key issues?" Katrina had learned early on that people enjoy having the opportunity to talk about themselves even more than talking about their friends.

"Sure. The advancement of women, first and foremost," she said as the intern nearby nodded in agreement.

"I also do less gratifying but equally important work in parliament. I serve on the EU Ethics Committee, the Animal Rights Commission, Banking and Finance..."

"Did Johanna serve in similar interests?"

"Oh yes, including the military. Blazing Amazonian women aside, she was a strong proponent of the demilitarization of the state." Ekstrand shook her head again. "She received a lot of threats over that issue in particular."

"Wasn't she ever afraid that those threats might turn into action?"

"You're not doing the right things if you don't receive threats of some kind." Ekstrand shrugged. "But she was brave. She never backed down." She paused. "At least not when she was with Kvinnor."

Katrina took notice of a slight trace of bitterness in Ekstrand's voice.

Ekstrand continued, "Even when she left the party, though, she never gave up on the women. She continued to advocate for an economic embargo in the Middle East for their barbaric treatment of women. The Saudis in particular were not impressed with that. Oh, the letters and calls we used to receive..."

"So she wasn't concerned that she was making too many enemies?"

"Enemies?" Ekstrand laughed. "My sister, you don't adopt our political positions if you only want friends. Oh, she had enemies alright." She began to tick them off on her fingers. "Abroad—the US, China, Russia, the Middle East, as I mentioned. At home—the armed forces. Pretty much all of the far right. The Scandinavian fur industry wanted to skin her alive." She shrugged in apology for the pun. "I will say this, though: for every enemy, Johanna had twenty friends. And they would fight for her ideals to the end." Her eyes cast downward. "Who knows what she might've accomplished had she lived."

"It sounds as if she left a legacy with Kvinnor," Katrina said gently.

"I'll be honest with you, Kvinnor hasn't been the same since she left for the Libcons. Johanna was very charismatic. Everyone was attracted to her... Everyone. Everyone wanted to get close to her. Though there was no one as close to her as me, mind you. We are—were—best friends." Ekstrand leaned back in her chair and closed her eyes. After a moment, she opened them and continued, her voice soft. "When she spoke to you, she made you feel like you were the only person in the room that mattered. Like you would say and do anything just to keep that glow around you."

Katrina let Ekstrand continue on in that vein for a while before deciding to tread carefully into her next question.

"Someone told me—I can't remember who—that you two had a falling out when she left the party..."

Ekstrand abruptly sat upright. "What? Nej, nej, nej. Nej."

It was the fourth no that confirmed Katrina's suspicions.

"Was I happy that she left? No, I was not. She threw so much away." Ekstrand pursed her lips. "But the Sisterhood is strong, and as with family, you can still love someone even if you don't agree with their choices." Ekstrand's eyes started to shimmer, and Katrina didn't think it was the usual political theater. "And I certainly did not agree with her choices."

"Why do you think she left?"

"I couldn't tell you what she was thinking sometimes with the Libcons' influence..." She looked away and went silent, lost in her memories. "Maybe it was her husband's doing. He *never* seemed comfortable around Kvinnor. Never."

Katrina latched onto that. "What about her family? What was your impression of Petter Lindström?"

"Her husband? Nice enough guy, I suppose." Ekstrand's expression said the opposite. "But I don't think Petter ever really *understood* her, what made her tick. She was good for giving him babies, though, I guess."

Hmm... Clearly, she was not inclined to be friendly with the husband.

"I think he was part of the reason why she left the party. Wanted a more mainstream life. Settled. Yet at the same time..."

"Yes?"

"Between you and me, I've always wondered about him. I always thought it was funny how Petter could not be bothered to contact the police until the next morning. A normal person missing a loved one would start calling around at least by midnight. Especially if your partner was high stature. *I* certainly would have. Odd... Don't you think?"

Katrina raised her eyebrows. That comment certainly gave her something to consider.

The clock ticked to the top of the hour. Right on cue, the intern reappeared with more hot water for tea and replaced the remaining cookies with a small tray of buns. Ekstrand took a long swallow from her cup and gestured for Katrina to take part.

"He could be jealous, you know, like he believed one of us would steal her away and keep her forever." She gave a small, secretive smile—one that also seemed like sadness. "So maybe he felt that if she was in a more mainstream party, she wouldn't be so dogmatic and so enmeshed with us strident women. The personal is political, and all of that."

"Did you keep in contact with him?" Katrina asked.

"Oh no. Our paths don't cross. Of course, he's now some spokestroll for Svensk Sanning, so I don't think they ever will." She scrunched her nose as though she smelled something methane-based. "Who knows what the story is with him now?"

A woman with a long blond braid came over. "Sister Ekstrand, we're going to be late for the rally if we don't head out soon."

Ekstrand smiled in apology. "Duty calls."

They'd long gone past the agreed-upon fifteen minutes.

"I understand. Thank you for being so generous with your time."

Katrina stood, shook hands with Ekstrand, and started to leave. To her surprise, Ekstrand called her back, and Katrina paused at the door.

"One more thing. If you need to find someone else who knew her well, try the Libcons' party leader, Tore Pantzerhielm. Not because I think he'll have anything good to say about her—he won't. But because it won't take but a few minutes with that blowhard to see the challenges Johanna was up against. He managed to shed at most two crocodile tears before accepting the position of party leader. With Johanna gone, there was no more competition."

Katrina nodded in appreciation. "Thanks for the lead. And again for your time. You've been very helpful."

On her way out the door, Katrina looked back and saw that Ekstrand's face had become serious. She spoke, and whether it was to herself or to Katrina, she couldn't be certain. "Anything I can do to help out the Sisterhood, I will. You can trust and believe that."

KATRINA WENT BACK TO the hotel room and found herself happy to find that Izzie was gone. She didn't mind sharing a room all that much, minus the snoring, but having some space to herself on occasion was nice. She flipped open her laptop and started typing up her report from her meeting with Ms. Ekstrand. While Katrina could tell Lindström and Ekstrand had indeed been friends, she'd detected an underlying tension, not so much in the words she'd said but rather in how Ekstrand said them. She would see what Magnus and Lena thought about it in their next meeting.

As she finished, she heard a familiar jingle coming from her computer, announcing a chat request. She toggled over to the next window. *Hector.* Katrina looked around and did a quick check of the room. Nothing around her indicated that she was anywhere other than her previously professed destination of Stockton, CA. She typed:

Hey Hector!

Can you talk?

Yeah, just give me a sec and I'll turn on the camera.

She quickly pulled off her bouffant wig and fluffed out her real hair. She whipped off her blazer and wrapped a lightweight hotel robe around herself.

What? Caught you in that ratty N'Sync fan club hoodie?

Ugh, of course he would remember that infamous moment. She quickly scanned the local Stockton news and weather before replying.

Something like that, she typed. She flipped on the camera and put on a smile.

"I'm back! Whew! You wouldn't believe how hot it is here. It's got to be a record in Stockton."

"Yeah, it's pretty hot here, too, believe it or not. How's your insurance case going?"

"Well, you'd never believe what happened during my first meeting with the local Stockton agents..." Katrina proceeded to tell Hector an adapted version of what working with the Swedish Division was like. Sharing her feelings and frustrations with a friend on the outside felt good, even if it was in the form of a series of half-truths.

"So, long story short, after several interviews, it's still not clear whose policy is going to cover the destroyed farmhouse. So I may have to be here longer than expected. Are you good with caring for my plants a little longer?"

Hector held one of her plants up to the camera and made a leaf wave hello to her. "Don't worry, Mama," he said in a high-pitched sing-song voice. "Papa Hector is taking good care of all of us. Even gave us some nice organic fertilizer as a snack. He sings us lullabies before bed..."

Ridiculous. Katrina couldn't help but crack up. That was what made Hector such a good friend, even if her chosen profession kept a barrier in their friendship.

"You are crazy," she said. "You know that, right?"

"I live to keep you entertained. No problem keeping an eye on things longer. I went in the fridge and tossed out the expired food so your place won't stink. You did have a visitor, though."

"A visitor?" Katrina's nerves heightened.

"Yeah, some older blond chick in some crazy high heels."

The director.

"I came in to water your plants, and she kind of sidled in after me, asking who I was. Can you believe that?"

Oh yes, Katrina thought. She could definitely believe that. "So what did you say?"

"I asked her who she thought she was, coming into somebody's apartment, and said if she didn't leave right then, I was going to call the cops."

Katrina's eyes grew wide, and she thought it nearly a miracle that the director hadn't garroted him on the spot for speaking to her like that. "What happened then?"

"Turns out she's from your job. Said her name was Sandra something. Anyway, she said she was in the neighborhood and was seeing if you were home."

Likely story.

"I told her you were in Stockton on business. She's at the same company. Shouldn't she know that? Weird."

Katrina absentmindedly rubbed a hand across her face. "Yeah, that's weird, alright." She tried to play it off. "But it's a big corporation, you know, so not everyone knows everyone's itinerary."

"I didn't think about that. You're right. Well, anyway, she turned around and left, and I finished watering the plants, and I haven't seen anyone else from your company coming by, so I guess the word got out."

Katrina had to end the conversation in order to think. "Well, thanks for checking in with me, Hector, but I've got to get these reports written up, or these Stockton colleagues will have my neck."

"No problem, Kat. Keep fighting the good insurance-claim fight out there."

Katrina laughed. "Will do. And thanks again for keeping an eye on things."

Hector made one of the plants wave again. "See ya."

After logging off, Katrina went into the bathroom to splash some water on her face. She looked up in the mirror, her brows furrowed in worry. She didn't know what that meant, the director slipping into her apartment, but she knew it couldn't be any good. *Just what the hell is the director up to?*

IZZIE CAME HOME LATER that night, making her usual ruckus. How she managed to be so stealthy as a spy and so noisy in all other aspects of her life, Katrina had no idea. She put aside the case report she'd been reading for research.

"Where have you been?"

"Oh, I went to the shooting range with Lena. You won't be surprised to know that I beat her in both speed and accuracy."

"So you're, like, friends now?"

Izzie shrugged. "I guess. Lena's not really that bad."

Katrina stared at Izzie as if she'd grown a pair of horns.

"Well, okay, she's kind of gruff, and I really do think she wanted to kill me the first day we met, but she's got a right to her attitude. She's been through some stuff."

"I don't disagree with that, Izzie, but I might be a bit more sympathetic to her plight if she wouldn't treat me like an unwanted wart."

"There's a wanted wart?"

"You know what I mean."

Izzie shrugged. "She's alright. I think you guys just have clashing personalities or something."

Hmph. Katrina wasn't quite sure what to make of that, but some part of her didn't like that her best friend was now hanging out with someone who pretty much hated her guts. But she supposed she was being petty. As Izzie got undressed and into her pajamas, Katrina told her about her call with Hector. She waited until Izzie came out of the bathroom with her toothbrush before telling her the most crucial bit.

"So then he drops this bombshell. The director tried to get into my apartment!"

Izzie spoke while brushing her teeth. "Whoa. What do you think she was doing there?"

"Beats me. That's what I've been sitting here trying to puzzle out. I don't have anything in the apartment that would be of any use to the director. I don't have anything nefarious to keep from the Division, either. And it's not like I can ask Hector a bunch of questions because then *he'll* get suspicious." Katrina groaned. "Sometimes, I think one of the hardest things about being a spy is trying to maintain a real relationship. Hector is my good friend, but I always feel like I'm only half a friend because I keep half of my life from him, y'know?"

"Nope, I don't." A blob of minty foam slid down Izzie's chin. She wiped it off with the back of a wrist and continued, "That's why you don't keep friends on the outside. Less complicated."

"What about you?" Katrina countered. "You talk to your parents all the time."

The toothbrush dangled from Izzie's mouth as she spoke. "Yes, but I've been honing my skills since I was a teen. I've been lying to them for so long that when I joined the agency, it just seemed like one more thing that became second nature."

Katrina had always wondered what the teenage Izzie had been like. Whenever she tried to ask her, Izzie's biography seemed to get pretty hazy, and Kat decided it wasn't worth pursuing.

"Well, you'll have to school me on it since you're the expert."

Izzie got into her bed and flipped off her light. "One day, grasshopper, I'll teach you to become as accomplished as I am. But tonight is not that day."

With that odd turn of phrase, she flopped over and was asleep in minutes, leaving Katrina alone to ponder the mysteries of friendship, lies, and what to do about the director's visit.

Chapter 15

Katrina didn't have to wait long to decide what to say to the director. Right after Izzie left the next morning, Katrina received a ping from her superior.

"Good morning, Agent Foster."

"Good evening, Director."

If the director was still in the US, the time was nearly midnight. *Does the woman not require sleep?* It wouldn't surprise her if the director simply willed herself to forgo rest should sleepiness appear at an inconvenient time.

"Let's get down to it, Agent Foster. After all, it is quite late, and I actually *do* require sleep."

Good grief. The director must've been a telepath or something. No other explanation existed for why the director seemed to be able to read people's minds.

Katrina quickly gave a review of her notes and apprised the director of their progress, careful to leave out the small details of the trashed hotel room and the mutual attraction with a fellow agent. She suspected both would get her sent packing back to the US.

The director, who had requested the update, seemed impatient upon actually receiving it.

"I think that's more than enough apprising, Agent Foster. Send anything else you feel is relevant to my assistant."

Katrina nodded, looking forward to wrapping up the call. The director unnerved her more than a little bit, and that interaction was no exception.

"Now, tell me"—the director fixed her piercing eyes on Katrina—"do you feel as though you've been successful in your mission thus far, Agent Foster?"

"Um... yes? I think we're making good progress." Katrina thought she'd established that in her report.

The director gave a swift shake of the head, though her hair didn't waver an inch. "Wrong answer, Agent Foster. The only successful mission is a completed mission. Everything leading up to that is just failure in the making."

"Yes, Director."

"And do you feel as though you are letting personal feelings get in the way of completing a successful operation?"

Magnus flashed into Katrina's mind, as well as her parents. "No, Director."

"I don't need to polygraph you to know that you're lying to me."

Katrina just barely suppressed a gasp.

"Think carefully before you respond this time, Agent Foster." She continued that unnerving stare as though she had again breached Katrina's conscience.

Katrina willed herself to keep her breathing even. It was not easy, and she briefly considered ceasing altogether. If she stopped breathing, that would be a welcomed respite from her current interrogation.

"I can explain—"

"Yes, please do, considering that's what has been requested of you."

"Well..."

"Exactly why are you having such difficulty with integrating your team? You're not going to complete your mission if you're limping along with only Agents Svensson and Figueroa. You need to figure out how to put aside whatever personal animosity is between you and Agent Lena Holmberg and get on with it. She's a well regarded and valuable resource. And frankly, if even Agent Figueroa can work alongside her, then I am somewhat amazed that you cannot."

Ah, Lena. Nothing involving Magnus or her parents. She breathed a sigh of relief. Then she felt confusion, wondering how the director had found out about the tension between her and Lena.

"If I might ask, how do you know these things, Director?"

"I didn't get this position solely on my good looks, Agent Foster." No other explanation was forthcoming.

"Yes, Director."

"Agent Foster, part of becoming an accomplished operative is commanding respect. The people you work with—the people who can also, I might note, make the difference between your life and death—need to respect you. Notice that I did not say 'like' you." She pointed at herself. "This may come as somewhat of a surprise, Agent Foster, but I am not universally liked."

Katrina wisely chose not to speak.

"I am, however, universally *respected*, a respect I've worked damned hard to cultivate." She shifted in her chair, clearly unaccustomed to having such personal conversations with underlings. "And it is that respect that makes agents give their all for our cause. It's what makes them perform at a higher echelon and what makes them willing to risk their lives. And it's what you need to develop with your peers. Simply being the smartest in the room won't cut it if you expect another mission." The director narrowed her eyes.

"I understand, Director. I will make that effort."

"Make certain you do. I will know if you don't." The director cleared her throat. "Okay, enough with the pep talk."

That was a "pep talk"? Called a failure, told to improve, and threatened with never receiving another assignment? Katrina was very much of the opinion that the director should not pursue a career as a motivational speaker.

"Thank you, Director." Katrina hesitated, unsure of the wisdom in her next move. "Um, Director?"

"Yes?"

"I, uh, heard from my friend that someone was in my apartment..." She cringed a little then screwed up her courage to keep going. "Based on his description, it sounded a lot like you."

"And?"

"So it *was* you?" Katrina was surprised the director didn't deny it, although maybe she shouldn't have been. "Why were you in my apartment?" She coughed. "If I might ask."

"Why *wouldn't* I have been in there? You didn't have any expectation of privacy, did you?"

Actually, Katrina rather thought she did, but that didn't seem the time to start a philosophical discussion on the right to privacy for spies.

"But what were you searching—"

The director cut her off. "That hefty young man caring for those sad houseplants."

"Hector." She was a little offended at that description of him. She supposed it was accurate but still rude. He just had big bones.

"Whatever. He made my job a lot easier. Just left the door wide open. You ought to find a better caliber of friends who know how to immediately close and lock a door behind them. Really now, Katrina," she chided her with a chuckle. "Now, with that last piece of advice, I believe we're done here. I look forward to my next report detailing your improved team cohesion. Director, out."

With that unceremonious dismissal, Katrina went out to find Izzie. In less than a minute, Director Jones had managed to admit guilt without being guilty, scold her for thinking her home wouldn't be entered, deflect Katrina's question, deftly distract her by saying something offensive about her friend, and then counter by accusing Katrina of not caring about her personal safety by having careless friends. Then she disappeared as quickly as she'd arrived.

Katrina had been played.

Master spy, indeed.

KATRINA STARED AT ALL the retro Americana on the surrounding walls inside the café, once again considering the love/hate relationship between America and Sweden. She hadn't seen that many Uncle Sams in one location outside an Independence Day parade featuring the Dancin' Uncle Sam Band. And even they had been even more subdued.

The décor was about the only American thing about the café, however. That day had to be the hottest of the summer, so far, with no air conditioning in sight—or iced tea. Persuading the barista that adding a scoop of ice to a cup would be perfectly reasonable took a bit of convincing and earned her a couple of odd looks.

"Then why'd you ask for tea?" was the surly response.

In truth, the place had only two things in its favor. One, not many people lingered around the café, which reduced the potential for someone to eavesdrop. Most of the customers got their purchases to go. And two, the pastries, however overpriced they might've been, were amazing.

Kat took a long sip of her mint iced tea and looked across the table at Isobel. "Can you tell me why you're drinking hot coffee in this weather?"

Izzie shrugged. "Force of habit, I guess. Plus, my grandfather always said that drinking hot liquids on a hot day can cool you down."

"How's that working out for you?" Katrina was skeptical.

"I'll let you know, if I ever cool off." Izzie tried billowing her shirt to dry off the sweat. "What do these people have against air conditioning?"

"Dunno. When in Rome..."

After Katrina's "pep talk" from the director, she'd made the regrettable mistake of agreeing to walk five blocks to meet Izzie at the café for *fika*. Afternoon had just begun, and the temperature had to be just under eighty. Because heat in Sweden was rare, air conditioning in Sweden was even rarer. The booth felt hot in the humid café, and it was going to be hell when the time came to unstick her legs from the sweaty vinyl.

The two spoke in hushed tones about their mission, excluding specifics and making it sound like they were talking about a book they were both reading, with slight name changes. They talked about the case and their theories about the suspects. Katrina also told her about her meeting with the director.

"Ha! You totally got worked over by her!" Izzie laughed but softened the effect by adding, "But any of us would have. That's one of the many reasons that she is 'universally *res-pect-ed*.'" Izzie did her pitch-perfect impression of the director.

While they sipped and chatted, a string of bells on the entrance jingled, and three men of Middle Eastern descent entered. From her vantage point, Katrina had a good view of every customer who came in, which was not an accident. Two of the men had full beards, and one was clean-shaven. The clean-shaven man wore a crocheted skull cap, cargo pants, and a tight-fitting T-shirt. The other two men wore loose-fitting black cotton pants and long tops resembling tunics.

Katrina turned to a topic that had bothered her from the previous night. "So what do you really think about *Leonora*? I'm not always certain of her motivations. Like I can't fully trust her. She does seem to be warming up to you a bit, though."

Izzie nodded. "It's like I told you. Len—Leonora isn't actually all that bad once you get to know her character. She's seen some things and was double-crossed more than once, passed over a lot, so I think she's just ultra wary of any outsiders now."

Katrina knew the two had met again for target practice at the Division's gun range that morning. She tamped down a feeling of envy that her best friend was out with someone that Katrina would *almost* consider an enemy. Well, maybe she wouldn't go so far as to say 'enemy,' but she was more than comfortable with thinking of Lena as at least a real jerk.

Two of the men got up to leave and told the third man goodbye—*Ma'a salama*. The third man then reached into his knapsack, pulled out a newspaper, leaned back, and signaled for a refill as though settling in for a nice long stay. The waitress did not seem pleased, but at least he didn't pull out a laptop. That was the kiss of death for customer turnover.

Kat and Izzie continued their coded speak. "Well, what about Mag—*Maxwell*?" Izzie asked. "You seem to be into him, and I still don't have a sense of what he's about. Seems a decent sort, if you like the strong, brooding, handsome type."

"Yeah, he's decent, alright..." Katrina kept up with the conversation but was distracted. For some reason, Katrina had a vibe about the man that compelled her to keep a visual on him. That's when she noticed something: though he held up the newspaper, he never flipped the page. Either he was an exceptionally slow reader, or the newspaper was simply a cover. At first, she worried she was being silly, but as time passed and the man—perfectly positioned within a good visual and hearing range of them—was still on the same page, Katrina knew her instincts had been right. They were being observed.

"Hey, Izzie."

"Yeah?" Izzie was preoccupied with brushing croissant flakes from her shirt. Katrina needed eye contact. She delivered a swift kick under the table.

"Yeow—what?"

Katrina opened her eyes meaningfully and tapped her right ring finger twice on the table. Izzie instantly transformed from mildly irritated to fully alert.

"We're at risk of overstaying if we're going to get from here over to there on time." She blinked on every word she wanted to emphasize—*We're at risk. Over there.* The key was to drop in enough other words so that you weren't constantly blinking. Katrina learned that early on in her Covert Communications of the Division course when the instructor rushed to her aid because she thought Katrina was having an epileptic fit.

Izzie gave a nearly imperceptible nod. "I know. But I can't figure out where"—blink—"I put the map." *Where?*

Katrina held her cup up to her lips and murmured, "Two o'clock."

Izzie's eyes darted the other way.

"*Your* two o'clock!"

Izzie dropped her napkin and glanced over when she reached down to pick it up.

"Ah. I see. Well, we better get going then." No need to trans-blink-late that one.

They unstuck themselves from the seats and left. The man remained in the café.

Together, they stood out front, pretending to rummage through their purses for the lost map.

"Okay, what's the plan?"

"You keep an eye on him. See if he alerts anyone else or tries to follow. I'll head to Division headquarters and see if they know anything about the guy by his description. We'll meet back at the hotel in an hour."

WITH MAGNUS OUT OF his office—she dedicated a brief moment to wondering where in the world he could be—the first person Katrina saw in NK's basement was Lena—not her first choice, as confidants went, but she wasn't in a position to be choosy. Plus, she would have the opportunity to put the director's advice to use.

"Lena!" Katrina hurried forward and grabbed her arm to stop her.

Lena looked down at her arm as though she'd been burned then back up at Katrina.

Katrina let her go and said, "We have a situation."

"Oh?" Lena seemed only mildly interested.

"Izzie and I were having *fika* when I noticed a strange man watching us. He came in with two other guys. Those men left, but he stayed. He was pretending to read a newspaper, but I could tell he was eavesdropping. It wasn't regular nosiness or interest in Americans. It was like he was listening for information." Everything came out in a whoosh.

Lena cocked her head. "A guy eavesdropping, you say? Describe him."

"Maybe five feet seven, light-brown skin, with a crocheted skull-cap over a shaved head, no beard, short-sleeve shirt." Katrina paused to consider further. "Middle Eastern descent. Spoke Arabic, but I don't know what he said to the men with him other than 'Goodbye.'"

"Did he follow you here?" Lena asked without any sense of urgency.

"Well, no. He stayed at the café."

Lena looked unimpressed.

"I have Izzie watching him, though," Katrina said. Something about Lena always made her feel defensive of what would otherwise be viewed as perfectly logical decisions.

"Okay... so based on what you said, you saw three men enter a café, drink something, and then one remained to read the newspaper—not following you—and you took that to mean you were being spied upon, correct?"

"Correct."

"Sounds like we ought to call in the guards. There's a national security alert!" Lena gave a brittle laugh that rang false. "Katrina, you're making something out of nothing. Rookie mistake. People behave oddly every day, everywhere. If every one of them was up to no good, we'd be overrun with crime, and murderers would be running rampant."

When Katrina didn't respond, she said, "But I guess I can help you out, if only to prove you wrong." Even support from Lena came with an insult. "I'll check the CCTVs nearby and cross scan the guy to see if he shows up in any databases. Good enough for you?"

"Thank you, Lena."

That wasn't validation, but Katrina would take any help she could get from her.

"I will say, though, as a seasoned veteran in this business, let me give you some advice. Quit searching for threats, and focus on the real ones right in front of us. There are plenty of them. Trust me." Lena gave a smile that looked more like she was constipated then walked away. "Give me a day or so, and I'll get back to you!" she shouted over her shoulder.

Katrina watched her walk off. While Lena was clearly helping only because she wanted to prove Katrina wrong, help was help, and at least Katrina could tell the director she was trying. Maybe Lena would never like her—and the feeling was mutual—but she would be *re-spect-ed*.

KATRINA FLUNG THE HOTEL room door open, and Izzie jumped up from the desk where she'd been servicing her handgun and pointed it squarely at Katrina.

"Jeez! Don't scare me like that." Izzie quickly lowered her weapon. "Thank God I have restraint."

Katrina brushed aside the perceived near miss. "Well, did you see him? What'd he do?" She was anxious for some evidence that her hunch was correct.

"Nothing much, actually. He had a refill of coffee before leaving. He stopped by a convenience store to pick up a pack of cigarettes then walked to the train station and checked the timetables. He slipped onto a southbound train right before the door closed, and I lost him. It was headed to Västerhaninge, if that matters. I think he would've gotten on any train to get away, though."

Katrina tried not to show her disappointment at Izzie losing him.

"Did he act suspicious?"

"That's the thing. If it wasn't for the fact that he was clearly *not* reading the newspaper, I wouldn't have looked twice at the guy."

Katrina flopped back on the bed and threw an arm across her face. She knew small signs and signals mattered. She wasn't going to second-guess herself on that, especially since she knew the exact same tricks of the trade. The smallest of tells could give away someone's true intention, and she had to be on alert for them at all times.

"Yet another unexplained piece. Just what we need." She then told Izzie about her encounter with Lena.

"She had to make a point of calling me a rookie and acted like I was making something out of nothing, like it was just nerves causing me to see dangers that didn't exist. At least she agreed to help, though. I mean, it's 'cause she thinks I'm wrong, but at least she's going to do it."

"Now see, that's nice. I told you she wasn't that bad."

"Well, she's not that good, either," Katrina grumbled.

Izzie didn't respond, and Katrina realized she was being churlish. "Okay, okay. You're right. The director was right. I'm just being petty."

"There you go, champ. It's the new and improved and trusting Katrina."

Katrina gave a small smile and kept her other thoughts to herself. *Trust... but verify.*

Chapter 16

"Press pass, please."

A front-desk security guard held out his hand, and Katrina placed her badge in his palm for inspection. Katrina hadn't dropped her suspicions of Lena or her fixation on the mysterious man spying on her, but she knew her best option was to journey forward and investigate the next potential suspect.

She arrived at the SVT television studio just in time for her meeting with Pantzerhielm. His personal assistant told her the man could squeeze her in just before his appearance as a guest panelist on the weekly program *Round Table Politics*.

Katrina was led to a pair of chairs near the set, where he was already seated. One assistant was spraying and fluffing up his hair while another powdered his face. He batted both away upon Katrina's approach.

"Katie Freedman, is it? So good to meet you!" He had that big, booming politician's voice.

"Lovely to meet you as well. A real pleasure." Katrina pasted on her biggest and brightest smile. Something told her that a little light flirting might grease the interview along.

"Ah, my dear. The pleasure is all mine." He pointed her to a seat. "Would you like something to drink?"

"Water would be wonderful, thank you."

He snapped his fingers at his assistant. "So this is about Johanna's assassination, is it? What makes you so interested in a decade-old assassination in our small but fair country?"

"We always find political assassinations so intriguing. As you know, we've had a number of high-profile assassinations and assassination attempts. In addition, Americans like to hear about them in other countries as well." She tilted her head a little in his direction. "Americans are always interested in Swedes and Sweden. Haven't you seen how we always talk about your 'evil socialism'?" She grinned to show she meant no harm.

Pantzerhielm let out a booming laugh. "Ah, yes. We use your gunslinging and warmongering and bootstrap mythology as boogeymen as well. Makes any proposal we bring forward seem not as extreme." He leaned forward as if to share a secret. "Personally, I've always loved Americans, particularly their women. So beautiful. So diverse. Quite the sampling of all the candies in the box."

Oh, good lord. Does he really think lines like that work? Katrina kept her gag reflex in check as she laughed and tried to steer the conversation back on track. "Speaking of women, I'm working on an article on one in particular. What can you tell me about Johanna Lindström?"

"Ah, dear Johanna." Pantzerhielm sighed. "She was very good at her job. And ambitious—so very ambitious." He pulled out the figurative knives. "As a result, there were two sides to her. Don't be fooled by the pictures of her smiling with that husband of hers and mistake it for softness. She could be nasty and cutthroat to achieve her political goals." He leaned toward Katrina again in a confiding manner. "Not that the public ever saw any of that."

Katrina thought that was a rather distasteful way to speak of the dead, but she let him continue.

"Your president at the time didn't like her, either." He paused. "Of course, the feeling was mutual, so it might not have been any big loss to her."

"How did the Libcons' leadership react to her party shift from Kvinnor?"

"The party was happy when she switched. While we don't value political personalities like you Americans do, I won't lie when I say the party leadership was anticipating a public relations boon when she left Kvinnor and joined us. She was beautiful, charismatic, a feminist without being a harpy."

Katrina had to try hard to not roll her eyes at that last bit.

"She got us lots of positive news coverage." He shook his head. "But her views..."

"What about her views?" Kat asked.

"Honestly..."

Experience told Katrina that anytime a politician began with 'honestly,' they were about to tell a whopper.

"Honestly, no one mourned the loss of Johanna *more* than *I*. She was a worthy political adversary that helped me become stronger, but as anyone can tell you, the woman had a lot of enemies. From all over. At times, it seemed like she was being deliberately provocative in her stances. I mean, talking about reducing the Swedish military weapon production? Are you kidding me? I don't know if you know this, but Sweden happens to be a very large weapons manufacturer."

"I did not know that," Katrina acknowledged.

"To vote for that would've been political suicide. It would've *destroyed* the party. By the time she said she wanted a severe—well, severe by EU standards, mind you—reduction in the availability of oil to curb greenhouse emissions... Hell, there was no way the party was ever going to consider her for PM. No way."

Katrina mulled over what that statement might mean. "Let's take a step back. You mentioned the excitement surrounding her departure from Kvinnor. What do you know of Sigrid Ekstrand, their party leader?"

"That hag?" Pantzerhielm momentarily lost himself. "Well, Sigrid was the party's second-in-command at that time. Their views were in lockstep until she left. Among those closest to Johanna, it was common knowledge that the split effectively ended Johanna's friendship with her. Not that you would've ever gotten either to confirm that publicly."

"Political alliances shift often. Yet people don't often make it personal to the point where they sever all ties." Katrina sensed they were beginning to drift in an intriguing direction.

He smiled and shook his head in a condescending manner. "You'd be surprised, my dear, how often the personal *is* political. I think Sigrid was mad that she couldn't keep sampling a certain *Svenska kakor*, if you catch my meaning."

Katrina's eyebrows rose. *Couldn't keep sampling a certain Swedish cake...* She tilted her head in skepticism. "Really? Are you saying they were a couple?"

"I'm not *saying* anything." He winked and waggled his eyebrows. "But there were rumors." He leaned in as though confiding with a best friend. "Had problems with the husband at one point. I heard them shouting over the phone once. Very *messy*. But they always made nice for the cameras and the kids."

Very intriguing...

"You mentioned rumors, but was there any evidence?"

Pantzerhielm waved his hands as though dismissing the idea that evidence should have any role to play in a juicy story. "Look, all I know is that everyone commented on how Johanna and Sigrid went from being inseparable to suddenly only speaking to each other through the media. 'I know my good friend Sigrid would support this bill.' Stuff like that. No one believed it was a coincidence that right after she left Kvinnor and Sigrid, Johanna and the husband were back to being a cozy couple." He took a sip of water and not-so-sur-reptitiously peered at Katrina's chest.

Pig.

"Speaking of couples... do you have a man back in America? Not that it matters here. What happens in Sweden stays in Sweden! Ha ha!"

She pulled back in her seat. The dude was utterly clueless at reading body language—that or just utterly determined.

"I'm married to my job, thanks. Anyway, you said 'right after.' Right after she joined the Libcons?"

He nodded. An assistant ran up and flashed him the signal for five minutes.

"Well, with my limited time, let's switch back to her assassination. Would anyone go beyond political means to prevent her rising in the ranks?"

Katrina noticed that he paused and averted his eyes before responding. A pause could just indicate contemplation, but the combined eye shift indicated that another prevarication was on the horizon.

"Like I said, there were a lot of people she got on the wrong side of, but I can't think of anyone who would go from grudge to gore." He seemed rather proud of himself for the alliteration. "I mean, that's not really how we do things here."

He looked over at his time-worried assistant, and Katrina knew her time was up.

"I've got to go on soon. I'm on a discussion panel for 'You and the EU.' Should be lively—be sure to check it out!" Then he flashed her the patented politician smile—all teeth but dead eyes.

"One more thing, Mr. Pantzerhielm." Katrina thought back to the men at the café and Pantzerhielm's comments about Johanna's opinions on the Middle East. "Do you and the Libcons have any connections to the Middle East?"

"What an odd question, my dear. No more than anyone else, I'd suspect." He flashed her another smile. "Now, you must forgive me, but I really must be going. Duty calls!"

After pretending to leave, Katrina hid behind a pillar and peeked out over at him.

The smile slid off Pantzerhielm's face, and he snapped his fingers at his beleaguered assistant. "Get my phone. Now!"

Chapter 17

Katrina found Magnus and Izzie in his office at Division headquarters. She told them of her interview with Pantzerhielm. Izzie seemed grossed out by the description of her interactions with him, while Magnus appeared as though that wasn't unexpected. Only when she mentioned Lindström's alleged romantic connection with Ekstrand did he seem surprised. Magnus turned toward Jens, who was lurking off in the background, silent as usual and sneaking glances at Izzie.

"Jens, have you heard anything about this?" he asked.

"I've never heard about it on the ground," Jens answered. "I don't know that anyone believed it was more than friendship."

It seemed, then, what Pantzerhielm claimed that "everyone knew" was largely limited to the political classes—or maybe just him.

Katrina walked over to the whiteboard by Magnus and started jotting down her ideas. "Motivations... Well, in addition to a host of political enemies outside her inner circle, it seems like she may have had a few closer to home. Pantzerhielm clearly hated her and clearly loved the consolidation of power that came from her removal from party leadership. He was a direct beneficiary of her assassination. Ekstrand, in contrast, resented Lindström and her star quality leaving Kvinnor and, possibly, her personally as well. In theory, either of those are enough to drive someone to kill. Whether one of them acted on it, though..."

Magnus tilted his head, taking it all in. "So what's the more powerful motivation? Power or passion?"

Izzie shrugged. "I don't know that those can be easily disentangled. Seems to me both benefitted equally. With Lindström out of the Libcons, both benefitted from the loss of her star power."

"And then there's her husband. Maybe he found out about the affair, and it drove him mad," Katrina thought out loud. "But that's all passion, though—no power. Unless we count his rising party membership in Svensk Sanning, and I don't know if it's significant enough to do so."

"Well, whoever it was and whatever drove them to do it, they need to have a connection to Surikov, and we don't have that yet," Izzie noted.

At that, the door flung open. Lena burst through with her usual tact and plopped down a stack of papers. Looking an uncomfortable mix of irritated and accomplished, she addressed Katrina.

"One, before you ask, none of the CCTV footage around the café of the 'suspicious guy'"—Lena had to make bunny-ear quotes with her fingers to remind Katrina of her skepticism—"was clear, so I sent it over to our A/V team to try to get a sharper image."

Only Lena could denigrate world-class technological experts as a group of audiovisual lackeys.

"And two, I know I treated you like you were crazy to mention brainwashing as an explanation for Surikov, but..." She took a breath as though searching for the inner strength to utter her next words. "You... were... right," she gritted out.

Katrina perked up. While she didn't like having to wait for the footage to be worked on, she could use some good news about Surikov, and it didn't hurt that it was coming from someone who looked like they were digesting razor blades in the act of giving Katrina credit.

"What did you find?" Magnus asked.

"I started searching like you asked—thinking it was a complete waste of my time—but lo and behold, there is some published but obscure work on the science of mind control." She pointed at the journal articles on the desk.

"Now, it's not the same name—they refer to it as 'suggestive-coercion research,' but when you go deeper into the details, what they're actually talking about is mind control."

"Hmm... Well it seems like Izzie was heading in the right direction," Katrina said.

Izzie looked quite pleased with herself, which was to be expected.

"So is it a big field?" Izzie asked. "How many researchers are there working on this?"

Lena turned toward Izzie. "Thankfully, for our purposes anyway, there aren't too many. I've got a list of ten researchers that I'm working on narrowing down. Isobel, I could use your help on this one—cross-referencing who might be the likeliest ones involved in this."

"You got it."

"It's no 'smoking gun,' as you Americans like to say, but I wouldn't be surprised if at least one, if not more, are involved in some capacity."

"Nicely done, Lena," said Magnus.

Katrina was excited by where things seemed to be heading. "Intriguing. Very intriguing." She started pacing. "Of course, we have to assume that the researcher or researchers weren't just acting out of curiosity. We also have to figure out why they would take a risk like this. And it's definitely a huge risk because their entire career would be ruined by an ethics violation of this caliber. Not to mention jail time."

Magnus spoke up. "Lena and Isobel, if you can get pictures of all the researchers, we can see if Surikov or even that head nurse recognizes any of them."

Lena and Izzie nodded in agreement.

With this new avenue to pursue, Katrina was ready to get back to work. "Jens, have the car ready tomorrow. I'm heading back to St. Gustav."

Chapter 18

The next day, Katrina once again donned the box braids and her camera glasses and set off for the facility. Given what they suspected about mind control, the more she thought about Surikov, the more he had her sympathy. Katrina hadn't forgotten his vile forum posts, but it seemed more and more like he was a pawn in a game well beyond his understanding. Knowing that he wasn't completely crazy, Katrina was eager to make another visit to him. This time, however, she was armed with pictures of the ten "suggestive coercion" researchers, courtesy of Lena and Izzie, and a better-guided arsenal of questions.

The first thing she noticed upon entry was that Nurse Ox was nowhere to be found—probably off somewhere in the building, making someone miserable. In her stead was a refreshingly polite attendant. Katrina explained who she was and why she was visiting. He reminded her of the visitor rules, and despite her best, most Izzie-like cajoling, the attendant would not budge and allow her to see the patient.

"Well, if I can't see Mr. Surikov today, is there anyone who works with him that I might be able to speak with?"

"Oh." He searched through a listing, dragging his finger down a list of names. "You'll want Dr. Patrick Abboud, then. Midmorning is usually a quiet time for him. Let's see if he's available."

The attendant took her through a wing different from her previous visit. While they walked, Katrina figured that would be as good a time as any to show him the pictures of the researchers. He seemed friendly and was more likely to offer information than his predecessor, Nurse Ox.

"Y'know, I don't recall seeing you before. How long have you been working here?"

"I don't actually work on this level at all. I'm just filling in. The regular nurse is at professional development training."

Rats. No point in showing him the pictures, then.

They walked down a carpeted hallway before stopping in front of an open office. He tapped on the door and quietly spoke with the doctor. The doctor was a small man with golden-colored skin, a balding cul-de-sac of black hair, and a small pointed goatee. He gestured for her to come in and stood up to greet her.

"This is Dr. Katie Foster," the attendant said. "She's here because she's doing research on one of your patients."

He took out a small cloth and wiped the lenses in his circular gold-rimmed glasses as he spoke. "It's a pleasure to meet you, Dr. Foster. Welcome back to our facility."

Clearly, he had some previous knowledge of her earlier visit. He was polite and professional, but Katrina could tell he had his guard up.

"A pleasure to meet you as well, Dr. Abboud. I recently met with a patient of yours, Mr. Viktor Surikov."

"I know. You made quite the impression on him." He looked severe. "'The American doctor. The American doctor. She knows. Ask her, she knows!' He must've repeated it twenty times a day the first week after you met with him."

Katrina gave a short laugh and tried to play it off. "Well, at least I'm getting praise from somewhere. Most of my patients usually spend their allotted hour telling me that I know nothing!"

He gave a small smile. "Well, let's not stand around, Dr. Foster. Please do come and join me, as I was just getting ready to enjoy a little *fika* down in the cafeteria."

Once in the cafeteria, they selected some tea and a few small buns. Katrina was delighted to see they had her favorite rooibos. They found an empty table and sat down. She let him have a few sips of his tea before she got to the purpose of her visit. Most people were a little more amenable to requests once they had a bit of tea in them.

"The attendant out front told me I couldn't meet with him unless it's during the official visiting hours and with preapproval—neither of which I have—so I wondered if I might speak with you instead."

He reached for a bun. "Certainly, although I'm not sure how I can help."

"I'm hoping I can get a more complete picture of him. What can you tell me about Mr. Surikov?"

He looked sternly over the gold rims of his glasses at her. "Nothing, actually. It's a little thing we like to call doctor-patient confidentiality. Surely you abide by the same thing in the US, no?"

Clearly the amenable-making qualities of tea had not yet kicked in for Dr. Abboud—most likely because all he had to work with was mint.

"Of course, of course. You misunderstand me, Doctor. I meant his *general* activities here, not his medical record."

Dr. Abboud still seemed wary.

"Has he been well integrated into the facility? It looks like there are a lot of activities here to keep residents busy while their minds heal."

"If they ever do," he muttered. "Well, you'd have to check with the activities director for specifics, but I don't believe Mr. Surikov avails himself of many of our facility's organized events. In terms of socialization, he keeps to himself—watches the television, and that's about it." He frowned slightly. "As of late, he's been going to the gym often, and we are glad for it. We like to encourage a healthy body to support a healthy mind."

"Too true," Katrina agreed. "Does he interact with anyone at the gym?"

"Not that I'm aware of. Not that he would tell me, but sometimes staff will report to me any signs of a social breakthrough with my patients, and I haven't heard anything on that front with Mr. Surikov."

Katrina drank her tea while she considered how to word her next question. "What about interacting through the computer? Is he ever back online? In the forums?"

"Oh no. Never. Terms of his court sentence, which is publicly available information. He's not allowed any computer access whatsoever." He squinted an eye at her. "So many questions. Are you sure you're not undercover from the Health Board?"

"Ha ha. Oh yes, the government has been paying to import Americans to spy on mental health facilities!" Katrina tried to laugh convincingly. "I'm afraid my motivations are not nearly so exciting. I'm a researcher. I'm curious. I ask questions." She shrugged and gave an impish grin. "It's what I do."

"I suppose so," he answered with a smile. "You never know when we'll be subject to a surprise inspection around here, so I thought I'd check." He waved a hand at her. "Go ahead with your questions then, Dr. Foster."

In that moment, Katrina knew that while she had temporarily disarmed Dr. Abboud, she would never be able to show him the pictures in her bag without reigniting his suspicions. Blown opportunity. She adapted and went on to her other questions.

"I wondered about his mother. Does she ever come around? Sometimes, mothers can bring comfort." She shrugged. "Of course, in our line of business, many also blame their mothers as the cause of all their problems."

He laughed. "Don't I know it! No, no visits from Mama."

Katrina deflected the conversation to a few interesting psychology journal articles she'd read, and they chatted amiably over tea and buns. She could sense the doctor was starting to loosen up.

"I have to tell you it was a very odd experience speaking with him. He had unique diction. So halting. Not like any other patients I've seen." She took a sip of her tea and smiled at the doctor. "Of course, I'm only a psychologist. I don't tend to see a lot of the types of cases you psychiatrists tend to see in a facility such as this. I mostly deal with the woes of the disaffected wealthy and their children's affluenza."

He nodded and leaned forward. "I'll confess when I heard about what had happened, I was a bit impressed with you, Dr. Foster. At least you got him talking. Mostly, he just mumbles with me. When I do get something coherent out of him, he seems to struggle to find words and he gets so frustrated when he can't..."

"Find them," Katrina finished.

The doctor smiled. "Exactly." He leaned back and started softly stroking his beard. "It's actually quite baffling to me. I first believed it might be consistent with his native Russian, but it has nothing to do with language acquisition. I can't pin down why he speaks that way. I've tried multiple drug therapies, but there still hasn't been any progress. But he has made my job interesting, for sure." He held up a finger to emphasize his point. "Usually, all they need is a little bit of time and the right level of antipsychotics or neuroleptics, and you can get them stabilized. But not Mr. Surikov."

Katrina could tell he was now speaking more to himself than her.

"No, Mr. Surikov is definitely keeping things interesting for me," he repeated softly.

She tried to steer the conversation before he started asking for her professional opinion on matters she knew nothing about. "He certainly is interesting to me as well. For my research, that is. Dr. Abboud, do you think there's any chance I can meet with him again? I'd hate to go back to the States so empty-handed."

He shook his head. "I'd love to say yes, but after what happened last time, I'm afraid it's simply not possible."

She dropped her head. "I understand. If he was my patient, I wouldn't want any setbacks either. Well, I'll let you get back to work. Thank you for the tea and your time." She rose to leave, and so did he.

"I'll tell you what. If the moment is right, I'll try to see what happens when I mention the 'American doctor.'" He hooked his fingers in the air to signify air quotes. "If he remains relatively calm, I'll see if he's open to another visit but with me supervising it."

"Thank you so much for considering it. I do hope we get to meet again."

"I hope we do, too, Dr. Foster."

KATRINA HAD AN UNEVENTFUL trip back to Division headquarters. On the way to Magnus, she passed Professor Rasmusson in the hallway, speaking with another agent. He looked over at her, and she tapped her special glasses in acknowledgement. He gave a knowing wink in return and turned back to his conversation.

She found Magnus in his office. "Did you catch all that?"

"Oh, yes," he said dryly. "What lovely chemistry you have with the doctor."

Katrina felt a blush coming on—ridiculous, but she enjoyed the slight undercurrent of jealousy that the oh-so-"professional" Magnus was displaying. It told her that whatever had simmered during their night on the town might have been buried, but it certainly hadn't fizzled.

"Don't be absurd," she said. "Izzie has been training me, in her words, 'on being human.' To that effect, I've been working on establishing rapport."

"Well, whatever it was, it certainly worked, because he had no problem violating our medical privacy laws for you."

She smirked. "My interviewing prowess aside, what did you think of the doctor? Any chance he's in on this?"

"I don't think so. He seems as perplexed as everyone else about the mystery of Surikov. Only he views it as a professional challenge and not as a security concern."

"Yeah, that was my take as well. So I think we can rule him out. While I wasn't able to extract too much from him, it does seem like we've got more to support the theory that he's a pawn in this. I'm a little perplexed by his sudden interest in returning to the gym. Dr. Abboud seemed to think it was a good thing, but I'm not so sure. Sort of makes me feel like he's training or preparing for something."

"Could be. Shame you didn't show him the pictures. It was the right thing, of course. I think if you had pulled those out, you'd have been kicked off the premises, but it's a shame nonetheless."

"With his guard up, I didn't want to take the chance of losing what could be a valuable asset."

"Agreed."

He checked his watch, which wasn't one of the fancy smart ones that could track a person and check their pulse or send out messages. Instead, it was an old-fashioned gold watch. She wondered if it was an heirloom or if it had some of Professor Rasmusson's handiwork in it. He caught her peeking at it.

"I know it's not fashionable, but it was my father's."

"Ah. So no spy surprises in there?"

"I didn't say that." He grinned. "Seeing as my father was a spy, you wouldn't be shocked to know that it holds a trick or two. But mostly, I just use it to tell time. Speaking of which, it's time for me to go to a meeting. Good work, and let me know how things progress."

"Will do. I've got to get started on a report for my director."

"Ah. Well, enjoy." He gave a salute as he left.

Of course, that wasn't all Katrina was going to be working on, but in that moment, what Magnus didn't know certainly would not hurt him.

Chapter 19

Tonight is the night.

Katrina stayed at her Scandinavian modular desk at Division headquarters, under the cover of working late. The best covers were those grounded in truth, and in Katrina's case, desk work was her boring reality. What the movies never conveyed was how *boring* being a spy could sometimes be. A lot of time was spent stuck at a desk, going blind at a computer. Too many details needed documentation, and reports needed to be written. The reports were not glamourous, and they didn't carry the James Bond-style élan of the general public's image of a spy, but it was, sadly, a significant portion of the job. Her cover story conveniently allowed her to get some of her work out of the way. Another wonderfully convenient part of her job was surveillance and trespassing, both of which were about to come in handy as she rather shortly would be breaking into Magnus's inner sanctum.

She eyed his office. The light was on, and she could see him working through the blinds. She hadn't forgotten those faded xeroxed papers he'd hidden from her, or his guilty look. She was certain that whatever was contained in those papers had something to do with her. She remembered where they were—bottom desk drawer, right side.

So she worked, and she waited.

Around 7:30, Magnus emerged. "Still here?"

She stopped typing and looked up. "Oh yeah. I'm finishing writing up a summary of my visit to St. Gustav. I'm outlining possible theories and potential avenues worth pursuing." That was completely true.

I'm also going crazy, waiting for you to leave. That was also completely true. *Leave, already. Leave! Leave!*

Not reading her mind, thankfully, he replied, "Good, good. Well, I'm heading out. Want to take a break and grab something to eat for dinner? My treat. I can expense it as long as we spend at least ninety-three percent of our conversation on work-related topics."

He flattened his blond hair against his forehead with his palm, which didn't make much sense, considering he was pretty much rocking a buzz cut. It would've been cute, had she not been so focused on doing or saying whatever was necessary to hasten his exit.

"No, thanks. I think I'll keep working. Once I get it all out and sent to my director, I'll be able to relax a bit." She resumed typing with a passing regret over her lost free meal and time alone with Magnus. Food wasn't cheap in Stockholm, and time alone was rare, but sacrifices were necessary sometimes.

He looked a little disappointed, which, again, would've been encouraging to Katrina under different circumstances. "Oh. Okay. Well, good luck, and I guess I'll see you tomorrow?"

This time, she didn't look up when she responded, "Yup. *Vi ses.*"

She heard him head out the door. He'd been the last one remaining.

Excellent. Let the games begin.

She continued to work for another twenty minutes on the off chance that he might return. She glanced in the direction of where the security cameras were positioned in the general office area. They didn't monitor what people were working on but rather their actions and demeanor. They watched to see if someone seemed oddly nervous, with a sheen of sweat covering their faces or a nervous tic—that sort of thing.

She'd never actually seen the security team that monitored them, but she wasn't worried. She hit the print button on her screen, and the printer began chugging out the pages of her report, including several additional report pages that she just so happened to remember that she needed to leave in Magnus's office. Another clever ruse, if she thought so herself.

She grabbed the pen that held her lock picks and got up. She headed to the printer, tucked the claimed pages into her decoy folder, and casually walked over to his office. She would do one folder in—her report—and one folder out—the xeroxed pages of mystery. *Easy peasy.* Confidence was everything. She just had to sell it. She lightly placed her fingers on the door handle. It gave easily, and the door swung open. *Victory!*

She was almost to his desk. She eyed her goal—bottom right-hand drawer—so, so close. *Yesss...* Just a little closer to where that mystery file was waiting for her. She could almost hear the papers calling her, taunting her.

"Almost there. You want us so badly, don't you, baby? Just a few steps more..."

As she approached the corner of his desk, she accidentally-on-purpose tripped, and the papers conveniently fell on the right side of his desk. *Oopsies.* As she bent to pick up the scattered papers, she flicked her pen into lockpicking position, and with her back to the camera and blocking its view of the drawer, she continued to pick up papers with her left hand while picking the drawer's lock with her right. After a few seconds, she popped it open, slipped out the file on top, and closed it. She deftly switched out the folders and slipped the decoy report onto his desk. With the file in her possession, she readied her escape from the office with the purloined papers in tow. *Excellent work, Agent Foster.*

She opened the door and ran straight into a familiar-looking chest. *Dammit. Magnus.* She looked up and saw those usually warm blue eyes giving her a hard stare. He snatched the file out of her hand.

"Well, well, well. Hello, Katrina. I must say, I didn't think you'd be in my office... seeing as you saw me leave earlier. But since you're here..." He grabbed her upper arm and firmly guided her back into the office.

Katrina tried to brazen it out. "Well, yes, I had remembered that I wanted to share my report with you. I figured I'd leave it on your desk so you would see it first thing in the morning." She pointed to deflect his attention while she retracted the lock-picking tools in her pen. "See? The report is right there." She quickly pocketed her pen.

He plopped her roughly into the chair across from his desk. He sat down on the opposite side and pulled open the bottom drawer. He made a sound of disgust in the back of his mouth.

"Shoddy work, Agent Foster. You should've relocked it before leaving. Also, I can still see condensation from your fingerprints. Surprisingly sweaty for someone who was only sharing a report."

Ugh. She forgot to put on the self-adhesive fingerprint guards. *Amateur hour.* Katrina sat quietly and scowled at him. She wasn't going to volunteer anything. If he wanted information, it was going to be up to him to extract it.

As the silence grew, Magnus seemed to realize that Katrina was not going to confess.

"Funny how I found you in here, when you were supposed to be 'finishing up.' Rather fortunate that this evening I decided to go to security to do an observation. Imagine my surprise when precisely twenty minutes later, I saw you get up, perform an almost comedic fake trip, and then fortuitously drop the papers right next to a desk drawer that you have previously taken a particular interest in. So very surprising, isn't it?"

Time to deflect and defend.

"Wait. Are you telling me that in your 'observation,' you sat there for twenty minutes, just watching me on the off chance that I might do something of interest? Do you do this often, Magnus? Kind of pervy, and just the sort of thing that should be reported to human resources, don't you think? I'm not certain that it's appropriate for my male superior to behave in such a manner." She placed her hand on her chest and gave her best impression of an aggrieved subordinate. "And I, for one, am now feeling quite vulnerable being alone with you, so I am going to leave now."

She started to rise from her chair.

"Not so fast, Agent Foster. I'm not finished with you."

Contrary to her expectation of his horrified reaction to being threatened with a sexual harassment claim, he relaxed and leaned back in his chair.

"Sure. We can report it together. And at the same time, you can tell them what you were doing breaking into my desk drawer. Does that sound good to you?"

Katrina sat back down and shot daggers at him.

Magnus gave her an annoyingly placid look in return as he pretended to talk to himself. "Now, what should I do about my intrepid but foolish colleague?"

She glanced over at where the camera was and told herself he couldn't do too much because security would see. Magnus smiled as he slid open his top center drawer, put his fingers on the back side, and apparently pushed some buttons. The camera swirled backward and faced the wall. *No more witnesses.* Her body instantly went into a defensive stance.

"Don't bother busting out any krav maga or some such on me, Katrina. One, because I know it equally as well, and we'd probably only accomplish knocking each other out, thereby creating a scene that would have to be explained to both our directors. And two, I only wanted a bit of privacy because I don't have a great feeling about how the next several minutes are going to play out in terms of our professionalism."

"Well, now I'm even more concerned," she murmured. But she was a little intrigued too.

"And just so we're clear, Katrina, I don't regularly watch you on any security cam." He tilted his head toward where the camera was positioned. "I guess I'm starting to learn more about you, and something about your demeanor just wasn't right this evening. You were textbook nonchalance... and that's what gave you away. Nothing about you has ever been flat affect and disinterestedness. That's how I knew you were up to something. That's called being a spy, not being a perv, Little Miss Run-to-HR."

Katrina laughed and threw her arms in the air. "Alright, fine. But you had me cornered—I had to come up with *something*. You were onto me!"

"Yes, when I have my suspicions, nothing's going to deter me." He smiled. "Plus, I knew something was up when you turned down a chance to join me for dinner."

"What?" she said in surprise.

His eyes warmed. "I don't think I'm out of line for pointing out that there's an elephant in the room that we'll discuss another time."

Maybe they wouldn't talk about it, and maybe they couldn't act upon it, but at least she knew it was mutual.

"Oh, you thought that I'd just drop all my work for the opportunity to go out to dinner with you? I, *sir*, am a dedicated agent," she joked.

"Why, I'd like to think that's precisely the case, yes," he joked arrogantly. "But really, the giveaway was not only that you passed up a meal with me, but that you passed up a *free* meal with me."

"Touché." She laughed.

That was true. Given the director's tight purse strings, she wasn't likely to pass up a meal that didn't have to be deducted from her budget.

Their shared humor slowly settled into an awkward silence.

Katrina wanted to make another joke to lighten the moment but wasn't sure how. "Well, I guess it would be inevitable that we'd start to learn each other's habits."

"Yeah, just goes with the spy instincts." He cleared his throat. "Look. I'm not supposed to share this, but the time you're spending hatching your little schemes is time you're not working on our mission. So, here." He tossed the file across the desk to her. "Read it. Maybe you see something of interest. Maybe you don't. But remember, regardless of what you see, you *did* ask for this. Please also remember that I am just the messenger."

Magnus's eyes no longer held humor or even attraction but something more along the lines of regret. She opened the manila folder labeled Classified and slid out the pages. Most were so heavily redacted that she couldn't see the point of their inclusion. One page, however, seemed to contain enough text to warrant reading.

Top Secret—Eyes Only

June XX, XXXX

Dear xxxxxxxxxx,

It has been brought to our attention that there are significant irregularities of concern regarding Agents Foster (M) and Foster (F). On a recent sojourn to Sweden during XXXXX, XXXXXX observed Agents Foster discussing XXXX with XXXX and XXXX. This was not intelligence that was made public to our agents or, indeed, XXXXX. The situation is unprecedented and therefore all the more dangerous. With the knowledge of XXXXX XXXXXXXXXXXX XXXXXXXXXXX XXXXXXXXXX XXXXXXXXXX XXXXX XXXXXXX XXXXXXX XXXXXXX XXXXX XX XXXX XXXXXXX XXXXXXXX XXXXXXXXXXXX XXXXXXXXX

*XXXXXXXX XXXXX XXXXXXX XXXXXX XXXXX,
there is suspicion that they XXXXXXXX XXXXXXXX XXX
XXXXXXXXXX XXXXX double agents.*

*The movements of Agents Foster must be tracked at all times, in-
cluding but not limited to when their progeny (Katrina (F)) is present.
After consultation with XXXXXX, it was determined that XXXXX
XXXXXXXXXXX XXXXXXXXXXXX XXXXXXXXX is the
only permissible outcome.*

*XXXXX XXXXXXXXXX treat as hostile XXXXXX by extra-
agency means, if necessary. Significant concern is that Agents Foster,
perceiving this to be their last chance, will attempt to
XXXXXXXXXXXXXXXXXXXX Berlin. Unclear if receiving assistance. All known contacts and assets to be surveilled during
XXXXXXXXXXXXXXXXXXX. Agents Foster must not
XXXXXXXXXXXXXX or we fear that XXXXXX XXXXXXX will
be the inevitable outcome.*

*Finally,   XXXXXXXX   XXXXXXXX   should   Katrina
XXXXXXXXXXXXXXXXX, post-haste.*

KATRINA GASPED FOR air. She hadn't even realized she'd been
holding her breath. In that moment, nothing—not the mission, not
the repercussions of breaking into her superior's files, nothing—mattered. She knew what it looked like, and she knew it didn't matter to
her. She refused to believe it. It simply was not possible. No way were
her parents Doubles.

After several minutes, she was finally able to raise her eyes to
Magnus's. She didn't like what she saw in return—softness, pity, the
last things she wanted in that moment. She would happily have taken
rage instead.

"I tried to access your parents' file after we spoke that first day,"
he said gently. "I was curious as to what had happened. Particularly

when you had mentioned Berlin was where they died, and Berlin is what I remembered everyone arguing about."

She nodded, still not trusting herself to speak.

"I went to the International Agent Archive room to see what I could find. Most of it was the standard stuff, nothing surprising. There wasn't anything about their deaths—just a listing of active dates in the field. When I pushed the hanging folders to the side to put the files back, I saw this manila envelope taped to the bottom of the drawer. Then... Then I read that," he finished somewhat lamely.

"This doesn't make sense," Katrina said, finally finding her voice. "Why was it that everybody tells me that my parents were heroes? That they were some of the best agents the Division ever produced?" She crossed her arms in front of her chest. "Explain that!"

He sighed. "I don't know, Kat. I wish I could. It says Eyes Only, so it's likely that not many people knew about it... whatever it means."

"And what do you think it means?" Katrina knew she needed to be objective, but a large part of her believed his next words would determine her opinion of him forever.

He watched her with eyes full of regret. "I'm so sorry, Kat. It's not clear, but it doesn't look good. If read one way, it seems like your parents were double agents."

"But if you read it another way," she protested, "it seems like they had *discovered* double agents, and maybe that's why they had to go to Berlin."

"Maybe." Magnus looked doubtful.

"Maybe?" Katrina repeated.

"Yes, maybe. Right now, the only people who know for certain are your parents—who are dead—whoever the author of this memo was, and whoever else laid eyes upon the unredacted version. And for all we know, those people might not even be alive, either."

"I guess that's fair," she said grudgingly. "I appreciate your honesty." She paused. "Do you think I'm a Double?" It seemed an important thing to ask.

"No," Magnus said without hesitation. Then he grinned. "A double agent would've done a far better job of breaking in." He paused as though in contemplation. "Actually, they'd be so good that they wouldn't even have needed to."

Katrina scowled. "Well, maybe that was just my crafty cover." She wasn't sure why she was even going down that path when even the hint of an accusation of dual allegiances would be a career ender, not to mention a life ender. Maybe the reason was the shock of unexpected news. Maybe it was because she'd so admired her parents. If they were going to be skilled double-crossers, then maybe she wanted to be thought of one too. That was utterly ridiculous, but she couldn't claim rationality where her parents were involved.

Magnus rolled his eyes. He got it. Somehow, he understood what it meant to want to emulate one's parents even with the knowledge that what they might've done was wrong.

He gave her a small smile. "I know you're not going to give this up, and honestly, if it were my parents, neither would I."

"Whether they're innocent or not—and I think they are—I mean to discover the truth. It's the not knowing that makes it unbearable."

He took in a breath as though resigned to say the next words. "I agree. Against my better judgement, I agree. So I guess we can—assuming it doesn't overly distract from the Blomqvist-Lindström mission, mind you—look into this further."

"Deal." She smiled and shook Magnus's hand to seal the agreement. "I like your thinking."

And I like your use of "we." She felt better knowing she wouldn't have to go it alone. If she had to prove her parents' innocence—and she knew, she just *knew* they couldn't have been double agents—she was going to need all the help she could get.

Chapter 20

After a largely sleepless night, Katrina had too many feelings that she just couldn't shake. And surprisingly, none of them involved Magnus. The memo about her parents—what she was able to read of it, anyway—had shaken her. The parents she knew were not the ones she'd seen in the report. And she had no idea which ones were the real Fosters.

Giving up on the idea of sleep entirely, she thought an early-morning jog might clear her head. Maybe the fresh air would give her some focus so that she could make sense of things. She pulled her hair back into a high pony puff, laced up her sneakers, and slipped out the door, leaving Izzie's snores behind. As she jogged, the images from the previous night bounced through her mind. *Berlin. Surveillance. Katrina. Danger. Classified. Doubles. Her parents. Unprecedented. Last chance.* Black bars of redacted text swirled before her.

She drifted back to moments with her parents to see if she could spot any signs. She couldn't, but that shouldn't have come as a surprise, not really. After all, her parents were accomplished spies, and she was only a child. *And when it comes down to it, can you ever really trust a spy?* Trying to replay memories of her past was an act of futility. All she could do was employ the skills she'd inherited from them and try to uncover the truth.

She didn't know what any of it meant. She didn't know who was surveilling whom. The double agent part worried her the most. *If my parents were double agents, what does that make me?* Not a Double—she knew that. But she didn't know what it meant to potentially be the daughter of one, either. Her mind wandered over to Magnus. She wanted to trust him—and trust him fully—but she always had that sinking suspicion that he was holding something back. His producing that file didn't help with that impression.

At a loss and with nowhere else to go, really, Katrina jogged back to the hotel, quietly changed without waking Izzie, and headed to work. On the way, her phone buzzed with a text—Lena. Katrina wasn't the only one up early.

Heard back from the A/V team. They tried everything they knew but couldn't get a clear shot of your 'perpetrator.' Sorry. Would have liked to prove you wrong.

Lena ended the text with a smiley face.

Katrina thanked her for the update. *Maybe Izzie is right. Maybe she's just really rough around the edges.*

Katrina figured she'd thank Lena in person, but she was nowhere to be found in the office, which was weird, but at least Katrina had the place to herself. After a few hours of work in solitude, Lena and the rest of the team trickled in for the morning meeting in Magnus's office.

Lena cleared her throat. "Glad everyone could make it. I think we've got some pretty compelling findings. I'm going to let Agent Figueroa provide the background information before discussing our target." She gestured over to Izzie. "Izzie? If you would..."

"Welcome, class. It's time to begin our lecture on suggestive-coercion research." Izzie had on a cardigan with leather patches on the elbows and had perched on her nose a pair of readers that Katrina knew she didn't actually need. Izzie was in the professor zone and was obviously loving every moment.

"Got your pens ready to take notes? Good, let's get down to it, then." Izzie fired up her presentation. "Suggestive-coercion research—or SCR, as I will refer to it from here on out—is the study of how to neurologically, rather than physically, guide an animal into a desired behavioral action. Instead of offering cheese to a rat to get it to go down a certain path or a shock to let them know they've gone the wrong way, with SCR, the animal is operated on and then manipulated."

She showed a slide of a rat with its head cut open. "Incisions are made, and receptors are placed on the animal. By activating certain parts of the brain, the researcher can guide them. It's super sciencey—mostly beyond me—but the gist is that it's been shown to work, and with pretty good results on animals."

"Long-term effects?" Katrina asked.

"Unknown. What is known is that common side effects are neurological decline and death."

"But this is on small mammals," Magnus pointed out.

"Yes, and how much do you want to bet that it doesn't take much to go from experimenting on animals to experimenting with humans?" countered Izzie.

"It's certainly possible although obviously illegal," Magnus said.

"Ah, yes," Izzie said. "I forgot there's one more slide that I wanted to share."

No, she didn't, Katrina thought. *She's just ramping up the drama. She's got more under her figurative hat.*

"Remember that picture of the rat from before?" She went back to the slide that showed the rat with the incisions. "Now, check out this pic of Surikov."

On the screen was Surikov's heavily scarred face and scalp. While the scars could have possibly been left over from his military career, it escaped no one's notice that the scar pattern around the skull seemed to mimic that of the rat's.

"I suspect that any potential concerns of illegality were overcome by a hefty chunk of dough." Izzie smirked.

"If they could get the SCR technology to human scale, I'd have to admit, then, that what you're showing is pretty convincing. Who of our ten researchers are the most likely suspects?" Magnus asked.

Izzie gestured at Lena. "Lena? It's your turn."

"So with Agent Figueroa's help, I really went down the rabbit hole on this suggestive-coercion research and investigated the possible candidates. Most were either too young, too dead, or too out of it."

"Too out of it?" Katrina asked.

"Yeah, one had a breakdown after attempting to experiment on himself. Anyway, I think I've narrowed our rogue researcher down to one person." Lena was practically glowing in triumph.

"Intriguing," Magnus said. "What'd you find?"

"Now, it's all based on animal research, as Izzie noted, but the first author in all the publications is always the same, a Swedish behavioral researcher named Rikard Westlund."

She showed his picture on the screen. He was a tall but slope-shouldered man, pasty, with short auburn hair.

"Hee hee!"

All heads turned to the back, where Jens had stood for who knew how long. Katrina was both impressed and creeped out at his ability to silently enter a room of spies with not a single one noticing.

At Magnus's raised eyebrow, Jens sheepishly explained. "Sorry to laugh, but he looks just like Ove Sundberg, but with red hair. He's on television."

Magnus ignored him and turned back to Lena. "What else did you find?"

"Well, I did some background recon on him. His lab had run into trouble recently, with two of his graduate students making claims against him."

"About what?" Katrina asked.

"Unclear. The claims were settled out of court, and all signed nondisclosure agreements. Both students are in labs outside Sweden, and I can't seem to get ahold of them. At any rate, not long after, the university dismissed Westlund for unethical practices... which could mean pretty much anything. But that's not the interesting part." Lena paused, apparently having a little drama in herself.

"Yes?" Magnus prompted.

"Not long after his dismissal, he was hired at a private research lab, where he garnered a multimillion-kronor grant to continue his work on animal behavior. But wait—there's *more*." Lena had transformed into a late-night infomercial. Katrina almost expected to hear that she was going to throw in a free set of steak knives for just the price of shipping and handling.

"He's loaded now. Rich. Really rich. Part of it was working for a private lab, as they pay more than the universities, but his bank account went up *way* more than his purported salary. I asked our money trackers to trace where the funds were coming from, and they're still working on it. So far, they've tracked it to several dummy accounts, located in a variety of countries."

That was exactly what Katrina was looking for. She steadied her breathing and tried not to look too hopeful.

"Timeline?" Katrina asked.

"You might like this. The private-research-lab hiring happened six months *before* Lindström's assassination, and his bank account blew up six months *after*."

"Wow. Just wow. This is great, Lena. Thanks for your hard work." Katrina still wasn't exactly a fan of Lena, but she did remember the director's lecture on leadership and professionalism, and she could at least say she did her part.

But for all Katrina's efforts, she received a stank face in return from Lena. *So much for positive reinforcement.*

"Excellent work, Agent Holmberg!"

Lena smiled back at Magnus.

Katrina tried not to roll her eyes. It really shouldn't matter since, after all, her findings benefitted the entire team, but Lena's blatancy was beyond irritating. Katrina just couldn't win.

"Well," Izzie said, never one to be left out of a conversation, "looks like it's time to visit our dear friend Mr. Westlund."

Chapter 21

That evening, Katrina woke up from a dead sleep. Instinctively, she clutched the knife under her pillow. *What was that noise?* Upon brief contemplation, it sounded like a moose trying to mate with a buzz saw. She turned toward the neighboring bed. Izzie was spread-eagle, mouth open wide, and snoring away. Despite the nasal cacophony, she was looking as peaceful as Katrina had ever seen her. Seeing her so serene almost excused the fact that her somniferous performance had cut right through Katrina's earplugs. *Almost.* After briefly contemplating cutting off Izzie's air supply in exchange for silence, Katrina gave up and rolled out of bed. *Might as well get some fresh air and a little peace and quiet.* She slipped on a robe and padded quietly over to the balcony. From the third floor, she had a good view of the city.

Once outside, she could feel another's presence. Katrina turned to her right, and on the neighboring balcony, Magnus was quietly smoking a cigarette. Katrina should've been surprised, but somehow she wasn't. She moved over to the edge of the balcony so that they were side by side, with only the railing between them.

He looked over and quickly stubbed out his cigarette. "I know, I know. It's not good for my health. I've quit."

Katrina stared pointedly at the still-smoking cigarette.

He shrugged sheepishly. "Maybe when the mission is over."

"Couldn't sleep, either?"

He smiled. "Your friend really is quite the dedicated sleeper. I wish I could sleep like that during an assignment. Instead, it's insomnia for me. Always. Until there's a resolution." They stood in companionable silence, staring out over the city below. The rest of the city couldn't seem to sleep either. The bars and clubs were still open. They could hear the muffled thump of Europop coming from one.

Katrina looked back at him. "Why didn't you tell me that you were next door?"

He shrugged and smiled. "Because I didn't have to."

"Can't argue with that logic." Katrina didn't bother to hide her exasperation. She was tired of all the games, all the secrets. That was her job, yes, but it could get very tiresome, especially because she knew it wasn't just about her profession, not with him.

"I moved in right after you told me your room was ransacked. I wasn't interested in losing any agents."

Magnus had opted for honesty.

"Thank you," she said softly.

He flicked the ash from his cigarette. She suspected he was completely unaware that he'd lit another one.

"Smoking kills, you know."

He shrugged again. "So does a bullet."

Katrina rolled her eyes in response.

He appeared self-conscious as he quickly stubbed it out. He sighed, and his face softened. "That said, given the risky nature of our line of business, I choose to play the odds that I'll survive the occasional cigarette or two." He paused. "You know a bit about that—the odds of survival—I think."

She nodded. "Yes. Yes, I do." She thought back to the day when her parents died.

"Rather miraculous, really. That you managed to survive." He seemed both impressed and slightly bewildered. "You'd think you'd be disfigured. A scar or two, at least."

"Some scars are on the inside."

"True. Very true."

She didn't know if others could sense the damage she carried within, but she did know she'd never told anyone that before.

"Well, that's not completely true. I do have a scar on the outside." She pulled back her robe slightly and placed her leg on a side table. She pointed at the back of her knee. "Right here."

Magnus reached through the railing and softly stroked the scar. She shivered, and neither of them wanted to acknowledge that the cause wasn't the evening temperature.

"A huge explosion, and this was it?" he murmured. "Simply miraculous." He leaned in closer and frowned slightly. "You know, has anyone ever told you that your scar looks just like—"

Katrina put her leg down. "Nixon. Yeah, I know. It's where the shrapnel burned my skin."

"Ah." He really had no right way to respond to that.

She peered over at him and traced the left side of his neck with a finger. He briefly closed his eyes.

"Tell me about this one, right here."

"Ah, that one. Well, I was positioned just off the coast of Madagascar on a rescue mission when we were ambushed by these pirates..." His eyes twinkled with mischief.

"Liar." She lightly batted his sleeve. "What really happened?"

"The usual time and place when stupid things happen. University. I was trying to impress a girl by juggling Aquavit bottles. Probably would've worked better had I not drunk half of one of them first."

Katrina laughed. "Idiot."

"I don't disagree." He grinned in return.

"I hope your strategy has improved since then."

"I'll give myself credit. I was a quick learner. Nearly bleeding out has a way of doing that."

She shook her head and laughed at the ridiculousness of it. *Men.*

They watched the cityscape some more. A couple ran out of the club, laughing and holding hands. Katrina wondered what the rest of the night held for them.

Returning her focus to Magnus, Katrina noted to herself that their time together didn't feel awkward, like before at the bar, or fraught like during her ill-fated attempt to retrieve her parents' file. It felt right. Maybe the privacy of darkness and being away from everyone else and the mission had something to do with it. Maybe the reason was that, at the moment, they were just a man and a woman, not two spooks well-conditioned not to trust. Or maybe it was simply that they knew more about each other.

Magnus softly bumped Katrina's shoulder with his own to get her attention. She looked up and swallowed hard at the expression in his eyes.

"Katrina?"

"Yes?"

"I know I'm not supposed to do so, and feel free to say no, but I would like to kiss you now."

"Yes, please."

He leaned over the balcony, and she met him halfway. As his lips touched hers, Katrina's mind, true to form, turned to the analytical. *Pro: I'm kissing a gorgeous man in one of the most beautiful cities in the world. Con: If caught, I'd probably be fired for this. Magnus definitely would be. Or worse.* Magnus cupped the back of her head to bring her closer.

Totally worth it.

She smiled against his lips, and he pulled back to look down at her.

"Another one of those calculated risks, Agent Foster?"

"Something like that."

He leaned back in and wrapped his arms around her, and Katrina quit calculating.

After not nearly enough time, the faint lines of daylight were appearing. The cloak of darkness that allowed them to disregard the rules was slipping away, never mind that the time couldn't be much past two in the morning. That was just the nature of being so far north. Of course, it would be just her luck that the light would be the one thing guaranteed to wake Izzie. She gave Magnus a small final kiss on his cheek and left his embrace. He understood.

"See you in a few hours," she whispered as she slid the door back open.

Magnus sighed, sat heavily on a balcony chair, and lit another cigarette.

"Snrxx... huh?" Izzie's head popped up.

Katrina had pulled the curtain back into place as soon as she came inside, but she wasn't quick enough. The light had woken and disoriented Izzie.

"What's going on? What time is it? Did I miss something?"

"No, Izzie, you didn't." Katrina touched her own lips in memory as she slid back into bed. "You didn't miss a thing. It's only two a.m. Go back to sleep."

Izzie happily complied.

Chapter 22

In the subsequent hours, Katrina worked to compartmentalize any thoughts she might've had about Magnus. She felt foolish all the while since she shouldn't have had anything to debate or contemplate. They'd both agreed to that kiss and both seemed into it. Maybe it would stick this time. Maybe they would move forward instead of back. Of course, moving backward was exactly what had happened the last time, not to mention that no one ever seemed to stick around Katrina's world very long. She reminded herself that anticipating rejection was just better and safer. That still didn't stop her from wondering what he was doing next door. *Is he already at the Division?* She had his number. She could call him and suss him out by initially talking about the mission and seeing where things went.

The mission.

Ugh. Get it together, Foster! You are not a teenager. You are a Level Four agent who won't remain one much longer if you can't get your act together.

She focused on getting dressed. She wanted to look good but not try-hard good—for herself, for her status as an agent, *not* for the handsome Swedish man who could be in the neighboring hotel room. Or in the lobby. Or at headquarters.

"You seem preoccupied," Izzie stated.

"Nope, not preoccupied."

"Are you sure? 'Cause I've been speaking to you for the past three minutes, and your total contribution has consisted of 'Oh?', 'Is that so?', and 'You don't say.'"

Argh. Izzie was right. "Sorry, I've just got a lot on my mind. I'm just running through scenarios." Strictly speaking, that was true. Katrina just conveniently left out that those scenarios had zip to do with their mission.

"Well, you can feel free to share some of those scenarios on the way to headquarters. I didn't do all that work with Lena on that Westlund dude for us not to nab him. I'm about due for an opportunity to utilize my interrogation skills." Izzie wove her fingers together, flexing and cracking her knuckles with a vicious satisfaction.

Katrina sighed and shook her head. The two of them would always have differing notions on the best ways to elicit information, but that's probably what made them such good partners—their different yet completely complementary skill sets.

"Alright, let me get this bag packed, and I'll give you one hundred percent of my attention as we head over." She crammed an assortment of clothes and accessories from Jens's costuming suitcase into a black leather sack that could be converted from a backpack into a tote.

"At least tell me what's up with all the clothes."

"You'll see. I have a feeling I'm going to need to make a costume change or two on the fly today."

THEY MET WITH MAGNUS and Lena at Division headquarters and headed toward his office. As Magnus opened the door, he gave her a warm but slightly guarded expression.

Ah, so he's a little worried too. Good. She gave him a small smile of encouragement to say, "Yup, we're on the same page." He gave a wink in return as she and Izzie passed through.

Once everyone had crowded into the office, he turned to Lena. "So what's the story?"

"Well, I've been trying to get ahold of Rikard Westlund. After we last met, I had some Level Threes watch the apartment listed as his residence. No one's seen any movement. They also spoke with a few neighbors on his floor, and no one recognized his picture."

"False residency?" Magnus asked.

Lena nodded grimly. "That's what I'm thinking. So then I called the company he works for, Vetenskapverket, and tried to get ahold of him there."

"Does he actually work there? Or was that a lie from him as well?" Katrina asked.

"That's what I had wondered. But he actually does work there. A Level Three found security footage of him walking down a hallway there to confirm it."

"Well, at least that's something," Izzie said.

"It was kind of odd, though," Lena said. "When I spoke to the secretary to make an appointment, he wasn't available today or tomorrow or any day within the month. She just apologized, said he was a very busy man, and hung up."

"When did you call?" Katrina asked.

"About twenty minutes ago."

That was all Katrina needed to hear.

"Let's roll." She popped off the wall she'd been leaning on, grabbed her black bag, and started for the exit.

Izzie quickly followed. Katrina's eyes met Magnus's, and he raised his eyebrows.

"No time to waste," Katrina said. "I don't believe for a second that he's just a 'very busy man.' The secretary has likely tipped him off, and I'm not going to miss my chance to see him."

Magnus held up a hand. "Wait. How exactly—"

Katrina cut him off. "Since we know where he works, my goal is to ambush him today."

Izzie's face made room for one of her signature frightening smiles.

"No, not that kind of ambush," Katrina warned.

Izzie's expression dropped comically in response.

"I just mean seeing him unannounced."

"Oh. Well. That works, too, I guess," Izzie replied.

Lena spoke up. "It's an ultrasecure building due to corporate espionage concerns. You can't just waltz in there!"

That was, of course, very true, but Kat had no intention of letting Lena get the upper hand.

"I am a creative and resourceful sort, even more so when on a time crunch. I do believe I can find a way. I have considerable weapons at my disposal."

"Didn't you say you weren't going to go in there with guns a-blazing?"

"And I still mean that." She shook her head. "You and Izzie. Not all weapons are of metal or bullets. Those were *not* the types of weapons I was referring to." And on that very unsubtle note, she looked back over her shoulder and gave them a confident wink. "C'mon, Izzie."

On her way out the door, she called back to the remaining members. "Magnus, Lena, I'll get you on the comms as soon as we've reached the building."

At her words, Magnus, whose eyes had seemed on level with her hindquarters, met hers. "Sounds like a plan."

Lena snorted. "Let's get the comms up. Five hundred crowns says she gets caught."

Magnus rubbed a hand over his face. He didn't take the bet.

KATRINA STRUTTED DOWN the hallway to the elevators, full of purpose. They didn't have a lot of time. She didn't know who knew what at the company, and she didn't want to run the risk of the secretary tipping Westlund off, which indeed might've already happened.

As the elevator closed, Izzie turned to Katrina and whispered, "Okay, that was pretty boss and all, but seriously, how are we going to get in there? No one's going to let us through the entryway."

"Honestly, I have no idea. Lena was just so smug that I had to come up with something." She put the address for Vetenskapverket into her phone. It was six stops away from headquarters.

They exited NK and headed down the escalator to the subway. At least her hunch about needing a costume change was right. By her estimate, from the time of Lena's call, they'd already lost about a half an hour, and that didn't include travel time. She wasn't going to waste even more precious time trying to find a bathroom to switch outfits.

That also gave her an opportunity to work on changing her clothing in the field. While they rode, Katrina converted her backpack into a tote for easier access. Not surprisingly, it wasn't very easy for a spy to alter their appearance while on the move. Katrina had found this out the hard way when she nearly failed her final exam in Sashay, Changé: Mobile Disguise Alteration, when she got her head stuck in her shirt. She learned an important lesson that day: turtlenecks should *not* be part of an agent's costume, no matter how well they paired with a trench, nor how well they hid bruises from practice chokeholds and garroting attempts.

Katrina was prepared. She had on a pair of black leggings, a long-sleeved white T-shirt, a lightweight olive jacket, and a black scarf—nothing flashy, nothing memorable. At the last stop, she and Izzie went off in opposite directions. It wouldn't help her to change outfits while still being seen with the exact same person.

The goal was to make the transition as seamless as possible within thirty seconds and without calling any attention to herself. She slid off her scarf and her jacket and tucked them into the tote. As she lost herself in the crowd crossing the street, she pulled her hair up into a ponytail, tied a bandanna around the top of her head, and put on a pair of sunglasses. The key was to appear intentional and to be confident. She glanced around surreptitiously. No one had paid her any attention. *Easy peasy.*

As agreed upon, she met Izzie near the alley behind Vetenskapverket.

"Nicely done, Agent Foster," Izzie said as she took in Katrina's appearance. "You look completely different."

"Nothin' to it," Katrina said with a smile. "Okay, you keep an eye out for the cameras, and I'll find a way in. Let me know when you spot them."

They both carefully scrutinized the outside of the building.

"Got it. We've got one on the ground level on the far-left side of the building and one in the middle of the third floor," Izzie said. "They have fewer than I would've expected for a research facility."

"Probably because most people try to go in through the front," Katrina murmured as she pulled off her sunglasses and continued to scan the building.

Across the front was a series of doors and windows, which in theory should all have been locked tight and, in accordance with all security measures, accessible only by card swipe. It should've been an insurmountable challenge. But what Katrina lacked in breaking and entering, she made up for in understanding the psychology of laziness.

"So what's the plan?" Izzie asked. "What, are you going to pretend to be a deliverywoman? Do you have a box tucked in that tote as well?"

Katrina ignored her as she continued to eye the building.

"Hush." Katrina felt triumphant as she spotted the opening she was searching for. "Aha... and there's my way in, just as I expected."

"Where?"

"See Door 1603? Across from the dumpster? There's a rag wedged in the door holding it open. I bet that's where the custodian heads out."

"What makes you say that?"

"Anyone who has to go in and out of a building frequently usually can't be bothered with swiping and entering a code each time. The most likely candidate would be a custodian. Plus, who else is walking around in a research facility carrying rags?"

Izzie gave an impressed nod. "So much for it being a high-security building."

Katrina smiled. "All the security in the world is no match for the most basic human impulse—laziness combined with a desire for efficiency." She surveyed the alley one last time. "Okay, you know the drill. If I'm not out in thirty, get me a distraction."

"You got it, Kat. Good luck."

Katrina pushed open the door and pocketed the rag. She saw a cleaning cart tucked in a corner, a cleaning apron left on the handle. *The custodian must be on break. Perfect.* She slipped on the apron and pushed the cart down the hallway before ducking into a stairwell. No one paid her any attention.

Finally inside and alone, Katrina turned on the comm. "I'm in. Disappointed, Lena?"

A decidedly male voice responded. "She's lucky I didn't take the bet, or she'd be a lot poorer now."

"You didn't take her money?"

"Didn't seem fair. I knew you would get in somehow."

"Good answer."

"So how'd you do it?"

"Well, I told you I'd use my weapons. In this case, as in most, I meant my brain." She paused. "Why, what were *you* thinking?"

Oddly, she could feel Magnus smile in her earpiece. "That's just what I was thinking as well."

Lena came on. "Just scope out Westlund and get out of there."

Now, how to access Westlund? Katrina needed to speak with him, and he didn't seem the sort that would deign to speak with the cleaning staff.

"How are you going to meet him, Kat?" That was Magnus in her ear.

"I'm going to be an inspector, I think." Katrina rummaged in her tote until she found her nonprescription camera glasses, a pair of heels, and a smart blazer. She whipped off the apron and slung it over the cart.

"Do you think anyone's going to buy it?" he asked.

Katrina slipped on her heels and pulled her arms through the sleeves of the blazer. "Well, we don't have much choice, do we? And really, there's only one person we have to convince: Westlund."

"Fair point. Good luck, Agent Foster."

She took out her ponytail and fluffed out her hair. She put on her camera glasses again, but that time, it was less for the remote visual capacity and more just to look smart. It seemed so odd that a pair of glasses somehow read "Here stands before you an intelligent authority figure." After all, a person could be dumb as a bag of rocks and still need corrective lenses.

She gave the cleaning cart a once-over for inspiration. She found a clipboard with a check-off list for each room that had been cleaned. She flipped the list over. *That'll do.* She stashed her bag underneath a pile of paper towels on the bottom of the cleaning cart then rolled it farther into the shadows of the stairwell. She hoped the poor custodian was on an extended *fika* break and wasn't frantically searching for their cart in a panic.

After reading up a bit on Westlund, Katrina came to the conclusion that the "Aren't we all such fine friends" approach would not work. She needed to reek of authority and power, which was more to her liking anyway.

She rapped firmly on his office door. "Rikard Westlund?"

The door cracked open. "Who are you? I'm not seeing anyone today. I'm busy." He had a backpack slung over his shoulder like he was on his way out.

Kat gave an internal sigh of relief. *Just in time.*

He attempted to close the door, but Katrina slid her foot into the opening. She gave thanks for the last-minute decision to pack the heels with steel toes.

"Sorry, you'll have to make an exception. I'm with the EU Council on Clinical Trials. Surprise inspection." Kat didn't give a name. She wanted to give the clear impression that he wasn't worthy of receiving one.

He peered at her, making no effort to relieve the pressure of the door on Katrina's foot. "No one said anything about an inspection."

"Yes," she replied dryly. "That's the surprise part."

He still didn't budge.

"Dr. Westlund, I am a busy woman. You can either open the door so we can proceed with the inspection, or I can report that you were uncooperative, which will launch a full inquiry to see if you are engaging in any practices not in accordance with the Clinical Trials Directive. You decide. Quickly, please."

That did the trick. The door opened, and a slightly wary Westlund moved to give her access.

He set his bag down on the counter with a sigh. "Well, come in, then. Let's get this over with."

With that veritable welcome mat rolled out, she entered and began touring the premises. She slowly scanned left to right to give Magnus and Lena a view as well via her glasses. The metallic environment was pristine: metal shelves, metal stools, and gleaming metal tops on the counters. Centrifuges, microscopes, and glass vials were neatly laid out, along with bins filled with syringes. She passed by a rack and noticed only one clean-room suit hanging against the wall. She didn't see any signs of lab assistants or coworkers.

"All by yourself?"

"At the moment. I'm at a stage in my research where I'm doing a lot of solitary work. Running statistical analyses... that sort of thing."

Katrina didn't reply but instead walked over to a series of conspicuously empty cages. "I suppose that's why there are no animals?"

"Yes, they're back at the basement lab for small mammals. Like I said, the actual testing has been done for some time. These days, I'm mostly analyzing the data and using the results to formulate new theories."

"And those might be...?" she asked.

"Proprietary. I'm sure you understand."

She made a noncommittal noise and stood silently, staring at her clipboard in an attempt to unnerve him.

"I-I don't know why you would want to meet with me," he said, clearly nervous.

"No need to be concerned, Dr. Westlund. The inspections are based on a random sampling of laboratories. You happened to be our lucky winner at this particular facility." She regarded her clipboard. "My notes indicate that you do experimentation on the modification of animal behavior. Is that correct?"

He gave a jerky nod. "Yes, that is correct. I do suggestive-coercion research—SCR—which involves technologies that redirect animal behavior remotely."

"What purpose does this serve?"

He shifted slightly before responding. "Actually, there are a lot of implications, positive ones. For example, take endangered species in captivity. Too often, they behave so aggressively in their new environment that they are too busy attacking one another to breed. Typically, to reduce aggression, the animal is neutered either physically or chemically. However, that has obvious drawbacks in breeding programs. Modify their behavior using small discs strategically implanted in the activity centers of the brain, and you've got an animal that will obey your commands, whether it is to interact peacefully, or..." He reddened slightly. "Encourage amorous activities." He cleared his throat. "So actually, doing this research is to the benefit of animals, for both their propagation and well-being."

Katrina carefully considered how to ask her next question. "And negative implications? Are there any?"

He stiffened. "None within the parameters of my IRB-approved grant."

"Do you think the procedure could be applied to humans? Think of the possibilities. The rehabilitation of criminals, easier international negotiations, weight loss..."

He flinched but recovered. "In theory, yes, I suppose you could apply similar principles to the modification of human behavior. You would need to adjust the algorithm to take into account increased mental capacity, apply more discs and strengthen the receptors, ramp up the remote access as humans are not stored in cages, but with a strong enough wireless signal to withstand interference—" He cut himself off. "But it isn't ethical, and it would never get approved, so there is no point discussing it further. No one would ever dare to attempt such a thing. In my field, we stick with the betterment of lesser beings."

What a curious turn of phrase.

He turned toward the door. "Is there anything else you need me to address, or are we done?"

"Not quite, Dr. Westlund." She continued to ask him some cursory questions to distract him from the path of her earlier questioning, stating that she wanted to confirm the accuracy of what was in her records. That custodial clipboard was paying off dividends. He confirmed his educational background and accolades.

"It seems you used to do a fair bit of outreach work. You used to serve as a consultant for several zoos and several political parties."

"Yes, I would sometimes be consulted regarding animal-welfare policies." He averted his eyes briefly. "But I don't do that anymore."

Liar. "Understood. I can see you're a busy man and evidently doing quite well, to head up a lab like this one."

He puffed up a bit. "Yes, all those years of hard work have finally paid off."

Since Katrina knew his bank-account situation, she found his comment to be more than a little careless.

"Is that why you left the university?" She didn't mention that she knew he'd been fired for ethics violations.

"Yes," he said dismissively. "They didn't appreciate the value of my work. Vetenskapverket does, however, and pays accordingly."

"And finally, where are you living, Dr. Westlund?"

He looked taken aback.

"Why do you ask?" His ego was once more replaced by wariness.

"I just want your most recent address in case we need to be in contact for additional information."

"Oh. Well, I moved recently. Trouble with an ex." He gave an address. It wasn't the one they had on record.

She stalled, asking him to repeat his address as she wrote it down, in order to give her team enough time to run the address. "How fortunate that you were able to find something so quickly, given the housing situation in Stockholm."

"Yeah, I was pretty lucky."

In her earpiece, Magnus muttered, "It's a fake."

Not giving any indication that she knew the truth, Katrina paused to draw out the tension.

A bead of sweat ran down his left temple. "Is there anything else? I'm afraid that in my situation, time is money, and I need to get back to work."

She gave a terse smile. "Thank you very much, Dr. Westlund. You've been most obliging."

Katrina left his office and hightailed it down the stairwell. By her estimate, the entire interview had taken around twenty minutes. She had maybe another five to retrieve her bag if she was going to meet her goal of exiting the site in a half an hour. The longer she was there, the more likely someone would take notice of her. Plus, she knew Izzie was waiting outside, just champing at the bit to rough someone up. Kat slowed as she reached the bottom of the stairwell and checked underneath. By an act of providence, the cart was still there. While it had been to her benefit, it did occur to her that Vetenskapverket really needed to hire more responsible staff.

Where is that custodian? Katrina grabbed her bag, discarded the cleaning pushcart exactly where she'd found it, and slipped out the door.

Chapter 23

"So I think we have our guy."

Katrina was feeling more than a little smug. She walked into Division headquarters with some definite pep in her step. In her mind, Westlund was definitely behind Surikov's transformation. And if he was behind that, then he was behind Lindström's assassination. All she had to do was find a way to link him to the death of Oskar, and she'd be golden. After her last talk with the director, and given how the new Swedish director was gunning for Magnus and Lena, they knew they couldn't nab him unless they had an airtight case.

She sat down in the closest chair and spoke as soon as the team gathered in the office. "Not only is he the primary candidate, based on Lena's research"—oh, how it pained her to say that—"but everything he said lines up with him being a person who had the knowledge, capacity, and skill to pull off scaling up the research from small mammal to human."

Magnus nodded. "Yes, I agree that all signs point to his involvement, but the question is, what's his motivation?"

Katrina considered that for a moment. In her rush of excitement, she'd considered the whodunit but not the why. "Money seems to be the driver to me. And career ambitions. And I suppose you can toss a large amount of ego into the mix as well. Before his surprise gig began at Vetenskapverket, he had two grad students leveling what were evidently credible accusations at him, and he'd been unceremonious-ly dumped by the university. He might have been talented, but no one would want his level of baggage. Who would want to hire some-one with that dark stain on his resumé?"

"And that raises another issue," Magnus said. "Even if he's the one, I'm not convinced that Vetenskapverket is the one fully bankrolling him. They seem legit enough, but his role within the in-stitution seems questionable, what with the dodgy secretary and the general lack of transparency."

"Makes sense to investigate them further, then," Katrina replied. "Lena, have your money tracers find out what Vetenskapverket is paying him and see if they're a shell lab of some kind or if he is legit-imately hired there but getting bankrolled additionally by someone else."

"Good idea, Katrina," Magnus agreed.

Clearly, Lena didn't think that was a good idea. The bristling neck hairs gave it away as well. She gave a tight nod.

"While Lena researches that, we have to continue building the case," Katrina said as she hopped out of the chair to pace the room. "To do that, we have to go back again to motivation. Why, specifi-cally, would he want to assassinate a politician? Nothing in our file on him stands out in terms of any political antagonism toward her. If anything, they were probably closer in alignment when it comes to animal welfare, if what he said is true.

"It almost makes me wonder, what if Lindström was just collat-eral damage? Wouldn't that be the irony of it all? After all of her con-troversial positions, she gets killed on the command of a mad scien-tist who just wants to test out if his research works on a human scale? All he would need is one high-profile success like that, and he'd have unscrupulous governments and terrorist regimes at his beck and call, paying him whatever he wanted in exchange for an assassin totally at their command. It's the only way it makes sense. Acting on a personal vendetta just doesn't add up. Perhaps Oskar was killed because he had figured out that Surikov knew more—specifically, he knew about Westlund."

As Katrina finished, she turned toward Izzie. She appeared as thoughtful as perhaps Katrina had ever seen her.

"That poor man." When Izzie received a bunch of bewildered looks, she explained, "Surikov, I mean. Not Westlund, obviously. Lindström is long dead, but there's a man out there who's still very much alive, who has to deal with the impact of taking a life. All against his will, I might add. To me, the question is, can this be undone? Or is he stuck that way forever—as just a human puppet on a string, ready to kill on command? If we know who Frankenstein is, then what do we do with his monster?"

"That's very compassionate of you to think that, Agent Figeroa," Magnus said. "But an even more pressing question, for me, is whether Surikov is the only one... or just the prototype? Did Westlund kill Oskar... or did he use more of his technology?"

The group fell silent in collective horror. No one wanted to consider the implications of that.

Finally, Katrina spoke. "Probably not, though. I mean, if that were the case, then St. Gustav would have more patients just like Surikov, right?" No one seemed much reassured by that.

"I think the first thing I'd do, if I had assassins on command, would be to find a way to get them to off themselves after the job was done," Lena said. "If you can control them, why couldn't you get them to commit suicide at completion? It would be a very clean way to wrap up a job, though that would mean throwing away a lot of resources each time."

"Possibly, Lena," Katrina said. "But we also have to remember that it's mind control but also mind control of skilled loner killers. How many people would fit a profile similar to Surikov's?"

"Whether there is just the one or more, I'm still not one hundred percent convinced that more of our politicians aren't at risk in this election year, especially if our hunch—and it's just that, of course—is correct," Magnus said. "Next week is *Almedalsveckan*..."

"Alma-what now?" Izzie looked confused.

"Almedalen Week, or Politician's Week," he replied, "is a large political gathering held each year. It's a time of political debate, and each of the major parties gets a day to discuss their political platform and—"

"Basically, it's a bunch of puffed-up politicians making speeches for the cameras," Lena interrupted.

"The point is..." He stared at Lena harshly. "Almost fifty thousand people are expected to be in attendance, so if Westlund's somehow still got Surikov activated, along with however many others, then that would be a bloodbath—with a completely captive audience."

He turned toward Jens, who was lurking in his usual corner. "Jens, I think it's time to discreetly hit up your contacts at the police and SÄPO. Let them know that it would be a good idea for them to beef up their presence."

Jens touched his cap and slipped silently from the room. At that moment, Katrina wondered two things: why had Izzie watched him so attentively while he left, and how had Jens—Mr. Chauffeur and head costumer—come to have considerable contacts within the police and intelligence community? *What is that man's story?* The more she heard, the more she wanted to get to the truth about his identity.

Magnus interrupted her thoughts. "Katrina and Isobel, you can take advantage of the fact that it's a huge media event and pose as members of the foreign press. No one will be suspicious if you're asking questions and taking in the crowd."

"That makes sense to me," Katrina replied. She definitely didn't want Izzie and her broken, butchered Swedish trying to fit into the crowd. "In the meantime, though, I think it makes sense to head back to St. Gustav. And just in case, let's preemptively make sure Surikov is where he's supposed to be and put in some surveillance to make sure he doesn't somehow slip out for a day trip."

SURIKOV WAS THERE.

Katrina didn't see him, but Dr. Abboud confirmed that Surikov had not left the facility. Kat was able to gain access under the pretense of gathering information on how Surikov might behave leading up to milestone events like Almedalen Week. Not surprisingly, Dr. Abboud said that was a great question and, indeed, one they had taken into consideration.

"Oh yes, given Surikov's role in a political assassination, we keep an extra eye on him during Almedalen Week, along with providing him with additional intensive therapy, not that it seems to make much difference."

"Do you think it's possible that he doesn't even know it's Almedalen Week?" she asked.

"Not likely. While he's kept from political forums, he still can watch TV. He still has access to calendars, so it's not like he doesn't know what's going on."

Although Katrina was glad Surikov was where he was supposed to be, she wasn't about to get complacent. She needed to come up with a way to surveil him. However accommodating Dr. Abboud was, Katrina had no way to show up each day and check on Surikov's status without arousing suspicion. Her solution was to get Magnus to place some Level Threes near the site to keep an eye on the exits. Kat might not know everything about what he was doing on the inside, but she could at least ensure that he wasn't getting outside. The Level Threes dutifully reported back daily that he hadn't left the premises. Everything seemed good, so she turned her attention to preparing for Almedalen Week.

Chapter 24

I am so sick of this wig.

Katrina subtly patted her own head. The heat of the day was making her wig itch even more. She quietly cursed and patted once more, showing considerable restraint when all she really wanted to do was rip the horrid bouffant wig off her head and throw the wretched thing into the trash—then light it on fire for good measure.

"It's your own dumb fault," Izzie said without sympathy as she watched Katrina continue to pat and curse. "You're the one who chose to wear it when interviewing politicians earlier, so now you're stuck with it. It's your identity now, American Bouffant Reporter Lady." She gave her own wigless scalp a traitorous scratch and shook her curls. "That's the price of being a boss."

"You're my best friend, Izzie, but please know that I totally hate you right now. Especially since you're right," Katrina grumbled as she patted her offending headgear again. Actually, the wig was the worst part of the whole thing. The rest of her ensemble was great. Her wedge sandals were comfy, and her cream sleeveless shirt and skirt combo had enough spandex that she could make a run for it if she needed to.

Everything else with their surveillance had gone surprisingly well also. Each day that week, the spies made a visit to Visby to attend the political event. Even with all the resources of the Division, no hotel rooms were available, so posing as a tourist group, they stayed in a small inn in rural Gotland and commuted in daily. The weather was nice, and the views were spectacular, so Katrina didn't mind.

The outdoor events during Almedalen Week operated like a well-oiled machine. All the major and minor parties had booths set up, filled with campaign memorabilia, pamphlets, and eager volunteers ready to explain why their party's platform was superior. For those uninterested in politics, there was no shortage of apolitical events and drinking to enjoy.

Katrina found the whole week interesting, though, and would've gone even if it wasn't a part of her mission. It was a prime place for people watching and learning more about Swedish politics and culture. Early in the week, she watched Ekstrand take the stage and found herself captivated by her strident speech on how women were better suited to take on many of the policy issues where the "patriarchy had failed," security being one of them. To Katrina's surprise, Ekstrand brought up Lindström to prove her point.

"It is approaching ten years since my dear friend, Johanna Lindström, was slain. Had women been in charge, we would have made sure that the streets were safe for females to walk at night and that the mentally ill would get the help they needed before tragedy could strike."

Petter wasn't wrong about her using Lindström's name to score political points, then.

Pantzerhielm was a dominant, commanding force onstage. He wore the mantle of party leader well, and he strutted across the stage as though he knew it. Katrina even thought he made a few good points on Sweden's role in the EU, and she was set to think better of him until he caught her eye and gave her a lascivious wink. *Blergh.*

Since neither of them were going to be able to pull off being "little gray men"—unremarkable and unnoticed—the Division issued Katrina and Izzie press passes. They were in an elevated media box to the left of the stage. As the majority of the rally was conducted in Swedish, Izzie was really only there to keep watch for anything suspicious and to serve as backup. To prepare, she mostly just milled about by the press box's table of refreshments. Magnus and Lena were positioned in the crowd. They were supposed to be interested citizens, which was easy enough since that was exactly what they were. Lena had pinned on a button supporting Kvinnor. All had on earpieces in order to communicate with one another.

While the rest of the team worked together, nobody saw any sign of Jens. Katrina figured he was probably with his mysterious SÄPO contacts. Whoever Jens's contacts were, they'd certainly listened to his concerns—the crowds were filled with officers, both in uniform and, from the unsubtle way they touched their hidden earpieces when speaking, poorly undercover. While they lacked the smooth style of the Division, Katrina was glad they'd taken Jens seriously and seemed to be on high alert. As far as the Division was concerned, any and all of the politicians presenting during the week were at risk.

Katrina tapped off her comm and spoke to Izzie. "Do you ever wonder what Jens gets up to? Or how it is he seems to know all these high-up security people... yet he's our chauffeur and costumer?"

"I think he said something about once working with the police chief. Or maybe they were army buddies or something like that." Izzie looked vaguely uncomfortable.

"Wow. How'd you know that?"

Izzie shrugged. "Dunno. Just came up, I guess." She didn't elaborate further.

Odd. Izzie wasn't the reticent sort when it came to gossip about others.

"Huh. I've never heard him mention anything about his connections. When'd he say that?"

"Don't remember. He probably brought it up at headquarters. Maybe you were elsewhere." She fell silent and gazed back at the crowd.

Definitely odd. And evasive. Katrina didn't press Izzie further, though. As curious as she was—and she was definitely curious—she knew she needed to focus on the job at hand and save any mysteries about secret conversations between Izzie and Jens for another time. So far, they'd made it through the week without issue, but she wasn't about to let her guard down. She covertly tapped her comm back on and scanned through the attendees.

On the last day of speeches, the time came for Johanna Lindström's husband, Petter, to make his appearance. Though not a top politician, he was probably the most widely known among the general public. He gave the introduction welcoming the party leader of Svensk Sanning.

"We've got to take our country back!" Lindström said. "We can do it if we work together to keep Sweden Swedish! The days of unchecked migration have got to come to an end. We can't take on the world's problems any longer. It has only resulted in devastating consequences. Believe me, I know. My children no longer have a mother, and I lost my devoted, beloved wife."

While that was true, Kat thought pushing the motherless-child angle was a bit much, as was the pointed reference to Johanna's devotion to him. Petter didn't seem to have a problem using his deceased wife for political gain, either.

Not everyone was convinced by his speech, however. Most of the audience turned their backs to Lindström in silent protest. Whatever goodwill he had engendered with Johanna's death seemed to have evaporated with his allegiance to Svensk Sanning.

Katrina made a point of observing who *didn't* turn. She scanned the crowd. Most of them were the usual suspects, with their shaved heads, Thor-hammer necklaces, and SS tattoos. No surprises there.

However, another was also scanning the rallygoers across the venue, a man with light-brown skin and a skullcap. Their eyes met, and a half-second lapse passed before mutual recognition. He was the man from the café, the one who'd pretended to read the newspaper. His eyes widened as Katrina mouthed, "You!"

He turned and started toward one of the exits. He was moving briskly but not quickly enough to arouse attention. Katrina looked back at Izzie. She was back over at the snack table by the far end of the box. She didn't have enough time to fully alert Magnus or Lena, who were farther away from the man than Katrina was. Everything was on her. She didn't know what that man was up to, but she felt strongly that he wasn't just an interested observer of politics.

"I see him! Giving chase."

Ignoring Izzie's yelp, Katrina hopped out of the press box. She wove her way in and out of the crowd, her progress maddeningly slow. She could hear Magnus, Lena, and Izzie shouting all at once into her earpiece, but all Katrina's focus was on maintaining her visual on the man. She couldn't risk losing him.

"Who are you chasing? Where? Report back, Agent Foster," Lena growled in her ear.

Before she could say anything, she was roughly jostled by a couple of bikers, and her earpiece popped out. *Damn.* Katrina briefly looked down, but it was an effectively discreet earpiece for a reason. She couldn't see it and certainly didn't have time to stop and hunt for it, so she kept going. She was on her own. She caught sight of the man again and kept working her way through the mass of people.

After what seemed like an eternity, she made it out of the park. Once free of the exits, both the man and Katrina took off at a run. She did the best she could in the platform sandals as she couldn't lose time trying to unbuckle them. The stupid wig started sliding off her head, so she yanked off the monstrosity before it could fall off entirely. If anything, being without it might make her run faster. As she ran past a trash bin, she tossed the evil thing in, never breaking stride. That was the safest way to dispose of it. She didn't need anyone picking up a hairpiece as evidence.

Her calves were starting to ache from running in the platforms, but she kept going, keeping a visual on her target. She gave him credit—the man was in good shape. He kept running and running and didn't show any signs of slowing down.

"*Vänta!* Wait!" she shouted. Katrina ignored the horns of cars as she darted across the street in pursuit.

The man clearly knew his way around the city and ran into a large shopping mall. He was clever, using the crowds to his advantage. She tracked him through a busy food court. They went through the back kitchen of an Italian restaurant. A pain had started in her left side, but she ignored it, grateful that she'd been able to run flat out that far, in heels, no less. She gave silent thanks to the hotel gym's elliptical machine as she kept running.

Through the back of the restaurant was a wide alley blocked off from the main streets with a chain-link fence. They came to a sudden stop. He was cornered, but so was she. He turned back to face her. She lifted her shirt and pulled her gun from her waist holster.

His chest heaved from exertion as he held up both hands. "Please don't shoot," he gasped.

"Then start talking, and keep those hands up." Katrina grimaced as she wheezed.

"It's not what you think," he gasped.

She leaned to one side and grabbed her waist. The ache from the stitch in her side had increased painfully, but she still held the gun on him.

"What I *think* is that you've been following me. I recognize you from the café."

"Okay, I admit it. I admit it. I was hired to follow you."

"Follow me?"

"And yes, I was also the one who trashed your hotel room."

She looked at him incredulously, her heart still racing and her breathing labored. That was *not* what she'd expected in way of an admission.

"I had..." He was still out of breath. "I had to make it appear to be a robbery. I was doing recon work on you, but that's not the point."

Not the point? The whole conversation was taking an odd turn, and Katrina was beginning to suspect she was quickly losing command of the situation.

"Who told you to do recon work on me?"

He looked around nervously even though no one was nearby. "You know, the grumpy chick."

Katrina mentally reviewed the "chicks" she had met in Sweden, and she didn't think he was talking about Nurse Ox or Ekstrand, which left...

Lena. The same Lena who so helpfully assisted her in trying to identify the very man right in front of her and had somehow conveniently kept coming up empty-handed.

"Why did she ask you to do that?"

He waved his hand. "Not important."

"Explain yourself!" *Dear lord. Why isn't the pain in my side letting up?*

"That's what I'm *trying* to do," he ground out. "I was also hired to dig up dirt on some suspects, but not by Lena. Listen, I think I know who's behind everything on your Lindström case. I pieced it together."

Katrina lowered the gun. She had no clue what was going on, and she wanted answers.

"I did work for Oskar too. I've seen the payments, and I've got some of his papers he told me to keep back in my flat. It wasn't just Surikov, it was—

His head snapped back, and blood poured from his chest. He dropped to the ground, his head landing with a thud. Katrina ran toward him and felt for a pulse at his neck but found none. She gazed into his unseeing eyes. The answer to completing her mission was dead.

Chapter 25

Katrina quickly looked up from where she thought the shot might've originated. It came from one of the taller buildings across from the alley. On top of the red roof, metal glinted, and a figure quickly pulled back.

The sound of running footsteps quickly approached from behind her. She turned with her gun up and saw Magnus, Lena, and Izzie running toward her. Izzie gasped as her eyes went from the body back to Katrina. Lena pulled up short when she saw the body and groaned.

"*Fy fan!*" Lena spat in a low whisper as she dropped to the ground and kneeled over the body.

Katrina's head whipped around to Lena. "You know him?" She decided to hold off on mentioning his confession about being hired until she knew more.

"Yes. That is—or at least that was—Ibrahim Muhammad." Lena appeared slightly green. "Ibrahim was my informant for ten years. Ten years!" Any grief Lena had been feeling was quickly replaced by anger. "And in broad daylight, no less. The Division is going to have fun trying to clean this up."

Magnus looked at the gun then down at Katrina. "What happened? Why did you shoot him?"

"I didn't!"

"I see a gun in your hand and a body on the ground. Explain." Lena had taken over the interrogation.

"I didn't shoot him!" She turned to Magnus. "I can't be sure, but I think I saw the shooter. Tall, so I'd guess male, and I saw a rifle. Up there." Katrina pointed toward the roof where she'd seen the figure.

"Agent Figeroa," Magnus said. "Get over there and see if you can find him. If the shooter's any good, he's already long gone and without a trace, but maybe you can find a witness who saw someone looking out of place."

Izzie took off.

Magnus turned back to Katrina. "Okay, then. What happened? One minute you were in the press box, *doing your job*, and the next, you ran off with no explanation at all."

"And you ignored all of us." Lena had to do her part to make a bad situation worse.

Katrina whipped her head back over to Lena. "Will you *shut up*? Let me explain. I was doing crowd observations—*like I was supposed to*—when I saw a guy that had been spying on Izzie and me at a café a while ago. It was that guy right there." She pointed at Ibrahim's body. "Izzie can corroborate that if my word isn't good enough for you.

"And if we're going to talk about demanding explanations, maybe you can tell me why he said he was spying on me!" she shouted at Lena.

Lena was silent, and Magnus spoke up.

"We will have to get into that and why I didn't know anything about Ibrahim later." He shot Lena an angry look. Turning back to Katrina, he asked, "Why didn't you say anything when you ran off? We were all shouting at you and asking for a report."

"Someone bumped me, and my earpiece fell out. I never even heard you."

"And the fact you have a cell phone in your possession escaped you?" Magnus huffed in frustration.

"I guess... I guess I was just running on adrenaline, trying to catch him. I couldn't risk losing him. I knew he was involved in some way." She looked back and forth between Magnus and Lena. "When I yelled at him to wait, he just took off. He never stopped, never tried to explain. He just ran. No one else was around, and I wasn't about to miss my chance. I thought if I could just catch up to him in time..." That sounded minor league to Katrina's ears even as it came out.

Lena was not open to explanations. Since the questions were no longer being directed at her, she was back in attack mode. "And so you figured you'd race in and save the day, huh? Be the hero. Now we have no informant, no information, and a blood-splattered alley."

She stopped her tirade long enough to survey her surroundings. A small crowd was appearing, their camera phones raised up against the fence.

"And now, we've got about five different camera phones trying to capture this moment." Her voice was lowered, but Lena might as well have been screaming for the impact each word had.

"You know, I'm starting to think that maybe they didn't send you here because you were so good. Maybe they sent you here just to get rid of you."

Katrina flinched at the direct hit.

Lena turned away and jabbed a finger into Magnus's chest. Her anger had found its way to a new recipient. "You know I respect you even if I sometimes question your judgment." She looked back over at Katrina as Exhibit A before continuing. "But if you don't put her behind a desk or, better yet, get her sent back, I will go over your head and do it myself."

"Lena, enough! We have worked together for years, but do not *ever* forget that on this mission, I am in command."

Lena had the good sense to take a step back and remove her finger from the center of his chest.

"Not to mention that we wouldn't even *be* in this situation if you had been open with us about your informant from the start!"

Police cars started pulling up. Magnus turned back to Lena.

"Now that the police have arrived, you will go over there, you will inform them that we've got a shooter on the loose, and you will tell them that they need to disperse the crowd and secure the perimeter. We also need some officers to watch over—but not touch—the body. As you so aptly noted, we have a fast-growing group of onlookers that we need to get rid of as soon as possible."

Lena gave his back a sarcastic salute but went over to the police cars without further argument.

Katrina spoke to Magnus. "I didn't get a chance to tell you, but he said he had figured it out. He had worked for Oskar too. Remember when I told you that Oskar had incomplete notes? He gave the rest to Ibrahim—a guy on the outside—for safekeeping. He said he thought he knew who was really behind the Lindström assassination."

"Of *course* he did. I *cannot* catch a break," Magnus said, mostly to himself. He rubbed his temples. "*Okej*, tell me precisely what he said. Verbatim."

"It wasn't much, I'm afraid. He said, 'It wasn't just Surikov, it was—' and that was it. Then he was gone," she finished lamely.

Izzie came back. "I spoke with a cleaner in the neighboring building. He said that office building has been vacant for some time. I went around the perimeter quickly, but I didn't see anyone."

Magnus sighed. "No. I had hoped, but I didn't expect that you would." His eyes went back over to the building where Katrina had seen the shooter.

"Agents Foster and Figueroa, start a sweep of the area. There's no doubt in my mind this was done by a professional, but maybe you can turn up a bullet casing, some gunpowder residue—anything." He looked squarely at Katrina. "And do it as a *team*. I'm going back to apprise the director of the situation, order our forensics to deal with this site, and get someone over to Muhammad's flat before anyone else can get there. Lena's informant seems to have had some information that was apparently worth dying for." With that, he was gone.

And not a second too soon, because Katrina could feel the tears that she had struggled valiantly to hold back start to give way. Yet another battle lost. She was tough, yes, but there was a man who died on her watch, and this was not the direction she was supposed to be heading as a new Level Four. She brusquely swiped at her cheeks with the back of her hand.

Izzie took one glance at Katrina's face and didn't say whatever she had planned. Instead, she gave Katrina's arm a pat and said, "C'mon, bud. Let's get to work."

They walked over to the abandoned office building. A red For Lease sign hung on the glass door. Not wanting to call any additional attention to themselves, they slipped around the back of the building and went up the fire escape. After carefully navigating the red tiles, they scoured the site quietly. The external silence allowed for endless castigations and questions to run rampant inside Katrina's head. *How could you have been so stupid as to just run off like that? Were you really trying to be a hero?* A nasty little part of her agreed with Lena. She wanted to make a splash on her first mission, and successfully catching a villain single-handedly would've accomplished that.

Piling onto her emotional upheaval was Magnus. She didn't like the look he'd given her—anger mixed with disappointment. She held no hopes for the two of them. She also held no hopes about having to report everything back to her director. She made a note to get her bags packed—just in case.

Magnus's assumption that the shooting was the work of a professional appeared correct. Katrina and Izzie couldn't find any traces of a shooter's presence—no casings, no finger- or shoeprints, no any-thing. The shooter was apparently a ghost.

They left the inspection of the body to the forensics team, who arrived, photographed, and bundled away the corpse with a precise and disturbing quickness, and headed back toward the ferry. An offi-cer opened the temporary barrier that had been erected so they could pass through to the main street. With the body gone, the crowd had started to thin, but plenty of gawkers still remained.

"Excuse us. Excuse us. Comin' through. My friend got a bit overzealous with the red paint for the political protests. Artists, y'know."

Katrina inspected herself. Her cream outfit was splattered in blood. Good thing they'd slipped up the back stairwell into the building earlier. No way would she have made it through the front door. Izzie was thinking of everything when Katrina was too much in shock to do so. She looked at her friend.

"Thank you," she whispered. "I hadn't even noticed."

Izzie shrugged. "That's what friends are for." She gave her another quick pat, careful not to touch any of the blood. "Don't worry. We'll get you cleaned up. I have a change of clothes in my bag. The dress may be a bit short, given our height differences, but it's better than what you've got on now. Once that blood dries, no one's going to be-lieve that's paint." She pointed into the distance. "Ah, there's a public restroom over there. Let's go."

Katrina numbly followed her lead. She could change clothes, but she didn't know if she would ever feel clean.

Chapter 26

Late in the night, Katrina and Izzie received a text from Magnus: *Emergency meeting. Seven a.m.*

At barely seven in the morning, the team gathered in Magnus's office.

Magnus was pacing, which couldn't be a good sign. He looked busted from a lack of sleep, but to be fair, after the previous day's events, no one was at their best.

"So many fires to put out," he muttered before clapping once to get everyone's attention.

"*Okej*, two things. One, the informant Ibrahim Muhammad's flat was searched yesterday. The door was left open, and everything was a mess, but we believe that to be a cover. His laptop was wiped clean, but they found a note that said, 'Once I followed along the trail of motivations, it quickly became obvious.' That's what I want each of you to do. Follow the motivations of every potential suspect, starting with Rikard Westlund. I want to know what exactly it was that seemed so *obvious*."

He continued to pace. "I also asked you to come early this morning so that we would have enough time to debrief the events of yesterday. And I'm not talking about the rally." He looked at Lena and Katrina. "Who wants to begin?"

"I will," Lena said. "I want to know why Agent Foster is still here after she blatantly broke Division protocol, got my informant killed, and wasted valuable Division staff time."

All eyes shifted to Katrina.

Ah, so that's how it's going to be? Katrina thought angrily. She was so stressed out that she'd barely slept the previous night. On top of that, it was too early in the morning, and Katrina had been through far too much to deal with Lena's crap. If she was going down, she was going to drag Lena with her.

"What *I* want to know is what your informant was doing following me."

Everyone turned toward Lena.

"W-What are you talking about?" Lena stuttered briefly, a dead giveaway.

"You know *exactly* what I'm talking about. Right before he died, Ibrahim said he had been hired to follow me, and he was the one who had been in *my* hotel room, on *your* direction, searching for information on *me*. Come up with a convincing story for *that*."

Katrina turned toward Izzie. "He said he was instructed to make it look like an attempted robbery."

"That little rat," Lena murmured. "To think I had trusted him..."

Heads kept turning back and forth during the exchange, to the point that it started to look not unlike a tennis match.

"Trusted him to what? Finish me off? And to think I trusted you! Despite my better judgement, I relied on you as a fellow agent. No wonder you weren't the least bit worried when I reported to you that a man—Ibrahim—had been watching Izzie and me at a café!"

At that, Izzie's mouth dropped open as she turned back to Lena. She looked shocked—and a little hurt.

"Wait, what?" Magnus asked. "Why didn't you tell me any of this, Katrina?" He, too, seemed a little hurt.

"I told Lena!" Katrina was tired of the accusations. "She acted like I was crazy, like I was seeing shadows where they didn't exist, so I didn't bother to tell anyone else until I knew more."

"I believed you," Izzie said quietly. She seemed to be seeing Lena in a new light and was re-evaluating all the things Katrina had warned of all along. Of course, Izzie might have also been remembering that her half of the hotel room had been equally violated in Ibrahim's quest for information. Either way, Katrina was glad for the support.

"Given everything I know now, it's no wonder our experts could never get a 'clean view' of his face to analyze. You never even asked them, did you?"

"Lena, is everything Katrina is saying true?" Magnus's blue eyes turned to steel. "Please tell me you *did not* waste precious time and resources doing recon on a colleague—a colleague that came *specifically* to help us do our jobs."

"I can't tell you any of that, because it's true. I never had anyone review any footage because it would have outed my informant. And yes, I did hire Ibrahim to spy on Katrina, and initially Isobel too. I mean, their arrival was all so suspicious—two completely green American agents sent here to help out on the murder of a top agent? I mean, it just didn't add up. I quickly saw that Isobel was talented, so she started to make sense pretty quickly. But 'Agent' Foster? I've yet to see anything here that warrants her arrival."

Katrina made a face that clearly said, "I'm just going to stay silent and watch this fool dig herself deeper into the hole."

Lena looked at Izzie and shrugged. "I am sorry for ruining your side of the room, though."

Izzie gave her a small nod in return.

Magnus, however, would not be so easily appeased—he was furious. "Lena, after all we've been through, I can hardly believe that you would compromise our mission out of sheer pettiness. I have stood up for you countless times across many missions, and this is what you do? I'd request that the director suspend you immediately, but you are one of only four agents, plus Jens, who knows about this case, not to mention that I clearly need to keep an eye on you."

He glared at all of them. "Apparently, I can't count on *any* of you to remember that there exists something bigger than yourselves and your stupid personality problems. *Skit.* I can't count on any of you to actually work as a team even when people's lives are in danger." His face was an alarming shade of red, and he looked ready to combust.

"What's worse is that *none* of you seem to get it. An already difficult mission has now been made almost impossible due to your collective screwups." He slammed a fist on the table, causing Katrina to jump.

"The media is all over this now, trying to figure out if it really was a drugs-related killing, or if that's all just a cover-up for a hate crime. We fed them the two possibilities, but it's only a matter of time before someone catches on that the evidence doesn't convincingly add up to either explanation. What I really don't need now is more problems and more interference, least of all from what was supposed to have been my team."

He spread both hands on the table and glared at them. "I'm giving you a choice, one that you have until the end of today to make a decision about. Either get it together and show up tomorrow ready to work so we can solve this thing *as a team*, or get out. If you're out, you'll either be packed on a plane back to America"—he turned toward Lena—"or stuck in a desk job. I would almost rather start from scratch than have to deal with this garbage again."

No one responded. Lena looked like she'd never seen such a display from Magnus. Jens, in his usual position by an exit, had a worried expression but seemed unsurprised at Magnus's stinging reprimand.

"Ugh. Get out! All of you, just get out." Magnus turned his back on them.

Jens had already disappeared. Lena abandoned her usual clomping for swiftness as she and Izzie scrambled out the door. Katrina was not far behind.

"Agent Foster. Katrina. Wait."

"Yes?"

"Come here, please."

She pushed the door shut and looked over her shoulder. "Why? So you can blow out my eardrums with another rant? I can beat myself up easily enough—I don't need your help piling on."

He had the decency to appear abashed. "I guess I deserved that."

Katrina walked back over and stood before him, face to face.

"Listen, I'm sorry about accusing you yesterday. Clearly, I was unaware of all the facts. Like Lena going rogue and sending an informant after you. While you *did* break protocol, it was wrong of me to prejudge you. I'm also sorry for getting so angry. That's not really who I am." He paused. "And that's not who I want to be." His face was starting to fade back to normal, with only a few red blotches on his cheeks.

"Apology accepted," she replied. "I probably would've reacted similarly in your position." She looked down briefly. "I *did* screw up. I got a man killed. Almost compromised the entire mission. Even if I didn't intend to do it, the outcome's still the same. Ibrahim's still dead, and we still don't know who's behind all this. So I guess it's my turn to apologize some more as well."

Magnus leaned against the wall and stared up at the ceiling. "I'm just... I'm just so frustrated with this whole thing. I had to listen to my director hand my ass back to me in eight different ways for an hour before you arrived. The way things are going, this is giving that man everything he needs to fire me."

He ran his fingers over his hair and blew out a breath. "That's not everything, though. When you disappeared, when I lost visual on you, I... I got worried about you." He reached out and squeezed her hand briefly. "I was so worried about you that I temporarily lost sight of the mission. I can't have that."

She looked up at him.

"Time worrying over you is time not spent focused on the operation. It's a zero-sum game. I can't jeopardize everything I have worked so hard for. I can't let the new director trash me and, by proxy, my parents' legacy. Your parents were like my parents, so you get it, right? I... I just can't do that. So from now on, we need to be professionals. That's it. Until this thing is over." He ran a hand over his face. "Damn. That sounded cold, even to me... and I'm the one who said it."

Katrina smiled sadly. "Yeah, but I get it. I can do the professionalism thing where we're concerned." She didn't like it, but she could do that—for him, for the mission, and most of all, for herself if she wanted to make it through in one piece.

"For all I know, my director is already making arrangements for me to pack it in," she said.

"I hope we can figure out how to do this, Kat. Don't let what happened yesterday shake you too badly. Despite what Lena says and your issues with her, you really are a good agent. You ask all the right questions, and you think in ways that pick up nuance, subtle clues. You're the one who spotted Ibrahim in a sea of people. I think that once you settle down and maybe stop trying so hard to prove yourself, you're going to be one of the Division's best. And that's not just my bias."

"Thanks, Magnus." She smiled then shook her head. "I mean, thank you, Agent Svensson." And with a very formal handshake, they parted.

Chapter 27

Katrina was running late. After what she'd been through the past few days, she almost couldn't be blamed for taking in the small luxury of sleeping in an extra hour. Just the stress involved with sending that report to the director should've warranted some additional time. She found a note next to her pillow from Izzie: *Tried to wake you three times! If I don't see you here at the memorial by ten a.m., I'm coming back and treating you to some water torture.* She knew Izzie would make good on her threat, so she raced around the hotel room to get ready.

Katrina went to Jens's clothing suitcase and picked out a black silk scarf. She draped it like a hijab over the top of her head. As she hurried out the door, she noted that the scarf not only made her respectfully observant but eliminated the need to try to do something with hair that was currently going undercover as an uncombable rat's nest. She did, at least, have the good sense to feel ashamed by that moment of disrespectful vanity, though, especially given that she was the reason for the memorial.

She slipped on some oversized dark sunglasses then raced down to the hotel lobby to find Magnus checking his phone.

"I'm here!" she said breathlessly.

"Good morning, Agent Foster. I was about to send Jens in there to drag you out. Isobel is already there with Lena."

The last forty-eight hours had been a "come to Jesus" moment in which all members assessed who they were and what they wanted to do with their lives. All agreed *who* they were—spies—and what they wanted to do was complete the mission. It was a struggle, but Lena and Katrina were able to tersely shake hands in an official détente.

Ibrahim's family had given him a public memorial. While the official word was that his death was attributed to a drug deal gone wrong, his parents didn't believe it. Their public memorial was a defiant gesture made so the public could see what a good, clean, and observant young man he was. If he had a little extra money now and again, it was from picking up side jobs, not from dealing drugs. Only Lena knew the true nature of those side jobs.

As the service was a public celebration of his life, they were able to slip in unnoticed. Forgoing the small neighborhood mosque, the family was holding the memorial in a large school gymnasium in Jordbro, just south of Stockholm. Inside was a large picture of a smiling Ibrahim with the caption "Friend, Brother, Son. Devoted."

The turnout was good, with family and his former university mates. The man must've been well regarded. Instead of taking some comfort in that, the fact only further compounded Katrina's sense of guilt. Seeing the many mourners brought it home that the world of spies was no lark—it came with tangible consequences. It was a world in which real people with real families could easily become collateral damage from real bullets.

They met Lena and Izzie by the guest book, in which none of them could actually sign their own names.

"Sorry I'm late," Katrina whispered.

"Given that you got him killed, the least you could do was get here on time," Lena whispered back. Her adherence to the truce was already losing grip.

Magnus wisely steered Katrina past Lena and an exasperated-looking Izzie.

"Was that really necessary, Lena?" Izzie asked.

Katrina and Magnus stood in the back of the gym. By instinct, Katrina surveyed the room. The majority of the people in the room were of Middle Eastern descent.

She leaned in and whispered to Magnus, "This room appears distinctly different from the halls of the Swedish Division headquarters."

Magnus pursed his lips slightly, which made him look uptight but not wholly unappealing.

"If you're making a not-very-subtle reference to our rather monochromatic agent population, we *do* have some agents of color," he said with a mild defensiveness. "But they're mostly placed on lower-level cases where we have to infiltrate a mosque or investigate immigrant berry picker smuggling rings. Or they get stuck inside on desk duty."

As though he could sense her bristling, Magnus turned a wry eye to Katrina. "Not everyone can get away with playing the foreign journalist or the researcher or the tourist."

Katrina gave the most righteously indignant "harrumph" she could muster without causing heads to turn her way.

Magnus smiled. "Sorry, but it's true. You can get away with that here because people see you as an American first. Ibrahim and folks like him do not have that luxury.

"In Sweden, our main targets tend to involve the moneyed, the powerful, the elite. If you're trying to infiltrate major corporations or political leadership, then you've got to be as inconspicuous as possible. These are not circles given to diversity. They're based on status or at least *perceived* status. To fit in, you have to look and speak like you summer in Torekov or went to school at Sigtuna or Lundsbergs. Often, that translates to white. It doesn't matter if you are born here or if you are a fluent speaker, you're still going to stand out in a room. With that crowd, if you don't have a convincing cover—like you often do—then you're going to be remembered, and people are going to be on their guard. I am told it used to be the same way with female agents in the past. We are trying, but we are also cautious. We tried using several Asian agents last year..." He winced as though remembering the outcome. "It did not go well."

They paused and refocused their attention on the proceedings.

"To Allah we belong, and to Him we return." The imam was concluding the memorial. He invited Ibrahim's parents to come forward and give their final words.

Katrina watched Lena. She was surprised to see the woman dab at her eyes while her jaw worked furiously to contain her emotions. Seeing Lena with emotions other than anger or arrogance didn't seem possible to Katrina. She didn't know if Lena was genuine or if everything was the carefully orchestrated act of a seasoned spy.

Izzie leaned over and gave her a small hug. Katrina felt a twinge of jealousy as she'd been friends with Izzie a lot longer than Lena. She supposed they'd bonded over their shared experience as seconds-in-command. She understood that. But she didn't have to like it.

Magnus picked up where he left off, and Kat turned her attention back to him. "To avoid a repeat of such disasters, we move slightly behind the rest of society to protect ourselves and our agents. As society advances... so do we."

Katrina was not impressed with what she was hearing but understood the logic. Yet she would argue the potential risk would be worth it if it allowed *all* agents to advance. The alternative—keeping qualified agents from high-profile cases until enough people of color entered the upper echelons of old-money, upper-class Sweden—might have kept agents safe but seemed patronizing. She wondered about the psychological toll it took on agents who were stuck in the undercover roles of nannies, custodians, and berry pickers, with no hope of advancing. Katrina didn't know the answer, and she had to concede that her perspective was likely influenced by being an American.

Katrina crossed her arms. "I still don't like it."

"I didn't think you would."

"I can accept it."

"Thank you. Although you don't have much say in the matter."

"I am trying to display a certain amount of graciousness. Don't ruin this rare moment."

"Ceasing to ruin the moment, Agent Foster."

Chapter 28

"What do you mean, 'gone'? He escaped?"

"Yes, gone. Although I wouldn't say escaped. It was more like he was voluntarily released into therapy, per a court order," Dr. Abboud explained sheepishly. "I guess they thought I wasn't making progress with him."

Katrina stared at him. She didn't know what she had been expecting to find at St. Gustav, but that wasn't it. With the Level Threes keeping an eye on the facility, Surikov shouldn't have been able to exit the building undetected. Heads were going to roll.

"It's not often, but it does happen on occasion. Someone will take him to do another evaluation."

"Another evaluation," she said flatly. She was so dumbfounded that she was reduced to parroting his words back to him stupidly.

Dr. Abboud began to look a bit uncomfortable. "Yes, well, they try out new practices, new therapies. But it's never long before he comes back. Although this has been the longest he's been away," he said as an afterthought. "And when he does return, he's a mess. It's like all the progress we made—no matter how minimal—disappears."

That's because they're using him to kill, and it's destroying him, you idiot. She was close to screaming at him. As frustrated as she was, though, she couldn't hold it against the doctor. He had no reason to suppose anything untoward was occurring. Most people wouldn't think their sickly patient doubled as an assassin.

She forced herself to paste on a smile. "Well, hopefully, this time will be different. Ah, I don't suppose you happen to have the name of the doctor treating him? I'd love to interview them as well."

"Oh yes, certainly. Here's a copy of the court order." He rifled through his files and pulled out a copy. "See? The *Allmänna Domstolar* said he is to be released into the custody of Dr. Sten Lundgren for 'intense therapeutic purposes.'"

Katrina's Swedish capacities did not extend to legal jargon, but she was able to piece together that the order had been—allegedly—sent from the general courts. She found the date on it: the final day of the political rallies, the same day Ibrahim was shot.

"Dr. Lundgren—got it." Katrina wrote down the name. "Do you think there's any footage of him leaving? Surikov, I mean," she clarified. She really wanted to see who had escorted Surikov from the building and past the Level Threes, because while she didn't doubt the court order was real, she didn't think for a minute that the good "Dr. Lundgren" was who he seemed.

Dr. Abboud appeared confused by her question. "I-I guess. There are cameras surrounding the facility for patient security. But I don't understand..."

"I know you can't share too much medical information about Surikov, but viewing generally available camera footage would be allowable and would let me see his disposition," she lied smoothly. She hoped he would buy it.

"Ah. Clever! Still ethical but very clever. Sure. Let's go down to security and see what's on video."

It didn't take long for security to pull the footage since Dr. Abboud was able to tell them which day to select. The security guard would fast-forward the footage then slow down whenever a person could be seen exiting the building. As Katrina watched the footage, she saw a nondescript black car pull up. At the same time, one of the Level Threes dressed as a gardener walked out of view. She looked at the time stamp—it was time for a shift change, but that Level Three shouldn't have left without having a visual on their replacement. *Slipshod.* They continued to stare at the screen.

"Stop. Put it on normal speed... Right there." They all watched as a man in a baseball cap and a strangely puffy coat was quickly maneuvered into the waiting car.

"Wait, that's Surikov," Dr. Abboud said. "How strange. Why was he put in such a bulky coat on such a warm day?"

To Katrina, the reason was obvious: to better disguise Surikov's thin frame in case the hat wasn't a sufficient cover. Also, maybe something was in the coat to help subdue him.

"Hmm... I wonder if Dr. Lundgren is employing the weighted-blanket technique. I read an article recently about that," he told Katrina.

"Quite possibly, Dr. Abboud. Quite possibly," she said, barely containing her frustration.

She reminded herself that he wasn't at fault. He might've been a learned man, but he was only seeing evidence that fit his particular framework.

She watched as a second man, a quite burly one at that, popped out of the back of the car to help Surikov get into the passenger seat. Katrina strained her eyes, but she couldn't see Surikov's escort clearly. The good doctor was doing a great job of shielding his face from the camera.

C'mon, she willed him, *just turn a little more... a little more...*

Then finally, a bit of luck: the doctor had to turn in order to get into the driver's seat of the car.

"Pause, please."

And there on the camera was none other than Westlund getting behind the wheel. The car sped off. *Son of a...*To further compound her rage, the other Level Three, posing as a dog walker, finally showed up for work just in time to miss everything. She referred back to the time stamp again: fifty-nine seconds. In less than a minute, an operation had been compromised because two shiftless Level Threes couldn't figure out how to do their jobs right. She would make sure Magnus knew about their failure to follow Division protocol, but she had a more immediate problem on her hands. She needed to find Westlund and Surikov and stop whatever Westlund was planning next.

"Well, that's that." Dr. Abboud clapped once and stood.

She snapped back to attention and rose as well. "Sorry?"

"I'm glad you had the idea to watch the footage of him. Sorry I couldn't do more for you in terms of supporting your research. I know you're only here for a limited time." He hesitated briefly before plowing forward. "Say, I'd love to share some of my theories on patient rehabilitation with you. Would you like to go for a drink sometime?" Poor Dr. Abboud looked hopeful.

"Yes, sometime, Dr. Abboud," Katrina said as noncommittally as possible. "That would be nice, but my first priority is to finish things here before my time is up." No truer words had been spoken by a spy.

Chapter 29

Katrina walked quickly from St. Gustav to the train station, her fear and frustration powering her along. Given the timing of Surikov's absence and the clean job of killing Ibrahim, she had little doubt that he was the shooter. It made sense—both Oskar and Ibrahim knew something, or at least they suspected something about the Lindström assassination that was close enough to the truth for them to be eliminated. She needed to find Westlund, and quickly. She needed to uncover his purpose and figure out why a "cleanup" was happening. She wondered if perhaps a decade later, Westlund might've finally perfected his research to the point that he was ready to go into full "manufacturing" mode, and that was why he wanted to remove all traces of anyone who might've known anything. If that was the case, they had no time to delay as the entire team was at risk.

Having learned her lesson from going rogue before, she knew she needed to contact the team. They would need all hands on deck. Standing out on the platform, she pulled out her phone. As she started to text, she was brusquely jostled from behind. She looked up in irritation, but so many people were milling about that she couldn't identify the offender.

"Rude," she muttered as she returned to her encrypted text.

Meet at HQ in forty-five. Surikov is missing. He left the same day as the Almadalen shooting. Rikard Westlund behind it. Details soon.

AS KATRINA EXITED THE elevator into the dark tunnel leading to headquarters, she saw two shadows move from a turnoff on her right. She could just barely make out the figures of Jens and Izzie, embracing. Then they pulled away from each other quickly and headed in opposite directions with Jens agitatedly brushing and smoothing his collar. Katrina's eyes bugged, but she kept going. However interesting that appeared, she didn't have time to follow that pathway.

By the time the team was fully assembled, Katrina gave an overview of her conversation with Dr. Abboud and what she'd seen.

"How did they get past the Level Threes?" Magnus asked.

"That's a conversation for another time," Katrina said pointedly.

Magnus got the hint. "Since we know Surikov is controlled by Westlund, let's find him first," he replied. "He's priority number one, and I would bet that he won't be quietly waiting around at Vetenskapverket very long. We can go back to the facility to pull the footage. That should be enough to hold him. Lena? Any updates from the money tracers?"

"No, none yet."

"Then head over there and verify his whereabouts, ideally with him but more realistically with his secretary. You know how to watch her for any tells. I need to get this as airtight as possible before I go to my director."

Lena gave a salute.

Katrina spoke up. "Izzie should go too." After Lena's betrayal, she wasn't about to let her head over there alone.

"Fine with me." Lena shrugged.

She and Izzie headed out. Katrina looked for Jens to see what directive he would receive, but he'd already disappeared.

"So... the Level Threes. What happened?"

At Magnus's voice, Katrina redirected her attention and related what she'd seen.

Magnus swore and made a sound of disgust. "Unacceptable. They're getting pulled. The stakes are too high."

"Agreed on the stakes, but instead of pulling them, switch up the surveillance teams," Katrina said. "Something didn't seem right, the way everything was timed so perfectly for Westlund to hustle Surikov out. If you just pull them, it may tip them off."

"You think they're moles?" Magnus asked sharply.

"I don't know," she replied honestly. "It could just be incompetence, but it's suspicious enough that I don't want them to work together again. If they put up a stink or make excuses, well, that will inform the next steps."

Magnus nodded. "Okay. Done. Anything else?"

"Not until we hear back from Lena and Izzie. I need to see Professor Rasmusson for a moment, and then I'll return."

"Need something new?"

"In a way. Information."

Magnus looked puzzled but didn't press her. "Well, in that case, I hope you find what you're looking for."

SEEING PROFESSOR RASMUSSON in his bustling lab was not an excuse. Katrina really did want to meet with him. She wanted to take the opportunity to speak with him as he was one of the few agents around to potentially remember her parents. Ibrahim's death had underscored the idea that longevity was not a common currency in the Division.

"Back for more equipment, my dear?"

Normally, Katrina would bristle at being called "dear" by a male colleague, but with Professor Rasmusson, it didn't bother her.

"You didn't break those glasses again, did you?"

She grinned. "No, not this time. They're holding up." She watched his employees testing out devices. "Is there somewhere we can speak privately?"

He followed her eyes. "If you want privacy, you certainly came to the right place, my dear. Come along." He escorted her to the back of the lab and into his office. After he shut the door, he gestured for her to join him in sitting at his desk. Professor Rasmusson reached over to a low cabinet and pulled out what appeared to be a brass plaque on a wooden base. On it was etched *Privat. Blå Rum, 206.*

"Prototype," he explained. "It's similar to the kronor device but on steroids. If you're wanting a private, unrecorded conversation, this can block out all forms of electricity for upward of three minutes. And what's more, I even added in a one-foot cloaking range. So not only is it unbuggable, as long as the speakers are within one foot of each other, no one's hearing a thing."

"Impressive!" Katrina genuinely meant it. She might never figure out the technology—that just wasn't her skill set—but she knew that creating a device like that was no small feat.

"Isn't it, though!" He looked pleased with himself. "It took quite a bit to get it to this working stage. I will remind you, though, do not ask for anything that requires electricity because I will not be able to help you."

"Got it." She traced her fingers over the plaque until she detected a small indentation over the *Å*. Right before she got ready to push the letter, she remembered to scoot her chair closer to Professor Rasmusson and leaned in.

"Good job."

She pressed the button. After an odd shimmery sensation, the room went dark.

"Professor Rasmusson?"

"Right here. The clock is ticking, my dear, so proceed."

"So, I don't know if you know this or not, but my parents used to come here. They were agents."

"The Huxtables," he answered instantly. "Yes, I remember them."

Katrina did not ask how he'd linked them to her all these years later. Professor Rasmusson might work in a lab all day, but he was still a spy.

"What do you remember about them?"

"Oh." He paused as though he needed a moment to ponder. "I did not interact with them often—they were mostly in the field and infrequently in Sweden, but they had a reputation for being two of the top agents... not just in the US Division, but out of *all* the Divisions. From my encounters with them, that reputation was well-deserved."

Katrina knew the question she really wanted to ask—if he had any reason to believe her parents were Doubles—but she knew she wouldn't get anywhere being that direct.

"By my estimate, we are fast approaching the halfway point, my dear. If there is anything else you would like to ask..."

That was all the nudge she needed.

"Did you find them... complicated? My parents?"

"Complicated? Well, no more than any other spies, I would imagine. Why? Did they seem complicated to you?"

She noticed that he'd answered a question with a question, but she answered anyway. "I only knew them as Mom and Dad. They were gone before I could see them with adult eyes."

"Very true," he agreed. "I myself did not understand my parents until I was in my twenties, and even then... it all starts to fade a bit with time."

"Did you trust them?"

"As much as I would any other agent, which is to say I am a believer in 'Trust but verify.' I did not find them untrustworthy, if that is what you're asking."

The lights started to flicker.

"By my guess, we have less than a minute, Katrina."

Knowing his job and going with her gut, she rushed out her final question. "Did you ever make anything for them?"

A small beat passed before Professor Rasmusson answered. "For them? No, my dear. I did not."

Katrina couldn't see his expression, but something in the way he said it made her think he was lying or at least was not being entirely truthful. She had no time to ask anything further, though, as the lights were fully up and she could hear equipment buzzing away. She pulled back from Professor Rasmusson and started speaking without concern for who else might hear.

"Well, thank you for your time, Professor Rasmusson." She got up to leave his office.

He winked as he slid the device back into the cabinet.

"Anytime, my dear, anytime. If you are still here in a few weeks, come on by the lab. I have an accent-adapting prototype that I would love for you to try out. It uses soundwaves to stimulate the vocal cords and the mouth to make a person sound just like a native speaker wherever they go. Perfect for maintaining a cover. Bring Agent Figueroa as well."

"Intriguing," she murmured. "Yes, if we're still here, we will come by."

WALKING AIMLESSLY THROUGH the halls of headquarters, Katrina considered her clandestine conversation with Professor Rasmusson. He was clearly being evasive with his answers, especially on the question of whether he'd made anything for them. She had a feeling he was leaning hard on the definition of "made" in his denial. She then thought about what he'd said about understanding parents: *"And even then, it all starts to fade a bit with time."*

That was certainly true. Everything leading up to the explosion, she could recall fairly well. *Everything after...*

Katrina remembered waking up and someone telling her that her parents were gone.

"Gone? Gone where? Another business trip? We were just in Berlin."

"No, not a trip. Gone for good. They're dead, Katrina."

Anything beyond that was mostly a haze. A perfunctory funeral was held, with no one she actually knew. Katrina had never met any grandparents or aunts or uncles, so she assumed she had none. She had a decent enough foster father, Luther. He kept her fed and housed and took her to school. They had regular outings to the gym, and she knew that every Friday night would be "puzzle night," when they worked on everything from jigsaws to brain teasers, but he was no parent, not really—not at all when compared with her own. In fact, the moment she turned eighteen, Luther pulled a Jens on her and completely disappeared. Katrina supposed that after the state money was cut off, he was no longer interested in the job. After that point, she was on her own. And that was fine—good, really, because it taught her independence. And if she had to choose between independence and being dependent upon others for help, she would choose independence every time. Besides, she wasn't alone. She had friends like Hector and Izzie. She had probably made a new, well, *something* with Magnus. So she had them, her job, and the memory of her parents. And that, she supposed, was enough.

Lost in past remembrances, and having covered all of the Division's headquarters she had clearance to view, she was facing Magnus's office before she knew it.

Chapter 30

In a surprisingly short time, Lena and Izzie were back. Katrina hoped that was a good sign. She mentally shifted back from thinking about her parents and Professor Rasmusson and what he had to say about her parents. Everything was about compartmentalization. Magnus was seated behind his desk. Per usual, the blinds were closed.

"What did you find?" he asked.

"Not Westlund, that's for sure," Lena said as she sat down in the chair closest to him. "I got into the building and was able to speak to his secretary. She gave me the runaround, and it was clear as day that she was lying to me about his whereabouts. Izzie managed to get over to his office while I distracted the front desk staff."

Izzie picked up where Lena left off. "I went over to his lab. Super easy to pick the lock. Given what he's working on, you would think it would have been more difficult. Anyway, there were no signs of his presence. Nothing in the trash, no coffee left in a cup, nothing. Now, maybe he's just super fastidious, but I don't think so."

Lena agreed. "I think he's pulled a runner. Whether that means he is hiding out somewhere in Stockholm, elsewhere in the country, or abroad, I do not know."

Magnus agreed. "Good work, you two. Not the outcome we wanted, obviously, but not entirely unexpected." He started pacing. "Okay, let's attack this on multiple fronts. Lena, put some Level

Threes on watch to see if he shows his face again. I doubt it, but it is possible that he's forgotten something and makes the mistake of going back to retrieve it. From Agent Foster's recon, we now know he uses disguises, so have them stay on alert. Jens?"

Jens stood up quickly and smoothed his pants.

"Use your airport security contacts to alert you if he shows up at any of the airports, but especially the ones with international flights. If he gets out of the country, it will be significantly more difficult to grab him."

Jens stared at Magnus a touch too long before giving a curt nod and leaving.

Katrina took in this new nugget of information about the mysterious Jens. *Okay, first the SÄPO contacts, and now he apparently knows decision makers for the Swedish equivalent of the TSA as well?* Maybe his "spy for the spies" act was just a cover. For all Katrina knew, "Jens" might not even be his real name. For all she knew, the guy could be the Swedish director parading around as a silent, sartorially obsessed chauffeur. She'd never actually met the Swedish director. *Hmm...*

Magnus managed to stop pacing. "So now, we watch and wait. Westlund will either slip up or start to make some moves, and we will need to have everything in place for when he does."

BACK AT THE HOTEL, Katrina went into her room and did the usual security check. Even though she knew the break-in had been part of Lena's scheme with Ibrahim, Katrina had begun a habit of checking for any disturbances in the room, and frankly, given her profession, she should've been doing that anyway. *All clear.* She tossed her coat over the back of a nearby chair. As it landed upside down, a folded piece of paper slid out of the lower left pocket onto the floor.

She squinted down at the paper. She knew her pockets had been empty, save for the "pocket litter" in her breast pocket that was consistent with the detritus a researcher abroad might have. This was something different. Katrina grabbed two wooden coffee stirrers and knelt down in front of the note. It appeared to be regular paper, but she wasn't about to take any chances. It could've been coated in toxic chemicals, and perhaps a fingerprint or two might be found on it, although she highly doubted that. Using the sticks, she expertly unfolded the paper. Inside was a bold typed note:

I know who you are. And I know what you are doing. Give up now, or end up like the informant.

A chill ran down Katrina's spine. She made a concerted effort to control her breathing as the implications of this note hit her all at once. *How could this have happened without my noticing?*

Katrina reviewed her day and recalled the moment when someone knocked into her on the subway platform on her way to headquarters from St. Gustav. It wasn't just a rude bump—it was a means of transferring information onto her person without her knowledge, a brush pass. *Classic move.*

At that moment, Izzie came through the door but stopped when she saw Katrina kneeling over the piece of paper.

"Whatcha got there? A love note? From Magnus? Not sure why you're praying over it, though." Izzie stopped joking once she saw Katrina's face.

Katrina smiled grimly. "If this is a love note, then things are worse than I feared. Someone brush-passed me today and left me this present."

Izzie peered over her shoulder and read the note. She gave a low whistle. "Well, that's not good."

"No kidding." She jerked her head in the direction of the kitchenette. "Can you grab me a baggie?"

Katrina kept up her spy tactics, but it was based more on muscle memory than presence of mind. She wasn't above admitting she was scared. The note hit too close to home, literally *and* figuratively. Mechanically holding the coffee stirrers like chopsticks, Katrina gingerly put the note into a plastic bag and sealed it. While it looked like a regular piece of paper, she hoped like hell that it had no tracker or embedded listening device in it, as that paper had followed her into Division headquarters and been with her throughout her interactions. She would have Professor Rasmusson examine it immediately.

Carefully carrying the bag, Katrina went into the bathroom and placed it on the counter next to the sink. She turned on the faucet full blast. Not eco-friendly, the method was still effective for masking sounds. She came back out to see Izzie peering out the window before closing the blinds.

"You think it's a legit threat?" Izzie asked.

"It must be. Someone went to considerable effort to make sure that I knew *they* knew about me. That's not a note that just 'accidentally' ends up on your person."

"Good point."

Izzie carefully took off her own lightweight jacket. She peered into the pockets and gave it a thorough inspection. "Nothing here."

"Well, at least you're still clean, then. Guess I better check on the others."

Katrina sent out a text to see if anyone else had received a message. All replied negatively.

"Great. I'm the lucky one." She then wondered if the note was another one of Lena's antics like the break-in. She sent out another group message.

Lena's reply came quickly: *Not my style. Sorry to disappoint, but if it had been me, the note would have self-destructed and put a hole in you.*

Katrina had to admit that that checked out. *So not Lena, then. But who would do this?* Whoever it was, she knew two things. One, her identity was definitely compromised, and two, she was in inescapable danger. Her situation was beyond the everyday occupational hazard of being a spy. She had become the target.

Chapter 31

Katrina watched Izzie carefully packing her weapons into a suitcase. Knowing that her cover was blown, Katrina had decided to send her to stay with Lena. *No point in outing two agents.* Part of her imagined the possibility of letting Izzie keep the room while she stayed with Magnus next door, but too many assumptions and too much risk were associated with that ridiculous train of thought. For starters, she couldn't guarantee he would even want her to stay.

Maybe he was like a male Greta Garbo, one of those solitary "I want to be alone" types. Maybe after all the daily pressures of spy middle management, he just wanted a space where he didn't have to be responsible to anyone or anything other than himself. Maybe he was one of those bro bachelor dudes. She'd never asked if he had ever been married or had a long-term girlfriend or anything like that. Not that there would have been a smooth, workplace-appropriate way to slide that into a conversation. And anyway, she wasn't thinking about those things—much. She was just thinking in terms of Izzie's safety. *Yes, Izzie's safety.* And it would just be spies bunking with spies. *No hanky-panky. Very practical-like.* And of course, she would never actually ask, not because she was a coward afraid of rejection—no, it would be because she didn't know if anyone else actually knew Magnus was staying next door. She wouldn't want to blow his cover, as it were.

Katrina didn't share any of those feelings as Izzie finished packing, nor as she walked with her over to Lena's. Getting there took a while because they had to do a series of doubling back and checks to make sure they weren't being followed. Katrina wasn't in a rush to see Lena's stupid face, but she was curious to see how the woman lived. She imagined a dingy, musty, furniture-free hovel where Lena squatted on the ground as she gnawed on a raw piece of meat. To Katrina's immense disappointment, it was nothing like that. She actually lived in a nice, if not fancy, part of town. Lena had a sparkling white, fully-appointed apartment that had a spare room with a clean fold-out bed ready and waiting for Izzie. Izzie had no problem making herself at home.

"Hey, new roomie," Izzie said cheerily as she tossed her bags onto the bed. "Don't mind me. I'm clean, won't sharpen my knives in bed, and I'm a quiet sleeper."

Katrina snorted at that last part. While she was somewhat surprised to find that she would miss having Izzie staying with her, she was definitely looking forward to being able to sleep without earplugs. She was almost convinced that subjecting Lena to Izzie's snoring would be a proper retribution for having Ibrahim spy on her—almost.

"Well, I better head over to headquarters and have Professor Rasmusson examine this thing." Katrina gestured to the note currently burning a hole—not literally, thankfully—in her pocket. "And I guess I better find out my fate. If I'm compromised, they'll send me home." *Or exile me to Siberia. Or a piranha-filled lake.* As had been drilled into her over and over, the Division was not a forgiving organization. She walked through the doorway.

"They won't send you home." Lena seemed quite confident.

"No?" Katrina turned back, feeling just the tiniest bit of hope.

"Oh no. You're in this now. You know too much, and you are in too deep, to the point that the enemy knows you. The only way you are getting out of this is either after the mission is accomplished... or in a body bag," Lena said with a smirk.

"Thanks, Lena. You always know how to say just the right thing." Katrina rolled her eyes and left.

Adopting a circuitous route and keeping a clear distance from passersby, she made her way to headquarters. She needed Professor Rasmusson's analysis, to have a clearer picture of what she might be dealing with.

EVEN LATE IN THE DAY, Professor Rasmusson had come back in once he heard the situation and what Katrina needed.

"Long time, no see, m'dear," Professor Rasmusson joked. "I got your message. Let's see that note."

Katrina retrieved the baggie with the note in it from her purse. It was clearly not Professor Rasmusson's first rodeo when it came to analyzing potentially toxic notes, because when she turned to hand it to him, he was wearing a full face mask and heavy rubber gloves. He gingerly took the bag and removed the paper with a pair of metal tongs. He placed it on a black metal device that appeared to be some sort of scanner connected to a monitor.

"We'll use this scanner for our preliminary check," he explained. "It won't detect everything, but it will pick up the most common threats. Based on the results, we'll see if a more thorough analysis is warranted."

He pressed a button, and a whirl of blue light scanned up and down the paper on both sides. The device beeped, and Professor Rasmusson peered at the monitor's readout.

"*Okej.* Negative for any embedded devices or major toxins. There are a couple indicators that are inconclusive, however, so I am going to do an additional check." He removed the note from the scanner and placed it in a laboratory glove box. With a dropper, he carefully administered a solution of three drops on the note.

"This will assist in a chemical analysis. Let's see if it will release any secrets about the person who brush-passed you." He set a timer. "The chemical reactions will take a bit of time. Don't go too far, though. I'll call you once it's complete."

"Thank you, Professor. I really appreciate you coming back in to do this for me."

"My job, my pleasure, m'dear."

Katrina left Professor Rasmusson's lab and headed over to Magnus's office, where he was inside, pacing away. She let herself inside and closed the door.

He looked up. "Never a calm moment, eh, Katrina?" he said, continuing to pace.

"Hey, I don't go looking for trouble. It's not like I don't have enough on my plate as is," she said as she sat down at the chair by his desk. She hoped that would encourage him to sit down as well. It did.

"I know, I know. It sure has a way of finding you, though. What's the latest?"

"The initial scan was clear. I'm just waiting on a more detailed analysis Professor Rasmusson wanted to do. So now, it's a waiting game, and I don't know what's better—a short wait or a long one."

"Well, you can count on him being thorough, so I wouldn't expect anything too quickly."

So they continued to sit, staring at Katrina's phone as though it would predict her future, while Katrina considered her fate.

"Assuming that thing wasn't embedded with some previously undetectable poison—in which case I'm already a goner—I don't have a lot of options, do I? At least none that are very good."

Magnus lifted his head from the phone to look at her. "As far as I can tell, you've got two options. Pack up and head home... if the

US Division will oblige to take you back—not likely—or we up your personal security and finish the mission."

Lena had said as much although without any mention of the additional security measures option.

"Well, both could have me ending up dead, but at least with the latter option, I can keep my dignity and maybe even solve this thing. Let's not forget that we still have Westlund on the loose."

"Yeah, that is not something I've forgotten, Kat," Magnus deadpanned.

"Speaking of personal security," Katrina said, "I noticed you're still at the hotel."

"Yes..." Magnus seemed puzzled by the topic change.

"Why are you still there even though you know it was Lena behind the break-in?"

He gestured toward the Fate Phone. "That's why. It might have been Lena's misguided actions that led to me being here, but given the way Blomqvist and Ibrahim died, it seemed prudent to me to stick around."

"You'll get no disagreement from me on that front. I was just curious." She gave a small shrug and smiled. "It wasn't a complaint. I like you being there."

He returned her smile. "And I like that you like I'm still there."

Katrina was saved from trying to come up with a response to that when the phone rang—Professor Rasmusson. She locked eyes with Magnus and took a deep breath before she answered.

"Hi, Professor. What's the story?"

She gave a sigh of relief. "That's great to hear. Yes, I'll be safe."

Magnus rolled his eyes and smiled at that last part.

"Okay, thanks again. Bye." She tucked her phone away.

"Well?" Magnus prodded.

"Good news. Just your ordinary LaserJet ink on twenty-pound paper. No toxins, trackers, or recording devices of any kind were embedded in the paper. At least, not with any kind of technology that Professor Rasmusson's lab could detect, and he seems to have everything."

Magnus looked like his heartbeat might've slowed down to the normal range. "I don't see a reason to inform our directors quite yet, then."

Katrina nodded. "This doesn't solve all my problems, but at least I know no one was listening in or tracking me. At minimum, my location within the hotel hasn't been compromised, nor has headquarters."

"Good, good," Magnus said. "Very good. So good. Super."

They smiled at each other.

"My thoughts as well, minus a 'good' or two." Katrina swiped her phone's screen. "I better let the rest of the team know," she said as she tapped out a message.

"Well, if you need me…" He rubbed the back of his neck.

"Yes?" She looked up, her attention on him.

"The risk still isn't gone. You need a plan. Plans. You have got to have one because there's still risk. And with Izzie gone, you are by yourself…"

Katrina squinted at him, trying to puzzle out the mishmash of ridiculousness coming from his mouth. "I'm not following…"

"Or rather, I mean, I'm saying remember that I am just next door. If you want to discuss strategies for moving forward…"

She raised an eyebrow.

"*Okej, okej*, I mean if you want *company*—totally professionally, mind you—well, just let me know, and I'll come over."

She grinned. "Thanks for saying what you mean. It's a deal."

Chapter 32

That night was quiet—a little *too* quiet. Katrina hadn't realized how accustomed she had become to Izzie's snoring and general ruckus. With the silence, she had only the noise in her head to keep her company, and those were klaxons she couldn't turn off or make sense of. She looked over at the clock, figuring the hour would be late, probably, like, around midnight at the earliest. It was nine o'clock.

Katrina tossed her head back against her pillow. She'd been in bed only thirty minutes, but the silence made it feel like forever. If she didn't come up with a solution, the night was going to be a long one. She needed a distraction, something to help pass the time. Katrina thought hard about what she needed, and she determined that she needed some... company.

Decision made, she got up and went to the door. Before she got there, she took a quick peek at herself—black tank top and heather-gray lounge pants, her hair in a high ponytail puff—nothing fancy, but decent enough. She looked down at her feet—cheap flip-flops. Hard to be stealthy flap-slappin' down a hallway in those things. She quickly switched them out for a pair of socks. She opened the door and peered carefully down the hallway left and right to see if anyone was out there. It was empty. She tiptoed over to the neighboring room and knocked. The door opened almost instantaneously as though he'd been waiting.

"*Hej.*" Magnus was barefoot, wearing a snug T-shirt and a pair of dark-gray sweatpants that was doing amazing things with his hindquarters as he turned to let her in.

"Come on in. Take a seat." Magnus gestured toward the couch.

Kat plopped down and looked at the TV screen. A cord attached it to his laptop.

"Not streaming, old man?" she joked.

"Not for this, I'm not."

"Oh?" That raised her curiosity. "What are we watching tonight?"

"Well, before you knocked, I was watching old footage near the area where Lindström's assassination took place."

"Ah," she replied. "So not a popcorn flick, then?"

"No, most decidedly not."

"What are you trying to find?"

He sighed heavily and dragged a hand over his face. "I don't even know anymore. A clue. Any clue." He sat back on the couch. "I guess I'm secretly hoping to see something unexpected, like someone who seems to be walking by or scouting the site or coordinating... Maybe Westlund in a bad wig with binoculars... I don't know. Just something."

Katrina could hear his frustration. The assassination was so long ago, but the impact was still ongoing.

"Well, let's give it a rewatch, then. Hit Play."

They watched the footage multiple times, focusing their attention on different quadrants of the screen, with Kat watching one quadrant and Magnus watching another, hoping that their concentrated viewing might yield something useful. It did not. Magnus shut the lid on the laptop.

"Alright, that's enough for tonight. My eyes are starting to cross from doing so much staring."

Katrina blearily rubbed her eyes in agreement. "Yeah, it was worth a try, though."

"Are you hungry?" Magnus patted his flat belly. "I somehow forgot all about it until now."

With everything that had happened that day, Katrina hadn't thought about eating either, but her stomach clearly had because it rumbled loudly right on cue. Magnus laughed.

"*Okej*, dinner, it is. We probably shouldn't go out together, though, on the off chance someone is watching the hotel. Is eating in alright?" He rubbed the back of his neck.

Katrina enjoyed detecting the tell that indicated his discomfort. Just to mess with him, she waited a beat before responding.

"Or we could stagger our exits and meet somewhere outside the city center," he suggested.

Kat shook her head. "No, apparently my stomach can't handle the amount of time needed to do that." It growled loudly again in agreement. "Eating in is good. And before you ask, anything is fine." She paused a moment. "Well, something meaty could be good."

He smiled. "I know just the thing." He went to his phone. "*Hej*, Jens. Can you pick me up something to eat?" He rattled off a list.

"Well, yes, that is a lot of food. No, I am not inviting you over. I'm just hungry. No... *håll käften*!" His eyes darted over to Katrina as his cheeks flushed.

"I am not discussing this further, Jens, so just shut up and bring over the food, dammit." Magnus hung up the phone.

"So Jens knew you were at the hotel, I take it?" Katrina asked as she held back a smile.

"Yes, although I am regretting that now... along with having him on the team," Magnus lamented like a beleaguered brother.

"You don't mean that," Katrina said.

"No, I don't mean it. We go way back."

"So what *is* his story, anyway?" she asked. "He seems so mysterious."

"His story?" Magnus looked away briefly. "Well, that's his story." He shrugged. "Not mine to tell, I'm afraid."

"Got it." Katrina appreciated what it meant to keep confidence and not spread someone's business around. That didn't mean she wasn't eager to find out, though. She would figure it out eventually and with Jens's permission.

"Okay, but at least confirm this for me. He's not actually the Swedish director under deep cover, is he?"

Magnus let out a loud bark of laughter in response. "Why in the world would you think that?" He looked at her like she'd lost her mind.

Determined to brazen it out, she listed reasons on her fingers. "One, he has all these high-level contacts. Two, he disappears all the time with no explanation. Three, he rarely speaks, perhaps in fear of being outed?" Well, maybe that last one wasn't her strongest piece of evidence. "And... I don't hear you denying anything, Mr. Answers-a-Question-with-a-Question."

He grinned. "Well then, let me be perfectly clear: Jens really is Jens. He is *not* the Swedish director, not remotely. The real director, as we've discussed, is a jerk. Now, anything beyond that is up to you to find out from him." He tapped the side of his nose. "I will give you one tip, however. Do not try to track him. You will *never* be able to do it."

Katrina made a face and started to defend herself. Magnus cut off her objection.

"It's not you specifically. *No one* can. If you try, he will detect it instantly, and he'll disappear right in front of your eyes, like that." He snapped his fingers.

"Hmm... Well, you've certainly given me something to consider..." she murmured.

A short while later, Jens knocked on the door. Kat assumed he knew what was up, especially since he was the one who installed cameras outside her room after the break-in. Still, she sidled across the room out of viewing range of the front door. Magnus used his foot as a wedge and cracked the door just wide enough for a bag and part of Jens's head to pop through. Magnus used one hand to grab the bag of food and employed his free hand to push Jens's head back from the doorway.

"Shove off... and, uh, thanks." He used his shoulder to push the door shut.

Katrina could hear Jens's laugh down the hallway. Magnus walked back over to the couch and dropped the bag of food on the coffee table.

"Let's eat. And if you like, we can even watch something that isn't CCTV."

Katrina left her hiding spot and headed to the kitchenette. She brought over plates and utensils then sat down next to Magnus. They found a movie to watch, *The Man from U.N.C.L.E.*, and started opening containers. Katrina's eyes lit up as she saw what he'd ordered.

"Traditional Swedish food. Nice!"

"Yeah, I figured you might like something traditional while you are here."

She piled some slices of *Kassler*, a type of salted pork, and meatballs onto her plate.

"You were definitely right," she agreed. "*Pytt i panna* too? I *am* a lucky girl." She loved that potato hash.

"I don't even eat these types of foods often. I'm more of a kebab and curry guy, but this is a nice change of pace."

They tucked into their dinner and chewed in companionable silence while the movie played.

"Thank you, Magnus. That was delicious." She closed her eyes in stuffed satisfaction and slumped against one arm over the side of the couch.

"Well, I'm just glad that you took me up on the offer after you blew me off last time to ransack my office."

She laughed and made to bat at his arm. He caught her wrist and tugged her back against the couch. And himself.

"Come here, Ms. Thief."

Her stomach muscles contracted as she resisted his pull. She raised herself back up. She needed to know where things really stood.

"Dude... enough with the mixed signals. I'm cool with pretending to be professional. I'm cool with going with whatever this is." She gestured between them. "But I'm not cool with the back-and-forth and trying to suss out which Magnus I will get on any given day."

Magnus grimaced. "I know, I know. I'm sorry. I am not handling this well. I'm not trying to mess with your head, and I'm not playing games. Please believe that. I just know I'm being watched by my director, and it's screwing me up. I've been wanting to be an exemplar, above and beyond reproach, but clearly I'm failing at that, and clearly it's not working, because I'm trying to pretend like we're just colleagues..." He took a deep breath. "When all I really want to do is hold you in my arms."

Katrina smiled. "Well. That can be arranged." She relented and leaned back against his chest. He smelled so good—nothing too cologney, just good. The rational spy side of her supposed their pheromones were simply compatible. The other side was chiding her and saying to just enjoy the moment. Katrina decided to listen to that side and snuggled in deeper.

"And just so we're fully clear, all of this is uncharted territory for me. I can assure you that I've never been this conflicted about another agent."

"That's good to know. I'm glad to hear you aren't harboring romantic thoughts about any other agents. I didn't want to have think about you and Lena like this." She raised their entwined arms in reference.

He shuddered and chuckled. She loved feeling the rumble against his chest while he laughed.

"That was *not* an image I needed at this particular moment."

"Apologies, sir."

Nicely bundled together, they watched the rest of the movie. How Napoleon Solo and Illya Kuryakin didn't realize Gaby was an agent was beyond her. It was so obvious. All the signs were there. *East German car mechanic, indeed.*

After the movie ended, Magnus made coffee for himself and tea for her, and they continued to talk about their mission. She also told him about her time with Professor Rasmusson and her attempt to learn more about her parents.

"That was a good idea. He was definitely around back then."

"Yeah, he knew about them and said they had a reputation for being some of the best agents. I asked him if he'd ever made anything for my parents. He said he didn't... but I'm not fully convinced. Something about how he denied it."

Magnus stroked his chin in consideration. "Hmm... well, there was no mention of him in the file we saw as an accomplice or anything else, but that doesn't mean much, given that we don't know who wrote the memo. It is entirely possible he could know more than he's letting on, though. Of course, even if he did, you would have a fine time trying to get it out of him."

"I don't know... I think I could probably give him a run for his money," she replied confidently.

"Oho! The hubris of youth," he joked.

"Hmm... I'll concede that you might be right... All that wisdom that comes with old age. You'd know all about that wouldn't you, old man?"

"Hush!" He pulled her back into his arms so they could snuggle again.

She worked her head back into a comfortable position on his chest. "Either way, he didn't give any indicators that he believed my parents were Doubles. Although to be fair, I didn't ask him outright. But enough about my parents. I've never asked you about yours. Are you close? Still with the Division? Retired...? If that's really a thing in our line of work. It must be nice to have parents you can get advice from about this type of life." Noticing that he wasn't saying anything, a terrible idea occurred to her. "I guess I made the assumption that you saw your parents. Are... Are they still alive?"

After a brief silence, he responded carefully. "I have not seen my parents in years."

"Dead?" Katrina asked, almost afraid to hear his answer.

"They're supposed to be."

She looked up at him in horror.

"No, I just mean to say that they're underground," he replied curtly.

Katrina could feel his pulse, and the tempo had shifted. He clearly didn't want to speak of them.

Whether he didn't want to or that was forbidden, it didn't really matter. Presumably, the fewer people who knew whatever his parents' circumstances were, the safer they—and possibly Magnus—would be, and Katrina understood. She wished her parents were just underground as well, but having been at the site of their deaths put that childish fantasy to rest.

"Ah," she finally replied. "Got it." She rose up to meet his eyes. "I wish I remembered you from when we first met. I wish I'd paid more attention to what was going on with our parents."

"Probably a good thing you didn't, seeing as I wasn't exactly the most congenial." He settled further into the couch. "I only remembered because I remembered you. You stood out, but what really stood out was your last week in Sweden. Your family and my family seemed like friends, but not at the end. They argued so much. Do you remember?"

"No. Everything from that time really is a blur."

"I think my parents felt bad after that... after what happened. Maybe it's because they didn't help them? I don't know. I just know that I heard them talking about it after I was supposed to be in bed. Mama was crying. I never heard them—or overhead them, as it were—mention it again."

"Oh." Katrina picked up her necklace and rubbed the pendant, almost like a talisman.

After a long moment, he picked up her hand and laced her fingers with his own. "Katrina?"

"Yes?" She couldn't quite describe it, but with her head on his chest, she could feel him thinking, debating.

"I don't want to talk about our parents anymore."

"Oh. Um, okay." She eyed him carefully. "That's fine. We can work on tomorrow's strategy—"

"I don't want to talk about that either. At least not right now."

She rose up off his chest a bit to regard him. As she took in that sleepy, hooded look, realization dawned. "Ohhh..." She cleared her throat. "If I'm catching what you're throwing, then it is entirely possible that I don't want to talk about those things either," she said with a smile.

He leaned down slightly, and she rose up, placing her hands on his chest to meet him halfway for a deep kiss. It was freaking fantastic. *And yet...*

"So we're kissing?" Katrina asked.

"Well, we *were*, yes."

"And we're working together."

"Well, we were working on something..." Magnus leaned in for another kiss.

She squinted in thought and didn't return the kiss.

"I can hear you thinking, Katrina..."

And because she was Katrina, she couldn't just turn off her brain to enjoy the moment. She opened it right back up.

"So just to confirm..."

"I meant what I said, Katrina. We're on the same page."

"If this got out, though—"

Magnus sighed and rose up, bringing Katrina with him. "Kat. I'm not going to say anything to my director, and given your situation, I can't imagine you would say anything to your director either. Right?"

"True..." she acknowledged. "But I bet anything that by now Jens has pieced together that it's me over here. Especially because I'm supposed to be right next door. No one orders that much food to eat alone."

Magnus seemed unconcerned with that prospect. "Probably." He shrugged as he leaned back over.

"And that doesn't bother you, Mr. Keep-it-to-ourselves-compartmentalization?"

"No," he said. "I know enough about Jens to ensure his silence forever."

Katrina opened her mouth to ask.

"And no, that was not an invitation for you to ask again," he said sternly.

She closed her mouth.

"We manage to compartmentalize everything else in our lives, right, Katrina? So let's just cordon off some space for this too."

His line of argument *was* convincing.

Magnus took the opportunity to kiss her again, but that didn't stop her from talking.

"So... we're going to do this? And just keep it in spy mode?"

He grinned. "Well, I don't precisely know what 'this' is, but whatever 'this' turns out to be is alright by me. Just let me know, okay? Agreed?"

"Agreed."

And with that accord in place, somewhere between that third kiss and her quasi-horizontal position on the couch, Katrina was pretty sure she'd lost her mind. Yet the absence of her mental faculties did not bother her in the least, as the results were so very, very good.

Chapter 33

Katrina was dragging the next morning, and not only due to the lack of sleep. The rational side of her had come roaring back, and she was weighed down again with the burdens of the mission and her life. Magnus's little line about compartmentalization was all well and good, but that didn't explain the next steps. Katrina knew she should just "live in the moment" and enjoy whatever was happening between them, but she just wasn't built that way. She was always thinking of the logistics. Of course, with a mastermind on the loose and with her cover blown, as well as the mystery of her parents, she had more immediate issues to consider. Her thoughts about Magnus were temporarily pushed back.

Also, no one at headquarters seemed to be nearly as weighed down as she was, which didn't help. To be fair, things weren't all sunshine and roses for the other agents. Katrina could acknowledge that much. But at least they could go about their spy day anonymously, without wondering who knew their real identity and what the consequences might be. They weren't on tenterhooks, waiting for the moment the director found out they were compromised. That was all on Katrina.

She didn't even have anyone to talk to. Magnus was holed up in an all-day meeting, and the other agents were trying to coordinate a new strategy for surveilling the suspicious Level Threes. So she sat alone at her desk and continued to work.

Somehow, the end of the day finally arrived. As she trudged down the hallway, ready to call it good for the day, she heard the laughter of Izzie, Lena, and Jens. They were making plans to go out. She guessed Izzie had the good sense not to bother suggesting that Katrina spend her off-hours with Lena because nobody asked Katrina if she wanted to join, which was fine with her. She was even more alright with being left out when she caught wind of what Izzie was saying.

"I can top that one. Let me tell you the story about the naked spaghetti-covered spy in training, Katrina Foster. Don't make that face, Jens. She gave me permission in exchange for skipping a knife lecture. *Anyway*, do you know what happens to your 'fast fashion' clothes when trying to escape a tunnel with a turbine generator at top speed after eating some 'probably okay' spaghetti? Thanks to Katrina, I do! It all started when..."

Izzie's voice trailed down the hallway as they made their exit.

"Great, one more humiliation," Katrina grumbled to herself as she headed out.

After leaving headquarters, Katrina made a point of alternating paths in case she was being tracked. She even walked with an NK bag so any onlookers would think she'd just been shopping inside. As Katrina walked, she noted how quickly the weather in Stockholm cooled as the summer began to fade. The day was still sunny, though, and she figured she would take a stroll through the park before heading into the hotel.

The park was well attended, with many people milling about. She found an empty bench, miraculously, sat down, and did some people watching—couples sharing a blanket, kids running amok with ice cream dripping down their faces. Watching the park-goers gave her the opportunity to keep an eye out while also doing some thinking. She ran down what she knew. Westlund was at the forefront of her mind. *Where is he? What is his next move?* She assumed Surikov was still with him, which doubled the danger.

Wrapped up in Surikov and Westlund were those blasted Level Threes who let them escape. She didn't know if that was just incompetence or they were planted in the Division, which would signal an even greater problem.

While she mulled that over, a woman sat down on the bench close beside her. Katrina turned and looked in surprise. Swedes weren't likely to just plop down and share a bench with a stranger. The woman's appearance was disturbing enough to jar Katrina from her thoughts about the mission.

What an odd duck. Her clothes were a weird blend of East Coast meets West Coast with a dash of flyover state: she had paired shiny leggings and a lightweight flannel shirt with the ends loosely knotted at her waist, accessorizing the outfit with spiked black booties and bamboo hoop earrings. Katrina stared, almost transfixed by her oddity. She wore thick, heavily penciled brows that made her look like the lovechild of Groucho Marx and a very angry jack-o'-lantern. Her face had a heavy layer of dark foundation spackled on, as though she were going for the quasibrownface common to many reality television stars. Her eyes were mostly obscured by sunglasses. She wore her hair in big barrel curls. Katrina didn't need to be a superspy to recognize it was a wig—a cheap one that looked of the synthetic Barbie variety, almost like she was trying to stand out and get noticed. Well, it worked.

"Hiya! Howzit goin'?"

Katrina pulled back in barely masked astonishment. The woman's nasal chirp was the worst attempt at an American accent ever. As such, it had the effect of instantly putting Katrina on guard. The odds of a woman randomly sitting down next to her and speaking to her in English—not to mention incredibly bad American English—was exceedingly small. Katrina decided to play along.

"Hello. I'm fine. How are you?"

The woman's mouth flopped open. "Ah-mairrr-ican!" she squealed. "So good to meet another countrywoman here around all these foreigners."

She seemed not to grasp that they—or Katrina, at least—were the outsiders or "foreigners" in Sweden.

"What'cha doin' here? What brings ya?"

The nasal questions irked Katrina, but she continued to roll with it. Clearly, the woman knew who she was or, at minimum, knew one of her identities. She'd introduced several covers and did not know which one was blown, so she kept her responses vague.

"Just hanging out at the park for the moment, enjoying the sunshine and *solitude*," she said pointedly. Suddenly, she didn't like the fact that her back was exposed to the rest of the park. The only positive thing was that they were in a public place. She looked around again before returning to the "American."

"What brings you here?"

"Oh, I'm just here for a good time," she said with an annoying tinkling laugh. "Heard they had great clubs here. Girls just wanna have fun, y'know?"

Katrina almost groaned at the outdated reference. *How old is she, exactly?* Under her makeup was tight skin that could have been of any age, natural or surgeon-enhanced. Kat reached down into her purse. The woman tensed.

Yup, not an innocent. A *regular* woman wouldn't think twice about seeing another woman reaching into her bag. Katrina pulled out what appeared to be a regular tube of lip gloss, and the woman visibly relaxed. She shouldn't have, though, as the reality was that while the tube was indeed filled with a lovely shade of coral gloss, the other end contained a stunning aerosol spray. Nonlethal, for sure, but it would create a cloud around the woman that would temporarily immobilize her so that Kat could get away. Now that Katrina knew what was up, her only goals were to keep surveilling and to keep the woman talking in order to get more clues as to what this joker's real purpose was.

"Indeed, they do have good clubs here," Katrina replied. "Where are you visiting from?"

"Oh, I'm from Springfield," she said. Given the number of Springfields in the US, that didn't exactly narrow things down.

"That's nice. Have you seen and done everything you wanted?"

"Almost. There are a few more things on my to-do list. I like to finish things from ay to sey."

Ah. That was the giveaway, as if Katrina needed one. No legitimate American would pronounce *Z* as "sey." They would say "zee." The "American" knew enough to know she couldn't say *zäta* and tried to shorten it to "sey" instead. Katrina smiled blandly at the imposter.

"Well, enough about me." The woman giggled. "How long have you been here?"

"Oh, with the crazy long hours of daylight, if feels almost like forever." Katrina tried to momentarily disarm her. "So what's your name?"

"Um... uh. It's Sydney. Oh yes, Sydney Bristow!" she finished brightly. Then she looked away.

A definite tell. When the woman turned, Katrina was able to see her face better in profile. She could see her eyes as well. They seemed scared... but they also looked familiar. With that closer inspection, and trying to peer through the striations of concealer and foundation, Katrina thought she'd seen the shape of her nose and mouth somewhere as well.

Who are *you?* She flipped through her mental catalogue. She knew, she absolutely *knew* she had seen her at some point during her time in Sweden.

The woman's eyes briefly flicked over Kat's shoulder and almost looked relieved at what she saw. Katrina flipped the lip gloss over to the spray side.

"Well, gotta go. Buh-byeee!"

The woman shot off like a rocket. At the same time, Katrina sensed a slip of paper sliding down the back of her shirt. And there it was, the purpose behind this suspicious encounter. Katrina turned back. Whoever had delivered the message was lost in the crowd. Using a napkin in her purse to protect her hands, she awkwardly reached back behind herself to retrieve the paper. It was another typewritten note. While she'd been terrified at the first note, this one just made her angry.

What is this? High school?

Chapter 34

S *can: Negative.*
    "Another note?" Izzie peered over Katrina's shoulder as she put away a mini scanner Professor Rasmusson had loaned her and inspected the paper. "What is up with all the frickin' notes? It's the twenty-first century—send a threat by text for crying out loud," Izzie grumbled.

"You better be glad they didn't, Izzie, because that would mean that they had my cell number... and probably yours too," Katrina said.

"Fair point. What's it say?"

I have the info you are looking for. Meet me at the entrance of the Solna police station. 16:45. I'll be wearing blue. Code word: Havrefras. Come alone!

Katrina had taken nearly an hour to get to headquarters. She knew enough not to continue back to the hotel, so she made her usually short journey to NK take much longer, until she convinced herself no one was following. She sent the team a message about the latest note, but when she got there, Izzie was the only one waiting. She told Izzie all about the bizarre exchange she'd had with the woman on the bench.

"There was something about her though. Man, I can't seem to shake that woman's face."

"Well, that makes sense to me. Based on your description, she sounds hideous."

Katrina rolled her eyes. "No, I mean I know I've seen her some-where. I just can't place it."

"Where does that leave you now?"

"Well, here's what we know—my cover may be blown, but we still don't know which one. If I had to guess, I'd say it was the jour-nalist one since I was the most public with that one. They know my general neighborhood if they knew my subway stop for the first note, and they kept eyes on the park on the off chance that I would be there."

"You think they know your hotel?" Izzie asked.

"Probably. But they must not know which floor or room, or they would've been in there by now. I don't know what their resources are, but I don't think it's a professional operation. If they were, her cos-tume and accent would be more refined. So probably not another spy agency."

"Unless that was a ploy to take you off your game."

"It could be. Everything is a question at this point. The first note was a threat. This second one promises information, allegedly. The first note had to be from Westlund or at least under his direction."

"Why do you think that?"

"One, this has to be related to this case, and Westlund is our key suspect. I don't know what he knows as far as my cover, but he must've connected me to the 'surprise' inspection at his lab and to my role as a reporter at Almadalen. I can't come up with any other explanation for why Surikov was there to assassinate not a politician but an informant—and only once that informant was speaking with me. He may not know everything, but he knows enough to see me as a threat, and he tried to scare me off."

"That does seem plausible. What about the second one, then?"

"That's what I'm puzzling over. It could be a misdirection at-tempt on his part. Or it could be that someone he's worked with is trying to sell him out. Maybe they think I can offer them some money or immunity or something. Or maybe things went sour, and they just plain want revenge."

"That also makes sense." Izzie eyed the note again. "So what's the next move?"

"Well, we're gonna go there. I'll meet with whoever this is, and you'll be my backup."

"Sounds good... minus the 'we' part. I can't join."

"Why not?"

"I wish I could go with you to keep a lookout, but I've been summoned to go on a mini mission with Jens soon."

Katrina gave her the side-eye.

"It's true," Izzie insisted. "Before he headed into the Swedish director's office, Magnus said he wanted us to keep an eye on those questionable Level Three agents at St. Gustav. He said that if they're moles, and moles with all sorts of access to the Division, then this is bigger than just one mission. Jens is supposed to drive and observe unseen, and I'm there for my particular skill set if muscle is needed. I don't like you going alone though. You should ask—"

"Don't say it," Katrina warned.

"Lena. I know. I know. But you need backup of some kind."

Given their shared history, Katrina wasn't convinced that she'd be much safer with Lena watching her back, but Izzie had a point.

"Alright, I'll grit my teeth and gird my loins." Katrina checked her watch. "But first, I've got time before I need to leave. And before your 'mini mission' with *Jens*, you have more than enough time to answer this question. What in the sweet yet unholy hell is going on with you two? And don't you dare lie or tell me it's none of my business. Spill it."

"What's going on? Nuuuthing..."

"Liar! I caught you two in a corridor once."

Izzie turned red. "Okay, okay. Nothing much. He's nice. We like spending time together."

"Oh, 'spending time together,' eh? Is that a euphemism of some kind?" Kat asked with a raised eyebrow.

"No! Jeez, Kat," Izzie said with a laugh. "Well, maybe a little. He's cool, though. He's not threatened by my love of weaponry and doesn't mind when I talk—he even encourages it."

"Why didn't you tell me?"

"I don't know! Probably for the same reason you haven't really said anything to me about Magnus. It's weird! It's like this thing that wasn't supposed to happen... but did."

"I get it. I totally get it," Katrina said. "The reason I didn't say anything about Magnus was that I figured the fewer people who knew, the better. To be honest, I kind of liked just keeping it to myself, but I shouldn't have closed you off."

"It's cool. Besides, the less I know, the less I have to testify about when Magnus eventually gets called in for 'fraternizing' with a subordinate."

"Oh my God. That's totally what's happening, isn't it? Or at least what it looks like." Katrina thought about it. "Wow, check me out. Katrina Foster—rule-breaking hussy romancing her way to the top!" She giggled at the sheer ridiculousness of it.

"Yep, and good for you!"

They squealed in mutual happiness and gave each other a hug, pleased to not have that barrier between them anymore. With the mission and Izzie staying at Lena's, they hadn't spent much time together. Katrina felt like she had her best friend back.

Katrina pulled away and looked at Izzie closely. "Okay, but tell me this. What's his story? Jens? There's no way he's just a well-dressed sorta-spy chauffeur who happens to have all these high-level contacts."

Izzie shrugged. "I don't know."

Katrina eyed her skeptically.

"Honest! Did you not hear the part where I said he lets me do most of the talking? Although now that you mention it, maybe that was by design..."

"Dang. He's just so mysterious."

"I like that, though. It's like a challenge when I do get any information from him."

"Freak," Katrina said with a smile.

"You know it."

Izzie checked the time. "Ugh, I gotta go... I still don't like this Solna meeting, friend. Just a gut feeling. Don't try to be solo hero. Promise me you'll talk to Lena first, 'kay?"

"I will. I don't want to, but I will."

"Alright... well if things go left, let me know, and moles or no moles, I'll drop the mission and meet you."

"Deal."

Katrina had barely left Izzie when she went around the corner and nearly ran headfirst into Lena.

"I was just searching for you," they both said at the same time. Then they looked at each other in mutual confusion as both knew the likelihood of either one wanting to encounter the other was below-the-ground low.

"Hey, I need you to serve as a backup," Lena said without preamble. She kept holstering and reholstering her gun in a nervous tic while she spoke, which was kind of freaking Katrina out. "I just got a tip that someone at a bank in Solnavägen is trying to take out a ton of money. Like the kind you'd take if you were going to flee. The bank is trying to delay him but can only do so for so long."

"And it's Westlund?"

"Well, that's the thing. It's not under his name, but I had the money tracers do an analysis, and their algorithm says there's a fifty-percent probability that it could be him."

"So... like a coin toss?"

"Probability *plus* experience tells me we need to get over there now and case the place and catch him." She eyed Katrina with her frosty squint. "What, do you have a better lead?"

"Actually, yes." Katrina enjoyed being able to say that. "I just got a tip as well. I'm supposed to meet someone shortly who can give us the information we need to catch Westlund." She might've been overstating that, given she didn't know who was behind the note or if they really had the information.

"Where'd the tip come from?"

"Well, an anonymous note. Where'd yours come from?"

"A lot more reliable source than that. Look, are you coming or not?"

Katrina had a choice. On the one hand, she had a note that gave a clear directive with a time and place, albeit from an anonymous and possibly unreliable source. On the other, a seasoned agent had a potential lead. Allegedly. Katrina considered the timing and couldn't put it past Lena that this could be another diversion, just like when she wasted time pretending to help Katrina search for Ibrahim. That level of betrayal didn't dissipate overnight. In Katrina's case, a note in the hand was worth more than two potential betrayals from Lena.

"I'm going to pursue my lead. I have a time, at least, and if they're a no-show—"

"So you won't be my backup? I guess my years of experience and successfully using informants to obtain evidence doesn't count for anything."

"I didn't say that. I just—"

"Whatever. Forget I asked." Lena quickly turned away and stormed off.

"I'm headed to the Solna police station, which is nearby," Katrina yelled toward Lena's back. "I'll meet you at the bank if the lead is a bust. Send a text!"

Katrina wasn't sure Lena had even heard her.

Under her usual layer of irritation at Lena, Katrina felt a small but nagging wave of guilt roil through her. *Lena actually asked me for help. Should I have gone with her?* Lena needing help—and from Katrina, of all people—was unprecedented. She reminded herself that Lena didn't want her specifically—Katrina was simply the only available person on the team. She also reminded herself that Lena was a big girl. She was a veteran who was more than capable of handling herself. Undoubtedly, Lena would have no problem taking down Westlund on her own, if that really was him at the bank. With that thought settling her conscience, she focused on her own mission.

Chapter 35

Katrina reached the police station with just seconds to spare. Having learned from her past mistakes, she sent out another message to Magnus, saying where she was going. Lena already knew, and she figured Izzie would tell Jens.

She looked around for someone wearing blue and realized that out of the rainbow of options, blue was not particularly rare for clothing. Everyone seemed to be dressed in blue, fitting the letter writer's description. *Which one can it be?* She couldn't exactly go around saying the code word *"havrefras"* to every person wearing blue. *Time to narrow things down.* Katrina eliminated any couples, as the point was to meet alone. Kids were ruled out, as well as a harried-looking dad trying to wrangle a set of twin toddlers and a dog. That left one person, a man in what seemed to be his early twenties in a newish blue shirt, a skinny white guy of medium build with dishwater-blond hair, pretty nondescript. He kept furtively looking down at his phone then around. Obviously, whatever he might be, a professional he was not. She approached him from the side.

"*Havrefras?*" she asked.

He peered at her nervously. "Oh, it's you."

When he spoke, she found a notable exception to his nondescript appearance—his teeth. They were brown and in varying states of decay. They looked like a set of overcooked crinkle-cut French fries. She was transfixed. *Focus on the task at hand, Katrina.*

"So... do you have something for me?"

His eyes darted toward her. "Do you know what *havrefras* is?"

"A cereal." *What is going on?* The note hadn't said anything about additional codes.

"Yeah, the cereal. Appears substantial from the outside, but it's actually hollow within."

"Okay..." Katrina had had her fill of weirdo interactions for the day.

"Full of fiber though, and low in sugar. So that's something," he mumbled before going back to his phone.

"I don't follow." As she said it though, Katrina had a sinking feeling in her stomach.

He looked up again and gave a grimy smile. "Sorry, lady, but there's nothing to follow. I was just hired to be the distraction. Cheers."

He saluted before racing away and hopping into a waiting car, which sped off. She saw no point in trying to follow. Katrina swore. *What was I supposed to be distracted from, though?* She would deal with that later. She took out her phone and texted Lena: *Dead end. On my way to the bank in three minutes.*

Lena sent only a one-word response: *Roof.*

The distraction. Katrina took off running.

AS KATRINA RAN TOWARD the bank, she kept watching the skyline. *Roof.* Lena was terse, but not that terse. She had to be in danger. Katrina made it to the bank. No police and no security teams were in action. Indeed, through the windows, the bank seemed to be having a normal day with irritated customers waiting for their numbers to be called before the bank closed. She headed around the building and searched for a fire escape. She saw the closest escape ladder and ran toward it.

As she got closer, she could hear pained moaning. *Lena*. Katrina looked up and saw Lena's back on the rooftop of the bank. She was kneeling on the ground. Above her stood a masked man dressed in black, a knife at her neck.

"Lena!"

At the sound of Katrina's scream, Lena turned just as the man slashed her neck. She went down. Katrina quickly scaled the ladder. As she flung her legs over the ledge to get on the roof, the man ran to the other side of the building, over the ledge, and down the opposite fire escape. Faced with a choice, Katrina went for Lena. Amazingly, she was still alive and struggling to get a thick rubber band around her thigh. She must have been slashed a second time as Katrina went up the ladder. The blood was flowing freely. Her neck was bleeding, too, but it didn't look as bad.

"Of *course* you would go after me instead of the man with the knife," Lena groaned as she flopped over in exhaustion.

Katrina knelt by her side and started tearing the bottom of her shirt to make a bandage. "You can complain later, Lena. Let's just get you..." She examined Lena's leg more closely. Band or no band, a pool of blood was already coming from her thigh, and the unnatural shade of gray on Lena's face did not bode well.

"Don't bother," Lena rasped. "It's too late. Femoral artery. Besides, I don't want to be a cripple."

"Don't say that. I'm going to get you out of here."

"Still with the heroics?" Lena gave a weak smile, always true to form.

"Oh, Lena." Katrina could only sigh, unsure how much time they had. "What happened?"

"Westlund ran out the bank as soon as he saw me. I followed and met the other guy with the knife. Next thing I know, you're screaming."

"Sorry."

"No, that was good. Turning my head kept his knife away from my jugular. Bought me some time." Lena grunted as she tried to adjust the band. Katrina reached out and squeezed the band with both of her hands, hoping the additional pressure would help the tourniquet give Lena more time. Lena didn't object to the assistance.

"Why didn't you contact me once you saw Westlund run?"

"I knew there wasn't enough time."

Katrina's bloodied hands were struggling to hold down the band.

"Plus, in case you didn't notice, almost everyone around me seems to end up dead."

"I didn't think you'd care if I died," Katrina noted.

Lena gave a half snort. "I wanted you gone, not because I hate you—although you *are* a pain—but because I wanted you and Izzie to be *safe*." She grimaced in pain before continuing. "They sent you here when they never should have."

"What do you mean?"

Lena gave her a look that conveyed her disbelief at Katrina's naivete. "I could never figure out why they chose you, of all people, to come here. Never made any sense."

"Well, I *do* speak Swedish, and I'm skilled at decoding..." She trailed off weakly.

"What, you think you're the only American agent who speaks Swedish? The only agent out of *all* the Divisions who can solve a puzzle?" Even in her current condition, Lena was still able to cut straight to Katrina's insecurities. "Wise up. Someone sent you here with an agenda. Either for what you know or what they think you know or to get you out of the way. Someone's using you for their own purposes."

Katrina didn't know what to say to that.

"Maybe it has something to do with those dead parents of yours. I don't know," Lena said with her usual tact. "What I do know is that from the very start, none of this smelled right. I thought we were being set up to fail."

At the end of things—and indeed, Lena was facing the end of things—Katrina could see her in a different light.

"I'm sorry, Lena. I'm so, so sorry. I should have gone with you. I had to choose between going after a lead and following you... and I chose wrongly. I figured you'd make it out okay, since, well... you're Lena." Katrina had to get it out while she still had time.

Lena coughed and whispered, "That's probably the most comforting thing you could ever say to send me on my way, Cowgirl." She started gasping and seized.

What seemed like hours was really only seconds. Her eyes went glassy. She was gone.

Katrina didn't have much time to think about what to do next. She felt a bullet graze past her arm.

"What the hell?"

She looked over her shoulder. The masked man was back. He was climbing back over the ledge as he fired. Apparently, he wanted to make sure he finished the job. Katrina rolled away from Lena and squatted behind a generator. She grabbed her gun. Oddly, the man kept approaching then turning, approaching then jerking and turning away again, like he couldn't make up his mind what to do next. Katrina wasn't about to wait around to get shot while he figured out what he wanted to do. Her hands still slick with Lena's blood, she wiped them on her shirt and pressed them against the dirty rooftop to use the grit as traction. It wasn't enough, but at least she had enough grip to not fear that the gun would slip, making her shoot herself.

He shot in her direction again, coming closer before turning away once more. Seconds mattered. The odds of her getting off a clean shot were low, but she had to try in the hopes she could get a bullet into his shooting arm to disarm but not kill him. That was the sort of thing Izzie could probably do with her eyes closed. Katrina had to strike the right balance: just enough to bring him down but not enough to kill him. She aimed, breathed in, and exhaled as she pulled the trigger.

His body jerked with the impact, yet he didn't go down. He turned and ran the opposite direction in earnest that time. *Guess he made his mind up.* He flipped his legs over the edge of the roof and started down the fire escape. Katrina raced over but couldn't catch him in time. She looked over the ledge just in time to see the shooter drop the rest of the way. Two men caught him and helped him into a car before speeding off. *Dammit.*

As Katrina pulled back from the ledge, something caught her eye: a scrap of black fabric clinging to an exposed screw. It appeared to be a lightweight cotton. It must have torn from the man's sleeve when he rushed down the ladder. She went back over to her long-discarded purse and searched inside until she pulled out a half-empty candy bag. She dumped the rest of the gummy raspberries and shook the remaining sugar crystals out. It wasn't exactly a sterile zip-top baggie, but it would have to do. She hoped it would give Professor Rasmusson enough to work with. Then Lena's death wouldn't be in vain.

She looked back at Lena, cold and unmoving, then took out her phone and dialed.

"Izzie?" Her voice was thick with emotions she hadn't yet had the chance to work through. "You've got to meet me in Solna *now*. Lena's dead."

Chapter 36

Lena didn't have any family. Rather, her file listed that she had an estranged brother, who, upon learning of her death overseas, wasn't the least bit interested in receiving her body. He said he always knew her work for a private security firm would end this way. He was, however, curious to find out whether she had a life insurance policy with the company. When told she did not, he quickly ended the call.

No one on Lena's team, however, wanted that to be the end of her story, so they gave her a tribute at Division headquarters. That wasn't traditional, but it was honest. Beyond her team, several agents said kind words about her skills as an agent and her tenacity. It was the type of gathering where someone saying, "Who knew that tough old bird could actually die?" was a sign of respect.

Katrina was there but apart, and she noticed eyes judging her. She spotted Izzie and went up to her. They hadn't spoken since the day of Lena's death as they sat with her body on the rooftop, waiting for the extraction team.

Izzie was inconsolable. Katrina had tried to explain what had happened, the decision she'd been forced to make, but it was no use.

"I mean, I'm not going to tell you it's your fault." Izzie paused. "But it *is* your fault. The *one time* Lena asks for your help, and you can't be there? *You're* supposed to be the one in charge of making all the right decisions." She started to move away before turning back to face Katrina. "I warned you. I told you something wasn't right, but you didn't listen. You knew better. Why did you think that it would be so simple, that the writer of some mysterious note would just lead you to all the answers? It doesn't work that way." She looked away. "It never does."

Katrina completely agreed with her. "Where are you going?"

"Back to Lena's apartment to clean it out. It's not like she needs it anymore."

If Katrina was seeking absolution or even a shoulder to lean on, she wasn't going to find it with Izzie.

Izzie sighed. "You're still my friend, Katrina. We'll be okay." She turned away. "Just not right now."

"Izzie—" Katrina started.

Magnus was suddenly at her side. "Let her go for now, Kat. She's not ready."

They didn't look at each other. Ever since Lena's death, Katrina had only interacted with Magnus in a professional capacity. She got dropped. She shouldn't have expected any other outcome. Thank goodness she hadn't made herself vulnerable. Thank goodness she hadn't let herself care.

"And you?" she asked. "Are you ready to speak to me?"

"That's what I'm doing right now."

"You know what I mean. For real, though, how are you holding up?"

"Well, I have lost a lot of colleagues, but I'll be honest. This hits hard. Lena was one of the first agents that worked with me when I became a Level Four. She only called me 'rookie' for the first year, but she showed me all the ropes..." He looked like he had more to say, but at the same time, both of their phones buzzed.

"My director," they said in unison.

"I've got to go. Well, I guess I'll see you at the next meeting," Magnus said before leaving.

Katrina swiped the screen on her phone. Word had clearly gotten out. She was scheduled to meet with her director at the top of the hour. The message specifically directed Katrina to take the call outside of Division headquarters. That couldn't mean anything good. She started back toward the hotel to await her fate, but she didn't get far.

Before she could leave the building, Professor Rasmusson contacted her. "Results are ready."

KATRINA HAD EARLIER given Professor Rasmusson the scrap of fabric for analysis. She hoped he'd found something useful, something that could help her find Lena's killer. As she entered the lab, she noticed all the lab techs suddenly found anything better to do than making eye contact with her. Lena might not have been well liked, but she was respected, and when it came down to it, she was one of them. The director had been right about that.

In contrast, if Katrina had ever had the impression that she was neither liked *nor* respected, that suspicion was conclusively confirmed in that moment. She felt completely alone and could only hope that Rasmusson wouldn't give her the cold shoulder as well. She crossed the lab and knocked on his door.

"Professor Rasmusson?"

"Come in, come in, my dear." He waved her in with one hand while hastily dabbing his eyes with the other. "Such sorry news. Lena. She wasn't terribly fond of me or my 'toys,' as she liked to call them, but she was an excellent spy, and I will mourn her loss as I do them all."

"I imagine that's a lot of losses." She stared down at her hands.

"Indeed." He cleared his throat. "Thank you for getting it to me promptly. Time was of the essence as any residues can degrade quickly."

He pulled up some images on his computer. As he reviewed the data, Kat could almost see him mentally shift from mourning Lena's death to getting back to the business at hand.

"The main thing was to ignore the data distraction that is the gunpowder residue. It isn't anything spectacular and tells us nothing that we do not already suspect, namely, that this is a scrap of shirt, probably from the sleeve of the person who killed Lena and shot at you. But take a look at this." He gestured toward a computer screen where several spiky graphs were displayed. "Once the chemicals from the residue are isolated, we can start eliminating other unuseful chemical factors. See this spike here? That indicates the presence of sodium dodecylbenzenesulfonate…"

Katrina's eyebrows rose.

"Which is simply a surfactant used in laundry detergent. You won't be able to track anyone with that," he said wryly.

Her brows lowered again.

"But here is something intriguing." The professor gave a slight bounce in his chair as he pointed at the screen. "This spike shows extremely high levels of temazepam, a hypnotic. At these levels, it would irreparably harm someone if this was being extruded through the sweat glands. However, in a laboratory setting…"

Katrina's eyes closed as she made the connection. Unless Westlund had had time to create another assassin while on the run, the man who stabbed Lena and shot at Katrina was Surikov. And Westlund didn't seem to be taking any chances if he was adding hypnotic drugs to the brain-altering technology.

"*Tack så mycket*," she said. "Thank you so much. I think I might be able to get justice for Lena *and* complete this operation."

"Then get on with it, my dear. If you need any help, you know where to find me."

Katrina nodded and left his office. She wanted to see if she could get herself together before meeting with her director. She was nearly out of the lab before Professor Rasmusson stopped her.

"Oh, and Katrina?"

She turned back toward him.

"I know this will not mean much now, but take it from an old man who has seen and heard it all. You did not kill Lena. The only person guilty of that was the man wielding the knife."

She gave a small nod. "I'll try to remember that, Professor." Katrina knew, though, that nothing short of capturing Westlund would ease her guilt.

NOT ONE TO COMPLETELY give up, Katrina tried to call Izzie three times. The first two went to voice mail, and the third time she picked up.

"Yes?" Her voice was curt.

Katrina wasn't sure where to begin, so she tried again to say that she was sorry and Lena had been valued, et cetera, but Izzie cut her off.

"You can stop now. I get it. You want to say the right thing, but frankly you're trash at it. So stop. Just stop."

"Sorry, Izzie. You know I'm not good at this type of thing."

"I know, so get on with it. What do you want?"

Katrina explained Professor Rasmusson's findings. "It was Surikov. He's the one who killed Lena." That might have been Katrina's way of redirecting her own sense of guilt.

"Okay, so what do you want me for?"

Despite their friendship, Katrina didn't know how to say what she really wanted. *Support. Your forgiveness. To be my best friend again.*

"We're all trying to figure out where Westlund and Surikov are," Izzie said. "If you do get a tip on Westlund, let me know, and I'll be there." Unsaid but clearly understood was "Don't bother me otherwise."

"Will do. Well, I guess that's it—"

"See you, then. Bye." Izzie hung up. It was, in all likelihood, the shortest conversation they'd ever had.

Chapter 37

"He came back, but he's not here anymore."

"What do you mean?" Katrina was back at St. Gustav, but unfortunately, she wasn't speaking with Dr. Abboud.

Nurse Ox was back at her desk, gatekeeping access. She shrugged a shoulder. "Well, I was trying to be nice about it, but what I mean is Surikov is dead."

Katrina gripped the counter to keep from reeling. "Well. This will certainly set my research back. When did this happen?"

"Late last night, from what I see here in his chart." She was hunched over and peering at the screen. "He was returned to the facility. The night nurse said he started raving about the voices again. Went on and on for several hours and—" She snapped her fingers. "He was gone. Said it was a massive brain hemorrhage. Nothing they could do." Her demeanor indicated that she didn't think they should have done anything for the patient anyway.

"They cleaned out his room a few hours ago. He must have been really looking forward participating in your study, because he left something for you."

Nurse Ox used her beefy arms to hoist herself up out of the chair and told Katrina to follow her down to the patient storage-locker area.

"The note said 'For the American lady,' so I figured that was you." She handed her the bundle. It was in one of those heavy white plastic bags that need to be durable enough for long-term use by their more unfortunate patients.

"You're welcome to toss it in the trash. I don't see anything that could be of any interest to anybody. But then, I'm not crazy."

She left the room smiling in a manner that once again made Katrina dubious of that claim.

Katrina sat at the table and opened the bag. Inside was a black shirt with a gaping hole in one sleeve where the fabric had torn. It was a match with the scrap she'd snagged. Several notebooks were filled with the repeated messages of "Beware the Voices" and "The Voices made me do it." She also saw a letter addressed to her. It was handwritten in block letters and, frankly, looked a bit of a mess, which she supposed made sense, given his mental health. But between the drawings and over the slashes, she was able to make sense of it:

DEAR AMERICAN LADY,

I WANT TO SAY SORRY. I DON'T KNOW WHO YOU REALLY ARE, BUT THE VOICES TOLD ME WHAT I HAVE TO DO. I NEED TO KILL YOUR FRIENDS. I NEED TO KILL YOU. I NEED TO KILL ANYONE WHO KNOWS. I DON'T WANT TO. I DO WHAT I'M TOLD. DON'T WANT TO. CAN'T FIGHT THEM ANYMORE. TIRED. SURI.

Katrina dropped the letter back into the bag. She thought back to his actions on the roof, the pacing back and forth. It all made sense. Surikov was fighting the SCR and the drugs, trying not to kill but ultimately not succeeding. Tempering her sympathy for him was the recollection that he didn't seem to have the same internal debate when it came to slashing Lena.

Katrina hurried out to the front desk. Nurse Ox seemed put out that Katrina had failed to immediately acquaint herself with the exit.

"Thank you for giving me the bag. A real shame about his death. Is his body here?" Katrina didn't think for a minute that a massive hemorrhage was what had killed him, at least not one borne of natural causes.

"Yeah, he's still around. Friday at midnight is cremation day. First thing."

It was already Thursday evening. Katrina considered asking to view the body but knew she didn't have the medical training to be of any utility. She was short on time anyway.

"Thank you, you've been a great help."

Nurse Ox, who previously looked a bit energized as she read a dead man's chart, went back to her normally churlish self and gave a short nod. Katrina tried not to run for the exit.

As soon as she left the building, Katrina whipped out her phone and dialed Izzie. It went straight to voice mail. "Izzie, I know you're really angry with me, but I need to be in two places at once and can't do it. Right now, I'm at the psychiatric facility, but I need to go meet with the director." She wondered if she was rambling. It definitely felt like she was rambling. "The point is time is of the essence because Surikov came back to the facility but is dead and set to be cremated first thing tomorrow morning, and I need you to get a team over here *now* before any evidence is destroyed. Based on how he died, I'm convinced Westlund killed Surikov to destroy the evidence."

Chapter 38

Katrina got back to her hotel room just in time for her call with the director. She knew the conversation was going to be one she desperately did not want to risk anyone overhearing. Sweaty and out of breath, she raced to her laptop. With Westlund still at large and his assassin dead, Katrina was not in the mood for an evisceration from the director. But if she'd learned anything from her mission, it was that the only thing she had full control over was her ability to adapt to her ever-changing situations. So she was going to gird her loins and endure whatever came her way as best she could.

Director Samantha Jones was already up on the screen.

"Agent Foster. Good of you to finally arrive."

Katrina consulted her watch. It was only thirty seconds into the top of the hour.

"Why don't we begin with your version of what happened, Agent Foster."

"Yes, Director." Katrina swallowed her emotions and concisely related the events leading up to Lena's death.

"I see. This is the second death on your watch, is it not?"

"That is correct, Director."

The director sharpened her gaze on Katrina. "And what, if anything, did you learn from this, Agent Foster?"

This is not the time to play it cool or be evasive. She laid out everything: the loss of respect from her colleagues—the importance of which she had been warned about—the guilt, and her vow to never forget that something greater than herself and her own ambitions existed. She also decided to preempt her own firing.

"I am profoundly sorry for my actions, Director. If you can just give me a few minutes to arrange a flight back—"

The director swiftly cut her off. "That's enough of the self-recriminations, Agent Foster."

Katrina, who had addressed most of her explanation to her knees, looked up.

"You made rookie mistakes. You're not the first. You certainly won't be the last. I've certainly seen worse actions during my tenure."

"I feel like I have blood on my hands."

"That would be because you do. What, did you think you're somehow special and unique because someone died on your watch? Get in line. Death is a regular part of this profession, Agent Foster. Sometimes, we're the cause of it, and not everyone gets a 'good' death. The key is to minimize the number of casualties by not making *stupid and preventable mistakes*."

Katrina nodded.

"Based on what you've said, it seems like you're figuring this out, however belatedly. It's up to you to decide if you can handle it, if you can learn from it... and if you can still continue to be one of our most promising spies."

"I... I'm glad you still have confidence in me, Director," Katrina said.

"Of course I do. How could I not, when I knew your parents? But it's more than your lineage. You proved throughout your training that you were more than worth what we've invested in you." She cleared her throat. "But this is it for you. The steps you take from this point onward will either make you or break you... perhaps literally. It's all on you."

"Yes, Director."

Kat was curious why the director was being so, well, nice. That was about as far from her usual demeanor as possible. It felt off, which only made Katrina feel even more like she was in a dire situation regarding her tenure with the Division.

"Um, Director?"

"Yes?"

"If I may ask, why are you being so sympathetic?"

The director paused an uncomfortably long time and sighed. "I have no earthly idea. I must be getting sentimental. I don't like this one bit, so consider this a one-time event in your favor. You never saw me this way, you will never see me this way again, and you will never, ever tell anyone that you did. If you make so much as an eyebrow twitch giving me away, I will kill you myself in an act of friendly fire that nobody will question. Understood?"

The steel was back.

"Understood, Director."

"Good. Because as I already mentioned, we have invested a significant amount of resources in you, which we would like to collect upon at some point."

"Thank you, ma'am."

"And speaking of investments, the Swedish Division invested a lot in Agent Holmberg. And that informant wouldn't have come cheaply, either. Rookie mistakes or no, you will not have the opportunity to balls it up on that level again."

Katrina dipped her head.

"Oh, and one more thing. I almost forgot."

Not for a moment did Katrina believe the director "almost forgot" anything.

"You have seventy-two hours to wrap this up. Fail that, and your butt will be on the next plane back to US soil."

"Seventy-two hours?" Katrina couldn't hold back her shock.

"Did I stutter, Agent Foster? Yes, seventy-two hours, also known as three days. And I had to call in a favor to get you that." The director's tone indicated she was greatly displeased to have to ask for a boon from anyone.

"Thank you, Director. I will complete this mission in three days." Katrina had no idea how that was going to happen, but she was determined to make it so.

"Anything else?"

"No, Director."

"Then get back out there."

"Yes, Director."

"And, Katrina?"

Katrina didn't think she had ever called an agent by their first name. The director must've been feeling positively sentimental.

"Yes?"

"It would not go unnoticed if you were to formally apologize to the Swedes. And do it in that flawless Swedish of yours. The fact you contributed to the death of their spy will go down a little easier that way."

Katrina had already apologized, multiple times, and given the way the Swedish Division agents looked at her—or rather, didn't—she was not of the opinion that another apology was likely to do any good. She didn't tell the director that, though.

"Certainly, Director" was all she replied.

"Good. Director, out."

Katrina didn't know what to make of that call, but she didn't think it was anything good. The director was not given to kindness or sentimentality. Either she was being nice because she'd lost faith in Katrina and, despite her words, had written her off, or she was being kind as a distraction before someone at the Division took her out—and not to dinner. She knew enough not to view the seventy-two-hour countdown as a binding, legally enforceable agreement.

Katrina needed a friend. Izzie was out for the moment, and Magnus was... complicated. She looked at the clock. She could give Hector a call. Maybe he could raise her spirits a bit. She breathed a sigh of relief when his face popped up on the screen.

"Hey, Kat!"

"What's going on, Hec?"

"Nothing." Then he smiled. "Everything."

"Sorry I didn't call sooner, but this insurance investigation has just been intense." She sighed. "It's like every step that I thought was going in the right direction turned out to be the opposite. The team of investigators have lost confidence in me, and if I don't produce results quickly, I'm likely to be canned."

At least she could be honest about that. So much in her life required deception that, as broken as she felt, speaking the truth in some capacity was a relief, even if he believed it was about an insurance fraud investigation.

"I'm sorry, Kat. It seems like that fraud case is really kicking your butt. You look rough."

Katrina huffed and smoothed out the corners of her eyes and tried to rub a bit of life into her cheeks. She wasn't so down that she couldn't work up a bit of vanity and offense at being called rough-looking.

"Oh relax, Kat. I just meant you seem tired." He took a swig of his ever-present Coke. "So can we talk?"

"Isn't that what we were doing?" she asked.

"I mean really talk. About important stuff." But he didn't look worried. On the contrary, Hector had a big smile and was bouncing a bit in his seat.

And just why is he so damned upbeat? That only made her feel more aggravated. "Alright, so tell me what's going on. What's this 'important stuff' you want to talk about?"

"So... it's this girl. I really like her. And I think she might be into me too."

Katrina's breath caught. *Where did that come from?* That was a weird response. She refocused to collect more information. "So tell me about this girl."

"It's like she's everything I could want in a woman—smart, funny, beautiful, and just mysterious enough to keep me on my toes."

"Sounds like a rare combination, one you don't see every day." She only partially avoided rolling her eyes when she remembered she was on camera.

She herself wasn't into Hector—not that way, anyway. They were just friends. But for some reason, one she didn't have the time or energy to explore, she didn't like the idea of him seeing anyone either. She theorized that was because she didn't have many friends to begin with and didn't want to share.

"So does this paragon of brains, beauty, and just enough mystery have a name?"

"Her name's Paula. Paula Swinton."

Katrina made a mental note to run a background check on her.

"What's a good first-date location? It's been so long that the last time I took a girl out it was to a video arcade."

"You *still* go to video arcades," she noted dryly.

"You know what I mean."

"Well, definitely not there, if you want a repeat date." Katrina did not have any more bandwidth to deal with foolishness. "Why don't you take her to a lecture or a performance? That way, you can grab drinks afterward, and you'll have something to talk about."

"I knew you'd know just the thing!"

She gave a tired smile. "Glad I could help."

Katrina remembered the director and her new timeline. "By the way, has anyone else from work been by my apartment lately?"

"Nope. No one that I've seen. There was some plumber who I saw trying to get in about an overflowing toilet, but I told him he must've had the wrong apartment because I'd just been in there, and there wasn't any issue."

Great. That could've been a coincidence, but Katrina had another thing to worry about.

Hector tilted his head and regarded her. "What's up? Problem? Is it more than the investigation? Anything I can give advice on?"

She shook her head. "No, it's just that I'm really tired. This insurance investigation is just really draining me."

"Oh, if that's all..." He still looked a little skeptical.

"Nah, I'm good. Nothing a nap and a more forthcoming claimant won't fix."

He brightened. "Alright, well I better go, then. Get that nap, and I hope things turn around with your insurance investigation."

"Thanks, Hector. See you."

She closed her laptop. Somehow, speaking with him accomplished the exact opposite of being comforted. Giving up on the idea that the day might be redeemable, she went to sleep.

Chapter 39

In the darkness, a masked man skulked on Katrina's balcony. Unbeknownst to him, Katrina was awake. He popped the patio door's flimsy security lock, slid open the balcony door, and promptly tripped over the thin wire Katrina had strung across the entryway as an old-school security system.

"*Skit!*" He hit the floor. "Ow..."

Falling on the floor should've been the least of his worries because as soon as she heard the door slide open, Katrina pulled her gun from under the bed, the silencer already in place. She trained the gun on the figure, who immediately put his hands in the air.

"It's just me. It's just Magnus." He pulled off his mask. The moonlight illuminated the angles on his face.

Katrina did not lower her weapon. *Oh, "just Magnus." The same one who's been incommunicado the past few days?* He could go straight to hell.

"And I should take comfort in that how, exactly, 'just Magnus'?" She didn't bother to hide her anger. "What exactly were you doing out there?"

"Uh, watching you," Magnus said lamely.

Katrina gave him a look that managed to be simultaneously disgusted and just a little bit bemused. "In the dark. While I slept."

He bowed his head.

"You know that sounds creepy, right?"

He had the good sense to appear abashed. "Yeah, I know."

"You haven't spoken to me in a week. What happened to all that talk about compartmentalization?"

"Can you put the gun away, please?"

"It's still not clear to me why I should."

"Hear me out, Kat, or at minimum, let me get up off the floor."

"Fine," she grumbled. "Whatever you have to say had better be good."

Magnus slowly, warily, dropped his hands.

"Can I sit on the bed?"

Oh, he's pressing his luck now. "No, because if I have to shoot you, it'll make a mess all over the sheets," Katrina said with her remaining bravado.

He took a nearby chair and sat.

Katrina sighed. "Why couldn't you just use the door, *like a normal person*, instead of trying to scare me to death?"

"Because I have reason to suspect that I am being watched."

"What?" Katrina finally lowered her weapon, putting the safety back on. She reached over to turn on the light.

"No, keep the light off. Moonlight is risky enough."

"What's going on, Magnus?"

"It's about all those meetings I've been having with my director. I've been given an assignment I know I cannot do, and I believe the Division is watching to see whether or not I have the disposition to carry it out."

"Can I help in any way?"

He smiled thinly. "Well, no. Not unless you plan on killing yourself at the end of the next three days."

Three days... "Hold up. I have three days—well, less than seventy-two hours now—to complete this mission."

"I know. I have three days as well," he said. "Apparently, the last two deaths have been too public, and the Division wants this wrapped up or shut down as soon as possible. Our directors apparently came to an agreement. You have three days to piece this all together and complete the operation. As soon as it goes to seventy-two hours and one minute, if the mission is not finished, I'm supposed to 'dispose of' you. Then I'll probably be next."

So much for the director saying Katrina would be on a plane back to the US. Although, to be fair, at no point did the director actually specify that Kat would be *alive* on the return flight.

"That explains her demeanor earlier," Katrina said, mostly to herself. "She was

oddly supportive."

Magnus seemed contemplative. "Or she saw you were feeling low, and she tried to encourage you in the hopes that you would get your confidence back and finish the job."

"Well, I told her I would get the job done, and I will... somehow. It's not like I have much of a say in the matter if I value my life... which I do." She looked over at Magnus. "And so you agreed to all of this? To off me? Did you know this could happen?"

"I'm not new to this, Kat. I know how the game is played. After Lena died on that rooftop, I knew what could happen. Or at least, I suspected as much, which is why I've been keeping my distance. If there was the smallest hint of anything more than disinterested professionalism between us, I knew they would just outsource the job to someone else, and I was not going to let that happen. I'm just sorry that I couldn't get close enough to tell you. I thought I would take the chance tonight, and... well, we see how well that went."

"Well, as excuses go, that's a pretty good one," she acknowledged. She gestured toward the bed. "Come on over."

Magnus grinned and sat down on the bed, wrapping Katrina in his arms. He put his nose in the crook of her neck, inhaled, and sighed. "Damn, I missed you. I missed this."

"Me too," she replied as she stroked the top of his head with her hand. "It really sucked not knowing what was going on. Why you ghosted me." She wouldn't tell him, but that had felt like one more loss.

He kissed her. "I know. I'm so sorry."

They both looked toward the patio. The early streaks of dawn were making their way across the sky.

"I've got to go. I've stayed too long."

"I know. See you at work... from a safe and professional distance, Agent Svensson."

Magnus grinned and kissed her deeply before getting up. He tip-toed back onto the balcony, being careful to step over the wire that time, before slipping back into the remaining night.

Chapter 40

W*ell, that's cute.* The situation seemed about right for Katrina's track record. She'd found a guy she liked, and he was in charge of killing her. She was just going to have to do everything in her power to find Westlund, because however much she valued solving her first mission, she valued her own neck even more.

Katrina looked over at Izzie's desk. She wasn't there. She wondered if Izzie had been able to get over to the facility in time before Surikov's cremation. That was a call she wasn't thrilled to make, but it needed to be done. Then she realized she had an alternative, one who just happened to be walking by.

"*Hej*, Jens."

"*Hej*, Agent Foster. Katrina." Jens pulled up next to her, wearing a three-piece suit. In the summer.

"I was thinking about looking for you."

"So was I, Katrina. I, uh... I just wanted to pass along a message from Agent Figueroa..."

"Oh, I get it. So you're like the go-between now for Izzie and me since she can't be bothered to speak with me?"

He frowned a little and played with the ends of his collar.

She sighed again. As she was about to use Jens for the same purpose, she knew she was just deflecting. "Sorry, Jens. It's not your fault. So what's the message?"

"Izzie was able to get a medical team over to St. Gustav in time. They switched bodies and brought Surikov back to headquarters for an autopsy."

He told her the findings. As Katrina had guessed, the cause of death was no accidental hemorrhage. The implanted device must've had a self-destruct function, because a small explosion had gone off in his front temporal lobe.

"Thanks for the update, Jens. I'll add that to the report. Surikov was no one's idea of an innocent, but given what was done to him, I hope he didn't suffer too much."

Jens shrugged. "I suppose that is everyone's wish. If you're going to die, at least make it as quick as possible."

They were silent while Katrina thought about Lena and how agonizingly long she'd taken to bleed out.

"Jens... how is Izzie? I know you've seen her. With your work on surveilling the moles, I mean."

He coughed uncomfortably and hooked a finger back in his collar. "Yes, I've seen her."

"And...?"

"She's had a shock. Give her some time."

Irrationally, Katrina became angry. Time was ticking away from her... and her life. "Well, what about me? Does she think that I didn't have a shock? I was by Lena's side as she died. Let me assure you it wasn't quick, and it wasn't pretty."

Jens put out both hands in a universal gesture that said, "Leave me out of this one." Then he said, "I don't know. For however tough she may be, she is struggling. She just needs more time to deal with it."

Katrina sighed. "Well, time is the one thing I can't give her. I have less than three days to complete this mission, and I need her. Talk to her for me, will you?"

He nodded. "I've got to go." He got up to leave. He shifted awkwardly in place, playing with the buttons on his sleeve. "I've made some spectacular mistakes. It's part of how I ended up here."

A clue. Katrina squirreled that away like she was collecting nuts for a long winter.

He cleared his throat. "You can come out of this thing on the other end, Katrina. I know it. It doesn't look good now, but as long as you can turn the corner, you won't be defined by a single misstep."

That was nice enough for him to say, but he didn't know what she was up against. Katrina just gave him a small smile. "Thanks, Jens."

WITH WESTLUND STILL unaccounted for and the clock in her head ticking ever more loudly since she knew the Swedish Division was gunning for her, Katrina knew she needed to contact the remaining people associated with Lindström. Clearly, Westlund wouldn't stop until everyone was dead. The remaining links were Johanna's husband, Ekstrand, and Pantzerhielm. She briefly debated with herself whom to contact first. Katrina thought about having to hear Pantzerhielm's greasy voice leering at her through the phone. *No thanks.* She would save his call for last. And if that was too late for him, she probably wouldn't feel too bad about the loss. Then there was Petter. *Ugh.* Kat had just decided to start with the least objectionable of the bunch, Ekstrand, when she was interrupted.

"Foster?" A Level Three came over to her desk and plopped a file down.

Katrina noted the lack of title from the underling but let it slide. "Yes?"

"This is the latest research documents request. It was meant for *Lena,*" the agent said with such surliness that she could have been Lena's protégé.

She thanked her and received an eyeroll in return.

Katrina went through the documents. They centered on Westlund. The bank was able to freeze all the accounts in his name, but given the amounts, Katrina assumed he had additional accounts under different names. More descriptions of his previous research were included, along with a list of some of the aliases he'd used. Then she spotted a rather curious sentence. Westlund had served as a scientific advisor on animal behaviors and welfare for Kvinnor.

Katrina sat back. *Well. That settles it.* If Westlund was clearing out—to use a Division euphemism—anyone with contacts with Lindström, Ekstrand was sure to be at the top of the list. She called the Kvinnor office and was put through to Ekstrand's cell with surprising speed.

"Sigrid Ekstrand?"

"Yes, Sister."

"Thanks for taking my call. It's me, Katie Freedman, the reporter whom you met a couple weeks back. I have an urgent matter to discuss."

"Oh yes, of course I remember you. The American."

Katrina paused, trying to consider the best way to warn Ekstrand about a deranged person that was after her, without sounding crazy herself.

"This is going to sound odd, Ms. Ekstrand, but in the course of my reporting, I've come across evidence that one of your former staff members does not wish you well. Rikard Westlund."

There was a long pause. "Rikard? The scientist? I'm afraid I don't understand what you mean, Sister. What's this about?"

"I know this is unexpected, but I have some urgent information that I can't tell you over the phone. We need to meet in person. The sooner the better." Katrina hoped her voice conveyed the urgency of the situation.

"Good lord, Sister. You were right about it being urgent. I can't imagine what is going on, but in my line of work... Yes, by all means, let's meet. I'm currently on my way to my brother's company. Can you meet me there in two hours?"

Katrina wrote down the address and got her "interviewing" bag ready. Then something compelled her to head over to Lena's old desk. Katrina sat in her chair, which felt beyond weird, and rifled through her desk. She didn't think she was violating any sense of privacy, given the fact that the woman was dead. She saw printed chat transcripts from Surikov's time in the forums. In them, he mentioned he needed a job.

"Come work for me" was the response. "As long as you're not afraid of hard work, I've got entry-level positions available. Scrap metals."

The company name was listed: K.T. & Anders Metallskrot Återvinning, a scrap-metal recycling business. Katrina read Lena's notes. Lena had indicated that the ownership was not straightforward. Anders was a common name, and the initials didn't help much either. She was going to have a devil of a time trying to trace the owner. *Ugh.* She literally did not have time for another hunt. She briefly put her head down on the desk and closed her eyes in frustration. That turned out to be just what she needed.

Like a swirl, the letters arranged and rearranged themselves behind her eyelids, and something hit her: K.T. & Anders became Ekstrand Metallskrot Återvinning—Ekstrand Scrap Metal Recycling.

Three people were now connected to Lindström's death, and Ekstrand was at the center of it. Westlund had worked for her. Then she had Surikov on the payroll after offering him work. All roads led to Ekstrand... whom Katrina had just forewarned. Katrina had been heading into a trap. Well, she still was, as it was going to be the only way to catch Ekstrand. But now, she would be prepared.

She patted the documents. "Thanks, Lena."

The time had come to assemble the team.

DESPITE ALL THE UNRESOLVED tensions, everyone made it to Katrina's desk in record time. As they stood around her, she quickly explained the evidence.

"Ekstrand is the mastermind?" Magnus asked.

"All the evidence points to her—" Katrina began.

"All of *Lena's* evidence," Izzie said.

Katrina did not miss the message behind the comment. "Yes, Lena's evidence. She left us the documents needed to figure out the rest."

"Well, at least you, Katrina," Magnus said. "I wouldn't have figured out her alias."

"Don't get too congratulatory, seeing how I just accidentally tipped her off. And we still don't know where Westlund is hiding, although if Ekstrand is the one guiding everything, he may be with her."

"Okay, team, no time to linger, especially because Katrina told Ekstrand she was on the way. Gear up, and meet at the car in ten."

They had a mastermind to catch.

Chapter 41

All that time spent chauffeuring paid off. Jens managed to dodge all traffic, taking back roads to the scrap-metal site. It was well off the highway and surrounded by a dense forest—the perfect location for processing junk, as well as the perfect locale for plotting assassinations, apparently. They stopped about a quarter mile away, not wanting to announce their presence by pulling up into Ekstrand's nearest parking spot.

Magnus led the group toward the scrapyard. "Okay, let's stick to the plan. Katrina, you go in the front, keeping up the façade of being a reporter as she doesn't know you know her true identity. Jens, you're on surveillance while Izzie and I find side entries. Comms on."

"Got it," Katrina, Izzie, and Jens said in unison as they split off into their respective roles.

As Katrina made her way past a gauntlet of rusted-out cars, she felt a breeze behind her left ear and turned as a bullet whizzed past, then another one. She ran behind one of the cars and crouched down.

"I've got fire!" she screamed into her comms. "Ekstrand came prepared." She rose up from the car to see Magnus and Izzie in hand-to-hand combat with four people dressed head-to-toe in black. They consisted of one man and three women.

"Keep to the mission!" Magnus yelled.

No way was Katrina going to leave her team. If Ekstrand had sent them, the jig was already up, and Katrina needed to protect them—no more leaving people behind. She wasn't alone. She watched as Jens leapt, silent as death, into the fray. He was a sight to see. She didn't know who or what he was, but his primary profession was clearly not driving. As Katrina ran toward them, she saw him fighting with impressive skill. It was like an elegant art for him, and he made it look almost effortless. He swept the leg of one man, getting him to lean back as Jens put him into a chokehold. He pulled the balaclava off the man's face.

"Persson!" Jens gasped. "I know this guy from... from before."

"I'm not after *you*, Jens," Persson grunted as Jens placed a knee in his kidney. "Back off."

"I'm not after you..."

In a moment while she was still fighting the remaining three attackers, Katrina locked eyes briefly with Magnus. She was the target. These weren't Ekstrand's hired help. With this level of skill, only one source was possible: the Swedish Divison. The assailants weren't likely to be actual employees but outsourced assassins.

Sonofa...

"'Cause I don't already have *enough* on my plate?" Katrina shouted at no one in particular. She wasn't naïve enough to assume they would play fair, but come on, she still had, like, twelve whole hours left in her seventy-two-hour death sentence. *Dirty.* There was no honor among thieves *or* spies, it would seem.

"Magnus, Izzie, Jens, go get Sigrid. I've got this." She didn't know how she was going to take on four assassins by herself, but she wasn't going to let them fight when Ekstrand still needed to be captured. She saw Magnus hesitate. "Go!" she screamed.

"Jens..." Magnus said.

Jens nodded, which seemed to give permission for Magnus to race after Izzie into the building.

The two tag-teamed against the four, and in short work, Jens had three of the assassins laid out on the ground. Alive or dead, she didn't know, and she didn't care.

"Great job, Je—" The words died on her lips as Jens took a bullet to the chest. She looked back at the remaining woman holding a gun. *Not another one.*

Katrina might've lacked the fighting skills of a Jens or an Izzie, but she had bravery and the determination that no one else was going to die because of her.

She bent down and barreled headfirst into the woman's stomach with a massive grunt. Temporarily winded, the woman fell, cracking her head against the ground. Katrina grabbed her gun and hit her across the face with its butt for good measure. She examined the gun. It wasn't a standard model. The markings indicated that the cylinder had the capacity to alternate between lethal and nonlethal chambers.

Katrina raced over to Jens and dropped to her knees to feel his neck. A pulse beat heavily against her fingertips, and she sighed in relief. She pulled back his shirt. Where a hole should've been, she saw only the end of a dart sticking out. The nonlethal option must've been some sort of knockout solution.

Grasping Jens under his arms, she dragged him behind some thick bushes, out of sight. "He's going to be so upset," she thought absurdly as she stared down on him.

His suit was a mangled, dirty mess, and his hair went well beyond mussed. But alive was alive, and he could always get a new suit.

Katrina went to check on the other bodies, keeping the stolen gun raised. The three Jens had dispatched were very dead. She stood over the woman she'd knocked out and considered the gun she held in her hand. Katrina knew it was kill or be killed with the Division, but it somehow seemed wrong to kill someone while they were unconscious. That didn't mean she was going to give that woman a chance to move, though. After carefully checking that the barrel was set to nonlethal, she pulled the trigger, shooting her in the neck. Katrina bent and opened the false bottom of her boot heel, revealing what looked like dental floss but was actually some of Professor Rasmusson's indestructible tape. She tied up the assassin as an additional measure as she didn't know how long the woman would be knocked out. And because Katrina was a true believer in petty revenge, she pulled out a tube of lipstick and wrote across the assassin's chest, "TWELVE HOURS." Maybe the Swedish Division would consider keeping their word next time.

Magnus. Izzie. She turned toward the scrapyard's building and broke into a run.

Fresh out the frying pan, into the fire.

Chapter 42

Katrina crept along the edge of the building. Upon finding a side door, she quietly slipped in. Magnus and Izzie were at the end of a long corridor, battling it out with three of Ekstrand's henchmen. She charged toward the fray, but they seemed to have things well in hand. By the time she got there, Magnus was tying up one slumped-over guy while Izzie knocked down two more with a quick side-to-side kick.

"Nice of you to join," Izzie said as she checked on the two figures on the ground. Both appeared to be knocked out cold. "Huh. Sometimes, I don't know my own strength," she said as she kicked the knife out of the hand of one. She turned back and looked behind Katrina, her face concerned. "Where's Jens?"

"He's fine. Just sleeping off a sedative dart in some bushes."

Izzie looked relieved. "Good."

One of her defeated henchmen started to moan. Izzie went over to that one and knelt over his prone body.

"Ah, excellent. If you're awake enough to moan, then you're awake enough to talk. Where is she? Ekstrand?" Izzie slapped his face a couple times, shaking him to attention.

As his eyes focused on her, they narrowed. "I'm not telling you anything, lady."

"Cute that you think you have a choice," she replied.

Magnus joined Katrina and placed a hand briefly on the small of her back. That was enough to convey what he was feeling.

Izzie opened the wristwatch Professor Rasmusson had given her on their first day in Sweden, and she turned the dial to the three o'clock position. A thin needle emerged—sodium pentothal. She quickly jabbed the watch into the captive's neck.

"Owww..." he whined.

Big baby. "Start talking!"

"Well, I always wanted to be a painter, but my dad said art was for sissies..."

Oh, for the love of... "Do you want me to deal with him?" Katrina asked.

"Nah. I've got this." Izzie smacked him again in the face. "Where is Ekstrand? I won't be asking a third time."

"Oh, her? She's in her office. She can see everything on the cameras, so she's probably going to go with her plan B." He furrowed his thick brows in concentration. "I think it might be poison... or gas. Maybe both."

Izzie cursed and, palming her hand over his face like a basketball, slammed his head against the floor, his head making a satisfying smack. "Let's get to her office before someone shows up here with a gas bomb."

But no bomb would be going off. Katrina heard rather than saw the arrival of mist.

Better protect my head, she thought as her body fell toward the floor.

"OH GOOD. YOU'RE FINALLY awake, Sister."

Katrina blinked with heavy eyelids and looked around. She had a next-level headache, but she forced her eyes open enough to take in her surroundings. She was inside a modern-styled office with wall-to-wall glass windows. Through the windows, the back of the scrapyard was visible, with rows of rusted and compacted cars. An assembly of cars lay on a conveyor belt, heading one by one into a giant compactor.

To her right stood a large man with a gun trained on her. Unlike with the assassins, she didn't think his weapon held any nonlethal alternatives. To her left was an even larger man with a rather nasty-looking knife holstered at his side. In front of her was Ekstrand, calmly standing by her desk, watching her. With a fancy silk scarf around her neck and a crisp pantsuit, she was dressed like she was going to a campaign stop, not plotting murder. The two people Katrina was most interested in, Magnus and Izzie, were nowhere to be found.

Katrina then did a check of her own body. She was not bound, which went counter to expectations. Pounding head aside, she didn't feel any other injuries. Her clothes were disheveled but at least still on her. Her weapons, however, were not. She wondered if she still had the floss in her boot heel.

"My, my, my. You've just been making all sorts of enemies, haven't you?" Ekstrand said. "I don't know who they were, but my thanks to them all the same as it gave me time enough to adapt plans. So, Sister, let's talk."

"Talk? And what's stopping me from taking down these two jokers and going after you?" she asked. She held up her hands as if to say, "No one even bothered to restrain me."

"While it's possible that you could take out my top men—I've certainly been watching your work—I'm not the least bit worried about you coming for me. I have been supplied with this very handy clicker." She gestured to a small black device in her hands. "Your fellow agents are *all tied up* at the moment in the scrapyard. One wrong move on your part, and your friends will have a rather explosive end to their mission. So please, let's have a civilized conversation while I wait for my extraction team to arrive."

Katrina didn't want to think about what that team might be like.

"By the way, thank you for the heads-up. It was downright sisterly, Miss... ah, I forgot. What name are you going by today?" She didn't give Katrina a chance to answer. "Before you called, I had planned to invite you over for a visit. I didn't think you would fall for my note-passing assistant again, though."

The bizarre woman at the park. Aha! That's it. Katrina *knew* she'd recognized that face. Under the bad wig and layers of makeup was the staffer that had served her and Ekstrand tea. Maybe she should have been grateful that it wasn't poisoned.

"She really did have a dreadful accent."

"Accuracy was not needed, Sister. She just needed to keep you distracted long enough for one of my body men to slip you a note to get you off track."

Apparently, men were good for something, at least, in Ekstrand's world.

"Why do you keep calling me 'Sister' when sororicide is clearly on your mind? Shouldn't that be the opposite of what you would champion?"

"Well, sometimes you have to cull out the disloyal and the ones that threaten the cause. *You*, Sister, are a threat to the cause. Still, I do want to speak with you. I was told you were valuable. I see no evidence of that, but if I can extract something valuable..."

Katrina simply stared at Ekstrand and remained silent.

"Maybe we'll have time to get to that later. Oh, in case you are wondering, *Katrina*, after seeing footage of you and that informant, I decided to call an old friend at your alleged newspaper. Worked there since the late nineties in the politics-and-investigation department and knows *everybody*. Imagine my surprise when she said she'd never heard of you."

Katrina didn't reply.

"And yet you had all these articles on the internet. And when my intern called the number on your card, I was assured that you were employed by the paper but were out of the office on assignment."

What are the odds I could pitch myself over the table and grab that clicker before Tweedledee and Tweedledumber could descend upon me? Katrina determined she needed a better strategy.

"I mean, it just didn't add up, a ghost reporter with all those articles. How could that be?"

"Could it be because you're an idiot?" Katrina smiled prettily at Ekstrand.

"I'm in *politics*, Katrina. It will take more than schoolyard taunts to rile me," Ekstrand replied. She held up one hand, inspecting her nails. "When my contact could not identify you but the 'newspaper' could, it told me that you were not what you seemed. What it told me is that you were both a troublemaker and a liar. Seeing that picture of you pointing a gun at that nosey informant during Almedalen Week confirmed any lingering suspicions. I assume you're working for the Division. Oh yes, I know about them. And Oskar. He couldn't stop poking around, couldn't stop trying to trace things back to me." She huffed. "Each time I thought this was over, that I could get on with my life, I would get notification that someone was poking around into Surikov or Johanna. I figured I was safe after I neutralized Oskar, but then they had to go and import some damned Americans." She laughed as though the idea was incredulous. "Once I heard you were in contact with Westlund, I knew it was only a matter of time."

"Oh yes, Westlund. How is he doing these days?" Katrina asked.

Ekstrand shrugged. "Beats me. I don't track the hired help once they've served my purpose. He's being dealt with."

"Let me get this straight," Katrina began. "You're telling me that a university researcher simply decided to take on a side job as an accessory to murder?"

Ekstrand rolled her eyes at Katrina. "It's not like I left him a choice. He had two options. Either he worked for me, or I was going to expose him for falsifying his research records. I knew about his research from when he did animal rights consulting work for Kvinnor. I then discovered that he was working to scale up the SCR beyond animals. Working on the technology to override free will in humans is illegal, as you know. He wisely opted not to have his career destroyed and did the implantation on Surikov."

"Why Surikov?"

"Why not? He was perfect. Well trained, had no close friends or family in the area, was already opposed to Lindström and her politics. And like any good soldier, he excelled at taking orders. Once Westlund performed the procedure on the guinea pig, I knew I had myself the perfect killing machine. He was the perfect soldier..." Her face twisted in dismay. "Until he wasn't. It reminded me once again that if one wants something done right—in this case, your disposal—one needs to do it oneself."

Katrina had to buy herself some time. "I don't understand. Why kill Johanna? To what end? I thought you and Lindström were friends—were more than that."

At that, Ekstrand's eyes flashed. "Ah, let me guess... Tore must've told you. Yes, we were lovers." As she spoke, fiddling with the clicker, Ekstrand set it on her desk. Katrina didn't even think Ekstrand was aware of it, and she was going to keep her talking to keep it that way.

"Then why...?"

"I simply could not believe it when she said she was going to leave the party. Was going to leave *me*. I told her to leave her husband, that we'd be an unstoppable force in Kvinnor på Toppen, that together, we could really effect change in a meaningful way. I said, 'No more provocative stunts for publicity, Johanna. I am talking about us doing the work to get seats in the *riksdag*, seats in the EU. Real power.'" Her voice turned bitter, and she started to pace. "I told her all that, pleaded with her. And do you know how she reacted? She laughed. Laughed right in my face. She said, 'You can't be serious, Sigs. Give up everything on a pipe dream? I don't just want a few crummy seats—I want to be Prime Minister.'" Ekstrand started pacing faster as she spoke.

Katrina said nothing in response and sat quietly while Ekstrand continued to rant. She was doing what all villains do when finally given the opportunity to speak. Ekstrand had to go on and on, *explaining things*. And Ekstrand was really making the most of her time *villsplaining*. It was quite tiresome, but it bought Katrina time to figure out what her next step was going to be before that team arrived.

"I knew at the moment she said she would never leave Petter, that she would never take the risk for our dream. She needed the happy family and the mainstream. When she signed on with the Libcons, she'd sold us out—not just me, but Kvinnor. I wasn't going to let her weaponize her charisma against Kvinnor, against me. If my supporters knew what she was aiming for, then Kvinnor votes would turn into Libcon votes, and I simply could not have that.

"She didn't get it, didn't understand. All our efforts were not supposed to be for the advancement of *one* woman but for *all* women. It was supposed to be about the advancement of Kvinnor, not her political career."

At that moment, Katrina saw Ekstrand's actions didn't have anything to do with love at all. It wasn't about love, it was about power—how to get it, how to keep it, and how to get more of it.

Speaking of power... "So, was Pantzerhielm in on this as well so he could become party leader instead of her?"

"Tore didn't have anything to do with it—not directly, anyway. He didn't want to get his manicured hands dirty. But he sure didn't mind making a considerable anonymous donation to Kvinnor when she died. I considered it blood money, payment for her death." Ekstrand took a deep breath and shook her head. "We could have been something incredible, something that the Swedish political establishment had *never* seen before. I believe that as much today as I did back then. If only she'd been brave enough. But she wasn't, and so it is up to me. Maybe I won't get to be PM, but I can at least get us twenty seats, maybe more—seats enough to really drive change."

"Yes, you can get those seats... only at the expense of human life." Foolishly, Katrina's mouth moved ahead of her good sense.

Ekstrand wheeled around on her. "That is what you don't get, what *she* didn't get. Sometimes, sacrifices have to be made for the greater good. What's a few lives if you can completely transform the system, really and truly bring female empowerment—*domination*—to the forefront? End the patriarchy for good? A handful of lives are nothing if you can accomplish all of that." Agitated, Ekstrand came from behind the desk and walked toward Katrina.

Now was her chance.

Speed. Speed. Speed.

Katrina grabbed the knife from the holster of the henchman on her left and quickly slashed the tendons of his wrists, making him scream in agony. She threw the knife and hit the other man in the neck. She didn't have Izzie's accuracy, so it didn't kill him, but it was enough to disarm him. Blood loss would take care of the rest. She had experienced that firsthand.

She then flipped the desk in front of Ekstrand, knocking her over. Katrina was fast enough to take down the men but not fast enough to get to Ekstrand, who scrambled for the device that had skittered across the floor and pushed down hard on it.

"Go ahead and waste your time with me," she taunted. "Do what you want with me. Your friends are already dead."

Knowing Ekstrand needed to be kept alive for interrogation, Katrina fought against the urge to kill her. Instead, she tied her up, using more of Professor Rasmussen's handy floss, and gagged Ekstrand with her own scarf. The man with the useless wrists didn't bother to move from where he'd collapsed.

Katrina looked out the giant glass windows and down to the scrapyard. One of those cars held Magnus and Izzie. She could only hope she would be fast enough to save them.

Chapter 43

Spotting them didn't take Katrina long. She just needed to follow the muffled shouts. She was relieved to see that the car was still on the lot, not on that ominous conveyor belt with the other vehicles ready to be smashed. She raced toward the rusted white Volvo with the windows busted out and found Magnus in the passenger side and Izzie in the driver's seat.

As she reached the car, she could see Izzie's hands were taped to the wheel and appeared to be cupping something. Upon closer inspection, Katrina saw the telltale blinking red light of an explosive device. Ekstrand hadn't been bluffing. Cords trailed to both of the door handles. If anyone opened a door—or pulled the wires too tightly—the device would go off. It was crude—a rush job, probably—but effective. Katrina leaned in to examine it more closely. As she followed the wires down, she could see a countdown clock—four minutes.

From what she could tell, Magnus hadn't been connected to the device, but he wasn't in much better shape. His mouth was gagged, and his normally angular face was rapidly swelling from whatever hits he'd taken. She looked down and saw his hands and feet bound with duct tape. His wrists were raw and bleeding from where he'd been unsuccessful in his struggle to escape. Katrina used her sleeve to clear out the rest of the glass in the window, reached in the passenger side, and quickly untied the cloth that had been wrapped around his mouth.

"Ekstrand?" Magnus asked.

"I've got her decommissioned in her office." She saw the question in his eyes. "Yes, she's still alive, but according to her, she's got an extraction team coming, and I don't know what that entails, but chances are we need to get our own backup here before hers arrives." She looked around and found a jagged-edged piece of metal and quickly sawed at the tape on his wrists. He tried moving them, but they'd been bound too long.

"I can't help you. My arms... My hands have gone numb."

"Don't worry, I've got this." She quickly tried rubbing his hands, but it didn't do much. "Okay, lean back and try to lift your feet. Do *not* touch Izzie or the wires."

It took a little finagling, given his height, but he was able to contort himself upward, and Katrina made short work of the tape.

"I'm still stuck," Magnus said. "I don't have any feeling left in my extremities. I'm too clumsy right now to get myself out."

"You won't need to. I'm going to lift you out."

Magnus appeared skeptical.

"You still have feeling in that cute butt of yours? Then I'm going to reach back in and hook my arms under yours, and on the count of three, flex your hips up, and I'm going to haul your carcass out this window. Got it?"

"Got it."

On the count of three and with some extremely unsexy grunting, Katrina hefted him and dragged him out the window. She couldn't hold him up, though, and he fell with a thud on the ground.

"Okay, let's get Izzie," he said, panting from the ordeal.

"No. You need to get to Ekstrand's office and get backup. She's got a phone on her desk." Then she remembered upturning the desk. "Well, there's a phone in there. Somewhere."

Magnus looked at her, something inscrutable in his eyes.

"Trust me. We'll be fine," Katrina said with more confidence than she felt, but it was enough to convince Magnus. He crawl-scooted his way with impressive speed back toward the building.

Katrina ran around to Izzie's side. She removed Izzie's gag and gently fingered the wires. The device had seven, most of which were probably decoys. Freeing Magnus had left them with only two minutes. They looked at each other. This was not good, and they both knew it.

"It's okay," Izzie whispered. "If we can't get it, just get out of here, and get safe."

An unwelcome tear slid down Katrina's cheek. "Stop that. You think I would leave my best friend behind? Not on your life!" As soon as the words came out, she heard the foolishness of it, which made both of them laugh and then, because emotions are funny that way, cry.

"I mean it, Izzie. Regardless of everything from the past week, you are my best friend. And I'm so sorry about Lena. I really didn't mean for it... I got arrogant—"

"I know, buddy. It's in the past, though. Totally history."

Katrina focused on the wires and her training so that she wouldn't fall apart further. She remembered the Division course Explosions 121: Try Not to Blow It. "Okay, so I've ruled out the brown, the two reds, the green, and the two blues. That leaves the yellow." She held the wire and her metal shard. "I'm going to clip it now, okay?"

Izzie nodded, eyes closed, mouth murmuring in prayer.

Twelve seconds.

Katrina took a deep breath then sliced the wire. The clock stopped. They sighed in relief, and Katrina flung open the door.

"Okay! Let's cut that thing off of you and—"

The moment Katrina cut Izzie free from the device, they heard a beep. Katrina and Izzie both looked down. The timer was off, but the beeping remained.

Izzie swore a steady stream. "This is more sophisticated than I thought. There must be a backup trigger..."

"Or maybe another cord?" Katrina dropped to her knees and followed the beeping.

There, under Izzie's seat, was a thin, clear cord, one that connected to her seat and to another box. The seat was the last trigger. The moment Izzie's weight was no longer pressing down on the seat, they were both going to be goners.

Katrina looked up at Izzie as she gently slid the box forward. It was roughly the size of a deck of cards and had an alphanumeric keypad below another blinking countdown—two minutes. *What am I supposed to do?*

Izzie must've read her face, as she started sobbing in earnest. Seeing her friend's pain, Katrina couldn't hold back her emotions any longer and started to cry as well. Izzie had been right—Katrina hadn't needed to try to apologize for Lena's death and to explain herself. Facing death tended to focus one's priorities. And in that moment, their friendship was fully restored.

Get it together, Foster. Falling apart was not going to keep them from getting blown apart.

"Okay. We're spies," Katrina said. "We're smart. We can do this. We have ninety more seconds to do this, and there's no crying in spying."

She looked down at the box again. With just a single cord, it was not a case of "clip the right one and escape." She then considered the keypad. *Maybe there's a code?* That was more Katrina's speed. *Maybe. Hopefully.*

"Okay, new plan. I am going to decode this. I think. But first, we need to get your butt out of the seat and replace it with mine."

Izzie looked as though she was going to object.

"We don't have time for arguing. I'm coming in through the passenger side, and as I slide onto your seat, you slide off and get out from the passenger side." They quickly executed the plan, and Katrina held the box in her hand. *Sixty seconds.*

Katrina ran through what she knew about Ekstrand. It was worth a chance. She typed in K-V-I-N-N-O-R.

A scratchy prerecorded voice spoke. "Incorrect. Two tries remaining."

Katrina thought about the other woman at the center of this. She tried J-O-H-A-N-N-A.

"Incorrect. One try remaining."

Katrina turned toward Izzie and said as calmly as she could, "You need to go. There's no point in both of us getting blown up."

"No!"

"That's an order!" Katrina's voice wavered, but clearly, if there was any time to pull rank, it was right then. "Either I'm about to join my parents, or I'll see you and Magnus back at headquarters. Either way, go."

Izzie started to object, but Kat cut her off.

"Go."

Izzie tried to smile but failed. "Okay then, girl, you got this." She gently kissed Kat on the cheek and ran away from the car.

Katrina thought about her parents, wondering if they'd known when they were about to die. Probably not, if Katrina was in the car with them. She started feeling sorry for herself. She had solved the mission, but at a steep price. She remembered the oft-spoken words of the director: "And should you die, take pride that you were fortunate enough to die for the Division." Taking pride was hard since Katrina had only been on one mission. She wished she would've had more time with the Division.

Katrina shook herself out of her pity party, reminding herself that she'd never been one for dramatics and wouldn't begin then.

Fifteen seconds. One last guess. Not Kvinnor, the party she loved. Not Johanna Lindström, the woman she claimed to love. Then it hit her. Ekstrand really only seemed to have two loves: power—and herself. Quickly, Katrina typed in E-K-S-T-R-A-N-D.

"Correct," the tinny voice said. "Oooh, you got it. But sometimes in life, that just isn't enough. Goodbye."

Ten seconds.

Katina dropped the clock onto the seat. Sweating profusely, Katrina raised her feet up on the seat, putting herself into a crouching position. She could use her feet to push off the seat in the final moments. She could never make a perfect transition, but she could give herself a good try.

At five seconds, Katrina propped her hands on the frame of the door and jumped out of the car. She tucked and rolled about six feet from the car. A piercing beep emitted from the device. Katrina got to her feet and ran, hoping like hell she would make it outside the blast radius. Her legs were like jelly, but she gave it her all. The beeps intensified.

Three.

Two.

One.

As Katrina flew through the air, with the heat of the flames at her back, her final thought was that in this case, that stupid little bomb box was right—giving it her all simply wasn't enough.

Chapter 44

Katrina felt perfect—not too warm and not too cold. Through her eyelids she could detect a soft, sunny light. She thought back to her final moments at the junkyard. *Am I in heaven?* She hadn't experienced such a level of peace in so long that all evidence pointed that direction. At least, she hoped that was the direction she'd gone. She gave a contented sigh. If this was to be her new celestial existence, she was cool with it. Heaven was nice—and quiet.

"Is she awake?"

"She's not snoring anymore. Still drooling, though."

"I do not think she would appreciate you pointing that out."

Not heaven, then.

With considerable effort, Katrina cracked an eyelid open and mumbled, "Not drooling. Water must've spilled."

Izzie gasped then tried to cover her relief. "Kinda viscous, though. And I can see some bubbles. Must've been carbonated."

At least her buddy was back and in fine form.

"Must've been." Katrina grimaced and tried to sit up. Attempting to move made it clear to her that whatever drugs she was on would need topping up, and soon.

Izzie gently propped some pillows beneath her while covertly doing the kindness of wiping the drool so that she could look at least halfway decent for Magnus.

"Amazingly, the doctors say you don't have much in the way of injuries," she said as she fluffed the last pillow.

"Tell that to my throbbing head and aching body," Katrina muttered.

Izzie shrugged. "Not in a life-threatening way, anyway, now that you're finally awake. The impact from the car bomb left you with a concussion, broken ribs, and some particularly awe-inspiring contusions. When we get back home, you can tell people you were doing some underground cage fighting as a cover story."

Katrina's eyes grew large in horror. *Just how busted up do I look?*

Perhaps sensing her alarm, Magnus came forward and softly brushed some curls from her face. "Well, I, for one, think the bruises just bring out the beautiful color of your eyes."

Izzie pulled a face. "Ugh. I don't think my stomach can handle that level of mush this early in the morning. I'm heading for the toilet." On the way out of Katrina's hospital room and into the hallway, she paused at the door and looked back at Katrina. "Glad you made it through. I couldn't bear..."

Izzie's crumpled face said all the things Katrina already knew about her dear friend.

She paused, collected herself, and tried again. "Glad to have my partner back." She quickly slipped out the door, but not before a single tear ran down her cheek.

Katrina looked over at Magnus and patted the side of the bed. He very gingerly sat down next to her.

"So what happened? The last thing I remember was the heat at my back and flying through the air."

"I ran out there just after it happened. After the explosion, you just lay there on the pavement like you were broken," Magnus said. "Didn't move at all. I will freely admit it—I was scared. So was Isobel." He paused as though remembering. "I'd never seen Izzie so terrified. Angry? Sad? Yes. But terrified? I didn't even know it was possible."

Katrina remembered how she'd felt as she prepared to leave the car. Yes, that level of fear was definitely possible.

"You didn't wake up for the longest of times." He shook his head. "But you're here now, mostly in one piece." His eyes started to warm. "Mostly in one very delectable piece."

He leaned down toward her, and Kat closed her eyes in anticipation.

Right on cue, a nurse bustled in. Magnus pulled back from Katrina as the nurse inserted something wonderful into her IV drip and announced that visiting hours were over.

"It's alright," he said. "I need to go talk with my director and prepare the report. I put off both of them until I could see you awake."

"And the, uh, *friends* that joined us early?" Katrina asked.

"No longer an issue. Having them forcibly retired seemed to send the right message."

When the nurse's back was turned, Magnus carefully kissed her one bruise-free patch of skin and left with a promise to return that evening. Katrina mumbled something, but she wouldn't have been able to vouch for what it was as she was starting to get that warm, vaguely celestial feeling again.

Right before Katrina slipped back under, she wondered what sort of scars she might have acquired. Already in possession of the Nixonian one, maybe she had collected the full presidential set.

Chapter 45

O ne week later.
    With fading bruises and ribs still wrapped, Katrina made a visit to the high-security prison. Though injured, she felt well enough to go and safe enough to go by herself. Knowing her audience, she took extra time to look her best. She wore a tight bun that concealed hair that was now uneven, as the fire had singed off a significant portion from the back. It took nearly an hour to slather on enough heavy-duty concealer over any of her skin that her clothes didn't cover, but it was worth it. She didn't want to appear vulnerable, not to the woman who'd nearly killed her.

The chair scraped loudly against the floor. Katrina made a point to hide a grimace of pain as she lowered herself into the seat. Through two-inch bulletproof glass she sat face-to-face with one Sigrid Ekstrand.

Ekstrand hadn't been in prison long enough to affect her appearance. Her dark, blunt bob still looked perfect. She showed no signs of being the least bit disconcerted about her new abode.

She leaned in and peered closely at Katrina. "I really did a number on you, didn't I? Good try with the concealer, Sister, but I can still see the bruises underneath, and I must say, they make me happy." She pulled back and crossed her arms. "It's just a shame you managed to live."

"Funny, I feel the same way... about you. I had hoped that maybe Sweden would make an exception and reinstate the death penalty just for you, but no such luck." As a general principle, Katrina was not much for capital punishment, especially given how it disproportionately affected people who looked like herself, but she wouldn't have batted an eye had Ekstrand been given a premature expiration date. Seeing her in person reactivated her anger at the woman. *How dare she murder so many for her own personal aggrandizement?* Life truly wasn't fair in that she would live while good people had died.

After fifteen minutes of mostly one-sided interrogation, a nearby guard indicated that her time was up.

"You forgot to ask me the most important question of all, Agent."

"And what would that be?"

"Where my resources came from, of course," Ekstrand answered. "You didn't think I could organize that whole thing on my own, did you?"

Katrina stared at her. Since they were out of time, the guard started to lift Ekstrand out of the seat. Ekstrand fought her off long enough to lean over and press her face to the glass.

"I'll let you in on a little secret—you've only cut one head off the Hydra, off The Voices," Ekstrand whispered.

"Nice try." Katrina rolled her eyes at her. "Let me guess? You'll only come back bigger and more powerful than before, right? I've heard it before. Sorry, but it ends with you."

At that, Ekstrand's eyes lit up with delight. "You really don't know, do you? Keep on thinking that while we bring on the new political order," she said. "Well, here's my gift for you in the form of a clue—go tell your director what I said. Let's see what that paragon of perfection, Samantha Jones, has to say. Good luck with that one!" She continued to laugh as the guard dragged her away bodily.

Katrina was ready to dismiss her posturing as a way to save face, but then she thought about Ekstrand's words back at the scrapyard, about how she had friends who said she might be important. As she left the premises, a wave of uneasiness passed over her. *Even if she had links to the Swedish Division, how did Ekstrand know about Director Jones?*

KATRINA AND MAGNUS met midmorning at their agreed-upon spot inside Kulturhuset. To the casual observer, they were just two strangers observing the same art installation at the cultural appreciation center. The quick brush of Magnus's pinky against Katrina's belied that appearance.

"You're looking better," he murmured with a warm smile.

"I'm feeling better."

He shifted, and Katrina noticed some discomfort in his demeanor.

"So... I've got some good news and some bad news," he began, rubbing the back of his neck in that familiar tell.

She laughed nervously. "I think I've had almost all the bad news I can take." She brushed the toe of one shoe against his. "Let's lead off with the good news first."

"Remember those Level Threes? How we wondered if they might be moles?"

Katrina thought back to their curious timing and also to Ekstrand's words. "Yeah."

"Well, not moles at all. Just lazy and incompetent. So we weren't compromised. Which is good news for us but obviously not for them. After their efforts, or lack thereof, we've invited them to pursue other career opportunities."

Katrina had a very good idea what that euphemism meant in the Division.

"And the other good news?"

"I received a commendation from the Division and was given a rather significant pay raise." Magnus was trying to look nonchalant and not succeeding one bit.

"Wow... that's great!" The wheels started turning in Katrina's head as she tried to work out what the bad news might mean.

"Well, the Division was pretty much compelled to. My director's words, not mine. As he so kindly explained, it was considered a reasonable form of payment from the Division because they couldn't exactly tell the media what really happened. This is my 'accolade.'"

"Well, whatever the motivation, you certainly deserve it."

"After being viewed for so long as undeserving, it was nice to finally get recognition. I've even got a new assignment: REACT-ULTRA."

They paused their conversation as a herd of school children shuffled past their exhibit.

"And is this the bad?" Katrina gave a nervous laugh. "Don't tell me it's something like you now have to take me out of commission *despite* our solving the mission."

"Don't joke about that. It could happen. Again."

Katrina's eyes grew wide.

"No, no, it's not that," he reassured her. "I'm just saying that I've seen that happen. You don't even want to put that out there as a possibility. Anyway, nothing to do with you." He tilted his head in consideration. "Although if it did, I'd have to lie to you about it anyway."

"Of course, you could be lying now."

He gave a small smile. "Of course, I could be lying now. But I'm not." He glanced over his shoulder and led her to a shadowed alcove in the museum. Once in the shadows, he took her hand.

"The REACT-ULTRA assignment means they're taking me off the grid. Underground. No contact."

Katrina nodded. *Ah.* She understood. That was the bad news.

"No contact equals no us," Magnus whispered stoically.

Katrina looked up. His eyes weren't able to conceal what his voice could.

"Well, it was nice while it lasted, wasn't it?" Like Magnus, she was pretty sure her eyes were giving her feelings away as well.

He looked around briefly before kissing her. "It certainly was. You made a miserable mission endurable. Given a case no one thought we'd solve. Then I met you. Bold, smart, sexy..."

Katrina raised her brows. "Everything you like."

His eyes softly flared as he wrapped his arms around her. "*Precis.* Everything I like."

They stood there, embracing in silence as the awkward realization of their impending separation settled between them.

He cleared his throat. "So..."

"I understand. Romance is at the mercy of our chosen employment." Katrina tried to smile. She couldn't.

"I wish there was a way we could keep the status quo. While I am excited for a new mission, it's not as if I could have passed this up. 'No' isn't a word that's understood by the Division in any language."

Katrina agreed. "No, it certainly isn't. Good luck with your new assignment, Magnus. You deserve it, and you'll be great." Somewhat to her surprise, Katrina found that she actually meant it. She didn't like what the consequence would be, but she meant it.

They kissed one more time before slipping back out of the alcove. They made their way to the exits, ready to head their opposite ways.

Katrina turned back to watch him as he went out the door. If this was goodbye, at least she had a good view of him.

She was not going to cry. She was not going to cry. She was not.

A traitorous tear escaped.

She quickly swiped it away in an effort to pretend it never happened.

Feeling impulsive, Katrina rushed back over to him. She grabbed his hand and slipped a card into his palm. "I know once you go underground, that's it, but if you ever need help, or you need to get a message to me, call the number on that card and say, 'Happy birthday, Mr. President.' Only that phrase, and then hang up."

He gave her a bewildered expression.

She smiled in return. "It's better if you don't ask. Just... If you need me, you'll know what to do." She squeezed the card and his hand one more time then turned away. That time, she didn't look back.

Chapter 46

Right before they left Sweden, Katrina learned what had happened to Westlund. He was finally found in a remote cabin on the outskirts of Luleå, with a single shot to the head and a suicide note. The official report said it was self-inflicted, but no one in the Swedish Division actually believed that. They tracked and destroyed his research. That was the story, anyway. Katrina wouldn't have been the least bit surprised if the Division had filed away the SCR procedures for their own use one day. But that was not Katrina's concern. Her mission was complete. She had lived to spy another day.

On the flight back home, Katrina distracted Izzie by asking her about Jens. Izzie was too busy blushing to freak out over the slightest shifts of the plane.

"Jens? Well, he said he wants to come out this fall for a visit."

"Wow! That's great, Izzie!"

Izzie waved a hand dismissively. "Eh, I told him I'd think about it. I'm young and carefree, you know? Maybe I don't want to get bogged down with just one dude."

Katrina didn't think that was the truth. However weird and unexpected their pairing was, Katrina had seen clear chemistry between the two of them. *What is making Izzie hesitate?* The story had more to it, but Katrina wouldn't pry, at least not while she was confined in a flying tube with someone skilled in weaponry.

"It was good while it lasted though, yeah?"

"Sure. He's a great guy, but whew! That man is a *project*, and I am not looking for that right now. It's just enough to deal with a crazed psychotic trying to kill off all of my friends. Anyway, enough about me. What's next for you and Magnus?"

Given all they'd just been through, Katrina was happy enough to ignore the deflection. "Well, his next mission is taking him underground. He'll be off the grid entirely."

He might have been going off the grid, but he'd left one more message. While packing her suitcase before heading out, she saw a manila folder tucked into a front pocket. Katrina knew she hadn't packed it, and her stomach lurched. If the mission had taught her anything, it was that no good ever came from surprise notes. She slipped on a pair of gloves and carefully lifted out the folder and raised the seal. A smaller sealed envelope was inside, and on the inside of the manila folder flap was a coded message:

K,

Professor Rasmusson gave me the contents inside. He didn't explain it and threatened me with 'premature expiration' should I open it. Given all the gadgets at his disposal, I was happy to follow orders.

Katrina smiled to herself as she read further.

Venturing a guess, I think it may have to do with your parents. Hopefully, it gives you some answers.

Until we meet again,

~M

She didn't tell Izzie about the folder, though, and wouldn't until she found out more. This was one of those times when it seemed like the fewer the people who knew, the better. The safer.

After arriving at headquarters, Katrina and Izzie went to separate rooms for what was laughably called a debriefing but was more like an interrogation. After a thorough physical and mental health "evaluation," Katrina was sent to debrief the director about the outcome of the mission.

At the conclusion of Katrina's report, the director closed her folder and rested her steepled hands on top. "Well, congratulations, Agent Foster. You managed to survive and, minus a couple of small deaths, managed to snatch victory from the jaws of defeat by identifying and capturing Lindström's true murderer, Sigrid Ekstrand. Your debut mission was a success." No mention was made of Katrina's having dodged her twelve-hours-shy-of-seventy-two-hour expiration date.

Katrina was glad Johanna Lindström's killer was found and that no other agents would be at risk, but it was no victory.

"Given that two people died on my watch, I don't know that I'd call it a success, Director."

Samantha Jones was clearly not accustomed to being crossed. "Tell me this, Agent Foster, did you conclude the operation having met your main objective—finding who was behind Blomqvist's death, Lindström's assassination, and the murders of anyone affiliated with the case?"

"Well, yes."

"Are you still among the living?"

"Yes..."

"In our line of work, anytime you make it back home, and *not* in a body bag, it should be considered a success. Take the compliment, Agent Foster. I assure you I don't pass those out frivolously."

Katrina could believe that. "Yes, Director."

Director Jones leaned back in her chair and studied Katrina. "So tell me, Agent Foster. Katrina. Is there anything else you'd like to share with me? I know you've been to Sweden before with your parents."

Katrina got ready to speak then stopped herself. She remembered Lena's assertion that Katrina being sent to Sweden was no accident. Katrina needed to discover more, she was sure, and she wasn't about to share any of that with the director. Not yet, anyway. She could learn to play the game as well.

She gave the director a bland smile and said, "No, nothing additional to share, Director, other than to say that the Swedish summers are just as lovely as I remembered."

The director looked at her shrewdly then nodded. "I see. Well, good. The Division heads thought you might enjoy returning there. Not that we're in the habit of providing agents with vacations and trips down memory lane."

Given everything Katrina had been through and survived, a "vacation" would not be how she would describe her time there, and the director's comment only deepened her suspicion that her mission location was no act of serendipity. She went for directness.

"Director, I find it hard to believe that I was sent to Sweden as an act of charity. Why did you decide to send me there as my first mission?"

The director's face was a mask. "Technically, it wasn't my decision. Not directly, anyway. My director informed me that you would be selected to head up the Sweden assignment."

The director has a director? Katrina was learning new things all the time.

"And for your information, that was on a need-to-know basis." She paused. "And you didn't need to know."

"Yes, Director."

They stared at each other silently, in mutual evaluation.

Director Jones broke the silence. "Well, good job, Agent Foster. You may leave now. We're done here."

Glad to leave, Katrina got up and went toward the door. She stopped when she got there, though. "Director Jones?"

"Yes?"

"There was one thing I forgot to mention. Ekstrand said to ask you about a group called The Voices. Does that mean anything to you?"

"Nothing at all, Agent Foster. Based on experience, however, I would not read too much into it. Just the ravings of a madwoman trying for a little last-ditch bravada would be my guess."

Katrina swore for a second that something passed over Samantha's eyes, but when she looked again, there was Director Jones, sitting calmly with neutral eyes and a placid smile.

"Go home and rest, Katrina. Take the weekend off to celebrate a job well done, and we'll see you on Monday. Excellent work on your first mission."

Someone else might have taken her statement at face value, but after previously watching her act kind while already having agreed to the hit on Katrina's life, she knew not to trust the friendliness in her tone, so Katrina simply inclined her head and left.

WITH EVERYTHING KATRINA had been through, she decided to splurge on a taxi to bring her home. On the ride back, Katrina thought about her meeting with the director. She still wasn't convinced by Director Jones's responses and definitely didn't trust her disavowal about The Voices, but that would be a problem that could wait until Monday. She believed strongly that The Voices—whoever they were—were real. Oskar had been right. The V was the key. It hadn't been for Viktor, and it wasn't the Roman numeral five—it was for The Voices. Like a sick calling card, it seemed their way of tagging their victims.

Overall, she didn't quite know how to feel about her first mission. Yes, she'd completed the job. Ekstrand was captured, and both cases were officially closed. But in the process, she'd lost one of Sweden's best spies and a valuable informant, and she also mourned the poor used-and-abused Surikov. She considered what she'd almost lost—her best friend, not to mention her own life.

Katrina settled back into the seat and leaned against the head-rest, smiling wistfully. The near-death experience aside, she did have a delightful bit of social activity with a certain Swedish agent, and she did learn a little more about her parents. That alone made it all worthwhile. She thought back on what Magnus had said about Berlin. *Germany.* Something told Katrina that Germany would hold the answers to her parents' deaths. She sighed. But for the moment, she was back home and feeling very grateful to be there. And hungry. The other feeling was definitely hunger. *Ugh.* And her place had no food.

Katrina got out of the cab in front of her apartment and saw Hector out front, dumping his recycling in the bin.

He looked up and grinned. "Welcome home!"

"Glad to be back."

Hector took her bag from the driver and carried it for her. "Going to stick around for a bit?"

Katrina sighed. "I hope so. A month away was too long. In the world of insurance, though, who knows?" She headed up the steps into the apartment building. "So how'd it work out with you and, ah..." She pretended to search for his date's name like she hadn't already run a full background check on the wench.

"Paula?" He shrugged. "Didn't work out. She was really sweet, but I don't know, something just didn't click."

"Sorry to hear that." *Not really.*

"Thanks. It felt good to get back out there, though. I'll keep trying."

"Good," she said. "You have value. You're a man who's employed..."

He raised an eyebrow, and Katrina laughed.

"Wait, let me finish! A man who's employed and kind and can cook? You shouldn't have any problems putting yourself out there again."

She opened her mailbox and took out a giant stack of bills and restaurant flyers. "And speaking of cooking... got anything for a hungry girl to eat?"

Hector grinned. "Of course."

She smiled in return and looped her arm in his as they walked down the hallway. She passed her apartment and carried her bags to Hector's unit. She was going to need to eat before dealing with anything—or anyone—who might be waiting for her at her place.

"I can always count on you to take care of me and my stomach."

He gave a small, wistful grin. "As always." He cleared his throat and reached for his keys. "So I've just tried my hand at *carne adobada*, and it's culinary magic, if I say so myself. Which I do."

Katrina laughed. "Such the modest chef."

Hector grinned. "You know me. Anyway, so the key to capturing the flavor is to first marinate the meat in..."

She let Hector wax on about his detailed culinary process. After everything she'd been through, it was just so *normal*, so familiar, that Katrina silently pledged to do whatever she could to keep it that way.

Chapter 47

Fortified by meat, Katrina made her way back down the hall to her apartment. Once inside, she set down her bags and got to work. She hadn't forgotten that the director and that so-called plumber had been to her home while she was gone. After checking and rechecking every nook and cranny, Katrina felt reasonably assured she was not being spied upon. She closed all the window blinds, drawing down the blackout shades as well, for her next act needed complete privacy.

She dove into her suitcase and pulled out the mysterious folder Magnus had given her. She sat down at her desk and opened it. After smiling again at his note, she tipped open the envelope. A single sheet of notebook paper fell out. The paper was old and softly frayed where it had been folded and refolded multiple times. She knew the drill—look for the obvious first, and once that was sorted, start delving into the obscure.

Katrina held it up to the light—nothing stood out. Then she placed it back on her desk and quickly scanned the sheet. Everything was coded, some of it written in different colors of ink. Only when she made it to the bottom of the page did she see a familiar design.

She looked down at her necklace then back at the paper—then back at the necklace again. It was definitely the same ice-cream-scoop-shaped swirls. She looked back at the words, really looked at them. The text was handwritten, and Katrina would've recognized it from anywhere. She was instantly transported back through time. Though alone, she covered her gasp with her hand.

"Mom?" she whispered through her fingers. Seeing her writing made it feel, if only for a fleeting moment, as though she was back in Katrina's life.

She then eagerly inspected the paper, front and back, for signs of her father's script. There were none. She could see encoded notes in the margins, but that handwriting wasn't familiar to her.

Katrina thought back to what she'd learned. Her parents had tried to receive assistance from Magnus's parents. At least one person in the upper echelons of the Division believed they might've been Doubles. Professor Rasmusson made that odd denial about creating any "toys" for Katrina's parents, yet he'd held onto this paper, whatever it was.

She had no idea what any of this meant, not the symbol, not her mother's coded words, none of it. But she knew it was important. It just had to be. She scanned the paper again. She mentally went through the most common transposition ciphers, but this wasn't anything she was familiar with. It was going to be a challenge, and if Katrina loved anything, it was a puzzle. She grabbed a pencil and a sheet of paper and got to work.

Katrina had a new mission.

Author's Notes

Some readers may notice that the subject of Katrina Foster's first mission sounds somewhat familiar. Indeed, the character of Johanna Lindström was inspired by the assassination of Swedish politician Anna Lindh.

Lindh was the Swedish Minister of Foreign Affairs until her death at 46 in 2003. A popular politician and member of the Social Democrats, she was expected to run for prime minister. She was killed in a knife attack while shopping at Nordiska Kompaniet (more commonly referred to as NK). She did not have any bodyguards with her. Lindh's assassin was a Swede of Serbian descent, Mijailo Mijailovic.

While the subject of Katrina's mission was inspired by the assassination of Anna Lindh, all similarities end there. The tumultuous life and death of Johanna Lindström is solely the product of my overactive imagination. Outside the fictional world, there is no Kvinnor på Toppen, no affair with a political party member, and no evidence that Mijailovic was anything other than a murderer.

In addition, although I cannot say with one-hundred-percent certainty, I am fairly confident that there is no organization in Sweden or anywhere else called The Voices who are set on destabilizing the entire global political system.

Acknowledgments

First and foremost, thank you to the fantastic team at Red Adept who took a chance on an unknown and made this book happen. In particular, thank you to my fabulous editor Rashida Breen. I showed up absolutely petrified with no idea of what to expect, and you immediately put me at ease with your infectious laughter and constant encouragement. Thank you for understanding the type of book I was writing, and for knowing exactly how to make it shine.

Everyone needs a circle of support, and I have that with my WFWA ladies: Barbara, Molly, and Rebecca. Your good humor and great advice helped me get this book out the door. Cathy Lamb—mentor! Coworker! Friend! Thank you for helping me navigate, well, all things book related. You are one of my biggest cheerleaders, but you also know when to tell me to stop procrasti-shoe shopping and get my rear back in the chair and write.

While it's important to "write what you know," there's something to be said for making sure not to write what you don't know. My thanks to those who filled in the gaps. Special shoutouts to Jessica Pickering, who very kindly used small and simple words to teach me firearms and what it's like to use them, and to Miles for distracting me through squats and weightlifting with tales of the police academy and what it's like to be part of a family legacy in law enforcement.

Beta readers were excellent for helping to save me from myself. An example would be one reader who pointed out that, in an earlier draft, Katrina's lead-lined suitcase would not only be impossible to hoist into the overhead bin but would absolutely catch the attention of the TSA—something a spy definitely wouldn't want. It's comments like those that really saved my bacon, so thank you.

And of course, a huge thank you to the family that puts up with my antics. My mom, who has been my constant champion from day one (like, literally from day one as she birthed me), and my husband who is endlessly supportive. Actually, this book is entirely due to him (but I wrote it, so, y'know, put any blame on me). I kept telling him about these wacky dreams I was having about these cool spies who would go on death-defying adventures. Perhaps because there are few things worse than hearing someone recount their hazy dreams each morning, he finally suggested that I start writing it down. Was this to prevent having to hear about it? Probably. Am I grateful? Eternally. *Tusen tack, min älskling.*

About the Author

Rayna Flye always wanted to be a spy, but as she's frequently afraid and can't keep a secret, it was never going to work. So she chose to write about spies instead.

By day, Rayna is a researcher, and her nights are spent trying to figure out how to get her characters out of their latest jam. When she's not writing, she can be found crafting or in the garden. A life-long learner, she skips the lesser C-SPANs to watch C-SPAN 3. Life goal? One day getting on *Jeopardy*. Rayna lives in Portland, Oregon, with her husband and their drooly Newfoundland. She is a member of the Women's Fiction Writers Association and a 2020 Pitch Wars mentee.

Read more at https://www.raynaflye.com/.

About the Publisher

Dear Reader,

We hope you enjoyed this book. Please consider leaving a review on your favorite book site.

Visit https://RedAdeptPublishing.com to see our entire catalogue.

Check out our app for short stories, articles, and interviews. You'll also be notified of future releases and special sales.

Made in United States
Troutdale, OR
10/25/2023

14003007R00207